Light Of Dawn

Aella C Grey

The Book:

In the riveting sequel to Shadows of Dusk, the fate of two worlds hangs in the balance as darkness threatens to devour everything in its path.

After Blair's harrowing, deadly attack, Lara finds herself thrust into a dangerous adventure alongside Darian and Val. Together, they must find Kieran, Zayne, Gray, and Cade while evading the clutches of the nefarious false Queen, whose dark ambitions threaten to tear apart the entire realm of Servilia.

As Lara uncovers the mysteries surrounding her lineage, she grapples with newfound powers amidst insurmountable odds. With everything hanging in the balance, she must summon every ounce of courage and cunning to stand against the forces of evil.

But the stakes are raised to unimaginable heights when a sinister figure emerges from the shadows, with his eyes set on Lara and a sinister agenda. The lives of all Servilians, including those she holds most dear, are at risk as Lara confronts her past and the true source of evil.

The question is, will she be strong enough to face the darkness before it's too late?

Prepare for an epic tale of courage, sacrifice, and redemption as Lara and her men embark on a treacherous journey to save their world from the encroaching shadows in Light of Dawn.

The Author:

Aella C. Grey is an author hailing from Winnipeg, MB, Canada, currently residing in the sunny state of Florida. When she's not immersed in the world of writing, Aella indulges in her other passions, such as playing video games, diving into captivating books, and cherishing quality time with her beloved dog and supportive husband.

With a vivid imagination and a deep appreciation for storytelling, Aella brings her unique perspective to the realm of fiction. Her love for literature and interactive entertainment has fueled her creative endeavors, inspiring her to craft compelling narratives that transport readers to captivating worlds.

Aella's writing draws readers in with dynamic characters, intriguing plots, and a touch of magic. Whether she's exploring mystical realms or delving into the complexities of the human experience, her stories are infused with emotion, suspense, and a dash of the unexpected.

Stay connected with Aella C. Grey through her website to discover more about her upcoming works, behind-the-scenes insights, and to join her on thrilling literary adventures.

Light Of Dawn

Unbroken II

Aella C Grey

aellacgrey@gmail.com
https://aellacgrey.wixsite.com/aellacgrey

Front cover image by artist, Amanda Dumky.
Book cover design by artist, Amanda Dumky.

Aella C Grey
aellacgrey@gmail.com

<u>Trigger Warning</u>

This book contains references or graphically described scenes and actions that could and likely will be offensive or disturbing to some individuals.

It is highly recommended that you review the below warnings, and please read at your own discretion.

These warnings include, but are not limited to:
DubCon/NonCon, Rape Ch.21 p157-159, Ch.51 p410-Ch52 p418, Sexual Assault, Sexual Harassment, Child Abuse, Foster Care Abuse, Alcohol Consumption, Post Traumatic Stress Disorder (PTSD), Blood & Gore Depiction, Dead Bodies & Body Parts, Physical Injuries, Scars, Death, Grief & loss depiction, Asphyxia, Strangulation & Suffocation, Blackmail, Captivity & Confinement, Torture, Imprisonment, Knife Violence, Murder, Physical Assault, Stalking, Whipping, Bondage, Orgasm Denial, Forced Orgasm, Light BDSM, Meat Consumption, Blood Ingestion

<u>Important Note</u>

Light of Dawn is, in no way, written to downplay or degrade the experiences many people have gone through and should be read as a fictional storyline, with fictional characters who have their own personalities and relationships.

<u>**Dedications**</u>

To every person out there who has read a book with multiple attractive
men, and thought, "Why not all of them?"
This one is for you.

And for those who push their traumas away, locking them in a box hoping
they'd never again see the light of day...
I see you, I hear you.

<u>**Song Playlist**</u>

Navigate to the **Light of Dawn** playlist on Spotify, by Aella C Grey

Table of Contents

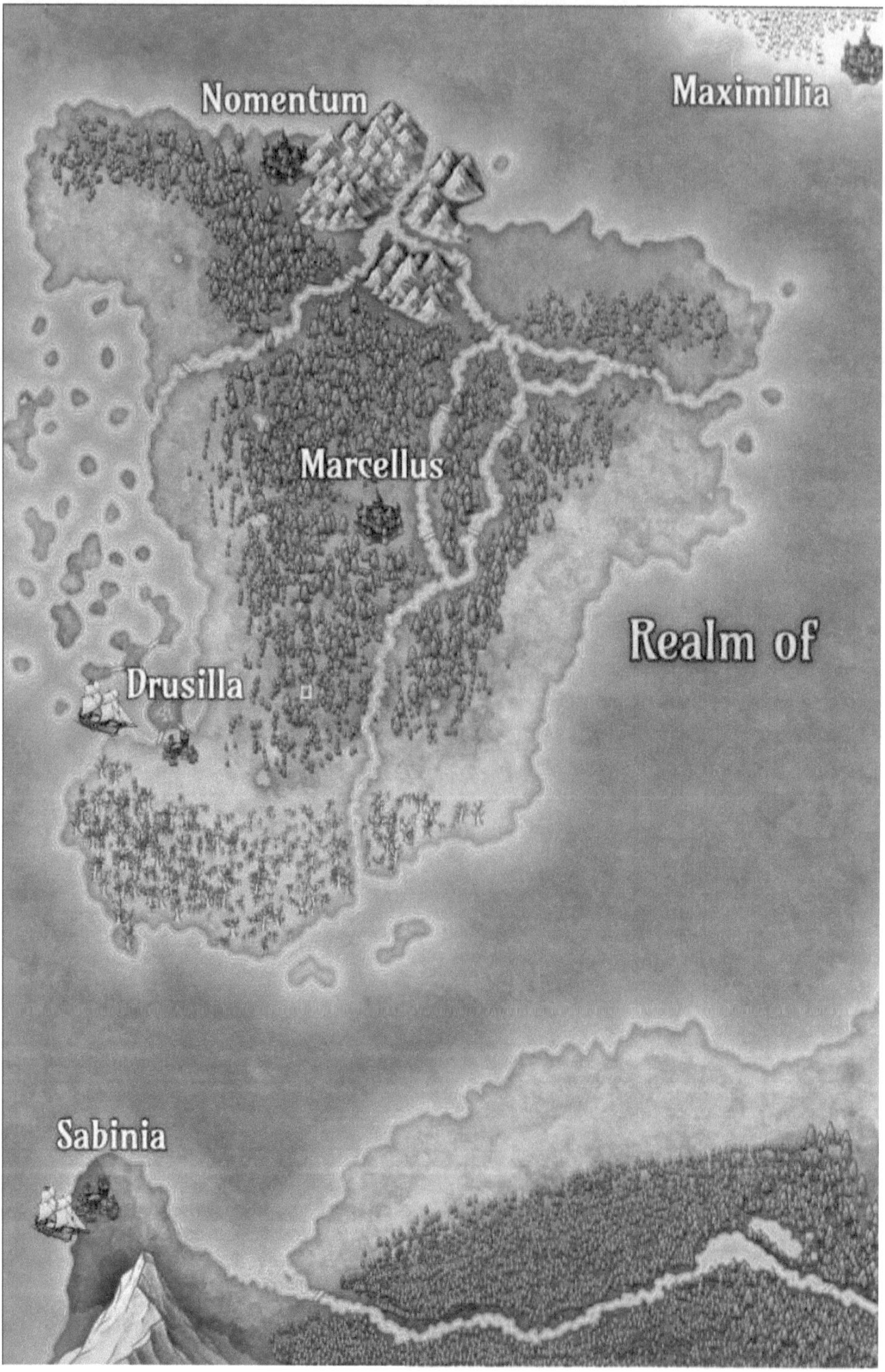

Nomentum
Maximillia
Marcellus
Realm of
Drusilla
Sabinia

Trebonia
Aveentia
Caesarea
Servilia
Lavinium

Chapter 1

Darian

Her life is slipping away.

That's all I can think of as Val holds her limp body in his arms. When he whined at the door after she left, most would have considered it an entirely canine thing to do, but I knew something was wrong.

He knew it.

I knew it.

Thinking back to her leaving, I should have seen the signs. There was no reason for her to go to the office; she knew the truth about the lake. Science can't detect or replicate magic.

It wasn't until the tracker on my truck showed it idle at the edge of the forest that I knew she had lied and that something was very wrong. What I didn't expect was to find my brother's right-hand minion here, covered in Lara's blood, with magic suddenly released.

And where the fuck is Caspian?

"What do we do, Darian?" Val's voice breaks me from my thoughts, and my gaze flicks to him before glancing at Lara's injuries again.

Blood still oozes slowly from her abdomen and wrists, her already fair skin has gone pale, and her breathing is dangerously shallow.

If we can't stop the bleeding, she'll be dead within minutes.

I won't let that happen. Not if there's anything I can do about it.

Lara belongs to me and my brothers. I'll fight Pluto himself if it means keeping her from the underworld.

Covering her abdomen with my hand, I blow out a steadying breath before reaching within myself, and my long-dormant magic stirs at my calling. It churns wildly within my body as I coax it to bend to my will.

It's become chaotic since magic was bound, and my well of power has hardly had time to fill. Swirls of ice curve over my arm as I channel a small portion to my hand, willing it into her body in an attempt to stem the bleeding.

Lara gasps sharply as the ice solidifies around her abdomen, but her eyes remain shut as Val's arm tightens around her, "You're alright. You're going to be fine." His voice is thick with concern, betraying the reassurance of his words as he runs his bloodied fingers through her damp silver hair.

My gaze drops to the thin sheet of ice along her abdomen, and my stomach turns in knots.

It should suffice for now.

Threads of my power feed into her abdomen, keeping it solid as I turn my attention to her wrist and repeat the action. It takes much less magic, but my well is still steadily depleting between the two threads.

This will keep her alive, but just barely.

"We need to get her to Lor. He will know of something to stop the bleeding."

Val nods, shifting to pick her up, "I can carry her to the jet-"

I shake my head, "No, that's not fast enough. I don't know what my magic reserves are like with magic being gone for so long, but we need him now. I'll get us to Haven, but you'll need to bring him to us while I focus on keeping her from bleeding out."

Val nods, stepping closer to me with Lara held tight to his chest as if she will disappear into thin air, but I can't say that I blame him.

I suck in a breath before resting a hand on his shoulder.

Teleporting this far under normal circumstances and alone is challenging, yet I'm about to attempt it with Val and Lara while keeping the ice on her body frozen.

"Wait," Val says nervously, and my eyes snap to meet his.

"What is it?"

"Are you sure about this? Are you able to get us there?"

"No. I'm not sure about anything, and the more you question it, the more I will too. But if we don't do this, brother, she dies. I'm not willing to accept that. Are you?"

His mouth snaps shut, and I tighten my grip on his shoulder as if that could help me focus or ground me. Steadily feeding my power into Lara's wounds, I picture our destination around us as my magic surges.

The power in the air becomes palpable as I open my eyes, and pieces of Haven come into focus. Lor's bar becomes more clear and crisp as the magic surrounding us thickens.

The forest and lake blur as my gaze lands on Lara's three friends a handful of feet away. My magic creates a fog surrounding us, and through it, a brunette with bright green eyes gazes back at me when the world around us transforms into a myriad of colors.

Chapter 2

Caspian

It's been hours since I left the house, and I'm sprinting through the dark forest with my pulse raging in my ears. As if I didn't already have enough problems, Blair had to go fuck everything up.

It wasn't supposed to happen like this.

I've spent weeks coming up with a way to release magic that wouldn't risk Lara's fucking life but came up short, so I was trying to buy what little time I could while keeping her at arm's length.

So much for that.

I suck in a deep breath, and the metallic tang invading my senses holds an air of familiarity as my chest tightens.

If Blair isn't dead already, she will be soon enough. Banishment be damned.

The branches of nearby trees lash against my arms as I propel myself forward. No matter how fast I run, it's not fucking fast enough. Lara's scent grows stronger with each step, and when I break the treeline to the water, it hangs heavy like an invisible mist taunting my inaction.

My gaze scans the area for a mess of silver hair, but there's no sign of Lara.

In the distance, near a tree that sits close to the water's edge, movement catches my eye, and I don't take a moment to think before I launch toward the heap of bodies on the ground.

My footfalls stop as I grimace at the tied and bruised visages of Lara's two work friends.

Of fucking course. That's how Blair got her to come here.

One of Lara's most significant weaknesses has always been those she cares about.

Hell, it's how I convinced her to start looking for the amulets in the first place.

I approach the two heaps on the ground and frown at their unconscious forms.

I could have sworn someone had been moving.

A crunch sounds out behind me, and I whirl around. My mind hardly registers the pain as my head snaps to the side from the force of the fist that's collided with it, and I stagger back a step.

"It's all your fault, you fucking asshole!" Tamara's voice rings out, and my teeth grind together.

I turn to look at her, but her mess of dark brown hair disappears from my sight within an instant.

Fuck.

I fucking hate that ability.

Within the blink of an eye, she reappears, giving a moment's notice to grab her wrist when she launches another blow aimed at my face. Jerking her to the side and contorting her arm into an awkward position, she shrieks in frustration, yanking her arm free with surprising strength.

I have to use both arms to keep her still, but if she truly wants to get away, she could with little effort.

All she'd have to do is her little disappearing act, and she'd be free within an instant.

I gaze into the burning rage in her eyes, "Where is Lara?"

She spits on the ground and disappears once more as my hands suddenly grasp nothing but air when a fist collides with my shoulder.

Ignoring the pain, I grasp and twist her arm as she whirls to the ground with a loud thud. The air escapes her lungs as she gasps loudly.

She should count her blessings that I don't fucking kill her right now.

Lara's the only reason she's managed to live this long.

"She's dead because of you, you despicable, good-for-nothing, lowlife scum piece of shit!"

And just like that, all the oxygen escapes my lungs as I stare at her wide-eyed.

Dead?

My lip curls as her green eyes burn bright, "You're lying." If looks alone could kill, I'd be the one dead with the way her face contorts with rage. It's convincing enough, but I can't believe it.

My entire body goes numb and cold simultaneously, as if doused in ice water from the inside out.

She can't be dead.

An unfamiliar feeling sinks deep into my gut as if a boulder rests at the pit of my stomach.

I don't know when it happened, but Lara somehow became this constant anomaly in the back of my mind. She's an existence seared within the very essence of my consciousness.

A presence that lingers as an echo no matter where I go.

I would know if she was dead.

Wouldn't I?

"Where is she?" My voice is no more than a whisper, as if speaking any louder would expose my desperation for her. I search Tamara's eyes as if they'll tell me where to go, even if she doesn't.

Whatever she sees only pisses her off more as she snarls, "Your brother and Val teleported her to Haven probably to have her goddamn funeral."

She disappears again, reappearing feet away, standing tall with her fists flexing as her chest heaves.

"I don't give a shit if Samira kills me when we return, as long as you get what is coming to you, Caspian," the venom in her whisper is unmistakable as she turns to walk away, "you know as well as I do that we can't escape her. I just hope when you do return, she finds out everything you've been hiding and kills you for it. And for Lara's sake, I hope that bitch does it slowly."

Her words hang in the air as she walks into the forest, and my knuckles turn white as grains of sand squeeze out of my fists. I push to my feet as conflict rages inside of me, and my teeth grind together.

If my assumptions are correct, Darian will find a healer, but knowing Blair, she likely had a fail-safe to keep Lara's wounds from recovering.

All paths lead to one future course of action.

My brother will bring her home.

Bringing my palm to my mouth to open the portal to Servilia, I pause as my gaze lands on the two bodies slumped against one another, and I click my tongue.

The urge to return home squeezes in my chest, rivaling the need to get to Lara.

Why the fuck should I care if these two die in the wilderness?

I let out a resigned sigh, stepping toward them and pulling out my phone.

This is a delay I can't fucking afford.

Darian better have a plan.

Chapter 3

Darian

My power wanes as Haven comes into focus, and my grip on Val's shoulder tightens.

Teleporting the three of us used much more of my power than I anticipated, and sweat beads down my temple.

I don't have much time before my magic reserves are spent, which means Lara doesn't have much time either.

Shouting catches my attention as I scan around us, noting the overhead ambiance of the nightclub with a sigh of relief.

I managed to get us into the club and delivered us right to Lor's feet.

Quite literally.

Lor drops to his knees and looks us over before settling his eyes on Lara's ice-covered abdomen, "What in all the gods' names is this!?"

I find myself unable to answer while sweat drips down my spine, and I try to catch my breath. The exertion of suddenly using so much magic starts to take its toll, and I'm struggling just to maintain the magic keeping Lara alive.

Thankfully, Val answers for me, "It was Blair. Lara took off, saying she was going to the office, but something didn't seem right. We tracked her, but it was too late. Blair had already done so much damage by the time we arrived."

Lor glances at me, then hesitantly back to Val, "And Caspian?"

Val shakes his head, "He wasn't there. When we arrived, Blair was in the water with Lara. Darian fought Blair while I pulled Lara from the lake."

Lor looks at me with concern painted across his face, "Is Blair still...?"

I know what he's asking.

He wants to know if my brother's banishment still stands or if I was able to kill Blair before her sacrifice.

I shake my head and drop my gaze to Lara's limp body between us, "I wasn't able to stop her before she took her own life. Lor, can you help her?"

He nods tentatively, "I'll examine the wound and get my supplies. Can you keep your ice intact for a few more minutes?"

"I can try. I don't know how much longer I have before my reserves are empty," I state, noting the already scarce magic inside me dwindling. I estimate I have another two to five minutes before the ice in her abdomen begins to thaw.

Lor jumps to his feet and hurries out of the room. He's only gone for a minute before he rushes back, sliding to his knees and stopping alongside us in one swift movement. He rolls out a series of herbs and powders alongside Lara's body.

"Right then. Let's test a small area first. Val, hand me her wrist," he says, holding out his upturned palm.

Val gently places Lara's wrist down, and Lor glances at me, giving me a single nod. Cutting off the constant supply of magic to her wrist, I feel the strain on my body slightly lessen, but my exhaustion still weighs heavy.

We sit quietly, watching as Lor tests his medicines on sample areas of her wound.

A minute goes by, and his frown deepens, "D, what was she wounded with?"

I shake my head, "I'm not sure. Assuming a dagger of some sort. Why?"

Glancing at all his herbs and her wrist still slowly trailing with blood, he responds, "Her wound isn't responding to traditional methods unless..."

His eyes glaze over as he gets lost in thought, and suddenly, he's off the ground and running out of sight again.

It feels like he's been gone for an eternity when he finally reappears next to us. He sets a pestle and mortar on the ground and begins mixing various herbs and powders, grinding them into a cohesive powder before he locks eyes with me.

My power begins to wane, and the steady stream of magic I've funneled into her abdomen has become little more than a trickle now as my exhausted body struggles to remain upright.

I didn't make it this far to fail her now.

Lor looks at me hesitantly and extends his hand. "D, I need your blood for this to work."

I extend my hand without a second thought.

The reason he needs it doesn't matter when I only care about keeping her here.

"Wait, why his?" Val asks suspiciously, holding his hand alongside mine, "Why not my blood instead?"

Lor shakes his head. "D is the only one here with royal blood. For this to work, it has to be him." He gently takes my hand, the question clear in his eyes, and I nod to reaffirm my decision.

I know only one ancient spell that can heal someone from the brink of death. I'm painfully aware of its repercussions, but I can't think of those now.

"Do it." The last of my power seeps into Lara's injured abdomen before fizzling out, and my chest is tight with countless emotions I refuse to acknowledge.

Not yet.

Not until she's safe.

At this point, I would forfeit my own life within a moment's notice if it meant keeping her alive.

I'd do anything to avoid a future without her in it.

Waiting with bated breath for the ice to thaw, I hardly register the twinge of pain in my hand as Lor cuts it open, allowing my blood to drip into the mortar.

Once the concoction becomes a thick paste, he takes a small amount and presses it to her wrist, "Ilvritia kir hylomn vren ptolyrian," Lor murmurs before turning his attention to her abdomen where the ice has melted, revealing the deep wound leaking blood once more.

He quickly presses the paste deep inside her injury before covering it with his palm and murmuring the exact phrase in the old tongue.

A wave of power crashes over me as the last word leaves his lips, over-taking the exhaustion in my body as I clench my fists against the ground to keep myself upright.

The oddest hint of a feeling echoes behind the chaos, dancing amidst the ocean of pressure surrounding me before it's gone, and I manage to suck in a ragged breath of relief.

Was that?

It can't be.

He takes her wrist and holds it up between us, and relief flickers across his features as I follow his gaze. The slice across her wrist has stopped bleeding, and the skin has mended together, leaving a pink scar parallel to the injuries she received from the hunter Caspian hired.

Val's shoulders slump as he dips his head forward, "Thank the gods."

I glance at Lara's abdomen, and the bleeding has stopped there as well. Where she once had a brutal injury is now a long pink line marring her fair skin between the tattered, bloody scraps of her shirt.

I tilt my head back and sigh deeply with relief, "How long until she wakes up, Lor?" He scans her once before answering, "Hard to say, D. Could be a few hours to a few days. Whatever poison was on the blade took a toll on her body. Had you not been there, she'd have bled to death. With-out knowing what kind of poison it was, I can only assume the rest is up to her. If she doesn't wake up in the next few days, she may need a proper healer."

My movements are sluggish as I turn to Val, "Let's get her up to one of the rooms to recover," I say before turning my attention to Lor, "Thank you, my friend. I find myself once again eternally in your debt."

He grins and shrugs, "I'm sure I'll call in the favor someday. Until then, enjoy your freedom, your radiance."

I roll my eyes as a smile tugs at the corner of my lips, and he lets out a genuine laugh as I push to my feet, swaying as the strain of depleting my magic weighs heavy.

My body feels like it's been holding up the world's weight as Lor pulls one of my arms over his shoulders, easing me against him for support. Val cradles Lara to his chest, and we make our way to the penthouse suite.

Once we settle Lara into the suite's king-size bed, I collapse alongside her, with Val lying on the opposite side.

Silence hangs thick in the air as I lose myself to my thoughts.

Caspian's absence, Lara's injury, Lor's spell to heal her, and the fleeting hint of whatever that feeling was while Lor cast the spell.

I can't make heads or tails of any of it, perhaps because I'm more drained than ever.

Val breaks the silence first as he runs his fingers through her long, blood-stained hair, "We never checked on her friends."

I drop my gaze to her peaceful face as her chest rises and falls subtly with each breath.

It's a sight I hadn't thought twice about leading up to today, but it's one I will treasure for the rest of my life.

She's alive.

"One of them was awake before I teleported us here. I'll get someone to go out there," I mutter, digging my phone from my pocket and lazily messaging a couple of contacts.

After sending somewhat of a rescue team to Lara's friends, I set my phone down, and sleep takes me.

Chapter 4

Darian

"Darian, wake up."

I feel someone gently shaking my shoulder, and I peel my eyes open to the source. Val's thick black hair is tousled and mussed from sleep, but the dark bags under his eyes indicate otherwise.

I frown and sit up slightly, "What is it?"

"One, you've both been asleep for nearly eighteen hours. Two, it's Lara. She's burning up."

He places my hand on her head. Her skin is damp with sweat and hot to the touch, so much so that my magic instinctively goes to the surface of my skin.

I let the chill of my hand stay on her head for a moment before glancing at her abdomen. The wound is shut and healed. There's no redness, swelling, or any indication of an infection. It's hard to say what could have caused her to have such a high fever.

"We need to find a healer," he says softly, leveling me with his piercing hazel gaze, "it's time to go back home, Darian."

My blood pressure rises as I look down at the pallor of her skin, which has returned, but the fever is concerning and could get out of hand fast without a true healer.

"Then we go home."

I adorn my father's sword after changing into Servilian clothes with robes that conceal enough that we won't stick out like sore thumbs or be recognized. Having been passed down from generation to generation, it feels reassuring at my hip as we make our way to the bridge between realms.

The club doesn't have the familiar aura of comfort and serenity it's so often accompanied with. Instead, there's an air of uncertainty and concern as eyes track our movements.

Val carries Lara alongside me as we pass by the same familiar faces in the crowd on our way to the waterfall.

These regulars have been coming for years, people who followed me here long before I made any name for myself.

These are the Servilians I protected from being used as pawns in whatever game Caspian was playing.

I pause, looking at those around us as Val stops beside me.

I can't leave them like this.

"They may have magic back, but they are loyal to you and won't leave without your blessing," Val says quietly, and a few people within earshot nod in agreement.

Sighing with reservation, I take a single step towards the crowd, and the earth in front of me shifts upwards by three steps. My gaze flicks to Val as a boyish grin creeps across his face.

Shaking my head with a soft laugh, I step to the top as the music volume lowers. Surveying the crowd, I meet the eyes of everyone in attendance before speaking.

"I wish I were giving you this news under better circumstances," I say solemnly, "Magic has returned, and yes, it has done so at a heavy price. My brother's banishment has lifted."

Murmurs and whispers rise from the crowd, and I raise a hand, waiting a moment for silence before I continue, "I will not demand you to remain here, nor will I force you to leave. You all may come and go as you wish. My journey returns me to Servilia, though I do not know what I will find upon my return. It has been decades without any knowledge or news of tidings, so if you should also find yourself traveling home, please take the utmost care with whom you trust. Much will have changed."

As I turn to step down, a young woman's voice rings out amongst the crowd, "So we can stay here if we wish?"

I nod, "Yes. I will maintain security here so that this will be a safe house for us on Earth. Use it as you see fit."

Murmurs continue as I step down the stairs and lead the way to the lake, with Val trailing close behind me. We navigate to the rock wall closest to the rippling water from the waterfall, where the portal is summoned. Val gently eases Lara into my arms, and I cradle her small form against my chest.

The moment her head rests against my collar, she inhales deeply and sighs. The action is so abrupt that I think she's awake, and my gaze flicks to her face, only to find her still resting peacefully.

The action sparks a pang of déjà vu as I'm thrown into the memory of settling her into my truck before moving her into my safe house. The action is so closely mimicked that I chuckle as Val uses his blood to draw a symbol on the rock wall before he turns to look at me, bringing me back to the present.

The wall shimmers as the visage of a forest with enormous trees and glowing moss comes into view, and we glance at one another with a nod.

Whatever comes next, we will face together.

Stepping through the shimmering rock sends a nostalgic shiver down my spine. When I open my eyes on the other side, buried emotions threaten to rise as I survey our surroundings, and Val gently takes Lara from my arms.

It has been far too long since I could step on Servilian soil.

The forest around us is thick, with towering, ancient, and majestic trees that dominate the area. Their height is so staggering that the tips seem to disappear into the heavens. Some of the tree trunks are sturdy and gnarled, with their branches reaching out like inviting arms adorned with cascading vines and beautifully delicate blooms. The familiar soft glow of moss creeping up their trunks gives the canopy shade a welcoming luminescence where light can't reach.

The gentle rustle of leaves in the breeze harmonizes with the chorus of birdsong to create a serene symphony, and my soul feels contented.

It feels good to be home.

Val steps up alongside me, and his voice is soft as he surveys the forest, "I never thought I'd ever see this again."

I chuckle under my breath, "Neither did I," I say, my eyes dropping to Lara's unconscious form cradled protectively in his arms, "nor did I expect to see it again under such circumstances."

Val looks down at her, and I see the mixture of worry and compassion in his eyes as he searches her face, "We will find a way to wake her up, Darian. She will be okay. She's a fighter, that much we know for certain." he says quietly, tenderly adjusting her in his arms.

I nod, and my lips twitch, "She is quite the stubborn little thing, isn't she?"

Val laughs as I turn my head to scan the area.

Considering the sun's placement through the canopy, I point in the distance, "This looks south, and if memory serves correctly, there was a farm along the southern road. Whether it remains after all this time is the real question."

Val nods once, and we begin our journey through the trees. Our walk is quiet as our footfalls meld into the orchestra of forest life around us.

Val gently shifts Lara in his arms, concern etched on his features, "What do we do if-"

"Don't," I interrupt him, shaking my head, "she will wake up."

He falls silent as we continue walking through the woods, and I'm lost in my thoughts again.

I don't even want to consider it.

There's no timeline in this life or the next where Lara isn't part of my life or the lives of my brothers. She belongs with us.

The unfamiliar clench of anxiety tightens within my chest, and I force the possibility from my mind.

No.

She will pull through this.

After some time, Val halts, looking down at Lara with furrowed brows and panic in his eyes, "Darian, her fever is spiking."

My pulse hikes, and I rest my hand on his shoulder, "I've got her from here, brother."

He nods, though I can see his reluctance to give her over. Knowing how much this woman means to us both, my chest tightens.

Within a few short weeks, she twisted our world on its axis, tipping it until everything hinged on her survival.

It's funny to think I tried so hard to find a way to keep her from death's clutch just for this to happen regardless.

When I finally got wind of the prophecy, it made me dread going to that damn cemetery for the simple fact that we were one key closer to what might be her death.

At least she's still here and breathing.

I repeat that thought over and over until it becomes my mantra. As I cradle Lara's limp form in my arms, my magic seeps through my skin to cool her off. Within seconds, she sighs and settles into me, making my heart clench at the sight.

Val and I stand there momentarily, watching her steady breaths until I snap us both to the present, "Right, let's continue then."

Finally, we breach the forest's edge, where a small tulosh farm sits alongside a small, worn-down road. The farm has been abandoned for years, and its dense vegetation is overgrown and wild-looking.

What used to be a fence surrounding the structure is degraded, and much of the wood has fallen to the ground, where plants have long since sprouted.

Hearing Val chuckle next to me, I turn my head to look at him with a raised brow.

A boyish grin creeps across his face as he snickers, "Imagine Lara's reaction to the different plants and trees. We thought she was excited about the moss. Just wait until she gets a load of the rest of our world." His snicker turns into full-on, near-silent laughter, infectiously making me chuckle.

An image of Lara twisting back and forth with her blue eyes as round as saucers flashes into my mind, and I can't help but laugh myself.

"She'll lose her mind when she sees this," I choke out before calming down.

I lead the way as we near the worn-down structure and pause abruptly as the faint scent of strangers hangs in the air. Cautiously, we crouch down, and I rest Lara's legs on mine for a moment before pulling the hood of my robe over my head. From the corner of my eye, Val mirrors the action.

The area is silent, but the scent is fresh as we quietly stalk alongside the building wall, with Val taking the lead. He turns to me with a nod before disappearing around the corner.

As I survey the treeline, I hear his near-silent footsteps fade away as I cradle Lara close to my chest.

Moments later, Val reappears around the corner and jerks his head towards the building.

"It looks like whoever it was didn't stay long. They must have been here overnight and left early in the morning."

"Let's settle in for the night; if our friends return, we'll deal with it then," I say as I move past him into the building.

I won't say it out loud, but the constant strain on my magic has drained me more than I'd like to admit.

Now that we're home, I'd prefer to be as rested as possible.

There's no telling what danger we could get ourselves into now.

Even when my parents were alive, the biggest lesson they instilled in me early was to keep your magic reserves as full as possible because you never know when you'll need to push yourself to the limit.

I wish I would have listened to that advice the day they died.

My attention snaps to the present as I cautiously assess the state of the building.

The house is somewhat run down. There's a hole in the roof, and vines have crept through the windows, extending along the walls and furniture. Val glances around the room momentarily and then shuts his eyes as the ground rumbles.

Within seconds, a large bed of wood forms against the wall, and thick, plush moss sprouts from the top to make it comfortable to sleep on.

Val's magic is a wonder to behold. I've seen him create entire farms for families who lost everything to fires or disease. He's always used it to help bring happiness in the short few years before I was forced to remain on Earth.

I kneel on the bed and gently settle Lara in the center as she seeps into the moss cushion. Anxiety tightens in my chest as I watch her slender form remain still, the only indication of her life being the rise and fall of her chest.

At least we have that much.

The hole in the roof slowly grows smaller as Val uses his magic to coax his vines to cover it.

"We should get some rest. There's no telling what we'll run into tomorrow as we head into town. I'll take the first watch," I say, rubbing my palms against my face as exhaustion weighs heavily on me.

Val nods and crawls into bed alongside Lara, resting his head on the thick moss. He shuts his eyes as I sit beside the bed, my back against the wall, facing the doorway.

There's nothing else to do but wait.

Hours have passed since Val fell asleep, and the sun has long since set with his slumber. Moonlight creeps through the vine-covered window into the room, casting shadows that dance along the walls beside me as I blink slowly, gazing into the dark.

It's a surprise I've managed to stay alert with the toll the use of my magic has taken on my body.

Two hundred years of banishment still allowed me to use my magic, but surprisingly, twenty-five years without it has made my reserves feel as though I'm only learning to tap into them again.

The wind howls eerily outside the house as Val's soft snores echo inside the room. The slow tempo of his breathing feels velvety to my ears, and I struggle to keep my eyes open.

I'll wake Val up for his watch if I can manage a few more hours.

Though, it may be easier to remain alert if I lean my head back against the wall.

As my head rests against the wood and my neck does not need to support its weight, my eyelids feel heavier. Staring at the doorway, I blink again, but my eyes do not open this time.

Chapter 5

Darian

My eyes open to an unfamiliar scene, and I'm clearly dreaming.

I'm standing on a sidewalk next to a school where parents are picking up their kids. Honking and lively chatter fill the air, but I can't seem to focus on anything.

The trees are a mixture of orange, brown, and red, and a bitter chill in the air nips at my skin as I scan the blurred area.

"Where are we?" Val asks, and my head snaps in his direction as he watches the fuzzy faces passing by.

My gaze lands on a young girl amidst the crowd on the sidewalk, no more than 20 feet away. She's the only person who isn't obscured in some way, wearing a baggy sweater that looks two or three sizes too big. She looks no older than thirteen, talking to some young boy I assume is the same age, though his face is as blurry and unfocused as the rest.

The roar of an engine captures her attention as a truck pulls up alongside them, and the passenger window rolls down. The young girl waves good-bye to the boy and pulls down her hood, revealing shoulder-length silver hair.

That has to be Lara.

My brows furrow as I watch her nervously climb into the truck's passenger seat.

"We're inside her dream," I say, taking a few steps closer. Her trembling voice echoes through the space as she apologizes profusely, and the area around us blurs together.

Val and I turn from one side to the other, scanning around as the dream becomes focused again. When my vision clears, we're positioned outside a house, standing before a bedroom window. With the cramped space inside, it must be the smallest room in the house, as the minimal light from the window illuminates the room just enough for us to see.

We hear Lara's cries first before a man comes into view, dragging Lara behind him before shoving her roughly into the room and shutting the door with a click of the lock. Rage boils beneath my skin as I watch the young version of Lara weep silently against the floor.

"Is this what she went through all those years?" Val's voice is barely audible but thick with anger, which mirrors my feelings.

I don't respond, but we both know the answer.

She went through worse than this.

What we're seeing is hardly close to the abuse she would have endured to get the scars she has on her back. The knowledge that this is only a taste of the horrors she experienced makes me regret every action for the last seventeen years of my life.

I should have saved her from this.

The dream suddenly shifts again, but instead of blurring out of focus, the moon and sun wink in and out of the sky, one at a time. Val and I look at each other with horror as we come to the same conclusion.

Days.

Lara was locked in this room for days.

We watch as the dream slows down, with Lara remaining unmoved from where she had fallen days prior.

"Are they going to leave her-" Val's hushed question cuts off as we hear the door unlock, and a young girl no older than Lara pushes the door open. The sound sends Lara into a panic, and she frantically crawls backward to the wall.

Her fear is palpable from where we stand, and my hands tighten into fists at my side.

It's taking everything not to just dive through the window to her, but I don't know what the repercussions would be.

The young girl hurries over to Lara, placing a glass of water and a piece of bread on the floor before her.

Lara looks up at the girl. Her face is heartbreakingly twisted in pain and sadness before she devours the bread, chasing it with the water.

My chest clenches as tears flow freely down her face. She sets the glass down with a tortured resignation painted across her features as if she dreads what will come.

A loud bang sounds down the hall, and the door to the room flies open. Lara's silent tears have turned into begging and pleading as the man from earlier grabs the young girl by the arm and drags her to the bed.

We watch in sheer horror as he unbuckles his belt and whips the young girl repeatedly while yelling and shouting at Lara.

He shouts that she is the one responsible for this child's torture and abuse, his voice ringing out loudly into the deafeningly silent air before Lara's adult voice cuts through in a shrill cry for it to stop.

The dream suddenly blurs again, and Val locks his gaze on mine as we wait for the scene to unfold. As the scenery around us comes into view, I first notice that we're in the countryside.

There's a long stretch of land on either side of the house. The home looks like one of those big front porch homes you might see on the front of a Southern Living magazine. We're standing off to the side of what appears to be a barn with connecting pens for various animals.

I spot Lara inside one of the pens. Her silver hair is tangled and covered with mud and muck as she uses some tool to sweep up the excrement from the floor.

Val places his hands against the wood ledge in front of us, his knuckles turning white as he squeezes, "I can't watch another one of these if they're all as bad as the last one, Darian."

I can't say I disagree.

Especially when I feel as though we're invading Lara's privacy, but part of me feels as though we owe it to her to suffer through this pain with her.

My jaw clenches.

"I don't want to be here either, Val. But it's not like we chose to be in her dreams. We don't even know how we got in here, never mind knowing a way to get out," I say quietly, keeping my gaze trained on the young version of Lara as she continues to clean.

Val falls silent beside me, and as the sound of an engine cuts off from the other side of the house, she freezes in place.

Then she's on the move, running from one side of the barn to the other, frantically trying to clean the goat pen and put the chickens in their coop when the back door swings open, revealing a different man than the previous dream.

"Were they all like this? She didn't have one good foster family?"

Val's rage is nearly palpable as we watch the man storm over to Lara, shouting in her face before grabbing a fistful of her hair and shoving her into the pig pen. He shouts something else at her before storming into the house, and Lara curls tightly into the fetal position in the hay.

She remains there for some time, and as the sky darkens, a chill sets in that feels like it's seeped into my very bones. I watch her shiver alone in the hay, and my heart wrenches as the pigs settle in against her.

The animals gave her more compassion than her foster families ever did.

Voices from the distance begin to get louder as time passes, and soon, a group of teenage boys file into the barn, pointing and jeering at her.

One of the boys steps into the pen, grabbing her by her arm, and she flails, throwing punches at him in a desperate attempt to get free.

Pride swells in my chest as one of her punches hits its mark, but it's quickly smothered as the other boys rush in to drag her out.

We follow closely behind as they bring her into a barren field where they have set up a roaring bonfire.

Dread coats my veins with what is to come next.

Val must have the same thought as he watches them haul her closer to the flames.

"She didn't have any burn scars, right?" He asks hesitantly, almost as if he's afraid of the answer.

I shake my head. "Not that I've seen," I say quietly, uncertainty thick in my voice.

While I thought I had every inch of her memorized, witnessing her traumas like this tells me there's so much more beneath the surface that we haven't seen.

It's a clear fucking reminder that not all scars are visible.

Val and I share a look, one mixed with apprehension and dread, as we turn to watch the rest of Lara's nightmarish memory unfold.

Chapter 6

Lara

My arms already feel bruised from the boy's grip on them.

No matter how I twist and turn, I can't free myself from their grasp as I stare into the mouth of the enormous fire. It spreads wide, but there's a slight hollow section in the middle, with one side not yet lit up.

They pull me to the unlit side and shove me into the center roughly. The force sends me painfully crashing to my knees. The small stones and sticks on the ground bite into my skin as heat licks at me from nearly all sides.

"My dad says you're worth less than the pigs!" Terrence, the biological son of my foster parents, screams at me as he takes one of the burning sticks and places it in the empty slot, catching the tinder on fire.

Panic settles within my body, and I crawl toward him, "Please stop! I didn't do anything!"

My pleas fall on deaf ears as the boys blow on the fire from all sides. The heat bears down on me as the flames grow more chaotic, and the fire engulfs the tinder around me in one large circle.

Amidst the shouting and hostility are familiar voices that seem out of place. Voices that bring a sense of relief to my mind, as if a damp breeze has cut through the intense heat threatening to consume me.

It takes a moment, but I recognize the baritone voice that shouts my name, cutting through the chaos.

"Lara! We're coming to get you!" the voice shouts, and my heart nearly skips a beat before my brain catches up.

Darian.

I twist in the direction of the voice, and my eyes lock onto the familiar mismatched gaze of the man who always seems to find me when I need him.

I hardly register the tears streaming down my face as I see who stands beside him. His long black hair flows loose down his shoulders, and a pair of piercing hazel eyes, bright with rage as they flicker against the burning from the fire.

Val.

Just as relief floods my body, my foster dad appears behind Darian and Val. His vile face is contorted into a twisted visage of rage as he approaches them.

Without a second thought, I launch myself forward. My warnings hang in the air between us, and I sprint over the white-hot flames of the bonfire. As I dash across the fire, ignoring the searing pain in my feet, Darian and Val jerk toward me with panic painted across their features.

I can't think about the pain right now.

Not when they're both in so much danger.

After an eternity, I reach them, falling forward into their awaiting arms, and I scream, pointing at my foster dad behind them, "Watch out!"

Val's hands tighten around my bruised biceps, and I suppress a wince as Darian cups my cheeks, turning my face to his.

"Lara, it's a dream. We are inside of your dreams. You need to wake up." His baritone voice is deep and sure, and even though this feels so real, the certainty of his words gives me pause.

I blink at him twice, and my brows furrow, "It's just a dream?" My body trembles, and I shift my gaze from him to Val, who raises an eyebrow in amusement.

"I'm not conjured by the dream. I guess I'm part of it for now, but I'm really real."

He grins, and I can't help the relieved smile that stretches across my face, wet from the tears streaming down my cheeks. The pain in my feet finally registers as they throb, and I lean on Darian and Val for support.

My mind whirls as it focuses and fixates in on the burns, but Val's voice cuts through and snaps me back to the present.

"Lara, you need to wake up from these nightmares."

I glance up at him as his words sink in.

Nightmares.

These have all just been nightmares?

I blink and glance around. The bonfire and teenage boys all look frozen in time. Turning to look at my foster dad, I see that he, too, is unmoving.

As the realization sets in, I remember that in my past, Darian and Val were not there to save me.

I ran across the red-hot coals to escape what I thought was certain death at the time and managed to flee into the house. My foster dad never showed up to the fire.

Instead, he found me in the house and punished me for leaving the pig pen by making me walk on my blistered feet for hours every day to clean.

I look at the boys as their faces ripple. It's as if they're an image projected onto a surface of calm waves.

With each wave, the truth settles deep within me, leaving no room for doubt.

I've been trapped in my past.

How long has it been?

My always simmering anger rears its ugly head once again, and I run at my foster brother, swiping my hand at his blurry face. The surface of the illusion tears, revealing a bright white light that quickly becomes blinding, and I bring my arms up to shield my eyes.

The light is so bright that it floods my eyes even with them squeezed shut, and I cry out as it erupts into every corner of my mind.

My eyes flutter open, and as the room comes into focus, I note the vines on the walls. On instinct, I attempt to recall what memory this might be from.

"Lara?" Darian's baritone voice sends a shiver of relief through my body, and I tilt my head slightly toward the sound.

His towering frame rushes toward me from the wall, and the warmth at my back tells me that Val was asleep in the bed alongside me.

Just like always.

Darian's impending form pulls me in, crushing me against him in a dangerously tight hug as Val encircles my back from behind.

I feel like a bean in a burrito. A very squished bean.

My chest feels like it will cave in from both pressure and happiness.

"As much as I'm enjoying this," I choke out, "I may die from lack of oxygen."

Darian eases off, settling on the bed in front of me. Val remains at my side but leans down on his arm, where I can see his face. Seizing the opportunity, I punch Val in the arm with medium force, and he recoils in shock. "What was that for?" He exclaims, feigning an injury as he rubs the spot.

My eyes narrow at him.

"That," I point my finger accusingly, "is for being a pervert when you were a wolf."

Val grins sheepishly and rubs the back of his neck with his hand as Darian barks out a laugh. I can't help but revel in the moment as emotion clogs my throat. The lightheartedness is a welcome contrast to the eternal dark of my nightmares.

"I'll admit, she's got you there, Val." Darian chokes out teasingly. His smile is infectious, and I can't help but embrace the smile tugging at my lips as he turns his mismatched gaze to me. "So, how are you feeling?"

I blink.

*How **am** I feeling?*

I glance over the length of my body, recalling the events leading up to this point. Through the nightmares, it feels like a millennium has passed, as if it had been in a past life or seen in a movie. I run my fingers across the pink line where the deep cut had been before putting my hand to my abdomen.

Frowning, I glance at Val and Darian.

"I don't understand. There's no pain, but I was certain I was going to die. Did I..." I trail off, panic rising in my chest, "Oh god. I died, didn't I? Am I dead? Oh god, are you guys dead, too?"

Each question I ask becomes more frantic, and Darian puts his palms up between us.

"Breathe, Lara. No one's dead here." He calmly and animatedly blows out a breath, indicating that I should do the same.

A pit of anxiety roils in my stomach, "Tammy? Candace? Henry?"

Darian pulls a lock of hair from my face, "I had sent a rescue team to them."

"The snake was that woman-"

He nods, "Blair."

"Right, Blair was the snake I saw. Who was the panther?"

Darian's lips twitch, "That was me, Sunshine."

I blink at him.

Talk about information overload.

My hands go to rub my temples, pausing when I see the thin pink line parallel to my scars from Cain.

"How am I healed right now?"

The muscle in Darian's jaw tenses, but Val responds, "You lost a lot of blood, Lara. You passed out on shore, and Darian stopped the bleeding with his magic before teleporting us to Haven. Lor healed you with a rather unconventional method that no one has used in quite some time. It worked, but you had a fever and weren't waking up, so we decided to find a healer here who may have been able to help."

Here?

Where is 'here'?

Val cocks his head to the side and brings his hand to my forehead, sending butterflies through my body.

"Thankfully, your fever has broken," he says with a soft smile, tucking my hair behind my ear.

The urge to lean into his touch is nearly overwhelming, and heat rises to my cheeks. I nod once, hardly absorbing the information as I fail any attempts to ignore the effect his touch has on me.

"What about my dream? How did you two end up there?" I ask, my voice coming out more breathless than intended, and I clear my throat awkwardly to mask it.

Darian sighs and leans down to rest his forearms on his knees as he contemplates his answer. The tension in his arms and neck tells me he's being particularly cautious, and my heart rate spikes.

It's as if he weighs a thousand worlds in his mind as he chooses his words carefully.

"Dream-weaving is not a power that Val nor I possess. In fact, there hasn't been a record of it in my or my parent's lifetime. It's more of an urban legend or myth that it ever did exist," he blows out a breath, and his gaze locks with Val's before he continues, "There are only two possible explanations for what happened. One is that whatever blade you were stabbed with somehow caused you to be stuck inside your mind and then sucked us both into it, which is unlikely."

His voice is soft as he adds the second suggestion, his gaze searching my face as he speaks.

"The other possibility is when magic was released, your power was released with it."

I'm so dumbfounded; all I can do is blink at him.

Me? Magic?

I shake my head, "That's impossible. I'm just an ordinary orphan girl who studies science. There's no way..."

I trail off, staring incredulously at both my upturned palms as if they could somehow give me an answer, when Val and Darian each grasp one of mine.

Their touch is comforting. They gently rub their thumbs along my skin, keeping my mind grounded as I take in the revelation.

I glance between them as butterflies continue to soar through my body, responding to their touch, "How could we know for certain?"

Darian rubs his chin, smoothing the facial hair along his jawline. "We were originally going to Trebonia for a healer, but perhaps we should search their archives instead. They have the second oldest library in the realm, with Lavinium, my home, being the oldest."

Val nods in agreement with an eager grin. "While we travel, we can try to replicate the act, just without the nightmares this time," Val says softly, searching my face with a tenderness that makes my chest tighten.

"We really aren't on Earth anymore, are we?" My gaze darts around the room again, soaking in the vines that stretch across the walls.

Now that I'm not half asleep and confused, I finally notice that they cover the ceiling and the window.

Somehow, though, I still feel drained, as if my energy has leeched from the very core of my being.

"We are not, though I suspect you'll enjoy it all the same," Darian's baritone voice echoes through the room as I yawn heavily. "Get some rest, Lara. Some real rest. We'll be heading out at first light."

"What if I don't wake up again?" My voice is no more than a whisper as if saying it any louder would breathe it into existence.

Val cups my cheek tenderly, and his eyes burn bright even in the dark, "Then you can use your power to call us back in."

I nod, feeling Darian's lips against the top of my hair, and Val eases me backward into the soft surface of the bed.

"Where did the moss bed come from?" I murmur, running my hand along the top, feeling it soft and plush against my skin.

Darian laughs under his breath as he lies alongside me while Val shifts closer from the other side.

Val's hand trails up the inside of my arm, dragging my eyes to his, and my heart flutters wildly in my chest. It's a conscious effort to keep breathing as my body responds to their proximity.

He opens his palm in the space between us as moss creeps slowly over his skin, circling his palm.

Air catches in my lungs as a single flower bud sprouts from the center before the green leaves of the bulb elongate, turning shades of blue, red, and silver, with speckles of orange all over.

The flower stops growing just as Val plucks it from his hand, tucking it behind my ear.

"My magic can grow plant life and move or shift the ground," Val whispers against my ear, snaking his arm across my abdomen before Darian's arm joins it.

I'm encircled from both sides, and bliss washes over me as I melt into them.

If I could remain in this room with them for the rest of my life, I would happily do so.

With my heart lighter than ever, I let sleep take me.

Chapter 7

Caspian

The scenery around me blurs, and the lake disappears into shades of blue and green before everything refocuses.

I never thought I'd return here.

Gazing at the forest, it's as if I'm viewing it from someone else's eyes as I head north at a brisk pace.

Now that I'm back on Servilian soil, I guess, in a sense, I am.

Though, the Caspian who was banished from this place hundreds of years ago is not the same Caspian returning.

Sure. I'm still me, but something inside of me has fundamentally changed. Some innate part of my being has been altered in my time apart from this place, and now I feel like I can actually fucking breathe.

The castle comes into view between the trees, and my momentary relief turns sour as my feet carry me closer to Lavinium. Even if I were tired the moment I stepped through that portal, I wouldn't have been able to stop if I had wanted to.

My feet make long strides past the front gate of the marble city that was once my home as heads twist in my direction. Baskets and various items clatter to the ground as a handful of people disappear into the nearby buildings.

Good.

This means they haven't forgotten what I'm capable of.

Or what I've done.

I turn the corner, and something comes flying at me in a blur. Acting on pure reflex, my hand snaps forward to grasp the fist hurtling at my face as I tilt my head slightly.

Why do they always go for the fucking face?

The way his mouth drops open, his face contorts, and the panic in his eyes all tell me he didn't think this through. He acted on pure emotion and only now realized his mistake.

It'll be his last.

My hand jerks back, bringing him falling into me, and within an instant, my other hand thrusts into his chest. His heart beats erratically against my tight grip before I tear it from his body.

It beats once, twice, three times before twitching weakly.

His eyes are wide as saucers as he clutches the gaping hole in his chest before dropping to his knees. I sidestep as he falls forward onto his arm, gasping and twitching before collapsing to the ground.

Movement catches my eye as a handful of onlookers scurry away to their homes. Even better.

If that wasn't enough reminder for them to give a wide berth.

I'm happy to assist with the natural selection process.

The warm heart drops from my hand, landing on the ground with a wet splattering thud, and I take a few steps forward before something small peeks out from behind the corner of the house.

My gaze slides to the young girl staring at me, her brown eyes wide and filled with terror. The look tightens my chest in a way I don't fully comprehend as I continue toward the castle.

The odd sensation fades with each step until I push through the castle's main entrance, and the large wooden doors groan as they open wide.

The hall leading to the throne room is smaller than I remember.

Everything about this place is less grand than it once was. It is as if even my memories of each slab of marble have been tampered with or skewed. My steps echo in the air as I near the center of the room, and I slow to a stop before the pristine white throne.

Hundreds of years still have yet to wear on it, and the stark contrast of black and gold that weaves throughout it only adds to the allure.

I'm surprised it's not covered in crimson, considering the amount of blood spilled to usurp it.

"It's about time you returned to me," Samira says coolly, and my teeth grind together.

I turn to face her where she stands at the side entrance from the adjacent hall, "Yet I still did."

"So it would seem," she whispers, her eyes narrowing as she takes in my full appearance, "You look... different."

I shrug. "It's been over 200 years," I say, frowning as I glance at the shadows dancing along the walls.

My voice comes out steady, but my pulse slowly hikes.

Sure, time might play a part in it, but knowing how different I feel coming back... I'd rather not take chances on playing a game of twenty questions.

No, it's better if she knows nothing about what happened during my time away.

The less she knows, the better.

That satisfies her as she steps closer, and my gut twists. I'm used to feeling the disgust accompanied in this gods-forsaken place, but being here now, like this, when Lara could be dying…

I'm crawling inside my skin, itching to get the fuck out of here but unable to leave.

"You have much to catch up on, my dearest." she says, stopping before me to search my face, "I wonder where we should begin." a wicked glint in her eyes sends a jolt down my spine as she spins, walking briskly from the room.

"Come," she says curtly, throwing me into motion as I fall into step behind her. "It is time for us to get reacquainted."

Chapter 8

Lara

As I gradually awaken and my senses come alive, the smell of forest rain and something reminiscent of sandalwood envelops me.

My eyes open to Val, his forehead against mine as he sleeps peacefully. The tips of our noses brush one another with each breath, and his long, dark hair frames his face.

I breathe in his and Darian's scent, fighting the emotions that tighten my throat.

I never thought in my wildest dreams that I'd find one person who makes me feel the way I do now, but the feelings Val and Darian bring make me wonder if this is just how it's meant to be.

Their bodies press against mine as we lay on the softest bed of moss, and my entire body is alight from their proximity.

The intimacy of the moment, listening to each breath with the gentle rise and fall of their chests, synced in a rhythm that's in tune with mine.

It brings a deeply ingrained sense of serenity to my soul.

I wish I could just pause this moment in time and never leave it.

Their arms draped possessively over my body send a nervous flutter into my core.

This is uncharted territory for me, waking up so intimately entwined with two men.

However, the more I consider it, Val had always slept curled alongside me. For Darian, it may have always felt like he was sharing me in some way, as Val always claimed his place alongside us.

I gather my thoughts and attempt to untangle myself from their embrace, but both men tighten their grip around my body. The feeling makes me flush from head to toe as my mind wanders, hyper-aware of every place where our bodies connect.

Val's muscles are hard as his arm flexes against my side to tug me closer to him, and my cheeks burn hotter.

He laughs under his breath, and his hazel eyes are half-lidded as they meet mine, pouring gasoline on the slow-burning heat inside me.

"Are you feeling feverish? You seem quite warm." His voice is hushed, but its teasing tone is unmistakable as my gaze drops to his lips.

Feverish? I feel like I'm going to break out in sweat from how hard my heart is pounding.

My face burns further at his implications, which aren't entirely untrue, but being this close to them makes me even more overwhelmed than before.

Darian's arm eases off my body, and his hand glides up my chest to my cheek, only making my body flush further as my heart skips.

"Lara?" His deep voice is still sleepy as he gently tucks my hair behind my ear.

Val's hand moves to my hip and squeezes. The action jolts electricity through me, and I gasp sharply, my mouth dangerously close to his. Val's gaze darkens, and I know he's all too aware of the effect they're having on me.

In a desperate attempt to collect myself, I blink and swallow thickly. "What? No, I'm fine." I say hurriedly, but my voice comes out breathless and husky.

Val's already staring at me with a knowing grin, reinforcing my desire to play off what is happening inside my body, and I scramble off the bed in a hurry.

Darian chuckles, and Val shoots me a boyish grin as if they both knew exactly what they were doing.

Asses.

Darian equips a long sword with symbols etched along the handle, reminiscent of the symbols that adorn his body. I watch as he secures it to his hip and wraps his cloak around his shoulders before handing me articles of clothing.

In fact, now that I'm looking at them, I notice that they're both wearing clothes made of cloth unlike any I've seen before, with leather reinforcing parts around their hips, thighs and along their ribs.

Other than the cloaks around their shoulders, the style of their clothes is more form-fitting, and my gaze snaps to the leather and cloth in Darian's hand as he gestures them toward me again.

"What are these?"

"We will need to keep a low profile as we travel and..." he trails off, pointing to my current attire as if that's enough of an answer.

I look down, noting the gaping hole in my blood-stained dress shirt, with the trail of crimson down to the waist of my pants with a grimace. My reluctance to change fades away, and I look up at both men with a nod.

"Okay," I concede, waiting for them to turn or leave.

Neither of them makes any effort to move, and after half a minute of them looking at me expectantly, I clear my throat.

Darian tilts his head with a raised brow, "What is it?"

"What is it?... What do you mean, 'What is it?' I need to change, and you both need to leave."

"Why do I need to?" Val asks innocently, and my face burns.

I want to crawl into a hole as every memory of changing and showering around Val comes into the forefront of my mind, and I shoo both laughing men to the doorway, "Don't remind me of your perversion."

They disappear around the corner, and I tug the old, crusted clothes off. My skin is still covered in dried blood that flakes with my movements before pulling the fresh clothes on.

Surprisingly, the cloth pants are breathable, light, and soft, and the shirt fits well, if not a little tight around my chest. I feel better as I tug the cloak over my shoulders, connecting the clasp in the center. The material is thick but feels like silk, the hem nearly touches the ground, and a smile tugs at my lips.

The clothes fit almost perfectly.

Exiting the room, I scan the run-down building we took refuge within, noticing the slightly decayed wooden walls, holes in the roof in some of the rooms, and the overgrown plant life that's crept into the cracks and crevices.

It's apparent that no one has lived here for quite some time.

Once outside, I spot Val and Darian a few steps away and quickly join them as they turn toward me. Val, in his human-looking form, is slightly shorter than Darian but just as muscular and broad-chested.

My footsteps slow as I get closer, and I need to crane my neck slightly with each step as they tower over me. It takes a conscious effort not to stare at their unfamiliar clothes and how the material hugs their bodies in the best ways as they stop murmuring to one another.

Val turns toward me with his brows furrowed before he leans in and sniffs, "Someone needs a bath." he teases, tugging the hood of my cloak over my head and tucking my hair behind it.

I huff, "At least I don't smell like a dog." I mutter, and Darian chuckles in response.

"We'll get a room in the next town, but," Val tugs on the front of my hood, lowering it, " we don't want to draw unnecessary attention to ourselves for now."

The amusement I felt moments prior is long gone, and I don't miss the uncertainty on his face or the feathering in Darian's jaw. I nod once before we start down the dirt road, and I break the awkward silence as the building slowly disappears behind us.

"So that place we stayed was just a house someone left behind?"

"It used to be a tulosh farm," Val answers, grinning when he sees my confusion. "Tulosh is a grain. It is most comparable to wheat, I suppose." He clarifies, and I blink at him.

Whatever he sees written on my face beneath my hood makes him laugh, "D, look at Lara," he chokes out, and my gaze collides with Darian's as he barks a laugh.

"What is so funny?" I ask, more with annoyance than anger, but that only makes Val laugh harder.

Darian is first to collect himself and answer, "It's plain as day on your face how excited you are about tulosh. We figured you'd be thrilled."

Val has finally stopped laughing and grins. "It's cute, really." He drawls teasingly, and my cheeks burn.

These men will be the death of me.

Chapter 9

Lara

After walking for what feels like an eternity, the sound of laughter, chatter, and the general humming of life echo in the distance.

A mixture of excitement and nervousness begins to brim within me as I glance over to Darian and Val. They both appear tense.

My nervousness only grows as Darian secures his hood lower over his face, obscuring him from view completely.

Val mirrors the action, making me more uneasy as I do the same, tucking in close behind the two men as the town comes into view.

The town is rustic-looking, with buildings made of various shades of dark wood. The signs hanging in front are adorned with the same symbols as those on Darian's body, and I can't help but wonder what each of them means.

I'm busy guessing what each symbol could stand for, judging from what I can see inside or the various goods hanging from the windows.

It's surprisingly busy as we get closer. There's a loud bustle of life as people stand near their covered stalls. Some call out to people passing by in another language, others package goods and make sales, and some chat with one another leisurely.

Surprisingly, in the chaos of chatter, I detect English being spoken in most conversations, and I file that information away for later. As I survey the area, I sense an underlying tension in some interactions between the townspeople.

Eyes shift every so often in our direction, but they don't seem to linger. It helps that we're not the only individuals with hoods up walking around.

I follow closely behind Darian and Val as we slowly walk through the crowded streets. As we pass by one stall, the seller steps toward Darian, and within the blink of an eye, Val has nonchalantly placed himself between them and gestures away to the man.

The interaction is over as quickly as it started, and I'm left wondering why Val suddenly acted so protective.

His reaction was almost as if he was Darian's bodyguard.

It's so bizarre that I'm lost in my thoughts and hardly notice when Darian quickly turns and cuts through a crowd into a building.

It's not until Val's hand suddenly grasps mine, making the air in my lungs catch that I'm jolted into the present, as he tugs me behind him and follows Darian into the building.

He pushes the large door open with his free hand and leads me to the counter where a mountain of a man with long braided hair is standing. I remain silent behind Val as he pulls out a pouch and hands something over with a clatter.

I spot Darian sitting in a far, dimly lit corner as Val's hushed voice reaches my ears, "A room for three for the night."

The man before him scrutinizes him. "We only have rooms with two small beds or one large one. Take your pick," he says gruffly.

Val chuckles under his breath, "We'll take the large." he mutters, gesturing toward Darian, and I quickly oblige.

I sit beside Darian, our backs to the wall as the patrons near us continue chatting. We stay silent until Val joins us and sits across the table.

"Any trouble?" Darian asks quietly, and Val just shakes his head in response.

"Good." Darian falls silent as a taller brunette woman approaches the table beside him.

"What can I get ya?" she says curtly, looking between us with annoyance.

Val slides some kind of currency to the table towards her, "Drinks and some rhil for each." he responds flatly.

The waitress nods once, shoving the coin in her pouch before heading towards the counter.

Leaning in Darian's direction, I whisper, "Why are we keeping such a low profile?"

Val shoots me a warning look, and my mouth snaps shut.

Darian is quiet for a moment before he answers, keeping his voice so low that it's nearly inaudible, "Before we lost contact with our world, things were," I see Darian's grimace from beneath his hood, "not great. There was civil unrest and many rumors floating about. Without knowing risks, I'd prefer to remain in the shadows as much as possible."

The waitress returns with our drinks and bowls of stew with various vegetables. I suppress a smile as she walks away, and as they both take their first spoonful of stew, Val and Darian groan in unison.

Even from what little I can see, my chest swells at the nostalgia on their faces.

The moment the spoonful of stew reaches my tongue, my eyes widen. The taste is unlike anything I've ever had. The broth is salty and fragrant, with spices that tingle my tongue. The meat is tender, nearly melting in your mouth, and the vegetables have absorbed much of the flavor in the broth, but they still maintain a slight crunch. Bringing the cup of frothy drink to my lips, Val and Darian pause as I take a long sip. The flavor is herbal, sweet, and crisp, with a hint of berries and something sweet like honey.

I put the drink down, heaving a contented sigh as Val flashes a grin at me from beneath his hood.

"Taste good, Sunshine?" Darian asks teasingly, knowing full well that I just downed half the cup in one go.

"Incredible. I've never had anything like it." I say, bewildered by the variation of flavors I just experienced.

Val snickers softly, taking another sip of his drink, and we silently finish our meal. Idle chatter fills the space around us, with people discussing the weather, family news, and small-town gossip.

Darian moves to get up when the door flies open, and three burly men in matching leather uniforms walk in, throwing the room into silence. The tension in the air is palpable as the other patrons watch the newcomers seat themselves at a nearby table.

An aura of arrogant authority surrounds them as they snap their fingers toward the waitress, who, to her credit, doesn't cower.

She crosses her arms before barking loudly at them, "What do you lot want?"

My jaw threatens to drop at her attitude towards them.

Hell. When I grow up, I want to be like her.

All three look up at her with an unsettling stillness that catches the air in my lungs before the one closest to her mutters something under his breath. She nods once before returning to the counter.

The room is filled with anxious energy as if everyone is waiting for something terrible to happen or someone to make a wrong move.

It reminds me of those Wild West showdowns in the last remaining seconds before both gunmen fire.

After a few tense moments, the woman returns with their drinks, and hushed chatter begins to sound off from the corners of the room.

Everyone glances nervously around their tables still, as if expecting something to happen.

As the waitress turns to leave, one of the men grasps her arm tightly, causing her to cry out.

My gaze flicks to Val and Darian as they visibly stiffen.

Darian's knuckles turn white on the handle of his cup. It's clear that they're just barely restraining themselves from intervening.

"Enough, Leon." one of the men says, gesturing between his companion and the waitress, "We don't need her spitting in our drinks another day."

"She needs to be taught some manners, Marcus. Anyone who disrespects us disrespects the Queen." Leon sneers, twisting the woman's arm into an awkward position.

She whimpers, and Darian moves as though he's about to stand, but a robed man calls out from the table before us, freezing him in place.

"Perhaps it's about time that yeh take yer leave, eh? Many of us would rather see yer false Queen's head on a pike than serve yer lot in here."

My gaze snags on the older man in a robe; his hair is buzzed short to his skull, with a grey peppered beard that reaches his chest.

"You dare disrespect her radiance!!" Leon shouts, shoves the waitress, and surges to his feet, and the chair he is sitting on goes flying backward.

"Aye, I disrespect anyone who sits the throne that ain't supposed to be 'ere." the robed man in front of us stands up slowly, placing his hands on his hips and cocks his head while looking at Leon.

"Why you..." Leon throws himself towards the robed patron, but Marcus catches him by the waist and casts an assessing glance around the room.

Others have risen to their feet as the electric atmosphere pulses into hostility. Recognizing they're outnumbered, the three uniformed men scowl at everyone before sauntering off, tipping chairs over angrily as they leave.

The moment the front door closes, the waitress swivels to face the older man in front of us.

"Cato, you dimwit. You could have been seriously hurt. I had it covered."

Cato waves dismissively before running his hand over his long beard. "Aye, aye. You had it covered alright," he says wryly before turning towards us and tilting his head thoughtfully.

In the corner of my vision from beneath my hood, Darian's hood tips forward ever so slightly.

"Well, I'll be a damned fool." Cato murmurs and Val swears under his breath.

Cato glances around cautiously as chatter livens up the room again.

Everyone returns to their conversations, and the waitress makes her rounds. He steps to the table, and my heart thunders, my pulse raging in my ears as Val holds his arm out.

Cato just snickers in response. "Don't bother telling me off unless yeh want the entire room to know who yeh are 'n who yer with, lad."

He pulls out the chair next to Val and sits beside him. Curiously, his gaze shifts between Darian and me, and I suppress the urge to squirm uncomfortably in my seat.

"What do you want?" Val's voice is low, but Cato just grins in response.

He doesn't answer Val as the waitress approaches the table, eyeing us warily. "Another round, Liv," Cato states dismissively, and she frowns before leaving the table.

Glancing around us, he drops his voice, keeping his gaze leveled on the other patrons as he speaks.

"I want what e'ryone else in 'is damned realm wants," he looks at Val and then to Darian as he continues, "Stabili'y 'n peace."

Darian's hood tilts with his head, his voice hardly audible, "Our desires align then, old friend."

Cato's eyes widen, "So it really is yeh then, eh?" he breathes, swallowing and assessing the group around us, "Yeh don't need to hide yer faces in 'ere, but we're gon' 'ave a chat 'bout where the bloody 'ell y've been."

Darian blows out a sigh, "Are you sure?"

Cato's grin widens. "Aye, aye, I'm sure as a toryian's arse. But yer gon' 'ave a world o' questions comin' yer way."

Sighing deeply, Darian pulls his hood back and looks at Cato.

I'm so focused on him that it takes a moment to realize that the room has gone silent. You could hear a pin drop.

With a twist of my head, my heart stutters as every head behind Cato and Val is locked onto Darian.

It's at this moment that I realize there's still much I have to learn about him. If he's claiming this much attention in a town he hasn't stepped foot in, in over two centuries, I can't help but feel as though I'm watching a crucial moment in his life as the eyes gazing at him widen in recognition, with varying emotions on their faces.

Val pulls back his hood, but as my arms move to do the same, he subtly shakes his head, and my hands drop to the table.

A man across the room slams his cup down as he pushes to his feet.

"Nice of you to finally show your face!" he shouts, and a couple of people in the room murmur in agreement.

"Och, 'nough o' yer gripin'. I'm sure 'is majesty has plenty good reason fer 'is absence." Cato waves his hand in the air dismissively.

His majesty?

I feel the blood drain from my face as my eyes slide to Val. His gaze locks onto mine before he nods once, silently acknowledging the realization that must be plastered across my face beneath my hood.

Have I been fucking someone in a royal family?

My head swirls with questions, but I can only watch as Darian rises to his feet, palms flat against the table.

"I'm aware there were rumors regarding my disappearance for centuries, and while much of the realm knew the truth, lies, and deceit tend to spread like wildfire in the absence of rain." He pauses as people in the room murmur to one another. They quiet down as he holds up his hand and continues, "My brother's banishment is no more, hence my return. What this means for everyone remains to be seen."

Cato rubs his beard thoughtfully as he watches Darian before glancing at the people around us.

Everyone in the room goes silent, and people begin to sit down as they maintain their gaze on Darian, Cato, and Val.

"Judgin' by the visitors earlier, I'm sure ye 'ave deduced things 'ave not gone well in yer absence," Cato says. Darian nods in acknowledgment before he continues, "Yer friends 'ave all but disappeared as well."

"What?" Val's head turns to look at Cato so fast that I'm nearly certain it cracked.

Cato's shoulders drop as he shakes his head. "Aye, lad. Kieran lost 'is mind 'bout twenty years back, started goin' after e'ryone 'round em. Locked 'im way out 'n the middle o' the ocean on 'n island north o' Trebonia." Cato hesitates, looking to the ground solemnly as he continues, "Gray shifted years ago 'n never changed back. Cade 'n Zayne 'ave been missin' fer 'bout ten years 'r so now."

I flinch as Darian's fist connects with the table, echoing through the silent room. The temperature of the room drops and panic rises in my chest as I exhale a breath that fogs in front of me.

What in the world?

Concern etches across Val's face, "Darian," he says in an attempt to get his attention, but Darian's rage is palpable as the temperature drops even further.

The surface of the table where his fist is freezes over first; the ice creeping from his knuckles nearly connects with my skin, but I quickly withdraw my hands.

Holy shit.

"Darian," Val repeats louder, with more urgency.

Darian's eyes remain glazed over, the muscle in his jaw feathering as he no doubt wars with his mind and the room temperature plummets. The air swirls in ribbons around him in a twist of icy fog, churning chaotically around his body as he remains still.

Everyone in the room stands up and begins to murmur to one another, but Cato is the first to speak.

"He's losin' control o' 'is emotions." His voice holds a tinge of concern as he takes a step back.

I push to my feet and meet Val's hesitant gaze.

"He's never done this before," he says, shifting his attention to his friend again, "Being without magic for so long has complicated things." He takes a healthy step back as ice spreads down the table and across the floor toward him.

As panic slowly fills the room, I turn to face Darian, trying my luck to get his attention.

The fog of my breath cascades from under my hood as I try to snap him out of his trance, "Darian." When he doesn't respond, I repeat more assertively, "Darian."

The creeping ice falters for a moment before speeding up and spreading toward the patrons, who rush out of the building quickly.

I move to step away, but my shoes are frozen to the ground, and out of sheer panic, I grasp Darian's arm, inhaling sharply at the cold that penetrates my skin.

It feels as though a million shards of ice have pierced my hand, and I suppress a whimper by grinding my teeth.

He would never forgive himself for losing control like this if anyone got hurt.

And if I can't get through to him, I'm as good as dead anyway.

Solidifying my resolve, I lift my free hand to cup his cheek, "You have to control it, Darian. There are innocent people here."

The cold seeps into my palm against his face, and the tear that escapes my eye freezes halfway down my cheek.

I hardly register the pin-needle sharp pain that peppers my forearms as the air around Darian forms thousands of shards of ice, and they swirl around him.

Closing my eyes even though panic grips me tightly, I exhale a steadying breath and try one last time.

"We will find and help them, Darian, but we cannot do this if you lose yourself. Come back. Please." I whisper, and the frost around Darian halts in place before surging away from him in a rush.

The force of it blows my hood off, and I turn my head instinctively.

A long moment passes before I open my eyes, relief filling me as the air around us warms.

I raise my head, finding Darian's gaze already on me.

His eyes soften as he searches my face, and my heart flutters erratically.

"Lara," he says softly, his gaze trailing down my arms to my hands, and he curses under his breath. I follow his line of sight to see countless red slices along my arms and shake my head.

"They're superficial, Darian. I'm fine." I say, internally commending myself on maintaining my composure as Cato and Val rejoin us.

"Och, lucky the lass snapped ye out o' it." Cato chuckles, "Don't think yer gettin' out o' 'ere without introducin' us." he tuts while crossing his arms.

Darian cradles my arm gently as he blows out a breath.

"Cato, this is Lara. She is a scientist from Earth," he pauses as if to calm his nerves, "Lara, this is Cato. He worked with my family for years before Caspian's banishment, and afterward, he coordinated with my brothers to keep things from falling into chaos."

Withdrawing my hand from his grasp, I suppress the wince as I cross my arms and shoot him a look.

"Ah, right. Your majesty." I drawl and raise a brow at him, "Were you ever going to tell me that **minor** detail?" I ask, not bothering to hide the anger that seeps into my voice.

Cato puts his palms up in surrender, "Trouble 'n paradise. If ye need m' I'll be outside." he says gruffly before sauntering out of the building.

Darian sighs, and his shoulders sag, "I never meant to withhold that information. It just never felt like the right time," he pauses, shaking his head slightly, "And I suppose a selfish part of me was afraid you'd see me differently."

My brows pinch together, "You should have trusted me," I say and shake my head before continuing, "Nothing could change my perception of you from our time together."

The guilt on his face is enough to tell me he's kicking himself more than I am.

After a long moment, Val clears his throat and snaps us out of our stalemate, "So what do we do now?" he asks softly.

Darian's gaze lingers on me before he answers, "We still need to research dream-weaving in Trebonia, but if what Cato says is true, we need to go north to find Kieran. You research at the library. Lara and I will go north to find Kieran and bring him to his senses."

Val sighs, "It's settled then. We go to Trebonia."

Chapter 10

Lara

Patrons file back into the room, with a few stopping to speak to Darian, conveying their desire for him to take the throne and reminiscing about the days when his parents ruled.

From what I overhear, his parents were just and kind. Their people loved them.

If what they say is true, what drove Caspian to ensure their demise?

Did he crave power so ferociously that no one could stop him?

Perched between Darian and Val, I watch the ongoing interactions with curiosity as Val orders another round of drinks.

They have continued to come our way, whether from Val ordering them or patrons buying a round for everyone and at this point, I've lost track of how many I've consumed.

Perhaps I should ease up, considering I've never had it before, but...
You only live once.

At some point, Val and Darian shifted closer to me, their legs brushing mine under the table at times, sending butterflies through my core as they continue their conversations.

As Darian listens to a young woman's story about her uncle who served under his father, his hand glides onto my leg and rests there.

My cheeks heat as his thumb traces back and forth, and all I can think about is how he tastes.

How he feels under me…

Inside of me…

A heady mix of desire and need swirls in my abdomen, and I shake my head slightly.

If I have more of those thoughts, I might just jump him in front of everyone.

I look at Val's slightly fuzzy-looking features as my bladder threatens to explode and lean toward him. Heat rises further to my cheeks as he leans in close to hear me, and the skin of his cheek grazes mine.

"I need to use the washroom."

My body's reaction to Val's proximity is visceral, and every part of me holds its breath as if waiting for the distance between us to close.

"It's right this way." He pulls back, searching my face with a slight chuckle before standing and nodding to Darian.

I push to my feet, internally praising myself for not swaying as he slides his hand into mine and intertwines our fingers.

The flush in my cheeks becomes an entirely new shade of red as he walks me to a corner of the room where stairs lead to the second floor.

I blink and look at him with my brows furrowed, "The bathroom is upstairs?"

Val chuckles under his breath, tugging my hand for me to follow behind him.

Oooookay.

He leads us down a long hall to a room with intricate carvings and the same symbolism that adorns all the buildings.

"What does this say?" I ask, pointing to the symbols on the wall on either side of the door.

Val follows my gaze and points to the first set of symbols.

"These are from the family who built this inn. It's their well wishes to all who stay here, and these," he adds, pointing to the other side, "are instructions on how to reach them in case there are any issues."

Some symbols look familiar, and I can't help but ask.

"What do Darian's tattoos mean?" I immediately regret my question as Val's expression becomes guarded. There's a long pause before he answers.

"Some are part of who he is and his place on the throne, so they speak of his royal bloodline and his duty to his people. Some are his promises to the realm, and others are of his duty to restore the peace between Servilians and the gods."

Pressing his hand to the door, he whispers words I don't recognize, and a quiet click sounds out from the wood. He pauses, glancing at me with a softness in his features that I can't seem to place before pushing open the door with his free hand.

The room is spacious and well-lit, with bright rays filtering in from outside. The glass-like window casts an array of colors on the walls, almost as if made of diamonds. The giant bed in the center of the room has a dark frame, with antlers carved from each post reaching the ceiling. On top of the mattress are plush blue and white blankets that look like clouds.

This is incredible. I've never seen anything so beautiful.

Val squeezes my hand gently, bringing my attention back to his face. The soft smile that graces his features makes my heart clench painfully in my chest.

I clear my throat, finally remembering the reason we came up here as my bladder threatens to explode, "The washroom?"

Val gestures to a door across the room and tilts his head, "Nice and private. Want me to wait for you?"

I shake my head, speaking more confidently than I feel, "No need. I remember the way back."

Val chuckles under his breath as I turn to the washroom. I exhale a breath of relief when the door shuts behind me.

Any more time spent with either of them would be disastrous in all the best ways.

After using the washroom, my gaze lingers on the stone tub and the various bars of what I assume is soap along the wall.

They wouldn't be too mad if I took a little bit longer than intended, right?

Having made my decision, I twist the single knob above the faucet and place my hand beneath the warm water that rushes out.

It only takes a few minutes to fill before I climb in. The water rises over my chest as I ease back with a sigh of relief. The dried blood on my skin flakes into the water, and memories of the lake flutter into my mind.

The sudden urge to scrub clean takes over me, as if soap could wash away the feeling of that woman's blade buried in my stomach or her mouth on my wrist.

I grasp one of the various soaps on the wall and give it a tentative sniff before doing the same to the next. With little knowledge about what soap is for, they all smell of citrus and floral, and I'm certain any of them would do.

Once satisfied that no specs of blood remain, I drain the murky water before pulling myself from the tub and getting dressed. The moment I tug the door open, my gaze falls on Val and Darian in the center of the room.

My gaze locks with Darian's first, and I blink at his tall form in clothing that hugs his body in all the right places. The flush I previously recovered from slowly creeps up my neck again, and butterflies soar through my body as I try to break the silence.

I look at Val, confused since he said he would be downstairs, "Everything alright?"

Val grins, "Everything is fine. It's late and we figured we should turn in for the night to get an early start tomorrow to Trebonia."

Darian steps forward, and my heart leaps into my throat as he steps closer. My head tilts to look up at him more with each step until he's standing right in front of me, and my breath nearly catches in my lungs as he pauses.

"Lara," he says softly, and my gaze tracks the movement of his mouth.

I'll never get tired of hearing my name on his lips.

"Hmm?" My voice cracks as a ghost of a smile creeps across Darian's face.

"You're in the doorway, Sunshine," he says, which snaps me back to reality.

I blink and quickly move aside to let him into the washroom, "Oh, right. Sorry."

Internally scolding myself, I walk to the bed and collapse face-first into it. It's soft and fluffy, like laying on a cloud that my limbs are slowly melting against.

The bed dips next to me, and my heart skips a beat.

Butterflies twist chaotically inside my body as I try to remind myself this isn't new. Val and Darian have laid in bed with me many times.

This is simply my body reacting to whatever remnants of the drinks we had that still exists within my veins.

I hear the door to the washroom creak open and footsteps stop next to the bed. The sound of clothes rustling and a loud thud echoes in the sudden stillness in the room before the bed dips on the other side of me.

Sleep almost takes me when feather-light fingertips trail along my back, immediately drawing my focus as someone leisurely traces my skin. The feeling is oddly comforting and equally good at distracting me from the fact that I'm in bed with two painfully handsome men.

The bed shifts again, and before I can react, arms slide under my body and lift me off the bed.

Automatically, I wrap my arms around Val's neck, and my eyes snap open to see him smirking at me as he cradles me against his bare chest.

My heart leaps into my throat.

His lips are hardly an inch apart from mine, and I'm hyper-aware of every place our skin touches.

Oh, god.

"What are you doing?" I ask, cringing when my voice comes out more breathless than confused.

His lips twitch, and he jerks his chin to my side. I turn my head, and my heart gallops in my chest as a shirtless Darian suppresses laughter. The corded muscles in his abdomen and arms flex as he pulls the blankets down.

Oh, I'm so screwed.

Val lowers me onto the bed and laughs softly before helping Darian cover the three of us.

Embarrassment coats my veins as my cheeks burn, and I don't need a mirror to know I'm red as a tomato, so I turn and bury my face into the fluffy pillow.

"You alright, Lara?" Val whispers close to my ear.

The pillow muffles my voice, and the desire coursing through my veins mixes with giddy excitement, "Mhm,"

My face only burns hotter when Darian chuckles next to me, as if he and Val both know exactly where my brain went the moment I saw both of them half naked.

Darian's baritone voice sounds out, and I can feel its rumble from how close he lays as he drapes his arm over my back, "Stop teasing her and let her rest, Val."

My chest tightens as I feel a soft kiss on my head from each of them before they settle down to sleep. My heart could beat out of my chest at any moment.

"Rest, Lara," Val whispers beside me and rests his arm alongside Darian's.

It takes longer to calm down than I'd ever admit to either of them, but I finally manage to relax as the heat from their bodies and the rhythmic sound of their breathing lull me to sleep.

Chapter 11

Lara

The faint sound of birds chirping is the first thing to catch my attention as I open my eyes. I'm standing on top of the terrace of a large stone castle with a beautiful marble railing in front of me that twists across either side.

The trees and buildings in the distance look misty, almost as if a light fog engulfs the landscape beyond. In the soft illumination of sunset, the ambient sound of sprawling life echoes out in the air.

I nearly jump out of my skin as a voice jolts me from my reverie.

"Beautiful, isn't it?" Val says beside me as he leans against the railing, and my gaze flicks to him before I scan the scenery again.

"Yes, it is."

Though my gaze is everywhere but on Val, it's as if a sixth sense is locked onto him. He steps in close, and I feel his hand on the small of my back. His thumb glides across my skin softly, leaving a blazing trail of electricity in its wake.

I feel confident this is simply a fever dream conjured up by my subconscious. It's not like we miraculously teleported somewhere.

At least I'm not dreaming of both of them.

"Am I interrupting anything?" his baritone voice behind me sends a shiver down my spine.

Definitely a fever dream.

Val casts a mischievous grin in my direction as I feel the heat of Darian's chest against my back, "Not at all. We were just observing the beauty of the world." My pulse jumps, and I nearly forget how to breathe.

"Impossible to acknowledge such a view when true beauty stands right before us," Darian says as his hand weaves into my hair, tilting my head to the side.

I feel his lips brush my ear, and my breath hitches. Val's hand has moved from the small of my back to my rib cage as he stands in front of me, watching my reactions with a look that sends the desire coursing through my body into overdrive.

I can't deny how badly I want them both. Not now. Not when everything inside of me craves to be close to them.

Locking eyes with Val as Darian softly kisses beneath my ear, trailing gently down the side of my neck, I realize that if I do this with them in my dream, I will not be able to look at them in the eyes tomorrow without feeling guilty.

Regardless of how badly I want them both to be mine.

My subconscious must know to shift the dream since Darian's kisses halt, and Val tilts his head as if confused.

"Are we incorrect in thinking you want both of us?" Darian whispers against my skin, and I shake my head.

"It's not that I don't want you both. I do… I just..." My heart sinks as I resign myself to admitting the truth no matter how embarrassing, "I can't do this with you two in my dream and act tomorrow as if nothing happened. Just because I'm dreaming of it doesn't mean I should take advantage of you both like that."

Val's lips twitch as he looks at Darian over my shoulder, and I frown, "What?"

Darian's lips press against the side of my neck, and Val squeezes my hip gently and leans in until his lips brush against mine.

"This isn't your dream, Lara," Val's hazel eyes are bright as my heart drums in my chest like I've run a mile in the past 30 seconds.

"What?" I ask breathlessly.

Darian's head leans against mine enough that I feel his breath skate over my ear, "You're both inside my dream, Sunshine. Now, let's wake up." he says, his voice husky as he nips my ear.

I gasp as my eyes snap open to the darkness of our bedroom.

The momentary relief that it was just a dream and that I didn't embarrass myself quickly diminishes as Darian shifts to prop himself up on his elbow next to me.

His free hand cups my cheek as Val's side of the bed shifts, and his hand traces my stomach, slowly swirling lower until he's running his fingers along the line of my pants.

I can hardly breathe as Darian leans down, turning my face with his hand on my jaw to give himself a better angle and access to my neck.

"Is this real?" My voice comes out as no more than a whisper.

He trails gentle kisses up my jaw before pausing when his lips are ever so slightly touching mine, sending every nerve in my body into overload.

The scent of forest rain fully envelops my senses, "This is all incredibly real, Sunshine, and if it is just a figment of my imagination, I never want to wake up because this is where I'm meant to be."

Val's hand slips beneath my clothes, and I inhale sharply as he softly circles over my clit with just enough pressure to send electricity through my abdomen.

Darian skillfully tugs his pants off as he gently presses his lips to mine, and it's only a moment before he moves. His kiss quickly becomes more passionate, and as I gasp at Val's ministrations, Darian deepens the kiss as his tongue finds mine.

Everything about this just **feels** right.

Being with them both is like finally placing a puzzle piece you thought you'd never find into place.

My heart races in my chest as Val tugs down my pants with surprising ease and positions himself between my legs.

His hand lifts my leg to rest on his shoulder before he leans down, and his breath cascades over my exposed pussy. I'm about to pull away from Darian to ask him if he's sure he's okay with this when Val's tongue glides all the way up to my clit and swirls over it.

"Fuck, you taste incredible," he mutters before his mouth is on me again.

Darian's kiss swallows my moans, and my legs tremble as Val continues to swirl and flick my sensitive clit. A chaotic euphoria grows in my core, and though I buck against him and grind through the movements, he doesn't let up.

He holds me firm as Darian kisses down my neck, sucking and nipping at my skin as he lifts my shirt and trails lower.

"That's it, Sunshine. Chase your pleasure, just like that," he says against my breast before taking my nipple into his mouth and sucking hard.

My mouth drops open, and I inhale sharply as my back arches, pushing me further into them.

He groans, and I glance down at the mess of dark hair from each of them as Darian's heated, mismatched gaze flicks to mine.

Fuck. This is the hottest thing I've ever experienced in my life.

Darian moves to my other breast and takes my nipple into his mouth, sucking hard as Val slides two fingers in.

The sudden intrusion, the pain, and the unending pleasure Val's giving to my clit sends my body into overdrive. My back arches into Darian, and I cry out huskily, gripping both of them tightly by the hair.

Val pulls back, and his breath skates over my soaked pussy, "She's close, D," he groans before flicking my clit with his tongue in a way that should be wholly illegal and slides another finger inside.

My orgasm crashes over me, and I cry out. It's loud enough that I'm sure the entire building heard it as he coaxes each wave of euphoria from my body.

 It's not until I'm begging him between pants to pause for a moment to catch my breath that he finally concedes, leaning back and letting my twitching legs rest on the bed.

I'm a fool to think that we're done until Darian rolls me on top of him, and I feel his dick throb between us. My mind whirls with the heady dose of desire and post-orgasm daze as our eyes meet.

I'm clearly a glutton for the best kind of punishment as my hand snakes between us to position him at my entrance, and I slowly sink the thick head of his cock deeper. My clit is still sensitive in the aftershock of my orgasm, and as I ease the length of his dick deeper, each shift as I accommodate his size sends jolts of pleasure through my core.

This feeling of fullness is overwhelming but everything inside of me craves more.

I need both of them.

My eyes find Val as Darian makes long, drawn-out strokes from below. I gesture for him to come closer, and he kneels comfortably on the bed before me, cupping my cheeks with both hands as his long, dark hair falls against my skin.

Val's bright hazel eyes search my face as he presses his forehead to mine before pressing a tender kiss against my lips. Tasting my arousal and Val is an intoxicating mix that sends my mind into a frenzy as Darian keeps his long strokes beneath me.

Val's kisses are cherishing, reverent, and savoring like he has all the time in the world, and there's nothing he'd rather be doing as he caresses my jawline and cheek with his thumbs.

Darian thrusts up with slightly more force, and Val swallows my moan into his mouth as Darian reaches down to circle my sensitive clit gently, and my toes begin to curl as another orgasm builds.

I feel Darian's urgency pick up, and I pull back slightly from Val.

I need them both more than my lungs need air.

"Stand up," I breathe, and he straightens up. My hands fumble with the ties on Val's pants as Darian's thrusts jostle my positioning. I tug down Val's pants until his cock springs free, and I swallow against the nervous tightening in my throat.

His dick pulsates between us, and I blow out a breath in an attempt to calm my nerves.

Giving head to above-average-sized men can be daunting enough...

Val and Darian are far beyond being above average.

I'm starting to wonder if it's a Servilian trait.

Tilting his cock up, I lean in and drag my tongue from the base to the tip before swirling my tongue around the top. Val's head falls back, and he mutters something in another language.

I use my hand to work the base as I swallow him until he touches the back of my throat, breathing through my nose to take him deeper, and his hand winds through my hair at the back of my head.

"That's it," Darian groans between thrusts, "You're doing so well. You take us both so fucking well."

His final note of praise is emphasized with a rough thrust that pushes me into Val's dick more, forcing his cock deeper than I intended, and tears spring to my eyes as I fight through the urge to gag.

Each time Darian slams into me, Val's grip on my hair holds me tight, keeping my head from pulling back, and I'm soon cresting another orgasm.

There's just something so hot about being fucked by Darian while Val makes me fight for breath, and as Val's breathing becomes as erratic as Darian's thrusts, I know they're both about to finish.

What I don't account for is the ice-cold sensation along my nipples, neck, and stomach as Darian slams into me at an angle that squeezes my clit, and my orgasm shudders through me.

My eyes snap shut, and the moan that tries to escape my throat just vibrates against Val as he squeezes my head further down his cock. He swears loudly as his dick swells as he comes, and I have no choice but to swallow with how deep he is.

Darian grunts before gripping my hips with his hands, slamming up into me in rapid succession before one final thrust, and I feel his cock throb deep inside of me as he comes too.

Val leans down after withdrawing from my mouth, his thumbs gently wiping the tears from my cheeks.

He gently kisses my lips before searching my face, "Never woken up from a dream like this before," he says before glancing at Darian. "You?"

Darian chuckles beneath me, his thumbs stroking my skin, "Never."

My cheeks burn, and both men grin as we extricate ourselves from one another.

"I'm going to need another bath," I say before Val hoists me into his arms and carries me to the bathroom.

Waking up that morning sandwiched between them has me blushing as I reflect on the events that transpired the night before. The only thing that makes me uneasy is that I somehow entered Darian's dream and dragged Val in with me.

I'm pulled from my thoughts as Val opens his hazel eyes, and they land on mine.

"Morning," he says softly, raising his hand to stroke my cheek, "What's plaguing that beautiful mind of yours?"

I sigh and frown, "Is this whole dream-weaving thing supposed to be chaotic like this? I can't control it."

Darian shifts on the bed, leaning over me and tucking my hair behind my ear, "It's been so long since there's been a dream-weaver. It's hard to say how it's controlled. Until Val researches it more, it will likely be trial and error. We'll just have to do what we can to roll with the punches until then." he says, reassuringly squeezing my hip, "You won't go through this alone."

He kisses my head tenderly, and both men get dressed as I shove my unease into a box and tuck it away.

Chapter 12

Lara

When we leave the inn, we're graciously given creatures called toryians to ride. They have similarities to but are also nowhere close to being horses at the same time.

I stare at the beast as big as a Clydesdale as it walks closer on its padded feet, and my heart leaps into my throat. Each toe has a deadly talon on it that is reminiscent of a hawk or eagle. Their bodies are muscular, sturdy, and covered with wiry fur. Their necks do resemble those of horses, but that's where the similarities stop. Their faces are short, with no eyes, but instead, they have two antennae hanging in front of them.

Darian helps me into the saddle, lifting himself onto his toryian as Val mounts next to us. The creature takes a step, and I lurch to the side as Darian leans in, his hand wrapping around my bicep to keep me on top of the beast's back.

This is going to take some getting used to.

It takes only a few hours of riding to get to Trebonia, and we pull our hoods over our heads as we arrive in the bustling city.

There are people everywhere. Their idle chatter blends into the background as we wind through the streets.

Val takes the lead with Darian between us to help keep him as concealed as possible while we navigate the labyrinthine roads toward the city's center. It's not long before a magnificently large tower comes into view, its imposing size hovering over the buildings beside it.

Darian slows, pulling his mount next to mine, and I can hardly hear his hushed voice amid the chaos around us.

"That is the library—one of the oldest in Servilia. If that building doesn't hold the answers, our only option is to go to Lavinium, where the marble archives are." He says solemnly, and though his voice is soft, there's an underlying current of hurt that reaches deep inside my chest and tugs at my heartstrings.

It's a pain I somehow feel so deeply that it could almost be my own.

We reach a crossroads, and Val slows to a stop, turning his mount to face us as a sharp twist of anxiety squeezes my insides.

My throat is tight, and I swallow thick against the emotion clogging it, "Are you sure about this?"

Val dips his head once, "Positive. Just keep this one out of trouble," he says, jerking his chin towards Darian with a grin I can hardly see beneath the shadow of his hood.

He steers his mount closer until he's between Darian and me before reaching under my hood to cup my cheek. The action is so tender that tears well in my eyes, and when he pulls away to place his other hand on Darian's shoulder, I feel the absence of his touch like an ache in my soul.

Watching Val disappear into the distance as he moves further and further away from us is so painful that it's a constant struggle to keep tears from falling as they pool in my eyes.

"He will be alright, Sunshine," Darian's quiet voice breaks through the cloud of sadness in my mind as he reaches between us to grasp my hand. "He navigated through this place for 200 years before becoming stranded on Earth. He knows how to handle himself."

The reassurance calms my soul, and I breathe easier, knowing this won't be the last Val I'll see.

Darian's grip on my hand remains steadfast as we slowly ease through the winding roads. Soon, the sound of crashing waves echoes in the distance, and the familiar scent of the ocean invades my senses.

The stone-paved road leads all the way to expansive docks that stretch far into the water, with countless wooden boats on either side—the chaotic waves of the ocean crash against the docks before spraying over.

The ships become increasingly large the further out the pier they are. The furthest ones could be a hundred feet long or more, adorned with carvings and statues.

We stop just off the coast at a stable filled with other toryians, and we place ours alongside them in stalls, filling their feed buckets and water before heading to the docks.

The area is even more impressive when not mounted on those giant animals. With my grip firmly in Darian's, he leads us to one of the smaller boats where a gruff-looking man stands with his arms crossed.

Darian releases his grasp on me as he approaches the man and exchanges words in a hushed voice. He hands him a small handful of tokens, and the man nods twice before jerking his chin towards the boat, mumbling something under his breath.

When he turns away to pull down the ladder for boarding, Darian laces his fingers with mine again and leads me onto the boat.

Even for being a smaller craft, it is still quite spacious. The back has a wheel and some sort of engine-type contraption that looks similar in a few ways to the engines on Earth.

Part of me wonders if the structures here are all created to work with magic in some way, shape, or form.

Darian sits near the front of the boat as the man who -I'm assuming- is the captain or owns the boat positions himself at the back. The engine-like contraption lets out a low hum as the ship slowly eases from its spot at the dock.

The man says nothing as he spins the wheel, and the boat turns to the side before picking up speed as the humming grows louder.

I lean toward Darian, keeping my voice low, "How does the boat run?"

Darian releases a soft laugh before answering, "Most here have some type of career or job that ties into their abilities. Boats here have a few ways they run, either by propulsion for those with the affinity for water, motor propulsion for earth, or what you would consider jet propulsion for air."

There's a long pause before he continues, "This one is earth-focused, so he uses his abilities to spin the wood propeller on the back." he says as the humming gets louder.

The boat hurtles forward over the water at breakneck speeds that would far exceed that of any on Earth, and it's only when Darian places his hand on mine that I realize I've been squeezing the edge of the wooden seat.

Releasing the tension in my hands sends a dull ache through my hand as Darian threads his fingers through mine, "We're safe, even here, Lara."

I blow out a breath and cling tightly to his hand.

"Do you know what it's like where we're going?" I ask, trying to keep my voice steady and my mind off the expanse of the water surrounding us.

Darian shifts closer and leans in. "From what Cato and some others said last night, Kieran is on the island by himself. They tried to build him a cabin, but he kept to the cave systems. They stopped visiting him when he nearly killed someone for getting too close, and that was nearly 20 years ago." He whispers, but apparently not quietly enough.

"Friend of Cato's, are you?" The man asks loudly from across the boat, and Darian only dips his head in response.

"Since you're his friend, I'll give you this one piece of advice free of charge. Don't go near the bloody madman. I have half a mind to just turn this boat around never mind wait for you both."

Darian nods once, and the rest of the brief trip is silent.

Soon, our guide is tying the boat to a newly conjured wooden dock along the rocky edge of the island. Finally on solid land, I observe the lush forest with relief and awe.

Its dense foliage has varying shades of green, yellow, and purple. Scattered across the area are tall trees that look like nothing I've seen before, and chatter of animals I don't recognize fills the air in the distance.

We make our way inland as the sun peaks in the sky, both of us remaining on alert as we scan the forest for any sign of life.

Soon, we come across the worn-down wood and stone cabin the citizens had created for Kieran. Though quite some time has passed, it still remains mostly intact. Vines and weeds have long since grown over the entrance, emphasizing the absence of anything living, and so we continue our search through the forest.

It takes some time, but we finally see proof of life as we find remnants of a fire pit near the entrance of a small cave. Darian takes some time to scope the area, but there's no recent sign of Kieran, so we continue north.

After what feels like hours of walking, I stumble over another log for the hundredth time as Darian's hand wraps around my arm.

He steadies me as I find my footing, "So, how did you meet Kieran?"

A sad smile graces Darian's features, and my chest tightens before he answers, "My family wanted the realm to prosper in the years that they ruled. My father had inherited the throne from his father, who was selected to rule based on magical affinity. When I was a child, mentors and teachers of different magics were paid well for their work so that the realm could benefit from magic wielders. Over time, the number of those who could wield declined."

I nearly tumble over a root when he catches me and continues, "When we heard of people who had strong affinities for different magics, my parents would bring them to the castle to be tutored and given a full royal education."

He turns to me, and I see his lips twitch slightly from beneath his hood, "It just happened that they had a handsome son who gets along with everyone, so Kieran and I met while being tutored."

My brows furrow, "What happened to his family?"

Darian shakes his head in response, "That is a story for him to tell. I'm afraid even I don't know..."

We fall into silence, and as time passes, I start to wonder if we'll ever find him.

That's when we see it.

The tree cover is so dense that it is almost dark as we spot some split logs and a frequented path-like area with grass, weeds, and other plants trampled from use.

We slow our pace as the path becomes more distinct, leading us directly to the mouth of a large cave on the side of a glowing moss-covered rock wall.

We stop in our tracks as the silhouette of a person lying next to the low embers of fire comes into view. Lowering our hoods, Darian holds his arm out in front of me, signaling me to remain where I am as he steps closer.

A mix of trepidation and excitement whirls through my body as I watch him slowly approach the entrance before he pauses, "Kieran?"

There's a long pause with no movement from the person by the fire.

"Kieran." He repeats louder.

Droplets of rain find their way through the canopy above onto my cheeks as I watch the man in the cave push himself to his feet and turn to face us.

His shadowed face turns to us, and his mussed blond hair falls forward, casting longer shadows over his eyes, obscuring them from our vision. He takes a step out of the cave, and the pallor of his skin is indication enough that he's not exactly well.

The torrents of rain continue to pour around us, and Darian takes a step closer, "Brother, can you hear me?"

The forest is nearly a monsoon now, the rain pelting through the tops of the trees as Kieran takes another step out of the cave. His silver eyes are glazed over, and though he looks toward us, it's as if he doesn't recognize Darian at all.

The downpour soaks us to the bone, plastering my hair to my skin, and Darian holds his hand out, palm facing Kieran, before taking another tentative step toward him.

With only mere feet between them, my heart thunders in my chest.

"Kieran, stop this." The commanding tone in Darian's voice is one that I haven't heard before, but it seems to do the trick as Kieran's head tilts peculiarly, almost in acknowledgment.

Suddenly, Kieran flails as if he's being attacked from all sides, and he releases a shout as he swats at the air. His eyes widen to saucers as they land on Darian, but not an ounce of relief shows on his face.

Instead, it's that of fear and terror.

The rain stops, and my gaze drags down as water sloshes against my feet. Instead of absorbing into the ground, the rain has begun to rise as my gaze flicks to Kieran again, and his features contort into a visage of panic and rage.

"Kieran," Darian warns as the water around us rises rapidly, and the realization hits me.

The weather did not cause the rain; it was Kieran's doing.

Holy shit.

The realization is followed by dread as I understand the gravity of our situation.

We're surrounded by water. Not just in the immediate area, but we're on a damn island.

Darian curses under his breath and starts to freeze the area around us, but without any notice, Kieran shouts, and bullets of water come at us from all sides—a dense sheet of ice forms around us, absorbing the impact before falling to the ground.

Kieran breaks into a sprint toward him, and Darian shouts, "Have you truly lost your mind, brother?"

Darian must anticipate Kieran's movement as he dodges the fists his friend hurls at him while deflecting the multitude of magical attacks Kieran throws.

As I watch the two engaged in battle, there's a commotion in the forest around us, and birds of all kinds begin to take flight into the air. That's when I notice the white crest of the nearly 15-foot wave in the distance rushing towards us.

He means to drown us all.

"Darian!" I shout in a panic.

Hearing the terror in my voice gets his attention as his gaze flicks to the impending attack, and he curses under his breath. The distraction costs him as Kieran manages to land a punch, connecting with his jaw. The attack is enough to make him lose focus as the next magical strike lands true, and Kieran releases a torrent of water into his friend's face.

It is unrelenting, and Darian begins to convulse as the water wreaks havoc inside his body.

But all I can do is watch.

I can only observe as two brothers fight, one nearly killing the other.

"Stop," I say, but my statement comes out quiet and more of a plea. Darian's hand reaches towards Kieran, and a knife of ice forms but immediately falls to the ground.

"Kieran, you're killing him!" I say louder, but my words fall upon deaf ears as he continues his brutal assault.

Fuck.

Unable to bear it any longer, I sprinted at Kieran as he nearly misses me with a long lance of water aimed at my head. I throw my entire body into his and tackle him to the ground.

I straddle his chest, holding both of his hands over his head as Darian coughs up water and vomits beside us.

Water sloshes against our bodies as I scream, "Kieran, snap out of it!" The wave in the distance hurtles closer, and I squeeze my eyes shut, wondering if this is it.

I open my eyes, and the forest is suddenly gone but so is Darian. Kieran is still here, and we're both swimming in what looks to be the expanse of the ocean.

What is this place?

Kieran's head bobs up and down in the water as he struggles to stay afloat. His arms flail out from side to side as he bats away creatures approaching him. One fin in the distance appears larger than the rest, and as it grows closer, Kieran becomes frantic.

"Leave me alone!" He shouts and tries to swim away from it, but the creature still closes the distance and tries to take a bite at him.

He throws himself underwater and narrowly avoids the attack, but as it swims away, it's clear that this is a regular occurrence.

Kieran begins to swim but as he tries, he doesn't actually go anywhere. He remains the same distance from me no matter how hard he thrashes.

"Must find land." He murmurs between gasping breaths, and the large fin reappears over the water, throwing him into a frenzy again.

The creature makes another pass at Kieran, and I look down, watching my hand wave from side to side in the water as I swim in place. A shimmer glides over my hand, and my eyes widen.

It's strikingly familiar, almost as if a kaleidoscope of colors is projected onto the surface, and the movement of my hand in the water disturbs it.

Frowning as suspicion coats my veins, I stick my legs out to feel for the bottom, and shock rifles through me when my feet touch something solid.

It's just like the dream that Val and Darian woke me from.

With the water lapping against my chest, I plant myself firmly, "Kieran!" I call out, silently hoping he doesn't try to attack me here, too.

My voice seems to snap him from whatever reverie has captured his attention, and his eyes widen to saucers.

"Who, who are you?! How are you here?! Where did you come from?!" He asks between gasping breaths as he swims over to me, somehow able to close the distance.

He closes the gap and grasps my arm, which suddenly feels like I'm being weighed down by a tonne of bricks. It takes a conscious effort to remain focused on the fact that we're not really in the middle of the ocean.

"Kieran, this isn't real. None of this is real."

His eyes are wild as he blinks, looking around frantically at the creatures circling us in the water. The moment he spots the fin of the giant creature again, his silver eyes flick to mine with desperation.

"You must go! It's not safe! It's coming back. I'll protect you, but you must get away!"

I frown at him. "Kieran, look at me. I'm not swimming. I'm standing up. The creature, the water, it's not real." I state, emphasizing my point by gesturing to my torso, half out of the water.

Kieran's bewildered gaze follows my movements, "Not real," he murmurs as his breathing seems to even out, "Not real. None of it is real."

He repeats it as if it is his mantra, and slowly, the creatures in the water disappear.

"Stand up, Kieran," I say as he tries to swim in place, and he looks at me as if I've grown a second head.

"Stand," I repeat as more of a demand, tugging on his arm that holds onto me with a vice-like grip.

He looks down at the water with trepidation before his face pales, and he stops swimming in place. He pushes himself to his feet, and as he stands at full height, I tilt my head to look at him.

"That wasn't so hard, was it?"

Surprise, bewilderment, and confusion are all plastered on his face as he stares at me.

"Who are you?" he asks as the room around us brightens, almost as if we're driving towards someone with their bright headlights on, and they're getting incrementally closer.

"My name is Lara. I came to find you with Darian." The moment Darian's name leaves my lips, the recognition registers on his face in a mixture of excitement and worry.

"Darian," he whispers, "He came for me." his voice is barely audible as the light around us gets so bright we both move to shield our eyes from it.

Chapter 13

Lara

When the light behind my eyelids fades away, I peel them open, seeing a mess of blonde hair against the ground. My clothes and hair hang heavily as water drips steadily off of me.

Heat rises to my cheeks as Kieran's eyes start to open from where he lays beneath me as I straddle his waist. Realizing I'm still restraining his arms, I release them, leaning back as his eyes, like liquid silver, flick to mine.

Relief flashes across his face as his once-pale skin gradually warms into a healthy, sun-kissed glow, "Is this real?"

"It is," A soft smile tugs at my lips, and I squeak as he suddenly sits up, pulling me into a tight embrace.

His grip is crushing as he shudders with his head buried into my shoulder.

"Thank you, Lara." he chokes out.

My gaze slides to a relieved Darian as he watches his friend before locking eyes with me. His gaze softens, and a mixture of awe and gratitude graces his features.

"Kieran," I murmur, getting his attention. "There's someone here you may want to see," I say with a slight tease before releasing him and standing up.

He twists, and the moment he sees Darian, tears well up in his eyes. He scrambles forward, splattering mud and muck around before he throws himself into Darian's arms.

I watch them embrace tightly, both men with tears streaming down their cheeks as they laugh. My heart squeezes in my chest as Darian presses his forehead to Kieran's, and they laugh even harder while holding each other's faces.

With pure joy and relief radiating from them, I nearly mistake it for my own, and a smile tugs at my lips.

After an extended reunion, they pull apart, and Kieran gazes around with a grimace.

"I don't suppose you'd be able to fill me in? I seem to be missing some crucial information," he says with a twinge of dry amusement before his gaze lands on me and his face grows serious. "I have a feeling that I have many amends to make, but first and foremost, I owe you my thanks and, more so, my life."

Kieran pushes to his feet and my entire body flushes.

I hardly did that much to be owed such a thing.

Darian stands as well, tilting his head curiously.

"What was the last thing you remember?" he asks, crossing his arms in front of his chest as I push to my feet to stand beside them.

"I was called to a farm just outside of Lavinium to heal a young child with a strange illness. The family was one I'd worked with in the past, but the child never had these symptoms. My magic was always used for the mother's ailments," he says thoughtfully, "When I arrived, the house was deserted as if everyone had packed up and left abruptly. I don't remember anything else after that."

My thoughts race back to the farm we first stayed in when we arrived, and as Darian's mismatched gaze locks with mine, I know he's on the same track as I am.

"We've noticed the same south of Trebonia. We will have to be cautious with our next steps," he says as he rubs his chin, "We should keep a low profile so no one knows you're back in society yet. With the others missing, I'm not convinced this wasn't a political ploy to remove any conflict for the throne."

Kieran's eyes snap to Darian, "Missing? All of them?"

"All but Valerian since he was on Earth with me. Rumor has it that after you went mad and were placed on this island, Gray shifted, Zayne and Cade went missing and haven't been seen since."

Kieran curses and drags his fingers roughly through his damp hair before pausing, "And Caspian?"

Darian's jaw feathers, and he shakes his head, "Haven't heard nor seen of him since magic was restored to Earth and his banishment was broken."

Kieran blows out a breath before turning his gaze on me, "And you? Where do you fit into all of this?"

I snort.

"Do you want the short version or the long one?" I ask with a raised brow.

Kieran laughs, "Oh, I'd say the long version, but judging by D's face, let's keep it short." He gestures to Darian, who shakes his head in feigned exasperation.

Suppressing more laughter, I give Kieran the mixed version as we make the long hike back to our boat guide, explaining my part in releasing magic and the events that led up to Darian's return to Servilia.

Kieran shakes his head.

"So Blair took it upon herself to become the martyr, huh?" he says rhetorically as we continue our trek through the woods, "As unfortunate the circumstances were, I'm thankful you remain unharmed."

The look he gives me is so genuine that my heart stutters in my chest.

He's right, though. I had yet another dance with death and somehow made it out alive.

Oddly enough, I feel stronger for it.

Darian nods in agreement to Kieran's statement, breaking me from my thoughts.

"Blair used some sort of poison on the blade that stopped her wound from healing, and it had some concerning aftereffects. Would you mind-?"

He hasn't finished his question before Kieran halts all movements and turns to me.

"I do not mind at all, you know that," he says, placing one palm on my cheek. The other weaves through my hair and firmly holds the back of my neck. He shuts his eyes, and goosebumps break over my skin as a tingling sensation travels from the top of my head to my toes.

"She's perfectly healthy. Whatever that evil bitch used is out of her system now." he says with a warm smile, "But how are you feeling?" he tilts his head slightly, but he keeps his hands where they are as he searches my face.

"I feel okay. No fever or anything that I've noticed."

Kieran nods and withdraws his hands, "Great. If that changes, just tell me, and I'll see if there's anything I can pick up."

"So you control water, and you're a healer?" I ask, and he grimaces as we continue to walk.

"Did I happen to use it on either of you before I...?" his question trails off.

"You did. It wasn't anything we couldn't handle." Darian says reassuringly, glancing at me as his lips twitch.

Kieran glances apologetically between us before turning to me, "So, where did you learn your magic?".

"She hasn't learned how to control it. She can dream-weave at times. As for what happened earlier, I'm not entirely certain what that was."

Kieran rubs his chin thoughtfully, "Dream-weaving, how peculiar. I haven't met one to date. Whatever ailed me presented like a dream, but my body seemed awake. I'm not sure what to make of that."

I nod.

"It was like the dreams you, Val, and I were in before. It was similar but also different. It was like a projection or something within Kieran's mind, keeping him trapped there."

"An illusion, perhaps?" Darian asks, and both of us nod in response.

"An illusion seems to describe it best," Kieran says as we break through the trees not far from where our guide had set up his makeshift cabin.

The man sees Kieran and falls backward, crawling back a few steps before his wide eyes lock on Darian, "Y-y-your Majesty, forgive me. I did not know." he says, rushing to his knees and dropping his forehead to the ground.

"Stand, you have done nothing in need of forgiveness."

The man's gaze falls on Kieran again, and he smiles, "Good to see you back, Lord Antonius." He rises, hurrying to the boat and placing the ladder down. We board the ship and sit near the bow as the captain pushes us off the dock and into the water.

"Back to Trebonia, then?" he asks, steering the boat away from the island as the boat hums louder.

Darian nods once before glancing between us, "Please, and would you happen to have a cloak you could spare?"

The captain hurriedly removes the cloak from his shoulders and tosses it to Darian with a laugh, "I'll not have it said that the bloody king and his companions went cold in my boat."

I watch as Kieran pulls the cloak over his broad shoulders and gives Darian a nod of thanks.

It doesn't take long to get to shore, and Darian has already given the captain extra coin to keep quiet before we disembark the boat when a nervous excitement washes over me.

Now to go get Val.

Chapter 14

Lara

I trail behind both men as they lead the way through the city streets, keeping our hoods low. We suddenly veer down one road and hurriedly turn off another busy street before I realize why.

We're avoiding busy roads where the guards do their rounds or patrol.

The sky turns into a beautiful array of pastels, and as the moon creeps into view, we finally see the top of the enormous tower.

My gaze travels up the length of it before comparing the size to the surrounding buildings.

The entrance must only be a few minutes away.

I'm distracted when suddenly Kieran and Darian turn around. They gently grasp either of my arms, drag me aside into an alley with urgency, and press my back against the wall of a building.

"What th-" I can hardly get the words out when Kieran's hand covers my mouth.

Glancing between them, the warning in their faces sends a chill down my spine, and it's only seconds before the rhythmic clank of armor sounds out from the road we were just on.

I don't have time to think when the metallic clink stops and Darian's large hand wraps around the back of my thigh, tugging my leg around his waist.

Kieran moves closer, and the two men crowd my vision as they tower over me before leaning in. My heart pounds so hard in my chest that I'm confident they can feel it when they move in sync as if we were a trio of lovers who couldn't wait until they got home.

They dip their heads to my neck and collarbone, and from under my hood, I see three very official and authoritative-looking men standing no more than fifteen feet away, staring at us.

Their gazes are a mixture of caution, wariness, and desire as we maintain the facade.

One of the guards glances at the other two before taking two steps closer. Before he can say anything, Darian grinds his hips into mine unexpectedly, and the gasp that leaves me comes out as more of a breathy whimper that halts the guard in his footsteps.

I'm fully aware that this is no more than a ploy to keep the guards from approaching us, but I cannot deny the overwhelming feeling of desire that still pools in my body as my fingertips dig into the material at their backs.

The guard clears his throat and glances around awkwardly as Kieran's lips press softly against my collarbone. Somewhere in my mind is the warring conflict that we already looked believable without him kissing me, but the way butterflies course through my body tells me I'm not upset about it.

My attention drags downwards where Darian's hard length grinds against me again, and his teeth nip at the tender skin between my neck and my shoulder.

They seem hell-bent on making this as authentic as possible and fuck if I didn't wish it was.

Between Darian, Val, and Kieran, I might just die.

Letting all my inhibitions go, the sounds that come from my throat aren't forced, but I don't put any effort into reining or suppressing them either.

My heart thunders in my chest as both men coax pleasure from my body, and after a few minutes of watching, the guards decide, albeit reluctantly, to leave us alone.

As they gain distance from us, both men pull their heads up, and the raw desire in their eyes sends heat to my cheeks.

I suck in a deep breath, but my voice still comes out husky, "A little warning next time would be nice."

Darian chuckles, "That was so much more fun, though."

My cheeks burn even hotter.

We extricate ourselves from one another, and my head is a mess of thoughts as we cautiously head down the road.

Is it normal to feel this drawn to multiple men?

Kieran and I hardly know one another, yet how is it possible for me to feel this way toward him?

Sure. My connection to him isn't as strong as Val or Darian, but it's still unmistakable.

What the hell is happening to me?

The sound of items crashing from inside a building up ahead sounds out into the dead of night, jolting me to the present as our pace picks up. We keep to the shadows, hiding along the side of a toryian stable as we eavesdrop on the commotion inside.

"I told you, I don't know!" One shrill voice screams into the air, and another loud crash follows.

"Then what do you know?!" A male voice asks, and I jump as a loud thud hits the wall alongside us.

"It was a man! He had long black hair! He asked about the queen and where some books on old magic were! That's it, I swear, I don't know nothing else!" the voice screams frantically, and I see Darian's lips flatten into a thin line as Kieran mutters something under his breath.

"Did he say if he was staying in the city at least?" the commanding male asks, his voice seething.

The person being interrogated coughs desperately, as if choking or struggling to breathe, before finally gasping out, "Peronia's." Voices chatter inside the house before the door opens with a crash, and the rhythmic clanking fades out towards the street.

Kieran looks at Darian, "Is that where we're to meet Val?"

Darian shakes his head.

"No. Peronia's is just where we say we'll go to keep them off our trail."

"Smart," I say, relief surging through my veins, "So where are we going to meet him?" Darian chuckles and glances to the building where the men just were before locking eyes with me again, "Inside, Sunshine."

I can hardly contain my surprise as they each take my hand, tugging me behind them as we slip past the broken front door.

Nervous excitement brims within me, and my gaze lands on a dark, cloaked figure in the back corner of the room.

I don't even need to wait for him to pull his hood down to know who it is.

Without a shadow of a doubt, I know that the figure pulling his hood to his shoulders, revealing his long, dark hair and bright hazel eyes, is my Val as my heart leaps into my throat.

Ripping my hands from Kieran and Darian, I sprint the short distance and hurl myself at Val, who deftly stands and catches me midair with a chuckle.

My arms snake around him, and his chest rumbles, "Missed me that much, huh?" Val says teasingly as he plants a kiss against my hair.

The truth is that I did miss him.

I missed him even while Darian and Kieran had my full attention in more ways than one.

Part of me wonders if I've bitten off more than I can chew, considering what happened between Darian, Val, and me, not to mention adding Kieran into the mix.

The other part of me -the one I'd much rather listen to- spent enough time being afraid of sex, of men and their intentions.

Val gently sets me down just as a body crushes into his embrace in a blur, and a smile tugs at my lips. Watching Kieran hug Val tightly in a mess of black and blonde hair as they murmur and laugh softly brings tears to my eyes.

I'm not at all surprised when I see Val's cheeks glisten with tears of his own as they talk amongst themselves quietly.

Darian embraces Val next, and the three of them grin from ear to ear as we sit down at the table.

A boyish grin creeps across Val's face, "It's good to see you well, though I suppose you could use some new clothes and a haircut." He gestures to the tattered bottoms of Kieran's pants, and in the corner of my eye, Darian's lips twitch.

Kieran feigns outrage and clutches his hands to his chest, "You wound me, clearly this is the new Servilian style."

"Remember that old veignon coat you used to wear?" Darian asks playfully, and Val's smile widens as he looks at Kieran, hardly able to contain his laughter.

Kieran's eyes widen as he glances between them, "That was a hand-made coat!"

"It looked like a cenirb attacked you and won," Val chokes out, his hazel eyes bright as his chest heaves.

My throat tightens with emotion as they reminisce about the old days together, and memories of days long passed with Tammy, Candace, and Henry flick through my mind.

Before loneliness can take root, Darian's arm snakes around my waist, and my eyes widen as he pulls me into his lap. His hand gently squeezes on my hip just as Val laces his fingers with mine, rubbing his thumb over my skin softly.

Darian levels Kieran with an unimpressed look in response to a statement I hadn't been paying attention to.

"Ouch. Can you heal my ego? I'm not sure I'll recover from that one." Val says with a laugh.

"Heal your ego? Not after your clear dislike for veignon craftsmanship. Though, maybe one of these days I'll cure your stupidity, but that day is not today." Kieran retorts sarcastically with a pause, and the three of them laugh.

I can't help the smile that tugs at my lips.

They truly are as close as brothers. Perhaps closer.

"So," Darian says to Val, leaning closer to me, and his hand eases onto my thigh. "What did you learn?"

The action is mostly innocent, but every place our bodies touch is alive. The gravitational pull I feel towards these three men is akin to the fronds of plasma when you place your fingertips against a globe.

There's no fighting it.

Val glances around, and I follow his gaze. No one is seated close to us, and although our reunion did draw attention, it seems everyone is giving us a healthy amount of space.

"I found one tome that mentions dream-weaving, where it's said that anyone with the ability to do so is blessed by the gods themselves, but I could have told you that much without needing the book." He grins at me with a wink. "I did find another that was a more theory-crafting type of book on wielding the ancient magics."

Val places the large book on the table before him and flips to a text-filled page.

Kieran blanches, "You stole a tome?"

Darian chuckles as Val shrugs, "I'll return it when we're done with it."

I fight a smile when Kieran rubs his temples dramatically, "It's a wonder they let you study there. You never abide by their rules."

Val ignores him. "The problem is that I can't read any of this. This is ancient Servilian, the word of the gods. The only ones left who can read this fluently are the seers," he says solemnly before shoving the tome into a leather bag at his side. Kieran runs his fingers through his tangled hair, "We go see the seers then."

Val sighs deeply, "And what about the others?"

Darian's gaze is downcast at the table as he responds.

"We keep our eyes and ears open as we travel. Sabinia has always been an ornery town, but perhaps rumor of our resurfacing may bring them out of hiding."

He glances at the others in the room, who murmur amongst themselves between stares before shifting me onto the seat beside him. The absence of his touch is mourned only for a moment before he grasps my free hand and pushes to his feet.

"We should get some rest and head out at first light," he says, tugging me behind him as he makes his way to the stairs with Val and Kieran close behind us.

The stairs to the room wind around in circles as we climb, and it's not long before we find ourselves standing in front of large, wooden double doors.

Kieran moves to the front to push them open, revealing a grand room covered in tapestries depicting various beings and animals. The windows twinkle against the soft light like diamonds, similar to the last inn we stayed in, as moonlight fills the room.

Darian gestures to the door across the room, "Bathroom is that way, Sunshine."

I release their hands as I walk to it before pushing it open.

The bathroom is enormous.

It's double the size of the room from the last inn, with an extra large wash tub that could fit an entire family. Taking off my shoes, I step onto the cool stone floor next to the tub, and Darian breaks me from my reverie by reaching over to turn the faucet on.

"Enjoy this one. We won't see another proper bath for weeks." With a genuine smile creeping across his face, his dimples on display as laughter breaks out from the other room, and my chest tightens with emotion.

How long has it been since he's been this happy, I wonder.

His eyes search my face, and his gaze softens.

I can't help but chase the feeling of seeing them this joyful, the warmth, the love, the innocent banter.

It's not hard to admit that I'd do anything to see a future in which they can be this way without worrying about their lives or the lives of their friends.

Darian is still looking at me with a tenderness that makes my chest tight, but somehow, as I've been lost in my thoughts, I've leaned in close. My cheeks burn as my brain catches up, and our faces are mere inches apart.

My nerves go haywire as he brings his hand to my face to cup my cheek and leans in, pressing our foreheads together.

"I have lived long enough to be loved, to grieve, and to know what a normal life is like, but none of it compares to the feeling of you being near me," he breathes, and though my body recognizes the action, the air gets caught in my lungs, "You have given me everything to be thankful for. You've given us hope for a future that would otherwise be impossible to imagine. I do not say this lightly, Sunshine. These may be my brothers, but we are yours. Not by any debt owed but by the life you've breathed into us. You belong with us."

His thumb traces my lower lip, and his gaze tracks the movement as I close the distance between us.

My pulse rages in my ears, and my heart beats frantically in my throat as he kisses me slow and long. Each movement sings in my soul as if speaking all the words he's left unsaid in a symphony only my very being can understand.

There's an undercurrent of desire that brims with each stroke of our tongues. An insatiable longing to be close teases the barrier between us but doesn't overwhelm the heartache feeling that pangs in my chest.

Love.

This is what love is, and I know with every fiber of my being that I would burn the world to the ground for this man. For Val. Maybe even for Kieran.

Darian pulls back slightly to look into my eyes, and a tear trails down my cheek. He catches it with his thumb and gently strokes along my skin before pressing a kiss to my forehead.

If he stays any longer, I'm going to be a mess of a woman and forego a bath altogether.

As if on the same line of thought, his gaze flicks to the bath behind me, which is now nearly full, "Enjoy your bath, Sunshine."

Darian gives me a soft smile before leaving the room to give me privacy and I quickly undress before easing myself into the steaming water.

Chapter 15

Lara

Still high off the euphoria of my revelation, the heat seeps deep into my muscles. They slowly loosen, and the tension in them releases as my head falls back into the water.

Staring at the solid wood ceiling while floating in the water brings memories of Kieran's illusion to the forefront of my mind. As my mind wanders, I dip my head further into the water, letting the crest of it cover my ears as I inhale deep, steadying breaths.

The water rumbles inside my ears as I focus on breathing, and time feels suspended as I let the water wash away the chaos in my mind.

I'm jolted from my meditation as Val and Kieran burst into the room, their eyes wide.

Kieran hurries over, ignoring my blatant nudity as he helps me to my feet, "Trouble downstairs, get dressed."

With water sluicing from my body, Val passes me my clothes, and I scramble to pull them over my damp skin as a crash sounds out from below.

Darian hurries into the room, settling his sword on his hip, "Shit." he mutters as shouting breaks out below.

"What's going on?"

"It looks like the rumors of our return surfaced a little faster than antici-pated," Kieran says with a grin as his gaze locks with Val's.

"Kieran, take Lara and go to the stables. Val and I will make a little spectacle of the guards before we meet you there."

Kieran ushers me to the doorway of the stairs leading to the alley behind the inn. Anxiety and panic build in my chest, and I know we're about to split up, but before I can say anything, Darian's lips crush against mine.

It's frantic and deep, but it's not a goodbye.

When we finally break apart, Val steps forward and snickers, dropping a kiss to my cheek before squeezing my hip, "Don't worry, Lara. I'll make sure he stays out of trouble."

"You stay out of trouble, too, Val. Please," I whisper, grasping his hand tightly, willing my heart to calm as dread pools in my stomach.

His humor softens, and he responds with a nod before another crash sounds out closer than the last.

"We need to leave. Now!" Kieran says quickly, gripping my free hand and pulling me close behind him as we scale down the stairs.

More crashes sound out from the building and my heart thunders. The adrenaline coursing through my veins makes my movements unsteady, and twice, I nearly stumble.

Kieran's hand in mine is the only thing keeping me balanced as we climb down the steps. Four moons scatter across the sky, but I can't spare a moment to soak it in as more crashes sound out from the inn.

After what feels like an eternity, we get to the alley, and just as I'm about to round the corner full speed, Kieran yanks on my hand, pulling me tightly against his chest.

My hands brace against him as I glance up to the warning in his eyes and any questions I have die on my lips. The rustle and clanking of quickly moving bodies rush past our hiding place, and I spy the faint details of leather and metal armor as more guards patrol the alley.

"Thanks," I whisper, and my heart gallops in my chest as Kieran leans in, brushing his lips against my ear.

"I owe you my life, Lara. You never need to thank me."

Unable to form words, I nod at him slightly in acknowledgment.

I don't feel as if he owes me anything.

I don't even know how to recreate what I did to help him.

The guards' hurried footsteps fade away, and Kieran slowly peers past me down the alley, "They're gone. Let's go," he whispers, leading me down the street to the stables.

We've only made it a step when the building behind us rumbles. The feeling is only rivaled by an earthquake as the ground beneath us shakes. I can barely keep myself upright when Kieran pulls me to the side, just narrowly avoiding the large piece of stone that would have otherwise killed me.

Holy shit.

Squeezing his arm with my heart in my throat, "Thanks for that," I say before looking at the rubble behind us, "Do you think they're okay?"

Kieran laughs as he leads us closer to the stables, "Okay? Sweetheart, they were the ones who brought the place down. I'd be more concerned with ourselves." he says as the clank of armor echoes in the air, and we hurry into the stables.

We untie the three toryians as shouting and more explosions sound out in the distance. Thankfully, the giant creatures remain mostly calm; their ears are the only indication of their awareness as they twitch towards every rumble.

I guess that's what Cato meant by being as sure as a toryian's ass.

Kieran's hands encircle my waist as he goes to lift me onto one of the mounts when the ground shakes beneath us, and before I can hook my leg over the creature's body, I slip through his grasp.

I collide into Kieran's chest, and he holds me tightly to his body while the world tremors violently.

"What was that?!" I exclaim, my voice sounding shrill amidst the chaos outside.

The tremors stop, and Kieran lifts me once more, gently setting me on the back of the giant animal that has yet to react to the commotion.

"That," he says with a matter-of-fact tone, "if I didn't know any better, I'd say that was Val wreaking absolute havoc." he finishes his sentence with a laugh.

My eyes are wide as I stare at him.

My mind has a hard time reconciling the gentle, fierce protector I know with someone capable of such destruction, but I'm quickly drawn from my thoughts at the sudden movement to our left.

"Time to go!" Darian shouts as he and Val move toward us. My gaze trails over them, their chests heaving with the mixture of dirt and blood splattered over their clothes.

· "Are you b—" Before I can get my question out, Kieran hoists himself onto the mount behind me, just as Val and Darian pull themselves onto their own with ease.

As Kieran leads the way to the doors, my eyes lock with Darian's, and whatever he sees there softens his gaze.

"We are fine. Tired and drained but unharmed." he says softly, glancing at Val as he continues, "Val did most of the work. It seems as though the guards here have orders to kill on sight, so there's not much we can do to spare them."

I glance at Val, only to find him already grinning at me, "Worried we'd get hurt?" he asks teasingly.

I look away with a huff, "Men," I murmur as Kieran's chest rumbles behind me with suppressed laughter.

The moment quickly turns serious as the clank of armor rhythmically thuds closer to the stable, and a knot forms in my stomach.

"Time to go." Val echoes Darian's earlier statement, and all three men spur the mounts into motion as we burst through the stable doors. There are more guards than I can count as they swarm the streets, searching for us.

As heads turn in our direction, shouting rises as they pursue us, and we race down the winding roads.

"Kieran," Darian calls out, "The civilians."

His voice is conflicted, and I glance around to see countless families, their eyes widening as they look into the sky. I twist to look behind us, following their gaze to see hundreds of arrows in ascent, slowing as they reach their maximum height. Their tips tilt downward as they descend, hurtling toward us.

They'd kill everyone?!

"Fuck," Kieran mutters, "Lara, take the reins," he says, handing them to me. The whistle of arrows grows louder, only adding to my frayed nerves as I pull the beast to a stop alongside Val and Darian.

The wind blows suddenly and hurries the arrows faster, and as they close in, families begin to run for cover.

Kieran raises his arms on either side of me, and I watch as a sheer layer of water forms around each arrow.

Darian is next. I watch as he moves his arm from one side to the other, his palm facing the sky above as the water surrounding the arrows freezes solid. They both jerk their hands in sync towards the guards, who stare at the impending attack with wide eyes.

I watch with little remorse as many guards succumb to the unexpected onslaught, and countless bodies drop lifelessly to the ground with arrows protruding from their bodies.

Crimson stains the earth around them as more guards hurry up the street toward us, and I hear Kieran sigh behind me. My attention snags on Val, who has dismounted and stepped toward the incoming army of men.

Breathing becomes a conscious effort as I watch the horde of guards close in on him as he reaches down, placing his palms against the road. The ground trembles beneath us, and the guards suddenly scream. Their terror fills the air as the ground swallows them to their chests.

Kieran is next to dismount and positions himself next to Val, mirroring his position with his hands against the road. The ground surrounding the guards quickly darkens. As they flail and squirm, the ground, which has now become akin to a swamp or bog, slows and labors their movements. The dry dirt they were once trying to dig and claw themselves out of becomes muddy and thick, like cement or quicksand.

No matter how hard they struggle, they cannot get out.

I watch with a mixture of awe and surprise at how easily these three men took down so many guards.

"Let's go while we can." Darian says as Kieran and Val return to their toryians, "It won't keep them there for long once the magic drains away, but they won't be able to follow us." he says quietly as a woman approaches us.

Her eyes flicker to the guards and us as she stands in front of Darian's mount with a basket clutched tightly in her hands.

"We know you must leave, but please, take this as our appreciation," She says, handing him the basket of goods, "Just know that the proud city of Trebonia recognizes the true king." she says before bowing and backing away to the building.

Darian gives onlookers a solemn nod, and we take off at a gallop, racing down the now-empty roads of Trebonia.

As we put distance between us and the city, we slow our toryians to a walk to give them a reprieve from our escape.

Darian takes a bite of a baked good from the basket before tossing us each one, "It's going to be a long journey to Sabinia. We'll have to take the boat from Aveentia and then make our way to the seers once we reach port."

"Why are the guards attacking you like this?" I ask, and Kieran fidgets with the reigns.

Darian just shakes his head with a pained confusion painted across his features, but I don't miss Val's uncomfortable look with Kieran.

Weighing my options, I decided silence is no longer an option.

"This is because of that 'Queen', isn't it? Who is she?"

With exhaustion etched across Val's face, he shakes his head, "Whoever she is, she's been elusive. Any attempts to get intel on her have come up empty. What we know of her came from the survivors of attacks from guards or army she raised over the years before we all became separated. We don't even know her name." Val says softly.

Darian rubs his jaw thoughtfully, and my heart stutters as Kieran's free hand gripping the reins drops onto my lap. My attention continues to drag back to his hand, and I glance around, trying to keep my mind on our surroundings.

"It matters not who she is or how she's remained elusive through the years. What matters is remaining in the shadows and avoiding innocent lives being lost. Too many were killed in Trebonia, guards or not." Darian's voice rings solemnly into the still air, and we fall silent.

After losing myself in my thoughts for some time, the first silhouette of farms outlines the darkness on the side of the road. Their lanterns are out, and it appears they all have gone to sleep.

Kieran's hand gently rests on my inner thigh, and my entire body pinpoint-focuses on his thumb, gliding up and down soothingly.

Once again, my brain goes into overdrive, and I wonder if he realizes what he's doing or how it's affecting me.

Did he do it knowing he was already distracting me with his hand in my lap?

Is this just soothing for him now that he's back to normal and his mind is at ease?

My breath hitches in my chest as his lips brush my ear. "Are you alright, Lara? You seem tense," he whispers innocently. While I'm positive he means it innocently, my intuition suspects that he likely knows exactly what he's doing.

Just as I go to remark, Val breaks the silence around us. "Darian, the air." The urgency in his voice has all our heads twisting in his direction. "It smells of death."

His words bring a cold wave of dread into my chest as Darian spurs his toryian into a full sprint, with us on his heels.

Chapter 16

Lara

The town inches closer minute by minute until finally, we near the gates.

Our toryians slow as the entrance nears. There's an unsettling, eerie stillness and metallic tang to the air and Darian motions for us to dismount.

Heart pounding in my chest, Kieran helps me to the ground, and a sense of wrongness hangs heavy around us.

I'm following close next to Darian as we stalk to the building beside the crossroads, not far from the inn where we met Cato. My hair is standing on end, and the shadows dancing behind the houses have me on edge as we reach the corner of the house, peering past it.

What I see next sends bile into my throat.

Dozens of lifeless bodies and severed limbs litter the ground, their blood staining the roads below them. A few remaining survivors huddle together at the center crossroads ahead; terror etched onto their features as they look at one another.

Motion above them catches my attention, and my gaze slides to a stranger with a billowing cloak standing on the inn's roof. Firm in his grip is the throat of one of the townspeople as he suspends the man midair from the inn's roof. The survivor's feet dangle and kick frantically, and he gasps, clawing at his attacker's hand.

We have to do something.

The robed man stands there as dark smoke billows from his robes, with horns jutting from the top of his hood and a scythe cast downward in his other hand. Dread pools in my stomach at the ominous power emanating from the assailant, and cold sweat drips down my spine.

A rush of air sounds out, and the man's head falls to the ground, spurting blood as his body falls after it.

I didn't even see the stranger move when it happened.

Whoever this person is, Val wasn't wrong when he said the town smelled of death.

This stranger embodies the name.

My breath gets caught in my chest as he crouches down before leaping into the air. A cold note of panic rifles through my limbs as the smoke around him forms into crescent shapes and hurtles toward the remaining civilians.

No!

Before I realize it, I sprint forward, ignoring Kieran, Val, and Darian as their grasp on my arms slips, and I hurtle from the safety of the shadows.

I reach the crossroads as the crescent-shaped smoke comes into contact with the remaining survivors. I'm only feet away as the elusive attack tears and rips through their limbs, blood sprays from their bodies, and my mind instantly empties.

I stare blankly as my body goes numb, and I collapse to my knees beside the mutilated pieces of their lifeless bodies.

I was too late.

That could have been me.

We should have saved them.

My gaze focuses as the initial shock wears off, and I realize I'm staring at the waitress Liv's bloodied face, her unseeing eyes open as she stares toward me.

Only mere days ago, those eyes were full of life and attitude that I found strength in and looked up to in the few moments I saw her.

My heart wrenches in my chest, my anger rising to the surface as the townspeople's blood mixes on the ground and pools close to my hands.

I push to my feet as the robed man lands nimbly in front of me, and my heart skips a beat before nearly stuttering out of my chest.

He raises his head to meet my gaze, and I glare into the eyeholes of a creature's skull mask where dull, emotionless violet eyes look back at me. Only the lower half of his face is visible from beneath the mask, and though his eyes remain unchanged, his lips part as if to speak, but nothing comes out.

The anger I so closely keep bottled up threatens to escape as my chest heaves, and tears stream down my face, "These were innocent people," I state, and though my voice trembles, it isn't with fear, "Leave here and never come back."

His gaze shifts as if it's going to look behind me, but I manage to keep his attention as I take an overly confident step toward him.

"I said leave!" I scream, and his eyes flash with something I can't quite place before a cloud of smoke engulfs his body, melding into the darkness before disappearing completely.

My head bows as I gaze upon the crimson-stained, lifeless body of Liv, and memories of her spunky attitude and how she didn't take any lip from any of the patrons as she made her rounds flutter through my mind.

It's not fair that her life was ended so quickly.

That all of their lives had ended so quickly.

Darian, Val, and Kieran are next to me moments later, and as Darian pulls me into his arms, a sob escapes my throat.

"Darian, they're all..." My voice cracks as I trail off, and his arms tighten around my trembling shoulders as something inside me fractures.

He leans his head against mine before pulling me tight into his chest, and my tears flow free as he whispers, "I know, Sunshine. I know."

I'm grounded only by how tightly he holds me as I mourn the innocent lives lost.

This shouldn't have happened.

Who the hell could do that to an entire town?

When my tears subside, Val and Kieran have gathered most of the dead at the center of the crossroads, and my heart nearly shatters seeing the heap of bodies stacked together.

"Darian," Val says softly behind me, "We found Cato."

His voice sounds so sad that I know he wasn't found alive, and I tighten my grip around Darian before releasing him to see his old friend one final time as I push to my feet.

I swipe at the tears running down my cheeks as Darian stands, grasping my hand tightly.

As we near Cato's body, I quickly glance up at him, seeing the muscle in his jaw flexing with tension. It's not until we approach the inn that a fresh wave of tears springs to my eyes when I realize Cato was the man dangling from the building.

If only we'd come sooner.

The temperature drops around us as Darian releases my hand to kneel next to Cato, slamming his fist against the ground.

The sound echoes into the silence of night air as Darian pulls his old friend into his arms.

I feel Kieran as he moves next to me, and I glance at him. The moonlight reflects off his glistening cheeks as he looks down at Darian holding Cato's limp body.

If Val hadn't been searching the library, we might have made it here in time to stop this.

My arms wrap around my torso tightly as a fresh set of tears threatens to fall, "I'm so sorry, you guys."

Kieran's arms snake around my shoulders, and I shudder as he pulls me into his chest, "None of this is your fault, sweetheart. We're just glad he didn't go after you too."

Val nods in agreement as he holds his hands to the ground. The area trembles beneath our feet as the bodies in the middle of the road slowly descend into it, and vines and plants carry bodies from nearby homes as they too are gently placed into the large crater.

I pull myself from Kieran's arms and approach Val as he covers the enormous hole with dirt.

Everything inside of me aches, like a pain that radiates from every corner of my mind and soul, as I glide my hand over his back to hug his shoulders tightly. My head leans against his dark hair as tears fall from my closed eyes.

Though I don't believe in the gods, nor do I believe in any higher power, I can't help but embrace their beliefs, if only for the moment.

If only so they could be at ease now.

Emotion clogs my throat as I find my voice, squeezing Val gently as he shudders, "May they find peace in the afterlife and have the gods' blessings for the terror they endured."

A long moment passes before Kieran inhales sharply behind us, and my eyes snap open as Darian curses under his breath in disbelief.

Where the bodies were buried, a singular golden tree now erupts from the ground, towering over us with branches that stretch far over the nearest houses, completely covering the area where the bodies now rest.

The iridescent bark of the tree shimmers in the pale moonlight, with the golden buds slowly unfurling into leaves before our very eyes.

"Impossible," Val mutters as we all gaze at the newly grown spectacle amidst the carnage that was here only moments prior.

I glance at Kieran and Darian, who stare at the tree in bewilderment, "What is the significance of this tree?"

There's a long pause, and Val turns to me, "This is the hylia ilvrost. They're trees which were gifted to us by the gods millennia ago. They were said to be proof of their blessings on Servilia. The dead forest used to be filled with hundreds of them years ago." he says quietly, gazing up at the tree with awe.

His quiet voice is filled with a mixture of tentative hope and awe as Kieran and Darian carry Cato's body to the base of the tree. Val faces forward again, and I watch with a heavy heart as the earth swallows Cato's limp form. The hole in the ground seals, and a long moment passes before Darian and Kieran return to our side.

A chill trembles through my body, and I shiver, "So, who was the man responsible for all this?"

All three men shake their heads, but Val answers as he looks at the inn's roof, "I'd heard rumors of men doing the bidding of the false queen when I was researching, but if that's what this was... It's my first time seeing it happen in person. I wish we got a better look at him. Did you notice anything?"

I frown.

"He had these lifeless purple eyes, and he was wearing the mask of some animal with horns."

Darian and Val glance at one another and then at me, "Purple eyes?" Val asks hesitantly.

I nod.

"They seemed dark under the mask but were purple. Why?"

"You're certain they were purple?" the expression on Val's face is weary as if he's hoping for a different answer than the one I'm going to give.

Darian curses under his breath, and my heart stutters, "Yes, I'm sure, why?"

The temperature around us drops as Darian paces back and forth before Val moves to calm him down.

My mind is chaotic when Kieran steps closer and speaks in a low tone.

"Zayne and Cade have purple eyes. They are blood-related brothers and the only people we've ever known to have them. Zayne was able to teleport and control darkness in various ways." His voice is solemn, and my heart nearly stops dead in my chest as he rests his hand on my shoulder. "We may have just come across one of our missing brothers."

"Why would he do this to innocent civilians?" I cut myself off at the first question.

Though my mind swirls with dozens more given the events, I can't imagine they're comfortable with the thought that their brother could be behind all of this pain and death.

Kieran shakes his head, "There's a chance it's not him, but we'd be fools to ignore the similarities. As for the why... that remains to be seen."

Darian walks towards us with Val on his heels, and a chaotic mixture of anger and sadness emanates from him as the muscle in his jaw feathers.

"There's nothing else we can do here. Let's salvage supplies from nearby buildings and head out," he says before going to the nearest house.

The sudden change to his demeanor has Kieran and I sharing a look. We split up to search for food and refill our water basins as Val brings the toryians to the crossroads.

Chapter 17

Lara

The first building I search nearly breaks me.

It's a small woodworking shop with a home attached to the back. Carved figures of a woman, man, and their child adorn the walls, and the bed frames have detailed portraits etched into them of the family.

Crimson stains the walls, and things have been knocked over as if they were running for their lives before they were cut down.

What truly shatters my heart is the small wooden figurine next to a large pool of blood.

A phoenix.

A bird with feathers of flames lies with a broken wing by the door. The image of a young girl clutching this in her hands terrified for herself and those she holds most dear, flutters through my mind.

Picturing her holding a figurine of a creature reborn of its ashes while being cut down makes my heart clench painfully.

Kneeling on the blood-soaked floor, my fingers encircle the small wooden item, and I hold it to my body, squeezing my eyes shut and swallowing the emotion in my throat.

Maybe one day, from the ashes, they too will rise.

It takes a moment to get my bearings as I tuck the trinket into the pocket of my robe and continue searching for supplies.

In the first two buildings I search, I find some fresh fruits and vegetables and some kind of dried meat. Too emotionally drained for a third, I walk slowly to the crossroads where Darian, Kieran, and Val stand, quietly talking to one another.

Val turns, his piercing hazel eyes searching my face as he tilts his head, "Find anything?"

Unable to speak, I simply nod and empty my pockets of the foods I found, handing them to Val and Kieran to load onto the toryians. With my pockets nearly empty, my hand grasps the small wooden phoenix as I silently wait for us to mount the toryians.

Kieran's footsteps get closer as he positions himself behind me, and as his hands move to my waist, he leans in, "Do you want to talk about it?"

He asks as if he knows the weight my heart holds as I stand there thinking of all the lives lost.

I shake my head, willing the tears in my eyes away as he gently lifts me onto our mount.

He sits behind me, wrapping one arm tightly around my waist with the other on the reins. His embrace is soothing to the piece of my being that feels like it could shatter at any moment, and I melt into it as his thumb gently caresses my stomach.

With a heavy heart and more questions than answers, we slowly leave the desolate town behind. We ride for hours in silence down the empty road.

As the sun rises, we pull our hoods forward to conceal our faces, and a few hours into sunrise, I shift uncomfortably in my seat.

Being so unused to riding, yet having ridden so much in the past few days, I have sores and chafing running rampant along my inner thighs.

At this point, I'm beginning to think it could be used as an effective form of torture.

Darian and Val lead their toryians off the road onto a little worn path next to a meadow, and we follow as they dismount. Kieran gets off first with ease before reaching up to slide me off the saddle.

He sets me on my feet gently, and as my trembling legs support my weight, the sores along my inner thighs radiate pain throughout my lower body.

I carefully move to a nearby log and stretch, wincing as my skin aches and footsteps approach me from behind.

Val.

"You alright?"

His voice is quiet, and though I want to lean into him, to use his strength, I just nod in response.

I'm not okay.

After seeing that town and those I had just met so full of life and happiness, I saw them die before my eyes.

My fingers trace the broken wing of the phoenix in my pocket as Val moves in front of me, handing me a piece of dried meat and some kind of root vegetable.

"It's okay not to be okay, Lara," he says, and I clench my jaw tightly.

Claire would eat this up.

The thought of Claire leads me to think of Tammy, Candace, and Henry. I silently wonder what has become of each of them while I've been wrapped up in my journey in this realm.

At least they're not surrounded by the dangers here.

Val's strong arms wrap around my shoulders, tugging me into his embrace, and I cave, snaking my arms around his waist as I cling tightly to him.

"I know you're processing what we saw back there and whatever you found in your search through the buildings," he starts, and my jaw clenches as I swallow, "But when you are okay enough to talk about it, might I suggest doing so with Darian first? He has taken this hard, Lara. I'm worried about him."

My eyes flick to where Darian sits at the base of a tree, with his eyes cast downward. His hand flexes open and closed as his jaw feathers with tension.

My heart twists at how distant he feels and closed off from me.

I've been so selfishly absorbed in my own sadness that I've neglected how Darian, Val, and Kieran were taking the loss.

These were their childhood family friends.

People who were remnants of Darian's parents and their reign.

Turning to meet Val's sad hazel eyes, I nod.

No matter how I feel now, I do not have a sense of duty to keep these people safe. On the other hand, Darian likely feels he failed his brothers by not being there for them, and now his people, as his brother fells them.

No amount of grief I feel could ever compare to those kinds of torturous thoughts in his mind.

Standing on my toes, I lean over to Val before brushing my lips against his, "Thank you, Val."

He shakes his head in response, gripping my chin as his hair tickles my cheeks and firmly presses his lips to mine.

"No, thank you, Lara," he whispers against my lips. He searches my eyes for a moment before releasing me, and I make my way over to where Darian is.

He hardly spares me a glance as I sit beside him quietly, and that's when Val's concern becomes all too clear. We sit silently for a long moment, and surprise rifles through me when Darian is the first to speak.

"He killed the children," he whispers, bowing his head, "He killed them all, even the children."

Shifting, I wrap my arms around his shoulders, "We don't know if it was him for sure, Darian," his head snaps towards me as if to protest, but I hold my hand out, urging him to let me continue, "Whoever was responsible for that, whether it was him or another, they will be held accountable. We will make sure of it."

He holds my gaze for a long moment as my heart thumps loudly in my chest before I reach into my pocket and hand him the small phoenix.

"I found this in the house of a small woodworking family," I whisper, my throat tightening, "I think you should have it."

He runs his fingers along the creature's wing. A softness graces his features before he shuts his eyes, and a tear trails down his cheek.

"My mother used to have an aespherion in the early years of my life," he says, his lips twitching at the confusion on my face. "They're what humans would call a phoenix," he adds, and I nod.

"When it turned to ash, I saw her crying as if mourning its loss. I was young then and didn't understand what the creature was, but when she cried, I cried with her as if it meant as much to me as it did her."

"I'll never forget how she held me that day, and as we sat there for the next hour waiting for it to reemerge, she used to tell me stories about Servilia and how we are like the aespherion in spirit. She cried not for the creature's death but for another cycle of its journey that had ended. As we watched the ashes start to move and breathe, she looked at me and said,

'From the ashes, we rise, Darian.' and damn, if that bird didn't look twice as impressive when it rose." He laughs softly as he looks at the figurine, and another tear trails down his cheek.

"Well, until they return," I whisper, and he turns his mismatched gaze to me. "We will build a better world for them to return to."

He blinks, his face flashing with an emotion I can't quite place before a soft smile tugs at his lips, "Yes, we will."

We sit for a while longer in comfortable silence until Kieran steps closer, eyeing Darian with concern as he holds out some dried meat toward us.

Darian shakes his head, "I'm good."

Kieran and I shoot him a look, "You need to eat, D. You used a ton of magic in Trebonia and haven't rested." Kieran's voice is more stern than I'm used to, and the contrast makes my lips twitch.

It's like a dad finally bringing out his 'Dad' voice to his kids.

"I'm really not-"

"Eat." Both Kieran and I say in unison.

Darian sighs in resignation, taking a slice of meat from Kieran and biting a piece off.

It's not long before we're back on our toryians, and by the time the sun goes down, my legs feel as though they've been filed down by sandpaper all the way to the bone.

The pain had been a welcomed distraction from the town we left behind hours before, but with nothing else to focus on, the pain has become unbearable as every step of the toryian rubs the sores.

As I uncomfortably shift in place, Kieran squeezes my thigh, "You alright, sweetheart?"

I adjust again, and pain radiates through my legs, "I've accumulated a collection of sores on my thighs, and they're very painful." Kieran laughs under his breath, and I tilt my head to glare at him.

"What is so funny?" I ask, my cheeks burning with embarrassment and frustration as he laughs louder.

"You're sitting with a healer, avoiding being healed." he muses as if thoroughly entertained by the thought.

He slides his hand between the toryian saddle and my thigh, his palm setting my skin on fire, and a flush crawls up my neck as warmth fills my body.

The tingle of his power seeps into my inner thigh as his fingers splayed wide, and my entire being is acutely aware of every movement he makes while his magic heals the sores. The pain in my leg eases as his thumb glides from side to side.

He's so fucking close to no longer touching my thigh, and my mind is a chaotic mess with every shift the toryian makes.

The teasing only serves to further the desire building in my body as he moves his left hand to mirror the action for the sores on my other thigh.

His hand placement feels too calculated to solely heal me, which only furthers the burning heat in my body as his power tingles against my skin.

The tip of his thumb is dangerously close to my clit where it rests in the space between the saddle, and I find myself silently longing for him to close that distance.

God, what is wrong with me?

Desire swirls through my body and the toryian shifts at the exact moment that he adjusts his hand. My breath hitches, and the air in my lungs catches as his thumb presses against my clit. Releasing the pressure against my clit almost instantaneously, my mind is a whirlwind of questions as heat pools between my legs.

Did he mean to do that?

Is he even aware of what the hell he's doing to me?

It takes a conscious effort to keep my breathing calm, though my heart is pounding so hard that it threatens to crawl out my throat.

Kieran's fingers twitch slightly, and my breath catches in my lungs again.

Do I want him to do this or not?

I know the answer is that I do.

That much I cannot deny.

Kieran's presence has the same magnetic pull that calls to me as Val and Darian do.

The issue is that I don't want it to happen entirely by accident.

The pause in his movements as his magic dissipates sends a mix of disappointment and relief through my veins. I expect him to withdraw his hand when he repeats the action more deliberately, as his thumb brushes gently against my aching clit, sending electricity down my core.

My heart pounds like a battering ram against my chest as he withdraws his hand to rest it on my lap.

The absence of his touch has me throbbing as if my body itself craves his touch in a way inexplicable by any words in the English language.

Butterflies soar chaotically through my body as his lips brush the shell of my ear, "Better?"

"Much." My voice comes out husky, nearly cracking as I try to calm my nerves, making him chuckle.

Just when I think that's the last of it and disappointment washes over me with a thin layer of guilt that I so badly wanted something when all he was doing was helping me, he pulls me flush against him.

My heart nearly stutters out of my chest as the length of him throbs hard against my ass, and I swallow audibly.

There's nothing more that I want than to just...

"Did you know," he whispers, "that my magic can also be used for other things?"

His hand reaches between my legs as he circles my clit with his fingers over the material of my pants, and I nearly moan in relief as pleasure builds in my core.

I pant as he pauses over my clit, and before I can protest, the tingling that usually ripples through my skin hits my clit with precision.

"Oh my god," I gasp as the inescapable euphoria wracks through my body, and my orgasm rages to the surface. My entire body shudders within seconds; my toes curl tight, and my legs twitch. I lean forward involuntarily and ride each wave of pleasure until his magic ceases.

Holy shit.

Kieran tugs me back against his chest as I struggle to catch my breath. My gaze flicks to Darian and Val, who look like they thoroughly enjoyed the show as they ride beside us.

"Any better now, sweetheart?" he whispers as his thumb glides along my stomach again.

I'm still panting as I hum lazily in approval, which only makes all three men laugh darkly under their breath, and I know it will be a long ride to Sabinia.

Chapter 18

Lara

We ride through the beautiful landscape for hours, with thick forests on either side of the road. A few times during our travels, we see others on their way to Trebonia, seemingly unaware of the desolate town they will stumble across on their way.

As the sun begins its descent from its peak in the sky, we slowly approach a small, lively town.

It looks like one of those 'everybody knows everybody' places, and Darian tugs his hood further down, positioning himself between Kieran and Val as we slowly ease our toryians through the crowds.

Val leads us to an inn near the outskirts of town and goes inside to get us a room while we unpack our goods from the toryians. Unlike the other places we've been, our hoods drawn forward garner suspicious looks from some townspeople as we haul our bags to the room.

I place the heavy bag of fruits and dried meat onto the floor by the bed and glance around the room. It's modest, with a single bed just barely big enough for the four of us, and I sigh in relief that we'll get an actual bed to sleep in.

"If we add any more to our party, I may need to sleep on the floor." I muse as I drop my bags onto the floor by the bed.

Val grins at me mischievously, wiggling his finger from side to side. "How quickly you forget one of my many areas of expertise."

To emphasize his point, he raises his free hand with his palm upturned as wood extends from the floorboards with moss to match the depth of the bed.

I blink at it before looking at him.

I don't think I will ever get used to that.

"Point taken," I breathe and throw myself onto the bed with relief as all three men sit alongside me.

Darian glances between us before leaning back onto the bed comfortably, "While we have time, let's try to recreate dream-weaving."

I blow out a nervous breath as each of them shifts to lie beside me, and butterflies soar through my body.

"Any tips for a newbie?"

"Don't kill us is usually my go-to, but I hope I don't need to remind you of that," Darian's voice drips with amusement, and I pinch his arm as Val snickers.

I think back to the other times I jumped into Darian's dream or pulled them into mine. Both times, I was asleep and under some sort of emotional distress, whether good or bad.

Considering the circumstances, I'd rather not recreate the emotional distress.

Inhaling deeply, I clear my mind, intending to jump into a dream and pull them in with me as I keep that at the forefront of my thoughts. Honing in on my breathing to allow my body to relax slowly, I ease into a relaxed, meditative state.

Claire had taught me early on in therapy how to meditate, saying it was an effective method of coping or processing traumas.

Though I never practiced it much, I am thankful for her guidance now.

In the quiet of my mind, I think of Kieran, Val, and Darian in an attempt to duplicate my previous efforts, but nothing happens.

I remain inside my mind and fully awake.

The three men alongside me are even breathing as they remain silent, and part of me wonders if they'd stay this way all night if I kept trying or fell asleep.

That's when the realization hits me. I wasn't always asleep. I jumped into Kieran's illusion while I was awake.

I remember wanting him to snap out of the illusion and stop hurting Darian.

That's it—an illusion.

Throwing caution to the wind and going off of gut instinct, I begin to create an illusion within my mind.

I start with a forest clearing identical to where I first met Val, with the moon shining bright through the canopy.

The grass waves in the wind, and I step into the center of the clearing and sit down, leaning back with my face upturned to the moon.

As I sit there, reminiscing about meeting Val, a pang of loneliness aches in my chest.

I wish he were here.

I fondly remember how he brought me blueberries, woke me up, and led me to water while I navigated the forest for an entire day.

The ache in my chest grows until his voice breaks me from my reverie, and my gaze snaps to him as he glances around in awe.

"I recognize this place."

His piercing gaze falls on me with a softness that makes my heart swell. The moon illuminates his face, and his dark hair flows with a slight breeze.

The illusion feels so real that if he hadn't been a wolf when we first met, this could have been a spitting image of our first meeting.

My lips twitch, and I can't help but laugh, "I remember being terrified when I first saw you. I was certain that if you were hungry, I was dinner." "I'll never forget the look on your face when I woke you up," he says, and I giggle as he sits down next to me, "You looked like you'd seen a ghost." The memory plays out in my mind, and a brief silence falls between us.

"I never did thank you for finding me in that house," I whisper, remembering the relief I felt at his vicious growl when he entered the room, even with my mind's state. Nothing could compare to the gift he gave me that night and every night that followed.

"I'd do it a million times over. My only regret is not getting there sooner," he says quietly, kissing my shoulder tenderly before tucking a lock of hair behind my ear.

"How are you handling the adjustment?" he asks, tilting his head.

I let out a wry laugh, "To what part? Leaving my life behind? Journeying through a whole new world? Seeing a tremendous amount of death in a short time? Or being shared by multiple men who each wield magic strong enough to make a grown man run scared?"

Val chuckles.

"Well, I was referring to being in Servilia and having magic, but I'll settle for an answer to all of the above," he says with a raised brow, and I sigh deeply.

"I worry about Henry, Candace, and Tammy, but my concern for them has been overtaken by the chaos that's been paramount since arriving in Servilia. Having magic that I don't entirely know how to use is daunting, confusing, and ultimately frustrating, though I've been so immensely thankful for it. Traveling through Servilia has had its moments of unparalleled beauty but also its tragedies that I will not soon forget in this lifetime. As for being shared by the three of you? I am still getting used to it, and you are just okay with it." I say, rubbing my fingers together soothingly.

Val grasps my hands in his and looks at them thoughtfully.

"It's normal for us, so it goes without saying that we'd be more than okay with it, but more than that, Lara, we want to."

"So you've all shared in the past?" I ask, suddenly self-conscious for some reason.

Val laughs and shakes his head.

"No, I meant it's normal for people on Servilia. From what I know, collectively, Cade is the only one who has been with someone for any given period, maybe a handful of weeks. We have mostly always been focused on running Servilia together."

I nod, my mind absorbing his words and the fact that this is new for all of us.

"Besides, I don't know about you, but something about this just feels right." My gaze flicks to him, but he's looking up at the moon. The glow against his skin almost makes him look ethereal as he continues, "I've lived a long time, Lara, and I don't think I've felt this strongly about someone a day in my life. Not until you. Darian is my brother, and I would lay my life down if it meant him living. That's how it's always been since we met, and he took me in. But now? Now, the only thing that would give me pause is not knowing you'll be okay. Not being there for you."

His bright hazel gaze slides to mine, and as our eyes meet, I know with every fiber of my being that I would do the same.

I would live for him as much as I would die for him, and the look in his eyes tells me that he knows.

A long moment passes between us, but it's a comfortable silence.

I'm lost in my thoughts as he slides his hand into mine, "So when do the others join the party?"

I bite the inside of my lip nervously, "I was thinking of pulling us into their dreams one at a time? Or, trying to, at the very least."

Val squeezes my hand once before he lays back in the grass beside me and laces our fingers together.

"Ready when you are."

I shut my eyes to focus, picturing Darian and Kieran in my mind. I picture myself pushing Val and me into whatever their minds have conjured when we've been resting.

Opening my eyes, I still see the moonlit glade and frown as Val squeezes my hand reassuringly.

"Try again. Picture your connection to Darian as an invisible path or a thread with Darian at the end of it."

Using Val's suggestion, I shut my eyes and return to my meditative state before creating the illusion. In the calm, peaceful darkness, a shimmering white-blue thread leads into the shadows, and I picture myself tugging Val along with me as I follow it.

The thread leads me to a door, and with nervous excitement, I tentatively push it open.

Stepping through the white-blue threshold, I open my eyes to see the crossroads again as a mixture of anxiety and dread wash over me.

The slight squeeze of my hand and Val's towering height beside me sends relief through my body that I managed to bring him with me, but as I glance at Val, he looks as concerned as I am.

We watch as the robed man cuts down Cato and the rest of the civilians before Darian sprints at the smoke-covered man.

"He's having a nightmare," Val says, and we break into a sprint to chase after him.

As we approach the crossroads, Darian's ice magic knocks off the smoke-covered man's mask, revealing a man with bright purple eyes, high cheekbones, and indigo hair. The memory of his mouth dropping open flashes through my mind as I gaze at his full lips and angular jawline.

Though his eyes were darkened and dull behind the mask, there's no doubt that the man in Darian's dream and the one at the crossroads were one and the same.

"Darian, stop!" Val shouts, rushing to stand between him and Zayne, "It's just a nightmare."

"He killed them," Darian chokes out with tears streaming down his face as he falls to his knees, "He did it, Val. I know he did."

Val crouches to wrap his arms around Darian's broad shoulders, and my gut twists.

"There must be a reason if it was him. If it truly was Zayne, we will find out why. Remember who he was, D. He was not one to be coaxed nor bribed," Val reasons fiercely as Darian wipes the tears from his face.

Curious of the extent of my abilities and wanting to remind him of all the people he has saved and helped and the good he's done, I begin reconstructing Darian's dream.

I start by removing the bodies first, and they shimmer before disappearing, replaced with various people I remember seeing from Haven.

I even go so far as to place the DJ in the center tree not far away.

Val looks around with a soft smile, "Darian, look."

Darian raises his head, and the look on his face tightens my chest as his gaze slides to me.

"If there is one thing Claire drilled into my head in the years of sessions with her where I was less than cooperative, it's that I cannot control nor am I responsible for the actions of others," I say softly, gazing around at the lively scene surrounding us as I continue, "You are the reason the people at Haven are alive today. You are not responsible for Zayne or those who have died at the hands of others while you've been away. You've protected and saved more than you likely know. Never forget that."

As I turn my head to look at Darian, he's already standing, and his muscular arms pull me into a crushing hug.

A sense of gratefulness washes over me, though I can't seem to understand why I feel that way, and I brush it off.

Okay, now for Kieran.

Darian releases me from his grip, and I suck in a breath before shutting my eyes.

Picturing another crystal blue thread, I pull it toward me instead of following it until the doorway is before me.

Hopefully this works.

I pull the door open and tug hard on the thread.

"You guys went to the bar without me? You know I love a good party."

Kieran's voice rings out, and Darian chuckles as satisfaction rifles through me.

"I forgot you never got to see it," Val says with a grin. "This is the safe house Darian built around one of the entrances to Servilia," he says proudly, arms extended to either side.

I shake my head, "I don't think this meager reiteration does it justice. It truly is a Haven."

"You did it, Sunshine," Darian says with pride as he tilts his head to the side, "How do you feel?"

I think over his question and assess my current state.

"I'm not sure. Everything is normal. I don't feel drained, tired, or weak. Creating the illusion in my mind, pulling Val in, and then transporting us to yours doesn't seem to have drained me, that I can tell."

"Okay, let's practice pushing people out and leaving yourself," he says, moving to face me, "Push me out."

I blink at him before my brows pinch together, "You want me to push you out? Why?"

"If you ever pull someone into your dream that you don't want there, or you jump into someone's dream accidentally, you need to know how to get them out or exit it yourself," Val explains, and Darian nods in agreement.

It makes sense in theory, but...

My brows pinch together as I focus, reluctantly picturing Darian being thrown from my mind. But my jaw clenches when I open my eyes to see him in front of me.

I glance between them, "Why isn't it working?"

Kieran gives me a knowing look, "You have to want it, sweetheart."

I shut my eyes, picturing the door I opened to Darian's mind before slamming it shut with him on the other side.

Opening my eyes tentatively, I still see the three of them standing there, and I groan in frustration, "It's not working!"

"Okay, let's just try this instead. Imagine waking from a dream, like throwing yourself into reality again. Try that." Val says softly, his eyes encouraging as he looks at me with reassurance.

Sighing deeply, I center myself and rein in my emotions.

I imagine the thread I followed to Darian's mind and follow it back out the door until I find myself in a comfortable place of darkness and will myself to wake up.

I surge forward into a sitting position and pant to catch my breath as all three men next to me stir.

Darian leans over to kiss the top of my head, "You did well, Sunshine."

"How are you feeling?" Kieran asks, holding his hand to the top of my head as his magic ripples from my head to my toes.

My muscles feel fine, but there's a deep-seated, dull, throbbing ache in my head and chest.

"I feel okay physically, for the most part," I say, bringing a hand to my chest, "But there's a strange sensation here and in my head that I've never felt before. It's dull, and while my body feels okay, I still feel exhausted."

All three men nod their heads in understanding. Darian brings his palm to cup my cheek. "It's from using your magic reserves in a way that is purposeful rather than reactionary. Emotionally charged magic is instinctual and doesn't cause as much immediate pain, but it will still drain your well of power."

"Using it purposefully is like training a new set of muscles that don't have any physical embodiment. It will get easier with practice." Kieran says as Val shifts to rub my shoulders.

My eyes slide shut as his thumbs dig into my tense shoulders. The massage is unexpected but entirely welcomed as the muscles loosen and knots get worked out.

The bed shifts, and my eyes flick open to Kieran pulling his hood over his head. "I'll grab some real food from downstairs, and then we should rest. We still have another day's ride to Aveentia."

Darian, Val, and I use the sink to clean off since there is no tub in this inn's washroom. By the time we're done, Kieran has returned with food.

We eat in comfortable silence, and soon, exhaustion sets deep inside my bones, and my blinks grow slower. Darian must notice as he takes my plate, and I yawn heavily.

"Off to bed for you," he says, passing my plate to Kieran and gently easing me into the center of the bed. My eyes don't open as I feel them lie beside me as we settle in for the night.

Chapter 19

Lara

When I open my eyes, I'm not sure how long I've been asleep, but I know for certain that I am not awake yet as my gaze scans the dark stone beneath my feet and the snow-capped mountain ranges.

The treetops in the distance are barely visible as an abyss of darkness lurks above them. I'm standing on top of what I can only assume is a watch tower or some type of castle.

The area is so serene and peaceful, but the encroaching darkness on the horizon is unsettling. It's an odd contrast that has my stomach doing flips.

My heart lurches in my chest as someone behind me blows out a breath of surprise.

"Lara?" Caspian's voice rings out into the crisp, thin air, and if I didn't know better, I'd say he sounds relieved.

The conflict of seeing him again brings emotions forward that I'd long since suffocated into a box in the back of my mind.

I twist to face him, taking in his mussed hair, the stubble along his jaw-line, and the bags under his eyes as if he had been awake all night.

A flicker catches my attention, and I glance at his chest with a frown before my gaze flicks to his.

Something about him just doesn't feel right, but I can't put my finger on it.

"Caspian," I say but abruptly cut myself off as memories flood my mind—Blair, the knife, Henry and Candace, Tammy, the amulets, the prophecy.

He used me.

He tricked me and then left me to die at the hands of that woman.

Yet he somehow had the gall to tell me he wouldn't risk me when it came to collecting the amulets.

Somehow, somewhere deep inside of me, I believed him.

Frustration and anger coat my veins like hot oil.

"You knew, didn't you? You knew the cost of breaking your banishment and releasing magic all along." I state, searching his face for any indication I'm wrong.

His gaze drops to the ground, and guilt flickers across his features, "Lara, believe me, I-"

"Believe you? I nearly died, Caspian. If it weren't for your brother, I would be cold in the ground right now."

His eyes flash, and I shake my head, "How am I to believe anything you have to say when everything was a lie or some cruel deception." I retort, and his jaw clenches shut as his gaze darts around us.

"Lara, you are not safe," he says in a rush, "If my assumption of how you managed to find your way here is correct, you must go. Now."

The command and seriousness of his voice send a cold note of dread down my spine, and the darkness slowly creeps closer over the tops of the trees as I frown in confusion.

"Caspian, what-"

The darkness suddenly rushes in, and he shoves me to the ground roughly, "Go, now!"

"Caspian!" I scream as I'm jolted awake and sit upright, gasping for breath as eyes dart around, bewildered as the bed shifts on either side of me.

Val's already sitting up, groggy but alert for danger, his voice thick with sleep. "Lara?"

"Were you just calling out for my brother?" Darian asks, his brows furrowed.

"I-" my voice cuts off as I hesitate on what to say, "I don't know what just happened." I frown and rub my palms against my eyes as I try to make sense of things, "It must have just been a bad dream." I say dismissively, and though I'm sure none of us believe it, no one questions it further.

Darian's gaze lingers on me momentarily before he glances at the window where soft arcs of light filter into the room, "The sun is starting to rise. We should go."

Kieran and Val yawn deeply, and their movements are slow as they climb out of bed to get dressed. I shuffle to the edge of the bed as Darian's hand appears in front of me to help me on my feet. Taking his extended hand, I raise my eyes to his mismatched gaze, and my heart gallops in my chest when he cups my cheeks.

He leans in, pressing his forehead to mine. "I am not going to ask you to tell me, but when you're ready to talk about it..." he trails off, but I know what he's trying to say.

The issue is that I don't know what to say, not that I cannot handle it. I just can't make sense of any of it.

Was it real?

How could I have dream-weaved to Caspian when I don't even know where he is?

What did he mean by that I'm in danger?

Does he know how I managed to appear in his dream? Is he going to use that information to hurt me?

Does any of it matter if it wasn't real?

My mind swirls with questions as I nod in response.

He kisses my forehead tenderly before covering his head with his hood. I'm on autopilot as I retrieve my cloak from the chair nearby, covering myself before following them out the door.

I'm lost in my thoughts as I trail closely behind Darian. We make our way to the stables before I'm lifted onto a toryian. It's not until Darian lifts himself onto the saddle behind me that I'm snapped back to reality.

I glance around as Kieran and Val position their mounts on either side of us.

"Not that I'm complaining, but why the change?"

Darian leans in, with his mouth against my ear on the other side of my hood, "I need you close to me." he snakes his arm around my waist, sending butterflies through my body as he steers his mount out of the stable.

We silently head further south as the morning goes on. Soon the forest opens to wetlands on either side of us, and only a couple of hours later, we come to a stone bridge with large cracks and crevices.

Val dismounts and puts a hand to the stone. I watch in awe as the cracks fill and weathered areas disappear before he mounts his toryian again with a grin.

My gaze flicks to the rushing river below warily as we start to move again, "Do others in Servilia do that for the bridges as well?"

Val's voice is oddly quiet as we cross the bridge, "They did at one point, but it seems as though nobody has in some time."

As we leave the rushing water behind us, the forest on either side becomes dense, and a sense of unease hangs over me.

Caspian's words echo in my mind like an alarm bell, and my already heightened anxiety begins to sink its claws into my mind. The forest has gotten so thick that I can hardly see a foot or so past the edge of the tree line.

The expanse of it brings fleeting memories of my past into the forefront of my mind, and my heart thunders in my chest.

Relax Lara. You're not in those woods.

I glance to the side in an effort to take my focus off, but as the minutes pass, my panic remains, building in my chest as my heart clenches tight.

It's as if someone has plucked my mind from my body and thrust it back into that cold forest.

With each long minute, the tree line grows closer, and the sudden urge to escape washes over me. My heart races, my chest feels so tight that it could implode, and my palms become slick with sweat as I frantically look for a way out of the forest.

I spot a break in the trees, and before anyone realizes what's happening, I've thrown myself off the toryian and to the ground as Darian's voice shouts my name.

Colliding with the ground as I land with a thud, the air knocks out of my already struggling lungs. My head is a mess of emotions, and I scramble backward as I stare at the encroaching forest that seems to get closer with each gasping breath.

Val jumps from his toryian and rushes over to my side, "Shit."

"Not safe," I mumble as I fight to reconcile my past emotions with reality.

The feeling of the unknown and the dark, expansive forest in a largely unknown world surrounded by death locks me within the fear of my younger self so many years ago.

Strong arms encircle my shoulders, holding me tightly as Val squeezes my back into his chest, "We're right here with you, Lara." he whispers into my ear, and though my pulse rages loudly inside my head, his words echo over and over again as he rests his head against mine.

Another warm body presses in from our side, and arms snake around us both, "Breathe, Lara." Darian's baritone voice rumbles loudly, and as he inhales deeply, I try to mirror the action and exhale a ragged half-breath.

Squeezing my eyes shut as my mind spirals, I feel gentle hands on either side of my face as Kieran presses his forehead to mine. The tingle of his magic washes over me, and all of the tension in my body recedes.

"Good," Darian says, "Again." he inhales deeply, and I manage to mirror the full action before exhaling.

I open my eyes, and they lock onto Kieran's silver gaze as he searches my face, his blonde hair falling over his forehead.

He searches my face, "You're safe with us, Lara. You always will be."

Whether due to the remnants of adrenaline still coursing through my veins or some confidence I didn't know I had, or maybe just because I want to feel something other than panic or dread, I lean forward to close the distance between us.

The moment our lips touch, desire swirls deep in my core, and it takes every ounce of strength I have to pull back instead of diving headfirst into a foursome on the side of a road after a full-blown panic attack.

"Thank you," I whisper, and as Val sits back, I can see he's just as affected from the heat in his eyes and the darkened look on his face.

I second-guess my decision to pull back entirely.

Darian's baritone voice pulls my attention back front and center, "What was that, Lara?"

Sighing, I shake my head shamefully.

"When you killed the people pretending to be my parents, I ran into that forest by myself, thinking you'd come for me too."

Darian's brows furrow, "That cabin was in the middle of nowhere, and there was snow on the ground."

I nod, squeezing my trembling hands together nervously, "I'm sure it seems so silly now, but I was young and lost for days. I hadn't slept much, and I had no food or water. I aimlessly wandered until I found someone's farm. How I didn't freeze to death still baffles me to this day."

I suck in a deep breath and continue, "Whether it was the feeling of being lost or the woods, I'm not sure, but there are times when I fall into that feeling again like a never-ending loop of memories that just builds and builds. Being amidst new scenery, in a world I do not know must have triggered it." I say softly, glancing up to see Val and Kieran looking at me with understanding in their eyes.

"I didn't mean to scare you all. I am so sorry." I say, shame sinking its claws into my mind as I consider what it must have looked like to them.

Darian's arms tighten around Val and me. "I am partially at fault, Sunshine. If it weren't for me, you'd never have experienced that."

I shake my head.

"No, I do not blame you at all. I wish I had not run that night," I twist to face him, searching his mismatched gaze, "My life would have been exponentially different had I not. Either way, I am here now, and that's what matters."

Bringing my hand to his cheek, my fingers trace the line of his scars before I lean in to press my lips to his.

Once again, I find it nearly impossible to pull myself back from his kiss, but somehow, I manage to do so just as voices down the road get close enough for us to hear.

Saved by the bell.

I gently pull Darian's hood over his head before doing the same to mine as exhaustion sets deep into my mind, "Shall we?" I say, pushing to my feet, and extending my hand to him, though I doubt he would need help.

Darian chuckles softly before taking my hand and rising to his feet. He hoists me onto the saddle and then settles himself behind me.

My cheeks burn as he throbs against my back, but it doesn't stop me from backing myself into him more.

I could be on death's door, and I would still want to fuck him.

"Lara," he says in a low tone, "There's no such thing as indecent exposure in Servilia, so unless you want to be fucked in front of anyone passing by, I suggest you stop."

The mental image of his warning sends a thrill down my spine.

"From what it looks like," Val snickers, grinning as he peers back at us. "She's not the least bit intimidated by that thought, D."

"Actually," Kieran chimes in, "It appears as though she might like it." he muses, and now my cheeks are burning again for more reasons than I can count.

"Remind me how many pairs of pants we brought for her?" Darian asks, and the realization of what he's asking makes me blink at Val.

Val, on the other hand, simply grins from ear to ear as he responds, "Enough to ruin this pair."

Chapter 20

Lara

Before I know what is happening, one of Darian's hands grasps the center of my pants from the front, his other hand grabs hold from the back, and he tears the fabric as if it were paper.

The brisk air hits my bare skin, and I gasp as Darian expertly and torturously slowly circles my clit. I lean forward, and my breath hitches as Darian tosses the reins to Val.

"You want to know what will happen to you when you do brazen things to get a reaction, Sunshine?"

With his now free hand, he slides two fingers along the entrance to my pussy, coating them in my arousal before easing them into my body as he continues to work me. I whimper, pushing back into his fingers in a desperate attempt to force them deeper.

I hardly notice the group of travelers as they pass by us. By the time they're out of earshot for me to answer, Darian squeezes a third finger in, and my chest heaves as I breathe through the stretch.

"You may or may not get exactly what you want."

He circles my clit in a way that has my legs twitching as he coaxes my orgasm closer, "That's it. Do you want me to fuck you, Sunshine?"

I'm panting and grinding into him, desperate to chase my own pleasure, when he stops and withdraws completely, "Words, Lara."

Mourning the sudden loss, my voice comes out as more of a moan as he adjusts himself behind me before he snakes an arm under my thighs to lift me. "Yes. Please."

I feel the smooth tip of Darian's throbbing cock notched at the entrance to my pussy, and he slowly eases me down.

Inch by inch, he sinks himself deeper into me until I'm fully impaled, and every step of the toryian below causes him to move inside of me.

"Is this what you wanted, Sunshine? You want me to fill this soaked fucking pussy of yours?"

He withdraws, snapping his hips into me, and I gasp.

"I said words, Lara."

His next thrust is rough, and I cry out before I manage to gasp words out between his sharp strokes, "Fuck. Yes."

A second group of travelers approaches us, and though we have our hoods over our heads, it's clear that Darian is fucking me as he draws in and out in long movements that only add to the pleasure building in my core.

Each time he buries deep, he holds me there for a moment as if reveling in the feeling, and fuck if it doesn't nearly send me over the edge every time.

Voices grow closer, and I peer at the strangers on the road from beneath my hood. My eyes nearly roll to the back of my head as Darian fills me to the brim before he pulls out again.

The travelers gaze at us with longing in their eyes as Darian continues to coax pleasure from my body with expert precision, drawing it out as long as possible.

For the next few hours, every time I'm close to my orgasm, he buries himself deep and holds me there, waiting for my squirming to stop and for my breathing to even out before he continues.

With each orgasm he coaxes to the surface, it takes longer to calm down, and at this point, I'm nearly coming as he squeezes me against him with no movement.

"Not until we get to Aveentia," he warns and withdraws completely as my orgasm threatens to crash over me again. I'm panting, and my body trembles from the intensity as I slowly come down.

My gaze lands on Kieran as he watches, the heat in his face just barely visible from beneath his hood as Darian lifts my body with ease, and I cry out as he thrusts in with one quick movement.

Another group of travelers passes by, and he leans close enough to whisper against my ear on the other side of my hood, "Do you enjoy being watched? Do you want them to see how I fuck you?" his voice rumbles deep in his chest as he slams up into me, before using one hand to circle my clit.

The orgasm he's denied to me comes back with a vengeance as I push myself further into him, desperately needing release, but he withdraws once again, and I have to make a conscious effort not to beg.

This has to be the best and worst form of torture.

In the distance, the town of Aveentia comes into view, and relief washes over me when I realize I'll be granted what he's denied for the last few hours.

He lifts my trembling body and sinks deep inside me once again, but this time, he doesn't hold back. His pace is urgent as he lifts me with one arm and slams into me repeatedly.

As the roads become more crowded, my orgasm crests, and I push back into each thrust. His dick hits every sensitive spot that's throbbing and aching for release as he pistons into me roughly.

My pussy clamps down as his fingers dig into my skin and his cock thickens. Complete euphoria takes over my body as I cry out. My vision turns white as Darian squeezes me tightly, filling me with his release.

His towering form leans over my back as my chest heaves, and I brace against the toryian for support.

Tugging me into his chest, he whispers into my ear, "You didn't think we were done yet, did you?"

He lifts me suddenly, and nervousness rises in my chest until Kieran's arms wrap around me. Surprise rifles through me as he settles me in front of him, straddling his waist instead of the saddle.

With our hoods melded and just the slightest hints of light getting in, I can see the mixture of desire and concern on his features.

As we approach the bustling city in the distance, more people pass by on either side of us, and Kieran's silver eyes illuminate in the low light as he searches my face, "Are you okay with this?"

Even though trepidation fills my veins at doing this so publicly, it doesn't tamp down the desire raging through me, and I nod my head, wrapping my arms around his neck.

There's a deep, slaking hunger raging inside my body with how close we are, and I know without a doubt that not only do I want this, but I crave to be closer to him in a way that cannot be described.

It's like the very essence of my soul calls to him, and being this close, breathing him in and feeling him around me, I know he feels it, too.

I lean forward, brushing my lips against his, "I need you, Kieran."

Emotion flashes across his face, and he presses his lips to mine as he moves to free himself from his pants. He settles the throbbing head of his cock at my still-soaked entrance, and he groans as he slowly inches in deeper.

Breaking our kiss, I cling to his shoulders as my mouth drops open. The pure, raw euphoria rifling through my body and crashing over my mind is overwhelming, and it takes everything in me to lean in to bury my face into his neck as he slowly fills me.

Much like my intimacy with Darian and Val, each movement feels like so much more than just sex.

My clit is still sensitive from my orgasm, and as our pelvic bones meet, the pressure sends electric jolts into my core.

I roll my hips, holding him tight to my chest as we move in sync. The groan that escapes Kieran's throat sends my mind into a tailspin, and I repeat the action as he pushes into me.

A whimper escapes my throat as pleasure builds in my body.

These men are more than the air that my lungs need to breathe. They're the sun and the moons in their constant dance as they orbit the world.

They're the first frosts of winter, the first blooms of spring, and the first rains of the year.

And what's more than that is that they're mine.

He pauses and shifts suddenly, snagging my attention as he pulls a wide, dark cloth from his bag. He holds it over my head and eases me backward so my face remains concealed.

The toryian is large enough that it's utterly unbothered by me lying further up its shoulders, and I have to keep both hands on the edge of the saddle as Kieran leans forward to drive into me over and over again.

With each thrust he presses down on my stomach, and the pressure releases a husky moan from my throat. His free hand moves to my clit, and the orgasm that was building gradually suddenly rises to the surface as his magic sends vibrations through my core.

I cry out as he pins me down with his hands, snapping his hips in quick thrusts, and I know he's close as he wraps his arms around my torso. I hold my hood in place as he eases me into his arms again, and we move in unison as he's buried as deep as possible.

Each movement is in sync as our hoods meld together, and I never want this to end. Our lips brush, and breathing his air is intoxicating as he presses them to mine.

My hand snakes under his hood and intertwines with his hair as his movements become more urgent. My body feels completely in tune with his as another orgasm crests, fueled by the need to brand my soul as his tongue dances with mine.

His cock swells as my orgasm crashes over me, and we come together. The pressure of him coming as he clutches me to him makes me cry out, and as the waves of euphoria fade, he presses his lips to mine once more.

Holy fuck.

Our chests heave as the lively sounds of Aveentia surround us, and he whispers against my lips, "Are you okay with what just happened?"

I hear the double meaning behind his question.

Am I okay with having climaxed in front of countless people?

Am I okay with being fucked by Darian and, subsequently, Kieran, both in front of countless people?

"Yes," I breathe and lean my forehead against his. "I am more than okay with it." My voice is barely audible amongst the noise surrounding us as I lean in to capture his lips as if to prove my point.

Our long, drawn-out kisses continue as he's fully seated inside of me, and as our toryian comes to a stop, he throbs again before he smiles against my lips.

"We better stop soon, sweetheart, or V might not get a moment with you for the rest of the day."

The threat is tempting, and I nearly grind into him again as he throbs twice, but the lively chatter around our toryian snags my attention, and Val's voice is thick as he calls over.

"We're at the docks, let's go."

I pull back from Kieran just enough to catch a glimpse of the town around us.

There are hundreds of people.

Some are looking at us, while others are minding their own business and moving along with their lives without a care.

"I'll help you off." his voice is low as he withdraws himself before he lifts and cradles me in his arms in one swift movement. The robe covers the tear in my pants as he swings his leg over the saddle and lands on the ground.

He sets me down gently as my shaking legs barely support my weight, and I take an unsteady step as Val lets out a dark laugh behind me.

"Don't think for a moment that you can escape me, Lara," he playfully squeezes my ass, "The moment we get onto that boat, you're mine," he warns into my ear, sending another wave of desire coursing through my veins.

Thank god Kieran is a healer, or I may not be able to walk soon.

We file onto a large ship filled with people, and Darian leads us to the back, setting our bags down along the wooden siding. I glance around, scanning the boat from beneath my hood, when Val's tall, broad-chested form approaches, backing me into the side of the ship.

The dark look he gives me from the shadow of his robe sends a thrilling jolt of heat to my core as his hands grasp the back of my thighs. He lifts me with ease and pins me against the wall as my arms wrap around his neck for support.

I see Darian and Kieran watching from my peripherals as Val frees himself from his pants and presses the length of his cock against my clit. His hands cup my ass, and as he pins me with his hips, the friction and movement against my clit make my legs twitch involuntarily around his waist.

"I never thought you were a fan of torture," I breathe as he glides himself along my entrance a few times, teasing me as my body demands more than he's giving.

The dark laugh under his breath makes my mind whirl, and I can't help the whimper that escapes as he pulls back slightly, but instead of teasing me again, the tip of his dick presses against the entrance to my pussy.

Val leans forward and presses a reverent kiss to my lips as he starts to ease himself inside of me. His dick pulsates and throbs as he slowly pushes deeper, and I moan huskily as my body stretches to accommodate his size.

As my pussy reaches the base of his dick, he withdraws slightly, and my mouth drops open as he thrusts himself in until his balls are flush with my ass. His thrusts aren't rough, but they press me hard against the wooden wall of the boat, and I grind into him, desperate to feel him as deep as possible.

"Do you know how hard I was," He breathes into my ear as he thrusts in again, "The entire time my brothers fucked you senseless on the road here?"

My mind whirls as he squeezes my ass with another thrust that makes the wood bite into my back.

"I nearly pulled you off their toryians and fucked you senseless myself. Do you know what kind of restraint it took not to do that? Do you understand how badly I needed to feel you wrapped around my fucking dick?"

His need to fuck me, mixed with the overwhelming desire raging through my veins sends me overboard, and I find myself cresting another orgasm as he continuously slams into me.

"Right there. Oh god, that spot V---" He covers my mouth with his, biting my lip as he hits one spot repeatedly.

I cry out as my entire body shudders, and he swallows my moans. My pussy clamps down on him as he suddenly swells, filling me with his release as I continue to pant through the waves of ecstasy of my own.

He holds me there against the wall as we both come down from our climax and as he presses his head to mine, my chest tightens with emotion.

As much as I lust for these men, they each hold such a delicate piece of my heart that only seems to grow with each moment I spend with them.

I lean in to kiss him as reverently as he does so often to me, and I feel a pang of emotion that I can't quite place as his hand cups my cheek.

After a long moment we break apart, and he laughs softly.

"You almost slipped up," he teases, and my heart stutters when I realize I almost said his name in front of all these people.

He withdraws and sets me on my feet as I blow out a shaky breath, "Almost."

My legs almost give out as I reach Darian and Kieran by the railing that overlooks the sea, and Val stands with his chest against my back.

I watch the coast slowly melt into the distance with a light heart.

"Onto Sabinia," I murmur, and all three men hum in agreement.

Chapter 21

Caspian

It's been hours since Samira left the bed. I listened to her footsteps echo down the hall until they faded into silence, waiting to be alone with my thoughts again.

Only then did a conflict of disgust and anxiety war inside my mind.

Disgust from Samira using my body for whatever the fuck she wants and anxiety from Lara appearing in my dreams while the bitch is lying next to me.

It was a relief to know Lara was okay, but finding out in such close proximity to Samira had me holding my breath until she left this morning.

She can't see in my head, but if she suspects anything,

All she'd have to do is command me to tell her, and I would.

There'd be no choice, no way for me to keep Lara's identity or this ability to dream-weave hidden.

Footsteps from the hallway sound out, and dread sinks into my gut.

"Caspian, my love," she coos, pausing in the doorway with her hand on her hip as she frowns, "Since when are you one to stay in bed all morning?"

She says it as if she knows me at all, and my teeth clench.

I release a sigh and move to sit up, but as the sheets fall down my chest, her voice sounds out, and my body stills.

"Stop."

My gaze flicks to hers as she eyes me like I'm a bowl of dessert served on a platter.

She cocks her head to the side, her brown locks of hair falling in front of her face.

"You want to fuck me. No, that's not quite right... You want me to ride you." She murmurs, taking a step closer, and my dick throbs.

By the time she's at the foot of the bed, I'm frozen in place with the sheet tented over my lower body from six fucking words.

It makes me sick to my stomach.

She leans forward and crawls over my legs, tugging the sheets off until I'm fully exposed, and she positions herself over me.

"You're going to fuck me like the King you are," she breathes as her hand glides over my chest.

What a fucking joke.

I'm no more of a king than she is a queen.

She glides herself against the length of my dick, and bile rises in my throat at how wet she is. The look on her face is pure anticipation as she rubs her clit against me, her breath hitching when I throb against it.

"Lean back," she says, pushing my chest as my body responds immediately.

She reaches down to angle the tip of my dick at her entrance before easing herself down, moaning loudly until she's sitting fully on me.

My expression schooled, her gaze flicks to mine as she begins to move and grind, chasing her pleasure before frustration flashes across her features.

"Fuck me, Caspian." she pants, "I need you to fuck me."

Within a second, I've flipped her onto her back, and I snap my hips against hers.

She never said to be gentle.

My pace is brutal since it's the only fucking thing I can control.

I might not be able to stop this, but I'll make it as unenjoyable as possible.

Her moans become as frantic as her erratic breathing, and it's not long before she orgasms. It's a conscious effort to keep my face even as she screams my name and pants.

My body doesn't stop, though. It keeps fucking her as she told it to, as if it's nothing more than her fucking sex doll.

I keep the bruising pace that would make any average person cry, but she doesn't tell me to stop.

No, she just grinds herself further against me.

Finally, she must have come down from her orgasm as she looks at me with half-lidded eyes.

"That's enough."

I quickly withdraw from her and throw the sheets off before pushing myself off the bed to move toward the bath.

I feel fucking filthy.

"Caspian," she calls out, and the edge of her voice sends a jolt of nervousness through me.

Even after what happened, my only concern is that she'll somehow know or ask about Lara.

I turn to her, meeting her deep red gaze.

"There are two kids—daughters of the rebellion—who live just south of Lavinium near the lake. Bring them to the cells to have them interrogated after you clean up."

My teeth grind together, but I nod, turning to the bath.

Someday.

Someday, I will kill her.

But first, I need to keep her from finding out about Lara.

Chapter 22

Lara

The journey takes two days, with brief rests for the captain to regain his strength and wield his magic.

Finally, Sabinia appears on the horizon. The coast nears as we approach the enormous dock stretching into the ocean, and people around us murmur amongst themselves.

A few feet from us, a small child tugs impatiently at her guardian's shirt, "Do you think we'll see the dragon?"

"I don't know, sweetie. I hope not."

I can't help but notice my three companions' glance as they eavesdrop.

"What is it?" I whisper, but Darian just shakes his head.

Even with his face partially obscured by the shadow of his hood, I don't miss the conflict that paints across his features, nor the slight temperature drop in the air around us.

My palms become clammy, and I grow increasingly restless as our boat pulls into port and everyone files into lines to disembark. Val leads with Kieran as we venture off the docks and into the quiet streets.

All the towns and cities we went to before were bustling and full of life, but Sabinia is the complete opposite for some reason.

Strangers peer out the windows of their wooden and stone houses before shutting them for privacy; others walking toward us veer off the road into nearby alleys.

It's all unsettling.

We file off the ship and venture through the nearly empty streets in eerie silence. When we finally reach the inn near the gates, I couldn't be happier about the prospect of resting on solid ground for a night.

I can't remember how many times the rocking of the boat woke me up. I lost count after ten.

At least I didn't get seasick.

The moment we step into the inn, eyes track our movements around the room. Val steps to the man by the entrance to get a room while the rest of us settle down at a secluded table in the back of the room as Val orders drinks and some stew.

The door blows open as a bald, one-eyed man walks in. The feathers of his clothes flutter in the wind as they brush against the bones of his necklace.

He looks straight out of a horror film where the swamp witch enters the movie scene.

"Shit," Darian mutters under his breath and lowers his hood as the man walks directly to our table and sits next to me.

My heart thunders in my chest, and I'm frozen in place.

The tension in the air is palpable, and everyone remains silent while the inn server approaches. She eyes the man warily before tossing a glance at the rest of us, and she places the drinks and stew on the table. She pauses, opening her mouth to speak when the man waves her off dismissively.

Anger flashes across her face, but something keeps her from arguing as she twists away and leaves in a huff.

When she gains enough distance, the man turns to face us, "I know who you are and where you plan to go, but you must listen to what I have to say." his hushed tone is barely audible through a thick accent I can't quite place.

Val and Kieran glance at each other in my peripherals before turning their attention to Darian as his jaw feathers, "Speak."

Giving one single nod, the man surprisingly turns to look directly at me as he continues, "As you are no doubt aware, there is a darkness spreading in Servilia. It kills our people, drains our magic, and turns families into foes. Some of this you have seen firsthand on your travels here, do you deny it?" I shake my head in response, and he turns his attention to Val.

Who the hell is this guy?

"I understand there is something you wish for me to read, but time is of the essence," his gaze scans over each of us before landing on me, "You must journey to the mountains above Sabinia where the great beast is caged and free it. Do this, and I will read the tome you brought from Trebonia." The air catches in my lungs as I realize this man must be a seer.

My voice is hardly audible as I frown, "You would help us? Why?"

The seer's gaze is piercing as he peculiarly tilts his head. His hand slides a few inches to grip mine tightly as a searing pain radiates through my skull.

I can't cry out, breathe, or blink as his voice echoes through my mind.

Know this, child born of the sun and moon. I help not from the good of my heart but because the gods demand it, and they demand much.

You alone must go to the mountain pass. Your companions shall fall should they decide to follow.

Do you understand what is required of you, child?

His voice fades away as Darian knocks his hand from mine, severing the connection, "Speak for all of us to hear," Darian says, his baritone voice lethally calm.

The seer stares at me for a long moment before turning his singular gaze to Darian with a wry laugh.

"You already know what must be done. The light must chase away the dark as they always do in their endless game of cat and mouse. This next battle is not yours to win, and should you decide to try, you will not see the dawn of a new era."

The seer's words hang upon the air before he continues, "The choice is yours, but for the good of Servilia, she must go alone."

Darian's knuckles turn white as he grips his mug.

"You have seen it? You've seen her return unharmed?"

The seer stares at him for a long moment before his gaze slides to me, and a shiver runs down my spine.

"She will return," he says softly, and the words he's left unsaid hang upon the air like knives about to fall.

The temperature drops and his eye glazes over before refocusing.

"Take the western path and follow it to the southernmost cave near the mouth of the volcano. There, you will find the caged beast that terrorizes our cities," he says as he pushes to his feet. "When you return, you shall have the information you truly seek," he says before striding out of the inn, and my heart thunders in my chest.

Alone. I must do this by myself.

Darian pushes to his feet without a word and makes his way to the back, taking the stairs up to the second floor of the building with Val at his heels.

My stomach flips anxiously as I glance at Kieran, "Damage control?"

Kieran nods as he gazes into his cup. "Much like the rest of us, he does not wish for you to go head-first into danger alone."

"The seer said something in my mind earlier that I don't understand. Blair said it as well before I—" My voice cracks, and Kieran tilts his head as he waits for me to finish. "He called me the 'child born of the sun and moon.'"

Kieran's brows pinch together deeply, "I'm not entirely sure what that means either, sweetheart," he whispers, siding my bowl closer, "But you'll need your strength, so please, eat."

My appetite is non-existent, even with the delicious aroma coming from it, but I know he's right.

We eat our stew in solemn silence as the other patrons chatter quietly. By the time we're done, Darian and Val still haven't returned, so we bring their bowls of stew with us as we turn in for the night.

Kieran pushes open the room's doors, and an icy wind blasts through the doorway as we step inside.

"Gods," Kieran breathes as Darian stands in the middle of the room, locked into an argument with Val.

Val's long black hair that flows to his shoulders has frost covering the tips. His clothes are ripped and tattered with dried or frozen blood along his skin as he stands next to the wall beside the bed.

"Val!" I exclaim quietly after the door clicks closed, and I set the bowls down before rushing over. Before I can get a step or two closer, Val holds his arm out, halting me in place.

My gaze slides to Darian as ice swirls around him ominously, and my jaw clenches as frustration bubbles within me.

"Do you truly not trust me enough to take on one task myself?" I ask loudly, and all three of their heads snap in my direction.

"Trust? You think this is about trust?" Darian asks in a low tone as he forms an ice spear. "This is about life and death, Lara," he growls, throwing the spear at Val, who absorbs the impact with a stone shield.

"Correct. That is why I am going—alone." I state bluntly, and Darian shakes his head, but I continue before he can retort.

I take two steps closer, craning my head to search his face, "I might have my own demons to work through, Darian, but I can do this. If the seer said I would return, I will."

The room warms as his magic retracts abruptly, "Please, Lara. I can't lose you, too," he says as he falls to his knees before me.

The sight shatters my heart into pieces and makes me equally enraged at Caspian for taking so much from him.

"You don't understand," he whispers. "We nearly lost you once, and that cost was almost too much to bear. I couldn't bear it. If anything happens to you, Lara..." His hands flex against his thighs, and he bows his head.

An entire realm depends on him, yet he here he is on his knees before me.

Emotion clogs my throat as I crouch beside him, taking his hands into mine.

"I will return, Darian. Nothing, not even the gods themselves, could keep me from you—from all of you. Allow me to do this," I say softly, pressing my lips to the back of his hands.

The pain on his face is so clear that it's as though I feel it myself, a deep agony that feels as though it could tear me in two.

He pulls me into a crushing embrace, nestling his face into the crook of my neck as he breathes me in. I'm vaguely aware of movement behind me, and Darian stands, carrying me to the bed.

He sets me down gently, kneeling before me as his mismatched gaze searches mine.

The conflict of wanting to protect me but knowing I must go alone wars behind his eyes as he straightens and removes his tattered shirt.

As he tugs the material past his tattooed chest and over his head, the corded muscles along his abdomen flex and ripple before he tosses it to the floor. He unties the knot at the top of his leather pants, and the deep V line from his abdomen unveils as his pants drop to the ground.

Val and Kieran undress, tossing their clothes to the floor as all three men straighten, and butterflies flip chaotically in my stomach.

They are breathtaking.

The sight of these three men bared before me is akin to staring at the beauty of a canyon before diving off the cliff.

My body heats, and my pulse hikes in anticipation.

I may not make it to the mountains tomorrow because I may very well die of happiness in their arms.

Kieran crosses his arms as he smirks, the muscles along his stomach flexing as he leans back slightly.

Val tilts his head to the side with an eyebrow raised as if he knows exactly what reaction they're eliciting from me. He leans his shoulder against the wall, comfortably shifting one of his ankles behind the other.

His movement drags my attention down, and my breath hitches before I gaze at his face, where a heated grin paints his features.

These men are mine.

Somewhere inside of me, I knew I belonged with them, but for the first time, the understanding has settled deep in my soul that as much as I'd claimed the space within their hearts, they'd filled just as much within mine.

They're mine, and no one can ever take them from me.

My heart thunders as emotion flashes across Darian's face, and he steps close to the edge of the bed. The V-shaped lines along his hips at my eye level make me swallow audibly as he leans forward, bringing my attention to his face.

I lean back slightly to get a good look at him as my heart leaps into my throat. The dim light flickers against his mismatched gaze as it darkens, the shadows accentuating the heat on his face as he closes the distance between us.

He pauses with his lips a hairsbreadth from mine.

"Whatever is to come, Lara, remember that you hold every inch of our hearts in your hands and are capable of so much more than you know."

He echoes my thoughts, and my heart swells in my chest as if threatening to explode.

Pulling back slightly, he searches my eyes, "You will return to us, if only for our selfishness."

My throat tightens with emotion as he crushes his lips to mine with an urgency unlike any I've felt before.

The desire already burning inside my core ignites, fueled by the gasoline of his words, and I return his passion with my own.

I could kiss him for the rest of eternity, and it wouldn't be enough.

The bed shifts and my eyes snap open as Darian trails his lips down my jaw and leans me back. His kisses sear down my neck as my gaze locks with Kieran.

His bright silver eyes burn into mine until Darian tugs my shirt over my head, tosses it aside, and continues to kiss down my chest. Movement on the other side of the bed catches my attention, and Val moves to lie alongside me.

My pulse rages in anticipation, and I'm certain that they know it.

Every part of me craves these men on such an intimate level.

Darian slides my pants down; his movements are slow and unhurried as Kieran kisses my shoulder tenderly.

Val wraps his hand around the nape of my neck, drawing my attention to him as his bright hazel eyes search my face.

"I knew from the moment I laid eyes on you in that forest that I'd never be the same." his voice is no more than a whisper, but my chest tightens with emotion as he leans in, pressing his forehead to mine.

Darian's kisses trail lower, and I inhale sharply. Kieran's fingers trail along the skin at my hip, and butterflies soar inside my stomach as Val leans in, pressing lips to mine in long, drawn-out kisses.

His kisses are devotion given form as his hand cups the back of my head, his fingers flexing with our movements as I eagerly return every vow he's giving.

My back arches as Darian's mouth trails up my inner thigh, and he's dangerously close to noticing how wet I am.

Our kiss breaks apart, and Val glances down my body, cursing under his breath, and I follow his gaze to where Darian is settled between my legs. His gaze flickers between each of us before locking onto mine with a grin.

This man is a king to his people.

He's the most important bloodline in this realm, and he's looking at me as if his rightful place is between my legs.

My cheeks burn as he leans in and drags his tongue along my center, and his eyes snap shut as he groans. My breathing picks up as his movements become more urgent as if this does just as much for him as being inside of me.

Val's hazel gaze slides to mine, "Hope you're ready for us, Lara," he whispers, and a shiver runs down my spine as he peppers kisses along my neck to my collarbone.

My hand snakes into his hair, desperate to touch him more.

Ready or not, this is all I want.

His lips trail across my collarbone to my chest before he takes my nipple into his mouth, and I gasp, feeling Kieran's lips against my stomach. My gaze drags from Val's dark hair, framing his face, to Kieran's mess of blonde hair, and I reach my free hand, tilting Kieran's chin towards me.

He instantly looks up and follows as I lift his face closer and cup his cheek, pausing as our faces are mere inches apart. My voice comes out breathless as Darian and Val work my body in ways I could never imagine in a million years.

"I need each of you with every fiber of my being, and no matter what happens, no matter what tomorrow brings, just know that I'm always with you. I belong to you just as much as you are mine."

Emotion flashes across his face as my lips find his. I eagerly pour everything I feel for these men into every kiss, every touch, every caress between us.

Kieran kisses me back fervently. Our tongues dance against one another as my orgasm crests, and it's not long before I'm on the edge.

"D," Val's voice is thick as he pauses, "I think she needs more."

Darian pulls back, and I suppress a whimper at the loss as he crawls forward. Val moves out of the way as Darian snakes his arm around my waist, flipping us both until I'm straddling his waist.

My heart rattles in my chest frantically as his large hands cup my ass, lifting me until he's notched at my entrance. Feeling Val at my side, a nervous excitement runs through my veins, and Darian throbs as he leans in to kiss me deeply.

Heaven is real, and it's here in this very room.

Kieran moves behind me, trailing kisses up my spine, and I shudder as Val moves in close.

Darian slowly pushes himself in, and my jaw drops open at the stretch, even with how wet I am. He's halfway in when it becomes painful, and I whimper.

He stills, but the desire coursing through my veins makes my mind haze as the pain suddenly dissipates.

I'm vaguely aware of Kieran's finger easing into my ass, the slight tingle of his magic easing my discomfort as both men stretch me to accommodate them.

My breaths come in heavy as I wrap my free hand around the length of Val's erection, and it throbs at the contact as I continue to glide my hand from base to tip.

"Lara," Val groans with his forehead against my cheek, sending heat further into my core, and I lean in to capture his lips again with urgency.

Darian makes long strokes, pausing just long enough for Kieran to position himself behind me, and my entire being feels alight.

Val kisses me fervently, his hands around my head hold me close to him as Kieran pushes in deep, using his magic to ease the pain of his size.

Thank god Kieran is a healer.

I feel Kieran's skin flush against my ass, and with Darian fully seated, even though my body feels like it can't take anymore, I can't help but feel as if it's not enough.

"Val," I whisper against his lips, and as if he knows what I intend, he kneels before me, bringing his dick inches from my face as I pump his length with my hand.

He groans, muttering a string of words in another language as he gently pulls my hair from my face. I lean forward to lick him from base to tip, and his breath hitches.

Kieran and Darian slowly pump in and out as I work Val with my mouth, the movement of each thrust pushing Val's cock further down my throat, and tears spring to my eyes as I fight for breath.

My throat contracts around him as his grip on my hair tightens, and he fights the urge to thrust into my mouth since I'm nearly suffocating on his cock already.

The desire in my body builds as my orgasm rages. The ecstasy in my core heightens with how full I feel. Darian and Kieran throb against one another with each movement, and Val struggles to maintain composure as I hollow my cheeks, taking him as deep as I can.

Suddenly, pleasure radiates through me in wave after wave of pure euphoria. My limbs tremble, and I push back into their strokes, my body clamping down as I moan.

The sounds are swallowed by Val's cock as he squeezes my hair, and my throat strains with how far he's pushed into it. The vibrations from my moans and fighting for air push Val over the edge as he stiffens against my tongue and throat.

His dick swells as his come fills my mouth, and I have no choice but to swallow it as he mutters a curse under his breath. His grip tightens in my hair as he squeezes my head as far as I can take him.

With the waves of my climax over, Darian and Kieran pick up their pace as Val withdraws from my mouth. My gaze drops to Darian's as he watches my expression. The moment our eyes meet, he thrusts in deeply, squeezing my hips as he swells and comes, with Kieran following right after.

"That was-" I breathe.

"Everything," Kieran whispers, placing a tender kiss on top of my head.

My throat tightens with emotion.

I know my life will never be the same again, and I couldn't be happier.

Darian and Kieran withdraw as Val tugs me in alongside them.

A serene peacefulness comes over me, even though I don't know what trials tomorrow could bring.

Chapter 23

Lara

The next morning, Darian meticulously packs a day's worth of food onto my toryian, and we say our goodbyes.

Val hands me a short sword that he attaches to the belt at my hip before he lifts me onto the giant creature. They walk me to the gate, and my heart feels like it's being torn in two as I steer my mount toward the mountains in the distance.

The journey is long and arduous as I navigate my toryian along the winding pathway westward up the mountain's cliffs. The higher we've traveled, the more narrow the path is, and soon it's just wide enough for a single toryian.

It's not long before the air becomes increasingly thin, and a series of cave entrances come into view.

The seer's words ring out, and I follow the path south toward the intimidating mouth of the volcano that dwarfs the other mountains. The jagged rocks at the edge of the narrow path crumble and roll down the side of the mountain as the toryian nears a large opening on the side of the rock face.

I twist the reins slightly toward the opening, thankful to have gotten some reprieve from the narrow path as I look around.

Just as I question whether this is my destination, a loud growl sounds out from inside the cave, making my mount side-step nervously.

It's a caged beast, Lara. Caged.

It's fine.

I dismount, letting the toryian stay behind as I cautiously close the rest of the distance on foot with my short sword in hand.

The entrance to the cave is intimidatingly large, and as I step inside, I feel as though I've ventured into the belly of the beast itself.

With adrenaline coursing through my veins, my hands tremble as I tightly grip the leather hilt of my sword.

A sudden roar causes me to jerk in surprise, and I lose grip as my sword clatters to the ground. Cursing under my breath, I move to grab it just as light fills the cave, and instinct has me hurling myself to the side.

Heat engulfs the space as my rolling comes to a stop, and my eyes snap open to white and red flames spewing into the space I was standing in moments ago.

Shock rifles through me as I follow the blaze to where an enormous black-scaled dragon stands. It must be over twenty-five feet tall, with giant wings that spread wide as it roars, the sound making the stone beneath me tremble as it echoes off the walls.

Something about this creature sends a pang of familiarity through me, but I can't quite place why as my gaze scans the length of its body.

There's one thing the seer was wrong about.

This beast is most definitely not caged.

It turns, and each step sends a shudder through the stone at my feet as its attention locks onto me like a predator with its prey.

Suddenly, I realize why this dragon is so familiar, and Darian's tattoos flash into the forefront of my mind as I gaze upon the life-sized and very real version of it.

If this is the same dragon, then it must mean this is...

'Gray shifted and hasn't been seen since.'

'Cade and Zayne have been missing for years.'

Considering Cade and Zayne have purple eyes, the creature before me must be Gray.

The molten gold hue of the dragon's eyes appears muted and dull as they lock onto me. His head snaps back, and a loud hiss sounds as he fills his lungs before releasing another torrent of flames.

I dive out of the way at the last second and sprint closer as the heat of his flames nip at my heels.

Fuck I hope this works.

As the last of his fire sputters, I sprint toward him, and he swipes at me with his long claws. One of his talons catches my arm as I dive to the side, narrowly avoiding his giant maw as he snaps at me.

Faster, Lara.

Surging forward as he swipes his tail at me, I take advantage as he turns his back, using my momentum and adrenaline to hurl myself up his hind leg.

The moment I'm on his back, he spins and bucks before releasing another roar, this one more pained than the last.

With his chaotic movement, he slams against the cave wall, and I drop to his back, squeezing myself onto his scales as he suddenly beats his strong wings.

He's about to slam against the wall once more to force me off when I squeeze my eyes shut and scream, "Gray, snap out of it!"

When the movement beneath me stops, I open my eyes to see his giant scaled body standing feet away, covered in red-hot chains that spike into his torn and bleeding skin with horror. His maw opens as he tries to breathe fire on them, but no flames come out.

I've entered into his illusion.

I push to my feet and take two tentative steps toward him. His serpentine gaze turns on me, his eyes like liquid gold watching me with rapt attention. The clasps that hold his chains together embed into each chain around his feet, with one around his neck, and I take another step forward.

"Gray, I know you don't know me but, I'm a friend of Darian, Val, and Kieran's. Please don't eat me." I say with a dry laugh and swallow audibly as he lets out a pained roar before thrashing in place, causing the spikes buried in his skin to bleed profusely.

"Stop!" I shout, quickly closing the distance to stop him from hurting himself more.

Just as I get close, his tail whips from the side and slams into my shoulder, sending me flying through the air. I land hard on my back with a thud, and the back of my head collides with the ground, sending stars into my vision.

I roll over and cough as blood drips from my mouth, and the severity of the situation sets in that I could very well die here.

Pushing myself to my feet, I solidify my resolve and sprint toward him again, every step more sure than the last. As his tail swipes at my legs, I leap over his tail before diving under his large body.

He swivels from side to side to try to catch sight of me, but I remain just out of view as I move with him beneath his chest.

Relying on timing, I remove the pin from one clasp of his deadly front feet before removing the pin from the other.

My heart races, but I don't stop to think before he can swipe at me again. I twist to grasp the long spiked scales along his side, ignoring the pain in my shoulder as I hurl myself on top of his back.

My mind is pure instinct as I keep my momentum. Hooking my fingers around his large scales to climb onto his spine, I crawl towards the clasp on his neck.

"Gray, if you can hear me, when I remove this, you're going to wake up. Just please don't eat me." I shout before I pull the pin, and the sharp spikes biting into his bleeding skin fall away, clattering to the ground. Gray's head angles back as he roars, and white-hot flames spew from his mouth.

They're so bright that I shield my eyes as he rears back, forcing me to roll off his back and fall to the ground with a thud. I land on my bad shoulder but don't have time to think as the light invades my senses.

When I open my eyes again, relief fills my veins to see the cave devoid of any dragon, but instead, Gray's nude human form lies on the hard stone.

He's not moving.

Fuck.

I push myself to my feet as I hurry to his side and roll him over.

"Please don't be dead, please don't be dead," I murmur as I hover over his body, "Gray, wake up."

Suddenly, he inhales a ragged, gasping breath, and his eyes snap open as he sits upright. His hand suddenly shoots out to grab me by the throat, and he squeezes tightly.

I claw at his hand as my head feels like it's going to explode, and his wild eyes scan the cave. It's not until stars fill my vision that his gaze flicks to mine, and he doesn't release me, but he lessens his grip enough for me to suck in a pained breath.

"It's rude," I choke out, "to strangle the help." I manage to say, and he loosens his grip but keeps his hand around my neck as I catch my breath.

"Who the hell are you?" he asks, but movement in the corner of my eye catches my attention as I see a billow of smoke form from the dark.

A woman and Zayne with his skull mask materialize from the smoke, and my heart stutters in my chest.

Shit.

"Darian's waiting in Sabinia, Gray," I murmur as the woman paces toward us.

Her hips sway from side to side, and her red eyes match her blood-red lips as she flicks her brown hair over her shoulder.

"My, my. What a nuisance you've all been," she says, her tone conveying pure annoyance as she puts her hand on her hip and eyes Gray.

"How did you do it?"

As if she thinks I'll just tell her.

"Who are you? What do you want?" I ask, trying to bide my time.

She sighs loudly.

"My name is Samira. You may know me as the Queen," she says matter-of-factly, checking her nails as if bored. "And I want to know how you keep freeing the pets I worked so hard to put leashes on."

She pauses momentarily. "No matter. If I can't have him, no one will." She sneers, glancing at Zayne, "Put him down."

She gestures toward Gray, and Zayne steps forward, his smoke concentrating near his hand as Gray curses.

No. No, no, no.

My heart thunders as I look for a way out of this, "Wait!"

She pauses, turning to me with a raised brow as she holds her hand out to halt Zayne's advance. I glance at Gray, who looks ready to fight but too drained to win, before my gaze slides to Zayne, whose dull purple eyes stare at Gray and me with no emotion or recognition.

Samira looks at me expectantly, and resignation burrows deep into my veins as I turn to Gray.

"My toryian is outside. Take him to Sabinia and find the nearest inn by the gates. Darian will be there with Kieran and Val."

He searches my face with a bewildered look as if I've lost my mind, "And people think I'm the crazy one in this gods' forsaken land."

Maybe I have lost my mind.

But I know that if I don't do something, neither of us will survive.

Pushing to my feet, the pain of my encounter with Gray's dragon form radiates through my body, and I turn to Samira despite Gray's hand wrapped around my forearm.

"Take me instead of harming him," Gray swears loudly, muttering something in another language.

Her red eyes narrow as they flick between me and Gray, and she cocks her head to the side, "Deal. Zayne, bring her. Leave the other one."

Zayne steps closer, and I quickly turn to Gray. "Tell them," my voice cracks, but I continue as Zayne approaches, "Tell them this is how it had to be."

"There are worse things than death, you know," Gray moves to stop me, but I just shake my head, and I take Zayne's outstretched hand as he leads me to stand next to Samira.

The last thing I see before the smoke engulfs my vision is Gray's golden eyes brimming with rage as the world goes black.

Chapter 24

Caspian

Something doesn't feel right.

Granted, that is the fucking statement of the century, but it's even more true since I returned. The two girls, no older than Rose and May, cry out as I carry their squirming bodies down the hall.

The cells aren't far from here, and each step feels like an eternity.

Even more than usual, the marble walls have an eerie sense of wrongness, and it's like even the air is imposing.

It's even more odd that she requested them be brought to the cells. Typically, she has a hidden entrance where she waits for me before she does her 'interrogations.'

I don't know what goes on beyond that fucking door, but it's not anything close to questioning.

No one ever leaves.

The two girls fight my grip as I round the corner, and the cells come into view. The scent of ammonia and mildew from long-rotted bodily fluids invades my senses, and I fight the bile in my throat.

I don't blame them for wanting to escape. The last thing I'd want is for this to be my final view.

Kicking the door open a bit, I toss each girl inside, and they land roughly, whimpering as they shift closer to one another, making my chest tight.

Memories of Rose and May holding tight to Lara's thighs come into my mind, and my jaw clenches.

She'd never leave them in here to this fate.

My body shuts the cell door and shoves the key into the lock with a click as it snaps tight. One of the two girls locks eyes with me, and the terror on her face is so familiar that it tears at something deep inside of my mind.

With the key in hand, I move to place it in my pocket as I turn away.

It takes every last ounce of willpower to open my hand, and the key clatters to the ground as I quickly pace away from the cells.

I don't bother to turn and look to see if they try to escape.

I don't want to know. It will just risk all of us more if I do.

The less I know, the better.

It's bad enough that I know Lara's secrets, and it's taking all my fucking willpower and energy to make sure Samira stays far away from her.

Which is nearly impossible since she's fucking paranoid as hell.

A door on my left opens as Tamara walks in, shooting me a glare.

"Throne room." she mutters, tearing her shirt over her head, "Samira said your brother is in Sabinia, and she wants you to send a message when she gets back."

If my brother is in Sabinia...

Fuck I hope they didn't go after Gray.

The idiot is going to get himself and Lara killed.

Each step to the throne room feels like it takes longer than the last, and warning bells go off in my mind as I walk through the last hall to the throne room.

Samira's voice rings out, and as I turn the corner, I school my features.

My heart nearly stops in my chest when my gaze falls to the center of the room.

Fuck.

Chapter 25

Lara

As my vision clears, my gaze falls upon a white marble throne before us as Samira moves to sit on it. I glance around with apprehension before I realize that this must be Darian's home, where he grew up.

Given the circumstances, the thought is oddly comforting.

Samira levels me with a deadpan gaze, "I'll be benevolent and give you one last chance to tell me how you lot were freeing my pets," she says, resting her chin on her palm.

When I stay silent, she sighs loudly in exasperation, "Fine! Have it your way. Zayne, get the answers from her."

Zayne's hand wraps around my bicep, his grip tight enough to bruise as I wince.

"Ah, Caspian, my love." Samira croons, and my gut twists nervously.

Caspian? Here?

My chest tightens as I turn, and my gaze locks with a pair of guarded emerald eyes before smoke engulfs my vision once again.

The Queen is working with Caspian?

She called him 'my love'.

Clearly, they do more than work together.

An odd mixture of jealousy and embarrassment coats my veins, and I can't quite understand what I just witnessed.

Had he fooled me all along? Is this the reason he wanted to come back so badly? To return to his lover, the Queen?

The smoke clears, and Zayne pulls me roughly to the stone table in the center of the room. The chill in the air sends goosebumps up my spine, and I shiver involuntarily.

He grasps my biceps, lifting me on top of the table as if I'm no more than a rag doll as the cold from the stone table seeps into my back.

I can't help but feel as though I've bitten off more than I can chew when he grips my arms and pulls them over my head.

Moving to my wrists, he pauses as his gaze lands on them. Whatever he sees there only keeps his attention momentarily before he clasps restraints around each. The needle-like pins dig into my skin, and I stay still as he moves to my ankles.

He pauses there, too, frowning before he clasps restraints around them and returns to my side.

"Not my first rodeo being restrained like this," I say, the nervousness in my voice betraying my dark humor as he tilts his head, "Doubt you and him have the same ideals for torture, though."

My stomach flips anxiously as his hand hovers over my chest, "This is going to hurt," Zayne's cold voice is quiet as smoke billows from his fingertips into my skin.

My entire body goes taut as pain radiates from my head to my toes.

It feels like Zayne's attached a live wire to my body through my chest and left the switch on. Every nerve is searing in agony, as if he's taken a red-hot knife, driven it into my limbs, and dragged it along my body, everywhere, all at the same time.

The pain recedes, and I gulp desperate breaths as my lungs finally fill. My vision flickers as tears stream down my face.

I've felt pain in my lifetime, arguably more than the average person, but this is nothing I've experienced.

This is pure torture to deliver the most pain possible.

"How did you free the others?" he asks in his cold, flat voice.

"Well, that depends on whose asking," I say between labored breaths with a dry laugh, "If it's Circe asking, I freed them by the method of 'Go fuck yourself.'" My laugh comes out strangled as he removes his mask, setting it on the table beside me.

Fuck.

I gaze at Zayne's painfully handsome face, and something inside me fractures. His violet eyes stare into mine as his hand grazes the top of my breasts, and I know what is about to come.

A single tear falls from my eye as smoke billows from his hand once again.

He continues this for an indeterminable amount of time until I'm on the edge of passing out, and he ceases the assault.

It could have been seconds, minutes, or hours.

From what it felt like, it could have been years.

Gasping for breath, my lungs struggle to expand as I cough and fight to maintain consciousness.

I murmur, and he leans over me, his face mere inches from mine, "Say it again," he says coldly.

"I said," I say, willing my voice to keep steady, "I forgive you for everything, Zayne."

He rears back as if I struck him, sending his smoke into my veins once more. He must have done something differently this time because an acute pain radiates at the back of my skull, and as I shut my eyes, I see my body on the table with Zayne towering over me as I float near the ceiling.

My hands shimmer in white light as I gaze at them, and my surroundings blur from the stone torture room into a haze of darkness before solidifying once again.

As the area around me refocuses, I take in the pristine white room with silver furniture and white cushions. A window to my side catches my attention, and the drapes billow with the wind.

I see golden trees in the distance, and a sense of peace surrounds me.

"Hylia ilvrost," I murmur, and a sharp gasp startles me. I twist toward the sound to see a man and woman in the center of the room.

His white clothes blend in with the rest of the room, but the intricately sewn gold stitching sets them apart. His short, pale blonde hair and blue-white eyes hold an air of familiarity as he gazes at me in shock.

The woman beside him mirrors his expression, her arms tightening around the chest of her silver robe as her silver hair flows against the breeze from the window.

"Eiara...?" The woman asks, gazing at me with eyes as round as saucers.

My brows furrow as the two look at each other, speaking another language.

"Who are you? Where am I?" I ask, and almost immediately, they tilt their heads in confusion.

"English? That language originated on Earth. Have you truly been there all this time?" The man says, his deep voice conveying pure disbelief as tears stream down his cheeks.

"Where else would I have been? That's where I was born." I ask, "Well, other than Servilia, I suppose." I say as both of them frown.

The room flickers dark for a moment, and I look around nervously.

"What is happening to me?"

"You appear to be astral projecting." She says, her voice thick with emotion as she clings to the man's arm.

"We do not have much time then," he says. "How did you get here, Eiara?"

I have a million questions, but I tamp them down to answer him.

"Someone named Samira, who claims to be the Queen of Servilia, took me captive, and she had someone torturing me for information when I passed out and, somehow, ended up here."

"Samira? She's been on Servilia!" the woman exclaims angrily. "Sol, can't we do anything?"

Sol? Like, the god of the Sun?

His fists squeeze tightly, and his knuckles become white as the muscle in his jaw feathers, "You know we can't, Luna. Sealing magic to stop Caspian was already more than we ever should have interfered."

Luna. The goddess of the moon.

If I had a body, the blood would have drained from my face.

This can't be real.

They can't be gods.

Anguish paints Luna's features, "Sol, they're torturing her."

"I'm so sorry," I say, my mind swirling with questions, "Who are you?"
"Eiara, we are your parents," Luna says solemnly, and the stark similarities between us suddenly make more sense.

"Is that," my voice wavers, "Is that my name?"

Luna nods and steps closer, "Whatever happens, Samira must be stopped, Eiara. We are limited in our ability to intervene with otherworldly affairs. The last time we did, the cost was great."

Sol steps forward to stand beside her, "Samira was a royal offering by her father in Vinaerus, a realm far less prosperous and fortunate than ours. In exchange for Samira's servitude in becoming my attendant, we would bless their land with magic and life. Things were strenuous at best after her arrival, and she had difficulty adjusting here."

He shakes his head, frowning as he recalls the events, "Shortly after she arrived here on Meloris, she disappeared. She had been missing for years and had evaded all our attempts to locate her, but not long after you were born, she returned," Sol's face darkens as he continues, "stating that Caspian's minions took her hostage and that his banishment was to be soon broken using blood magic."

Sol scoffs, "Little did we realize she managed to somehow sneak your blood into and adjust the spell we were casting to bind magic from Earth. When we returned from completing the ritual, you had disappeared, as did Samira."

Tears stream from Luna's face as she gazes at me longingly, "We scribed for you for months, years even, and heard nothing of your whereabouts. We thought perhaps you were dead, and the price paid for binding magic on Earth." She says as she shudders and wraps her arms around herself.

My vision flickers once more, and the two glance at one another, sorrow etched deeply on their faces, before Sol speaks again.

Sol's deep voice resonates through the room, "If your powers have manifested to allow you to astral project, then hear me when I say this, my daughter."

Everything in me aches at those two words, and though I have no physical form, my being still longs to move closer to them as they look upon me with a mixture of longing and fondness.

"There is a darkness spreading across the land of Servilia, and though we have no right to ask it of you, I'm afraid you may be the only one able to halt its steps before it's too late. It is a terrible magic, one that drains the land of its luster and people of their fortitude."

My vision flickers, the darkness taking hold for a long moment before returning, and my anxiety begins to build.

"How? How can I manage to do that? I don't even know how to fully control my magic. It just happens."

Sol's gaze softens, "Trust yourself. You are the daughter of the sun and moon. Sol and Luna. You are the brightest of both our lights, the goddess of elements." His face brightens with pride, and he continues, "You must trust that while you are the beacon that guides others like ships to the shore, so too shall it guide you."

My vision flickers again, and Luna's face becomes solemn, "We love you, Eiara Ptheron, we always have and always will." She says as they cling to one another, and my vision darkens.

Chapter 26

Caspian

I need to fucking do something.

Anything.

The moment I saw silver hair in the middle of the throne room, I nearly lost my shit, and it's been hours since Zayne disappeared with her.

No.

If Samira knew who Lara was, she would kill or do worse things than have Zayne interrogate her for answers.

That's the tiny fucking shred of hope in this scenario.

I pace back and forth in the bedroom, my pulse roaring in my ears. There has to be something I can do without making Lara more of a target.

If Lara can dream-weave and was there when Gray was freed, there's a good chance she was the one who freed him, and Samira just hasn't figured that out yet.

She might be smart, but she doesn't have all the clues that I have.

Not yet, at least.

Footsteps echo down the hall, and I know Samira is drawing closer.

My mind races as I consider my options.

All of them lead to her asking who Lara is.

All except one.

Fuck. If this goes sideways, I will lose my mind more than I already have.

When the footsteps approach the doorway, I school my features, grab my shirt, and begin pulling it over my head.

"Caspian," she says, pausing as she looks me over appraisingly, "Well, that's a welcomed sight."

I force a twitch of my lips. "I was thinking," I start, glancing out the window before returning to her. "If this person Zayne is interrogating was close to my brother, why not use her to draw him out?"

She eyes me warily, "Draw him out..." she echoes, crossing her arms thoughtfully, "Well, she hasn't given him any information as of yet outside of calling me 'Circe' and telling me to 'Go fuck myself.' I will consider it."

I fight the urge to smile as pride swells in my chest.

If anyone knows how stubborn that woman can be, it's me, but I'm fucking thankful he hasn't broken her yet.

Her gaze travels along my body before locking with mine, and dread sinks into my gut.

"I think we have a little free time before I... draw him out, though," she murmurs, taking a few steps closer.

At least she's not asking about Lara.

Small victories.

"Once we're done, we will go see Zayne's progress. If he hasn't gotten more information on how Darian is freeing the others, I will use her to my advantage."

Small victories.

Chapter 27

Eiara

As consciousness returns, the first thing my mind registers is the throbbing pain throughout my limbs.

I imagine it's akin to being run over by a semi-truck, only for it to back up over you and then run you over again. My eyelids are heavy as they open, revealing Zayne's shadowed face as he stares at me with no emotion in his eyes.

"How did you free my brothers?" he whispers.

My gut twists as I think of what's to come with my answer, but I say it anyway.

"Let me talk to the real Zayne, and maybe I'll show you how," I whisper back, sliding my gaze to lock with his as his mouth snaps shut.

The muscle in his jaw feathers as he places his fingers on either side of my skull, and I can't help the whimper that escapes, knowing the pain I'm about to endure.

"You will die if I continue," he says softly, his tone still indifferent as he tilts his head, "But you know this."

I nod slightly, holding his gaze, "And I will forgive you, even in death."

A moment later, his magic seeps into my skull and wreaks havoc on my body. After what feels like an eternity, my body is numb as his assault recedes.

It feels as though my mind is in a pure state of delirium as I peer through puffy and swollen eyes.

My gaze lands on Samira at the foot of the table. She stares at me with curiosity as movement behind her catches my attention.

Caspian stands a few feet beyond her, his green eyes bright with anger as he scans my body. Whatever he sees must be enough to warrant action as he steps forward.

I'm not sure why, but instinct has me suddenly thrashing against my restraints, ignoring the jolts of pain from the movement, and he halts.

"I have nothing to tell you," I choke out between breaths as Zayne's dark magic wraps around my limbs to keep me still.

"Be that as it may," her eyes light up as she snickers darkly. "You may still prove useful in other ways."

My chest tightens as she walks closer with a dagger and bowl. My anxiety heightens as I remember the last time one of Caspian's minions took a blade to my skin, and my chest heaves.

"I'll never deny having a new pet." She grins as she slices my arm open, holding a cup to the wound. She murmurs a series of words over the cup, and my gaze flicks to Caspian as my head begins to spin.

"Enjoy your sleep."

I don't know how long I've been running.

All I know is that my limbs are stiff, the frost in the air burns in my lungs, and while panic overwhelmed me at first, I find myself struggling to remember what or who I was running from.

Passing by another fallen pine tree that's strangely familiar, I slow to a stop, turning in a circle with a frown. The forest is a place that would usually strike fear into my heart, but now I only find myself searching rather than attempting to escape.

What is this place?

I turn in circles again and scan the fallen tree, noticing it shimmer and my memories come flooding back. This was the forest where I ran from Darian as a child. This is where I once thought it all began when, in reality, it began long before my memory would recognize.

Zayne's torture flutters through my mind as I recount the moments leading up to this.

It's just a dream.

An illusion.

Just as the thought crosses my mind, everything goes dark.

~

I've lost track of how many dreams or illusions I've been thrown into.

Whenever I realize I'm trapped inside one, I end up stranded in another.

I open my eyes knowing I'm once again stuck inside another conjured illusion, but nothing happens. I frown from where I lay on the closet floor, waiting for any indication of my memories fading or the illusion changing, but this time, I remain.

The shadows in the corner of the room dance as my eyes adjust to the dark, but oddly, even though minutes pass, the shadows twist and twirl like ribbons amidst the darkness surrounding them.

Zayne.

It couldn't be him…

Could it?

Dragging myself to my hands and knees, I crawl apprehensively toward the dark corner, and the shadows seem to overtake everything as I squeeze my eyes shut.

It's just an illusion. Nothing can hurt me here. Not really.

I open my eyes and groan as the illusion has changed, gazing up at my bound arms that suspend my body from the ceiling. Shadows again dance around the dark basement in all the corners of the room.

One corner is so absent of shade or color that it's like an abyss threatening to swallow me whole as I stare at it.

No, not this one.

A rhythmic thud snaps me from my trance. My body trembles uncontrollably as I fixate on the stairs, and the footsteps halt.

A slow creak sounds out, followed by a blinding light that sends a shiver of pure terror down my spine as my foster father's silhouette comes into view and steps closer. By the time he reaches the bottom of the stairs, his hand shoots out to grab me by the throat with a bruising grip.

He says nothing, though his hand squeezes my throat tightly.

That was the difference between this foster parent and the rest. He never said anything demeaning or hurtful.

He simply came, did anything he felt like, and left. The eerie yellow light of the main floor became the ominous foreboding of more abuse, and the moment it flicked on, I'd recede into my mind to block out the pain.

Today is going to be no different.

Releasing my neck, he walks to the rack on the wall beside me and grabs the baseball bat with one hand and thin-strapped whip with the other, making my heart drop into my stomach.

Fuck.

I choke down my whimper as he moves to stand behind me, and I stare into the light pouring in from the top of the stairs as he brings the whip down along the already tender skin of my back.

He brings it down again and again until finally, I can't take the pain anymore, and the next thrash of the whip makes me cry out in pain.

The whip falls to the ground in a soft thunk, but the air gets knocked out of me as the bat collides against my side. The pain radiates into my lungs, chest, and spine as I struggle to breathe before he repeats the action to my other side.

This is where I die.

I'm sure of it as I cough up blood that spurts from my mouth and drips onto my chest.

Staring into the light as I hear the whip retrieved from the floor behind me, my mind struggles to remain calm as panic and chaos consume it. The shadows in the corners dance around as if taunting me with their elusiveness and ability to stay concealed.

For a moment, my eyes strain as a pair of purple eyes stare at me from the shadows of the abyss. I hardly feel the whip come bearing down on my back as I try to decipher which is reality.

It's not real. None of this is real.

The next strike hits, and I muster every ounce of strength to yank my hands apart.

To my surprise, the chain clatters to the ground, and I sprint up the stairs at full speed, only to halt as I reach the top.

The main floor hallway is gone.

Three doorways stand against the wall before me, each covered with vines and various flowers. Glancing back, the stairway to the basement has disappeared along with my foster father, replaced by one long floor of vines, so my only option to move is forward.

It's... a maze?

As I observe each entrance, a nearly imperceivable movement catches my attention on the right, where a thread-like wisp of smoke trails between the vines through the center of the door.

Throwing caution to the wind, I decide to follow it.

Pushing the vine-covered door open, a narrow pathway with large bushes on either side comes into view, and I cautiously move forward to the end, where the path suddenly cuts left.

After what feels like an eternity of crawling beneath giant boulders that could crush me, running from plants that want to eat me alive, and narrowly avoiding a wall of spikes that threatened to impale me if I didn't move fast enough, I finally come to a solid oak door.

The wisp of smoke weaves into the center of the door, intertwined with a thread of white that dances alongside it.

I swallow nervously, placing my hands on the heavy wood door before using all my weight to push it open.

I first notice the hustle and bustle of a busy town as the sun sets as I stand a handful of feet away, obscured by the treeline.

I made it out.

Movement next to me catches my eye, and I see Zayne in his mask, staring at the civilians with his dull, emotionless eyes. My heart skips a beat as I realize what we're about to do.

I need to stop him.

Without hesitating, I hurl myself at him which catches him off guard. He stumbles slightly before realizing I'm no longer enthralled, and though I had the upper hand to start, he's quick to recover.

His shadows twist into crescents as he hurls them at me, and I dodge behind a tree. My pulse rages as the tree topples over, groaning as it collapses to the ground.

The commotion draws the attention of nearby civilians who quickly shout for everyone to flee.

My momentary distraction costs me as Zayne suddenly teleports in close, grabbing my throat with a bruising grip.

His hand squeezes my neck as I claw at his arm, and my senses go haywire. It's as if some part of me recognizes the ominous essence that emanates from his hand.

It's like when you feel around an apple for the rotten spots.

Somehow, it feels like the core of my being rebels against this essence. While fighting for breath, my fingers trace along his arm to his hand, and lastly, his fingers, where I find what I assume to be a ring on his third finger.

This is nothing like dream-weaving or breaking an illusion, but I don't have much choice as my lungs contract in a desperate plea for air.

Pulling strength and confidence from my practice with Kieran, Darian, and Val, I shut my eyes. Squeezing my hand over the ring and willing my magic through my limbs, I silently pray that this will work.

I picture a white thread coming from my chest and guide it to the ring, flooding it with everything I have.

My eyes snap open, and where I pictured the thread, a ribbon of light winds around my arms and hands as it flows into the object in my grasp.

Stars flicker across my vision, and it takes all my focus to flood the item as resistance pushes back against me.

Zayne's crushing grip lessens as I feel my strength waning.

It's now or never.

I urge everything in me into the item, and the resistance collapses as the ring around his finger shatters into dust. My legs tremble beneath me as they threaten to give way, and our hands drop between us as I suck in a ragged breath.

My knees buckle as they struggle to hold me upright, and I watch with tears in my eyes as Zayne's dull, lifeless eyes regain their vibrancy in the shadows of his mask.

"You," he whispers, and tears of relief trail down my cheeks.

My legs finally give out, but before I can fall to the ground, Zayne catches me in midair. His arms wind tightly around my torso, holding me against his chest as he shudders.

My throat is hoarse as his bright violet eyes search my face, "Do you know who I am?"

His arms tighten around me as he nods, "I do." he says quietly.

A tense moment of silence passes between us, and I'm almost afraid to ask.

"How much did you see?"

My traumas are my own. No one else needs to bear witness to those horrors.

It's bad enough that Val and Darian did.

His lips thin under his mask, "All of it."

My mouth goes dry.

Part of me knows he's referring to the illusions, but I can't help but wonder if he saw more than that when he was inside my head.

"How did you-?" I begin to ask, but the crowd growing in the area draws our attention.

"We should go find Darian and the others." He says softly, sparing one final glance at the town before smoke engulfs us.

The familiar sign of the inn where Darian and the others were staying comes into view, but my heart sinks into my stomach when the building itself looks as though a bomb exploded with debris everywhere in the road and gaping holes in the side of the building.

I glance around apprehensively as Zayne moves to my side.

He turns to peer down the adjacent alley before shaking his head, "This has Samira written all over it."

I hurry into the destroyed inn, silently praying that everyone made it out alive. Stepping over the rubble, I survey the flipped tables and toppled chairs that litter the area. My mind races as it imagines all the horrendous things that could have happened to Darian, Val, Kieran, and Gray as I note the dried blood all over the room.

They can't be dead.

My heart races in my chest as I see the corner of a dark cloak on the ground.

No. No, it can't be any of them.

My heart tells me that Darian, Val, and Kieran are safe and alive, but my mind's convinced this is one of them. I launch toward it, kneeling beside the large, blood-soaked body.

Bile rises in my throat as I roll the heavy torso over, nearly sobbing in bittersweet relief when I realize it's none of my men.

"Lara," Zayne's quiet voice carries in the still air as he approaches me from behind, "We should go."

Nodding, I push to my feet, but before I move past him, his hand gently stops me.

"Here," he says, his violet eyes peering from behind the mask as he extends something toward me.

My gaze drops to the dagger he holds between us. It's the length of my forearm, with a marble and leather hilt, with symbols etched into the blade itself. Taking the dagger from his hands, my fingers trace the engravings gently, "It's beautiful."

"Keep it," he says before he moves to secure the sheath on the side of my hip, "Consider it a gift."

I don't have the heart to ask why or where he got the blade as I gaze at it for a moment more before gently putting it in its rightful place.

We slowly make our way out of the inn's ruins and cautiously walk down the deserted streets. As we survey the rubble and torn-down structures, no building was spared from destruction.

"Do you think they were taken?" I ask hesitantly, and his silence doesn't make me feel any better as I consider that all four of them could be under some sort of control.

We make it to the docks, and my heart sinks.

They're not here.

Chapter 28

Eiara

I'm equally terrified and hopeful that they managed to escape before the town was attacked when sudden raucous laughter erupts behind us, and we spin around.

Samira's humor dies down from where she stands behind Caspian and another man with short silver-white hair that falls forward over his forehead. His purple eyes are nearly identical to those of Zayne's, which is enough to tell me that this is Cade.

"I see you somehow managed to not only break free but also steal my second-most prized possession," she sneers. As she glances around, her sneer turns into bitter happiness.

"I'm glad you found the message I sent to Darian, though," she says, and my gaze slides to Caspian.

His eyes are shadowed as he looks at us, his jaw clenches, and though he appears normal, there's something unsettling about him.

Samira notices me staring at Caspian and inhales sharply.

"Ah, yes. I suppose the young lady has yet to see why my love is an otherworldly treasure." she croons, leaning forward to trail her fingers down his cheek, and anger rifles through me.

He shows no reaction beyond the muscle in his jaw working as she continues.

"Caspian, my love, why don't you show them how weak they are in the presence of a god? Kill them."

Caspian's movement is slow as if dragging out his actions intentionally as he takes long strides forward. His eyes flick to Zayne before landing on mine, and my heart thunders in my chest as he extends his arm. A sword made of smoke materializes out of nowhere, and dread settles in my stomach.

"Shit," Zayne mutters as Caspian blinks out of sight.

He narrowly avoids the first attack as Caspian reappears on the other side of him before he teleports again, hurling another brutal strike that he dodges at the last second.

Zayne's teleportation is not slow by any means, but Caspian is doing it within a fraction of a second.

It happens so fast that my eyes have a hard time keeping track of him as he disappears and reappears.

How Zayne is keeping up with the movements, I have no idea.

So far, Zayne's only dodged the relentless assault without any attempt of retaliation until Caspian's next strike is unavoidable, and his sword swipes at Zayne's chest.

My heart races as Zayne's scythe materializes at the last possible second. As the two weapons collide, a surge of power rushes outward from them, throwing me backward, and I land with a thud.

I cough and sputter, squinting through the dust as it clears. Relief washes over me when I see Zayne mere feet away, kneeling with his scythe braced behind him, panting from exertion.

Not far off from him is Caspian, who -on the other hand- looks hardly winded. Caspian's immense strength sends a cold note of dread down my spine as he stands tall. His broad shoulders rise and fall with his even, steady breaths as he points the tip of his sword at Zayne, readying himself for another strike.

"Cade," Samira's voice rings out, "Help Caspian put them down," she says with a dark laugh.

Cade steps forward to stand next to Caspian, and my heart wrenches in my chest.

There's no way Zayne can take on both of them without help.

I place my hand on Zayne's where he grips the scythe. As his violet gaze finds mine, a soft glow brightens between us, and we glance down. I watch in awe as his scythe, once shadow and smoke, has now solidified into a glowing swirl of darkness and light.

Movement over his shoulder shocks me back to the present, and I'm about to warn him of the impending danger as he counters the attack. The force of it sends Caspian staggering backward, giving Zayne a fraction of a second to recover before Cade jumps into the mix.

One of Zayne's counter-attacks catches Caspian's arm, and blood trails down his sun-kissed skin just as Cade uses a blast of air aimed at his brother. The gust collides with Zayne's chest and sends him crashing to the ground before me.

Caspian blinks out of sight, and my mind goes blank.

I don't think as I launch myself forward in front of Zayne.

Caspian reappears, and his eyes widen as his attack aimed at Zayne is now dead center to my chest as his blade sings through the air.

He suddenly adjusts mid-strike, his sword jutting off to the side as his momentum sends him crashing into me, and we tumble to the ground. Within seconds, Zayne's at my side, pulling me upright as Caspian collects himself only feet away.

We hear a tut and direct our gaze to Samira, who watches me with rapt attention. Her gaze flicks to Zayne's scythe before meeting mine.

"Who are you?"

I narrow my eyes on her as Zayne's arm snakes around my waist, and his smoke engulfs us.

"My name is Eiara. Eiara Ptheron."

Her eyes widen with recognition, but before she can say anything, the world around us darkens as Zayne transports us away.

When my vision comes into focus once more, it's to the quiet ocean waves as they lap softly against the white sand of an empty beach.

If we weren't running for our lives, this place would have brought an air of peace.

"Well, Eiara," he says softly as he removes his mask, tossing it into the sand with a thud, "I believe I now owe you my life twice over."

I shake my head, knowing I would still be under Samira's control if he hadn't helped me from those illusions and that maze.

"You had already saved mine; consider us even," I say before glancing around. "Where are we, anyway?"

"The dead forest." His gaze turns to the ocean as if he could see them in Sabinia from here. "We're north of Sabinia. It's as far as I could get us with the magic I had left. They'll likely assume we remained on the continent, close to Lavinium. No one travels here."

His words send a shiver down my spine, and as I look upon the decrepit forest, I hardly want to know why people avoid this place.

We slowly walk through the scarce dead lands, and even the air feels imposing as if our presence disturbs the area as we suddenly bring life to it with each step.

"What happened here, Zayne?" I ask, and though my voice is quiet, it almost seems to carry on the wind as it eerily blows between the carcasses of trees.

"Thousands of years ago, this was a holy place," he says, scanning the trees. "Rituals of compassion, love, devotion, and happiness were abundantly performed here. Our kind held feasts and festivals where we celebrated life, gods' blessings of magic, prosperity, and everything else good in the world."

His violet gaze slides to mine for a moment before he continues, "As time passed, our ability to bear children waned. While some hoped things would improve, others pointed fingers at the gods, claiming their blessing was a curse. Thus, the rumor that magic would be our demise rather than our deliverance was born. With each decade, rituals and celebrations ceased almost entirely, and instead, animosity grew as people blamed the gods for our plights."

His hood falls back with a gust of wind, giving his dark hair an indigo hue as the light hits it, and he doesn't bother to pull it back up.

"When this forest began to die, we thought it a blight, a plague, or illness of some sort, one that not even our best scholars or botanists could solve. The loss of this forest wasn't enough to curb the rumors in the end, though. Even as the trees died and decayed, our childbirth rates remained as they were, and then magic began to disappear slowly from most of the population. The rate of its descent has accelerated throughout a handful of decades."

I frown.

"Even with magic dissipating, the rates of childbirth remained unchanged?"

He nods solemnly, "That is correct. I'm sure you can imagine the civil unrest when Servilians began to realize we had lost favor with the gods in all ways and still were plagued with our inability to repopulate the land."

I shake my head, "That sounds terrible."

"It was," he whispers, and I fall silent, losing myself to my thoughts.

As the sun finally disappears beyond the horizon and each of the four moons rises high into the night sky, we settle down to rest near a collection of trees.

It's the first time since being in Servilia that I've seen the moons rising without immediate danger, and I find myself watching each one with a renewed sense of awe.

My limbs feel like bricks as I ease myself down next to one of the tree trunks, and my stomach gargles as hunger pangs begin to make themselves known.

I do my best to ignore them, tilting my head as Zayne steps close and removes the robe from his shoulders. His muscular form is impressive. It is as if his entire body is honed for a deadly combination of agility and strength.

The black cloth shirt he wears flows open at his chest, with reinforced leathers along his forearms. Adjusting his clothes, he settles in beside me, and his shoulder leans against mine as he eases back against the tree.

"When you were under her control, what was it like?" I nearly regret asking as his face darkens, but he answers after a few long moments.

"I was aware of what was happening the whole time," he says softly, "Each town I destroyed, each person I killed, each child I murdered," he says, gazing into the sky as his hands flex into fists.

"I tried for a long time to escape, but at some point, the death and torture became too much, and I receded into my mind. At least, until you showed up," his gaze slides to mine, "When you ran into the crossroads and yelled at me to leave, I half expected to cut you down, but somehow whatever compulsion she used didn't seem to recognize you as part of the task, so I left that place as fast as I could."

My heart twists painfully in my chest.

I can't even imagine how horrific that would be.

"When you gave yourself up to save Gray, and she made me torture you for the answer," his voice wavers before he continues, "I thought I'd killed you when you didn't wake up. So when you finally came to, I moved to your head. I searched inside of you for your magic and tied mine to yours temporarily under the guise of getting the answers I sought."

"I didn't know what she had planned for you, but if I could help somehow, perhaps that was how I'd be able to while under her command. What I didn't account for was my consciousness being pulled in with you," He tilts his head as his eyes harden.

"Tell me," he says as the air around him stills, and he searches my face. "Do those men still breathe? The ones who did those things to you?"

His question is so familiar that I let out a small laugh, closing my eyes and tilting my head back on the tree.

"If you wish for them to draw their last breath, you may be fighting for a place in line."

Silence falls between us, and my eyelids begin to droop. As the wind picks up, the brisk air blows across my skin, and a shiver trembles through my body.

"You're cold," he states as another wave of chilled air glides over my skin.

Stubbornly, I shake my head, "I'll be fine."

Zayne shifts next to me, and my eyes flutter open as his arms hook under my body, lifting me gently before sitting me between his legs.

What the-

His arms encircle my collarbone, and he leans back into the tree, bringing me with him as I ease into his chest.

My heart thrashes in my chest wildly.

"What are you ---?" I begin to ask before he uses one arm to cover us both with his robe. Within seconds, the delicious warmth from his body seeps into mine.

Oh.

"Get some rest, Eiara," he says softly as his breath skates over the shell of my ear, making me shiver once more.

I blow out a shaky breath as my body relaxes, molding to his, and I lean my head back to rest on his shoulder as my eyes slide shut.

And soon, I drift off in the comfort and warmth of Zayne's embrace.

Chapter 29

Eiara

As I slowly rouse from my slumber, my eyes squint to adjust to the brightness of the morning sun. Without any actual tree cover, the bright rays of early morning are inescapable, turning the back of my eyelids bright pink.

A flush creeps up my neck as I feel Zayne's arms still curled around my back and shoulders. Somehow, I managed to twist in the night, curling into his chest and using him as a pillow.

My ear lies flush against his chest, and the steady rhythm of his heartbeat threatens to lull me back to sleep if I close my eyes again.

The thought is tempting.

I feel the slightest movement and glance up to see him already awake, gazing out into the distance before his piercing, violet gaze slides to mine.

My heart drums within my chest as he tilts his head slightly, and his gaze draws me in like a magnet.

There's this inexplicable pull, as if we're two worlds orbiting one another. Gravity exists as a living, breathing thing between us.

I must be imagining this.

What the hell is happening to me?

"Did you sleep alright?" he asks softly, searching my face.

I nod, not trusting my voice as I extricate myself from his embrace to stand, doing my best to avoid staring at him as he pulls his cloak over his shoulders once more.

Turning around, my breath catches at the two small golden saplings only mere feet away that were definitely not there before we fell asleep.

Zayne moves closer behind me as I stare at them in disbelief, and his voice sounds out close to my ear, causing my entire body to shiver involuntarily.

"Do you know what they're called?" he asks quietly.

I nod.

"Hylia ilvrost," I say, "I've seen them twice, once at the crossroads south of Trebonia, and the other time was when---" My voice cuts off as I struggle to find the words to say.

How does one tell another of their godly heritage without sounding conceited?

"When Samira had you questioning me," I say cautiously, and he winces at the memory, "I somehow astral projected when the pain became too intense, and during that time, I met my real parents. When I first appeared in the room with them, a forest of hylia ilvrost was outside the window."

A long moment of silence passes, and I turn to face him, only to find that he's wide-eyed, staring at me with a mixture of awe and disbelief.

"You're a---"

"Don't," I say, shaking my head, "At least not until I'm ready."

He dips his head slightly in acknowledgment, "So you had never astral projected before?"

Taking a breath to center myself, I shake my head.

"That was the first and only time. Much of my experience with magic has been mostly reflex or incidental minus two instances."

"I see. What other abilities have you discovered? Besides changing my scythe." he adds with a smirk.

I laugh under my breath. "Another incidental change," I assure him, "mostly dream-weaving and dispelling whichever illusion or magic Samira used on you, Gray and Kieran. I've yet to understand my magic in its entirety. I hardly know how to use it on command."

He nods.

"Regardless, knowing your abilities and what you are only reinforces that you're much more of a target for Samira. We'll have to be cautious while we're in Drusilla."

The pangs of hunger return as a mixture of nervousness and impatience washes over me, "How far is Drusilla?"

He scans the area before returning his gaze to me, and a soft smile graces his features.

If I didn't already think he was painfully attractive, this would surely be the moment as the morning light gives his skin a warm glow.

"If we were to walk there, it would take us two days or so." he finishes, and I read between the lines as he moves to stand before me.

My heart races at his proximity, "But we are not going to walk there, are we?" He laughs under his breath, which sends my nerves haywire.

"You're a quick study," he teases, "We'll arrive just outside of the town. If I don't get food in you soon, I'm concerned whatever creature is in your body making those sounds will demand a sacrifice."

I blink at him before bursting out with laughter.

"I am quite hungry," I agree as he drags his hand up my arm, causing electric butterflies to race through my body as his magic engulfs us.

When the smoke clears and the forest around us comes into focus, we make our way to the road.

I wrap my arms around my torso, feeling exposed without a hood to conceal myself with. Glancing at Zayne, I frown when we step onto the road, and he makes no effort to pull it over his head.

"I know I do not have a cloak, but shouldn't you have yours on?"

He shakes his head.

"My mask and magic make me more well known as Samira's puppet. No one save my brothers and a few others should recognize me like this," he says as the city comes into view.

It's similar to Trebonia's structures; most are wood or stone, with thatch-like roofs, and some are weather-worn. As we approach, civilians bustle about, minding their business and paying us no mind. Here and there, someone will take a second glance at us, but no one seems to do so with recognition.

Their glances are more curious than anything.

Zayne leads us down the main road before turning down a less busy side street. We walk to the end, where a small, secluded shop is. He pushes the door open to reveal a cozy yet intimate dining area. There are two small tables along the wall, with two chairs across from one another at each table.

Following his gesture to one of the tables, I sit facing the shop window as he makes his way to the front counter. After he exchanges words with the woman working, she hands him two cups, and he makes his way back to the table, glancing at the window once before sitting across from me.

He extends a cup between us, and I gently take it, swallowing a grateful sip as the flavors hit my tongue, and I look at him in disbelief.

"It tastes like some kind of fruity beer," I say, blinking at how familiar it is.

He laughs softly before taking a sip.

"Servilia has fermented drinks similar to that of Earth. This one is made from pruvyarial and is quite good for you."

The woman working the front counter brings two plates over and sets them before us, and my mouth instantly waters as I eye the thick cuts of meat with some type of gravy and mixed vegetables.

We eat in comfortable silence. Every now and then, when someone walks by the window, I watch in apprehension until they disappear out of sight. Zayne orders us both another serving with some fruits, and once we are done, he leads us to the main road again.

The streets are beginning to fill with people as the sun gets higher in the sky, and everywhere, decorations are being hung or set up across houses with countless people carrying trays of food down the street.

The look on my face must be clear as day because Zayne laughs beside me.

"It's the annual celebration of harvest," he says, moving closer to avoid someone carrying an impressive armful of food. "It's one of our largest and oldest traditions that's never died out," he says, eyeing me thoughtfully in a way that makes me want to squirm.

His hand suddenly grasps mine before he leads me down the street, following the waves of people headed in the same direction.

The further we walk, the closer we must get to our destination as the crowd grows. Where before, I had a foot of space between Zayne and me, we now brush arms against one another as he holds my hand firmly.

With the ocean on the horizon, people line up in droves to board ships that line the docks. Others set up their tents along the water, and some boats return from what looks to be another mass of land not far offshore.

"Those are the isles of Drusilla. They're small islands that people use for celebrations, but any other time of the year, they're used mostly for catching m'kot," he says, glancing around before leading us to a higher location.

"M'kot?"

He nods, stopping near one vendor to get two large drinks, "Various species of creatures of different shapes and sizes that we catch from the water."

"Oh, so, fishing then," I say contemplatively.

A soft smile creeps across his face, "Fishing." he agrees.

Chapter 30

Eiara

We finally crest the top of a hill along the busy dock. From here, we can see each island stretching out into the water and all the tents below.

It's surprisingly quiet even with the crowds forming below since only a handful of people sit nearby, and those who are are too engrossed in their own conversations to pay us any mind.

Zayne lays his robe on the ground, gesturing for me to sit first. I keep the view of the islands in mind as I sit, easing back onto my palms as he takes his place next to me. We're half facing each other, half facing the water, as a nervous excitement rifles through my veins.

I have always been a sucker for these kinds of things.

"So what kind of celebration happens?"

"You see the boats over there?" he asks, gesturing to six large boats at a dock in the distance where no one is bringing loads of food but rather crates and barrels onto them.

I nod, so he continues, "Each of them is loaded with materials that interact in particular ways to create beautiful displays of light. When the moons reach their peak, they will take up positions between various islands along the coast. The celebration begins in earnest once the last light show happens."

Fireworks?

Watching Servilians so peaceful and happy, their lively chatter as they help one another prepare and find places to watch the celebration, sends a tranquil kind of serenity through my body.

A handful of families with children catch my gaze as they talk in a large group. The kids don't wander too far off from their parents, and it tugs at my heartstrings when I see the strangers around them interact with the kids as if they were their own.

It strikes me that these people may be the only ones who have managed to bear children, and my chest tightens for all different reasons at the revelation.

As the food boats slowly make their way from the dock toward the islands and the sun slowly begins to set behind us, the excitement that echoes over the docks is mirrored within me as my heart thunders.

The misty and faded edge of the first moon becomes visible over the horizon, and the air erupts with cheers as people clank their cups together.

Zayne holds his cup out between us, and I knock the side of mine to it before taking a deep sip. The liquid almost feels carbonated as it bubbles, with a sweet, fruity taste that goes down smooth, but as I go to take another sip, he puts his hand on mine to stop me.

"It's quite good for you, but it is potent. The taste can be misleading to those unused to it," he says, and his eyes widen as I take another sip.

"I can drink like a m'kot, you know." I tease with a matter-of-fact tone, and his eyes widen, half in bewilderment and half in amusement.

All around, people are dancing and singing with one another, and some are hoisting children onto their shoulders for a better view while others play some kind of game on the long grass.

It's not long before the second moon appears, and the crowds erupt once more. Everyone clanks their drinks together to celebrate, and I laugh as we follow suit.

Taking another sip, a fuzzy feeling tingles in my fingertips, and warmth pools inside my body. Heeding Zayne's earlier warning, I place my drink on the robe between us.

"So, tell me about yourself," I say, and he laughs lightly, setting his drink next to mine.

Leaning back on his palms, he tilts his head thoughtfully, and the dark blue tone of his hair shines against the moonlight.

"What would you like to know, Eiara?"

The sound of my true name on his lips makes my heart flutter wildly in my chest.

"Tell me about your childhood."

"My youngest years were not the happiest," he says softly. His voice is quiet enough that I have to lean closer to hear him.

"Cade, my sister Breisha and I grew up in a small town outside Lavinium. We had a small farm where we grew certain rare herbs that the King and Queen enjoyed for their feasts. Cade was the friend maker and extrovert between us, so he spent much of his time outside with his friends." As he speaks, he leans forward and gazes at his upturned palms.

"My magic surfaced when I was five, which was quite early for powers to present themselves. At that time, Cade was living in the castle with Darian as his magic was strong." He pauses as if struggling to find the words to say, "My magic surfaced amidst a temper tantrum I was having. It was so minor and quick, I don't think anyone noticed it but me."

His voice is so solemn that everything in me knows this is a difficult memory for him, so I reach over and slide my hand into his.

Without missing a beat, he laces our fingers before glancing up to meet my gaze.

"That night, I laid in bed across the room from Breisha, terrified of the shadows as they moved along the wall. I thought they were monsters that were coming to get me since they had followed me all night, and," he says as his voice cracks, "My parents and Breisha died that night."

After a moment, he continues, "I ran away after it happened and didn't return to Lavinium for three years. By then, I'd come to terms with what happened and learned how to control my abilities, but I needed to face my brother and take accountability for it. Little did I know my brother was there and saw me fleeing amidst the destruction I left." he says with a wry smile, "It changed us irrevocably, and Cade became a shadow of his former self. When I returned, the King and Queen welcomed me with open arms into their family and helped me further my training until they died."

The crowd erupts in cheers again as the smaller moon appears. Because of the noise, I shift closer to Zayne, holding my drink in my free hand between us.

"To every moment, and every decision, whether good or bad, that makes us who we are today," I say.

He watches me contemplatively before lifting his drink to mine and taking a long sip. Still feeling fuzzy in my fingers, the sip I take before I set my drink down could hardly be called that.

I shift to the side and lean my head on his shoulder comfortably as the moons brighten against the darkness of night that dominates the sky.

"Thank you, by the way," I say as he tilts his head down and slides his gaze to meet mine. " For sharing the memory with me," I whisper, and he inclines his head in response.

We remain like that in comfortable silence as the final moon begins its ascent over the horizon, and cheers erupt louder than before. We join in, taking another sip of our drinks with everyone around us.

Zayne leans back on the palms of his hands, with one comfortably resting behind me, and stretches his legs before crossing them at his ankles as he surveys the crowd around us.

He looks relaxed, but the assessing look in his eyes tells me he's been searching for any sign of danger while we've been here.

Surprisingly, the notion brings peace to my mind, allowing me to fully immerse myself in the moment as the final moon peaks.

Suddenly, in the distance of the water, rapid bangs go off as bursts of flames spiral high into the sky before exploding into a symphony of light. The air catches in my lungs as I watch in pure awe at the different colors and shapes that appear.

A blue swirl of light brightens the area around us, and smaller white lights shoot out from it, mimicking what I can only assume are shooting stars or a meteor shower.

The blue hues turn red as countless aespherion burst from the sea, their bodies made of pure light as they ascend into the sky and soar in circles. The warmth in my body and Zayne's presence brings me a sense of contentment that allows me to appreciate the celebration.

My heart swells as the crowd cheers, and every new display brightens the night sky. A smile tugs at my lips at the awe painted across everyone's faces as the light illuminates them.

I glance at Zayne, and my heart stutters as I find his eyes locked on me with a softness I've never seen before.

It's as if, after all the horrors we've both endured, this moment is a reprieve that we didn't realize we needed until faced with it.

He scans the crowd again as the light show stops, and everyone sits down with their heads bowed.

Zayne notices my confusion, and his lips twitch.

"It's customary for everyone to give thanks to the gods for continued harvests, although it may not be required of you," he says with a twinge of amusement before lowering his head as well.

It couldn't hurt, right?

I bow my head.

Though I'm uncertain of my place or role in this world, I am confident that from what I've seen, being thankful and forgiving the past will be crucial in determining its future.

Forgiveness is the first step with those who unknowingly or unwittingly played a part in the horrors Samira brings to this realm.

But people are more than their traumas.

That much I've learned in my life.

Our experiences may shape us, but our conscious decisions and how we treat others make us who we are. Considering the history I've been taught, reconciled with the information Luna and Sol gave me, my heart clenches in my chest.

Picturing everyone in this town and their unspoken prayers waiting to be heard as they each go through their struggles, I silently hope that each of them finds their prayers answered.

Forgiveness begins with hope.

Hope, the sister to love and happiness, is the silent fuel to an otherwise uncontrollable wildfire. Once the flames of perseverance catch and begin to spread, you find yourself amidst an inferno of dreams that refuse to be diminished.

I open my eyes slowly as murmurs and hushed voices fill the air.

"Eiara," Zayne says softly, and I glance at him only to find him wide-eyed, staring towards the isles.

I follow his gaze as more people chatter and point in the same direction.

"What is---?" I ask, but my words hang in the air as I see it.

On the closest island, in clear view of everyone on shore, stands one tall hylia ilvrost that shines bright like a beacon, reflecting the moonlight against the ocean water.

"May I ask what you thought of?" he asks quietly, still staring at the tree across the water in disbelief.

I pause for a moment, reflecting before I answer.

"Hope," I whisper to him, "I thought of hope."

My gaze travels along the crowd, and my chest swells as faces light up and they talk to one another in excitement.

As the camaraderie and raucous laughter begin anew, I watch the interactions longingly, with Kieran, Val, and Darian weighing heavily on my mind.

They'd be just as joyful knowing another one of their brothers is free from Samira's grip, and pangs of sadness from missing them come in waves.

The logical part of my brain knows that Samira would have bragged or said something had she killed or taken Darian.

The illogical part of me won't believe they're okay until I can physically see them, even with logic taking control.

Zayne shifts next to me to drink from his cup, and I do the same as he leans back comfortably. I'm so engrossed in my thoughts that I hardly notice families with young children returning from the crowd into town.

I'm pulled from my thoughts as a soft gasp catches my attention, and my head turns quickly to a woman lying on the ground, her legs wrapped around her partner's head while another kisses down her neck.

My entire body flushes as I tear my gaze from them and bring my attention forward.

The crowd below has dispersed, with groups of individuals making themselves comfortable. Some are already looking quite intimate, and I don't need to ask how they plan to continue the celebration.

As my heart gallops in my chest, a cawing in the distance rings out, and within seconds, Zayne's on top of me. He quickly presses me to the ground as his entire upper body covers mine, and if my heart was galloping before, it's a whole stampede now.

He curls the cloak over my hair and leans down until everything in my vision is him. The weight of his body on me, our foreheads touching, and his breath cascading over my skin sends a shiver down my spine.

"What---" I begin to ask as the cawing draws closer, and Zayne's eyes flick to mine.

Even from the shadows, I can see the warning in them as he listens intently. The cawing fades into the distance, and Zayne's body relaxes. His weight presses further onto me as he releases a tense breath.

My mind registers the stressful moment, but my body hasn't gotten the memo as it basks in the sensation of being below him with our lips a hairsbreadth apart.

Just as his eyes search mine, I know he's going to pull away to put distance between us, and without hesitation, I press my lips against his.

His eyes widen, and I wonder if my brazen act has been ill-received when his eyes slide shut and his soft lips move against mine in response.

It's as though fire has ignited within my veins, and I want nothing more than to add fuel to it.

My hands find their way to his neck, and I curl my fingers through his hair as our tentative kiss deepens. Zayne's hand grips the back of my thigh tightly as he pulls my leg around his waist.

It's as if my entire being craves more, and I hungrily press my body against his. We both pause as the caw in the distance rings out again.

Zayne pulls back slightly, the apology clear in his eyes.

"It's no longer safe here, Eiara," he whispers against my lips before gently pressing them to mine.

I nod, ignoring the desire pulsating deep in my core as he pushes to his feet.

He extends a hand to help me up, quickly retrieving the cloak and securing it over my head. We walk to the nearest building, keeping to the shadows as the cawing gets closer. My heart pounds in my chest as we duck into a small covered crevice between two buildings and wait.

As the creature becomes louder, Zayne's towering form presses further into me, and I flush from head to toe once again.

My pulse rages in my ears as another caw sounds out directly over us, and I don't dare breathe. Zayne's hand slides into mine, and no more than a moment later, the creature's call comes again, but thankfully, it's gained some distance from us.

Relief coats my veins as I let out the breath I'd been holding before we slowly return to the shadowed road and follow it toward the city's gates.

"What was that?" I ask, scanning the sky anxiously.

"That was my brother," he says, and my eyes widen, "he was likely scouting for the false queen. It seems too coincidental that it happened right after the hylia ilvrost showed up."

We turn a corner as the gates come into view down the road.

"Where will we go?" I ask.

"North to Nomentum through Marcellus," he says, entering the toryian stable, "It's a city in the mountains where an old friend of mine lives. She may be able to help us locate the others while we evade Samira and her puppets."

Zayne gears up one of the giant mounts before moving to the entrance and glancing around.

"Stay here," he whispers before disappearing around the corner. My stomach flips as I wait for him to return, anxiously counting the seconds.

I'm on the verge of leaving to look for him when he reappears with leather bags in hand, tying them on either side of the toryian.

He reaches for my hand, helping me into the saddle before mounting behind me. My mind flashes back to the ride to Aveentia, and my cheeks burn.

This is going to be a long journey.

Chapter 31

Eiara

At some point in the journey to Marcellus, in the dead of night, my legs began to feel like sandpaper again from riding for so long.

Once Zayne helped shift me sideways, I finally fell asleep against his chest, listening to the steady rhythm of his heartbeat.

With the sun high in the sky turning my eyelids pink, I squint and yawn deeply.

"Sleep well?"

I glance up to see violet eyes peering down at me before they return to the road ahead.

"I feel like I overslept," I mumble, rubbing the sleep from my eyes. Yet, I somehow feel like I could continue sleeping for another ten days.

Zayne's chest rumbles with quiet laughter. "You did manage to sleep most of the ride there," he says softly, angling his head to smirk at me, "We should be there shortly."

I settle my head against his chest again, enjoying the brief comfort of his strong heartbeat, when a whizzing sound rings out behind me.

What the---?

His grip tightens on me as he spurs the toryian into a full sprint, and an arrow rushes past his right shoulder. My eyes widen as more arrows fly past us, and my pulse skyrockets.

The toryian suddenly loses its footing, sending us flying forward as it tumbles. Zayne wraps his arms tightly around my back, cradling my head to his chest as we fall.

I squeeze my eyes shut as I brace for impact, surprised when I feel nothing more than pressure from our tumbling. When our rolling stops, my eyes open to see Zayne's dark smoke surrounding my legs, dissipating with the cloud of dust around us, and my chest tightens.

Movement catches my eye on the treeline as a handful of men wearing leather and masks stalk out from under the canopy with arrows trained on us.

Who the hell are these guys?

Does Servilia have criminals and bandits of their own?

Zayne stands as if unbothered by the attackers, helping me to my feet as he stands next to me, keeping the men on his right.

"Are you alright, Eiara?"

My pulse thunders as I blink at him, "I'm okay."

We were just attacked, thrown from our mount, with weapons pointed at us, and he's doing a check-in with me?

He tilts his head as his gaze flickers from each arrow pointed at us to the man holding it nocked.

One of the men who I'm assuming is the leader, gestures to the groaning toryian lying on the ground, and one of the men beside him turns his arrow to aim at the creature.

Panic rises in my chest.

The toryian didn't do anything to deserve this.

The man draws his arrow to his shoulder, and my heart skips a beat.

"Stop!" I blurt out. The men turn to look at me with confusion, amusement, or just a raised brow.

My heart thrashes wildly as I put my palms between us, "Please, don't."

Laughter erupts from the group, and I frown, glancing at Zayne, who shows no concern as he assesses the men in front of us. The men continue to laugh as one of them steals our supplies off the back of the toryian.

"Why are they laughing?"

Before Zayne can respond, the men's voices ring out, "We're laughing because you won't be able to use the animal anyways."

"I give him a couple hours at most before a yritae gets him"

Another man elbows the first with a grin. "Aye, it's better off dead,"

The leader tears his eyes off Zayne to scan me from head to toe. His gaze flicks to Zayne again as he speaks, "We'll give you a chance to live, kid. Give us the girl, and you can run off to your friends and pretend this never happened."

I blink at our attackers, feeling the blood drain from my face.

Zayne raises a brow ever so slightly and tilts his head to the side, "I will treat you with the same courtesy. If you leave this place, I will let you all live," he says quietly. "This will be your first and only chance."

The men laugh again, and I shake my head.

"Can't say you didn't warn them, bunch of brick-brained idiots." I huff, and Zayne's lips twitch in response.

"What did you say?!" A man in the back shouts, stepping forward angrily.

"Let's just kill him and be done with it." Another says, gesturing towards Zayne.

Four men raise their bows in our direction to emphasize the threat.

Logic tells me that Zayne is strong enough to handle these men, but irrational thought sees the weapons trained on us, and my pulse hikes.

How are we going to—?

Before I can finish the thought, hundreds of small, dark crescents hurtle through the air, but instead of aiming for our attackers, they strike the bows and arrows.

Within seconds, shards of wood fall from their hands to the ground, and the dark smoke disappears like wisps into the air. The attackers look at the ground with wide eyes before their gaze fixates on Zayne, taking a healthy step back.

"The hell just happened?!" A man in the back exclaims.

The leader narrows his eyes on Zayne and grabs a dagger from his side in the blink of an eye.

He moves fast, raising his arm to hurl the dagger in our direction, but his movement stops abruptly as a spear of Zayne's magic juts out from his neck.

The smoke dissipates once more as blood spurts from the gaping wound, and the man gargles with wide eyes before falling face-first to the ground.

The others collapse to the ground of the same fate, and I almost forget how to breathe.

"Holy shit."

A groan sounds out, and my gaze slides to the giant, injured toryian as I sprint to its side, leaving Zayne behind. My heart squeezes as I survey the two large arrows lodged in its front leg.

I shift closer to its giant body, "Oh god."

My hands hover over the injury as I look for a place to grab hold of the wooden shaft.

I've never had to remove an arrow before.

Swallowing my nerves, I wrap my fingers around the solid wood, placing my other hand on its leg for leverage as I pull up with all my strength.

The first arrow dislodges just as the toryian kicks its leg out. A flash of black surges between me and the giant creature as pressure erupts in my stomach, and I fall backward to the ground.

I glance down with wide eyes to see Zayne's magic dissipate from where it softened the blow and my fall, but the kick to my abdomen was a message in itself.

Message received.

I cough, pushing to my feet and positioning myself by the giant creature's leg again.

"Listen, I know it hurts, but I'm just trying to help. Just stay still!"

Much to my surprise, the toryian stops shifting and twitching in place. Only the steady rise and fall of its chest gives any indication that it's alive as Zayne pulls the remaining arrow out.

The moment the arrow is free, a steady stream of crimson seeps from its leg, and I glance around, looking for something to stop the bleeding. I glance over the bloodied bodies on the ground and Zayne's dusty cloak with a frown.

I'd rather not give the creature an infection.

Infections exist here, right?

Can they even get infections?

The only remotely clean article of clothing is my shirt, and I flush, tugging my mostly unmarred shirt over my head.

My nudity is the least of my worries as the creature's antennae shift, and I press the material to the wound to stem the bleeding.

The crisp breeze licks my skin, and goosebumps cover my arm and neck as I maintain pressure on the wound. Zayne shakes off his cloak beside me before securing it over my shoulders, and my mind races.

What are the chances that toryians heal as fast as Servilians?

A long moment passes, and as I lift my shirt from the wound, more blood oozes out.

"Fuck," I mutter, "Fuck, fuck, fuck. Come on," I say quietly as panic builds in my chest.

What if they were right?

What if killing it is a mercy?

I glance at the giant creature's head as its antennae flicker toward me, and my heart fractures.

No.

There's no way I'm leaving it to die here.

"Come on, just stop bleeding. Please," I whisper, tears welling up in my eyes, "You'll be okay, just... the bleeding needs to stop. Please, please, please."

My eyes squeeze shut as my whispers become a silent, chanted prayer, and I beg internally, hoping that it will just take some additional time for the wounds to heal. I'm silently praying that toryians heal as fast as Darian and Caspian as I feel Zayne at my side.

"Eiara," he whispers gently near the shell of my ear, "Eiara, let her go."

Her.

He gently tugs my hands, but I shake my head as a tear trails down my cheek.

"Not yet, not until she's okay."

Zayne's fingers entwine with mine as he pulls my hands back, "Open your eyes and see," he says softly.

My eyes flutter open to look at its leg. The now crimson-stained shirt lies on the ground where it fell after Zayne lifted my hands, but where the arrows were once lodged is nothing more than pink scars.

I stare at the healed wounds in astonishment.

"Did you---?" I ask, turning my gaze to him as he shakes his head, "Then how...?"

Holding the back of my hands in his, he upturns my palms.

"My magic doesn't have the ability to heal, only destroy. The answer to your question lies within you, Eiara." His voice is soft, but the words that come from him echo in my ears loudly, as if forcing me to see the truth. "Whether you're ready to accept it yet or not."

He helps me to my feet as my mind whirls, gently walking me back a few paces before helping the toryian to its feet. My eyes fall to the heaps of bodies nearby, and guilt coats my veins as I tighten the cloak around my chest.

"Does it bother you?" I ask, and his gaze slides to me as he grabs the bloodied shirt from the ground. Pouring water from our waterskin onto the cloth, crimson seeps from it and splashes onto the ground as he tilts his head.

"Does what bother me?" he asks, and the muscles in his arms flex as he wrings the material before repeating the action.

"With the challenges Servilia faces with repopulating..." I trail off, uncertain how I can finish the sentence without sounding accusatory, and he steps closer to the toryian, laying my shirt over its neck to dry.

Why the hell did I ask that?

He says nothing as he lifts me into the saddle before mounting behind me, and his proximity sends a shiver through my body as the cool breeze blows under the cloak.

His arms tighten around my waist as warmth seeps into my back, and I lean into him, hoping to absorb more of it. I feel his lips brush the shell of my ear, and my pulse rages.

"The moment they considered hurting you, they gave up their claim to life. They're lucky I gave them an option at all."

He eases the toryian into motion, and his next words send a shiver down my spine for all different reasons.

"I would cut down an army of Servilians if it meant keeping you safe, Eiara."

Chapter 32

Eiara

It's not long before I've put on my damp shirt, and the forest line gives way to the large wooden gates of the city. As we approach, the guards peer out at us, and the gates open with a heavy groan that echoes into the still air.

Zayne ushers the toryian slowly into the quiet city, and I must admit. It feels strange but oddly refreshing to navigate the roads without either of us concealed.

The civilians chatter quietly amongst themselves, and some leisurely walk the streets while others hold up trinkets and produce they're trying to sell.

Leaving our toryian in the stable beside the only inn within the city after giving it plenty of food and water, we make our way inside.

My stomach growls loudly as the smell of fresh food wafts through the air. Between that and the promise of a soft bed, I've never been more excited.

There's only one table taken in the dining area, where four patrons glance over at us as we enter. Their stares linger for a long moment before they return to their conversation.

I follow Zayne to a table only a few feet from the others and take one of the two seats along the wall. The sound of clattering echoes from the kitchen area, and I track Zayne's movements as he walks to the counter.

Everything about how he moves is equal parts graceful, mysterious, and intimidating. Looking at him like this, you'd think he could kill a handful of people, but as I watch him speak to the man at the counter, taking two cups in his hands, how disarming he is to people is intensely misleading to the devastation I know he's capable of.

None of these people realize how strong he is.

As he returns, placing the cups on the table between us, the men nearby begin to chatter even louder, and we share a look as we eavesdrop.

"Did ya hear about Cathorn's reappearance?" the man with a long, black beard asks, and the men around him nod.

"Aye, just in the nick of time, too. Can't bloody stand these zealots working for the queen. Gutless lot, if you ask me."

"Right after he shows up, the gods' tree suddenly pops up too. Can't be a coincidence, eh?"

The men all murmur in agreement as a tall blonde woman approaches the table with a food tray. Her footsteps slow as her gaze falls on Zayne, and she sets the food down as her eyes narrow on him.

"Zayne bloody Nereus? Is that you?" She asks, and his gaze widens as he looks at her.

"Gods, it's been nearly a century!" She exclaims, and I glance around to see all eyes trained on him as he inclines his head.

"It's been too long, Rosaline," he says, and her face lights up.

"Did I hear that right?" the man with the long black beard asks. "Is this the legend himself in flesh and blood? We were just talking about Darian, too!" he adds, clapping his friend on the back with a laugh.

Glancing between them, and then at Zayne, who looks uncomfortable with all the attention he's suddenly getting. I suppress the giggle building in my chest by taking a long, drawn-out sip of my drink.

The woman across the table glances between us and shoots him a glare.

"I could have sworn you said you weren't interested in settling down," she says suddenly, and I nearly spit my drink out before choking on it and coughing.

Oh my god.

Recovering with tears in my eyes from choking, I look at Zayne, whose face embodies pure exasperated boredom as he sighs, taking a sip of his drink, "That was the truth."

My eyes flick to the other patrons observing and snickering amongst themselves before I glance at Rosaline, who is pointing at me, and I blink.

"Then what are you doing with her? You never travel with anyone except your brothers!" She chews out, and I take another sip of my drink.

"Aye, I can see plain as day why he's traveling with her," One of the men says with a laugh.

"If you looked that good, we'd all be traveling with ya, Rosaline," the bearded man says with a loud laugh.

I raise a brow at them, "Bold of you all to assume she'd even want any of you."

Rosaline's eyes flash with surprise, but she quickly recovers, tilting her chin up with a huff.

"I'd never stoop so low, even in my most desperate hour."

Damn straight.

She turns, glancing at me with a soft look as she walks away.

"I wonder if she rides as good as she looks," one of the men further away from us says, eyeing me, "You here for the night?" he asks louder, and the men at the table murmur.

Zayne's jaw feathers and his knuckles turn white around the handle of his cup as he looks at them. The man with the beard notices first, smacking the first man with the back of his hand to quiet him down.

Deciding to ignore them, I return my attention to our food and take a bite. It's lost most of the heat from when it came to the table and is nearly room temperature in the time it took for our interaction to end.

I glance up at Zayne, whose food remains untouched, and sigh. My hand brushes his thigh, gently pressing against the cloth of his pants, and his violet gaze softens as it slides to mine.

"Your food is getting cold," I say quietly, and he glances at the food in the center of the table.

"Well, I'll be damned, look how strung she's got him," the man in the far back says as Zayne takes a bite of his food, and everyone in the room goes silent.

"Oh, how the mighty have fallen," he says, utterly oblivious to the ribbon of smoke curling behind him.

I sigh loudly.

"I didn't realize you had a death wish," I say, watching the smoke as Zayne continues to eat slowly beside me. The man's brows pinch together, and I mouth 'turn around,' using my finger to point behind him.

He turns apprehensively as Zayne's smoke wraps around his throat, squeezing tight enough that the man's skin turns red and swells as he claws at thin air.

The men around him grow nervous as the surprise attack doesn't let up, glancing at Zayne, who continues to eat his food nonchalantly.

Staring at the man's head, which now resembles a cherry tomato, it takes everything to avoid laughing, "I don't think he deserves death, Zayne,"

Zayne glances at him, and the smoke releases from the man's neck as he sputters and coughs, gasping desperately for air.

"Next time, don't be a raging asshole," I say, taking a bite of bread as the men around him pat his back and scold him.

We continue our meal in relative silence, the other patrons slowly becoming more rowdy as the evening drags on. Not long after, we made our way to the room, where I take a much-needed bath before flopping into bed.

"Does it not bother you when men act like that?" Zayne asks quietly beside me from where he lies, staring at the ceiling.

I turn onto my side and contemplate his question for a moment.

Truthfully, before I met Caspian and Darian, the slightest comment from a man like that would have sent adrenaline coursing through my veins. Somehow, that life feels like an eternity ago, and instead of being afraid of what they could do, I find myself more inclined to react to them instead of shutting down completely.

"Stuff like that used to. A long time ago and, until fairly recently, I used to be terrified of men like them."

His violet gaze slides to mine, "What changed?" he asks, running his finger along the scars on my wrist.

"Darian, Val, Kieran, You, and believe it or not, Caspian," I say thoughtfully. "Each of you has helped me learn a deeper connection to who I am, and I find that the more I learn, the less afraid I am of random men and their intentions."

"Who did these?" he asks, trailing his thumb along my wrists again. I track the movement as my pulse hikes. The carefully closed-off box where I've pushed all my emotions during that encounter is one I'd rather never reopen.

For years, compartmentalization and avoidance were my primary coping mechanisms until Caspian and Darian showed up, and I used to think that telling them my traumas made them real.

The truth is that terrible things happen, and maybe part of leaving these atrocities in the past is acknowledging them in the present.

Claire would be proud.

"His name was Cain," I say as my throat tightens, "Val killed him," I whisper, remembering the blood as it sprayed onto the surface of the furniture next to the bed.

Zayne nods, bringing my wrist to his lips and gently pressing a kiss on each of the scars. My heart beats faster in my chest, whether due to the memory or Zayne, I do not know.

Perhaps both.

"Good," he whispers, releasing my wrist but shifting to lean on his arm. He mirrors my position as he looks down at me, searching my face.

"Can you tell me about it?" he asks softly.

The look on his face is not one of judgment, scrutiny, or sympathy. Instead, it's an expression of knowing, an understanding that sees directly into my soul, into the essence of my being with all its flaws, which has me inhaling a ragged breath.

I swallow, preparing mentally to open that long-sealed box of emotions.

"Cain had been hunting me for… I'm not sure how long, and finally caught me when I was alone and lost. He knocked me out and brought me to some rundown house in the middle of nowhere." I say, unable to suppress the shudder that makes its way through my body. "When I came to, I was tied to the bed, and he had all but undressed me," I whisper as Zayne's thumb glides over my wrist in a comforting way.

"Did he---?" Zayne's question hangs in the air, but he doesn't need to finish it for me to know what he is asking, and my eyes squeeze shut.

I nod.

My heart rattles inside my chest as the memories drive adrenaline into my veins, and it's a conscious effort to keep my breathing even.

Zayne gives me time to collect myself, silently supportive as he gently rubs my wrist.

But there's one overwhelming thought that has plagued me since it happened—one lingering toxic thought that I've pushed down, suffocating until it fits inside the box with all the emotions I've avoided.

My chest tightens, and my breathing picks up. I'm not sure how to say this without sounding pathetic, weak, or vulnerable.

I open my eyes to meet his, tears welling in them against my will as I expose myself completely.

"Through everything that's happened in my life, I can't help but-" my words get caught in my throat, and I swallow before continuing, "I used to wonder why all these things happened to me, but there's always been this thought..."

My chest tightens painfully, and the tears I had been holding back trail down my cheek unbidden. Zayne's free hand moves to my cheek, wiping the rogue tears gently.

My breath hitches, but I know I've made it this far in bearing my scars open that I must push through.

"Part of me wondered if I did something to deserve it, like some kind of penance for some misdeed I'd done in my past that I no longer remember."

Tears trail down my cheeks steadily, but Zayne holds my gaze as a fierce look graces his handsome features.

"Do not blame yourself for the actions of others, Eiara," he says, searching my face, "never in a million years could you do an act that would earn such consequences."

I shake my head.

"Eiara, you did not deserve it," his voice is quiet but stern as he takes my chin in his hand and tilts my head to face him. "I want you to say it."

My heart stutters as his violet gaze burns bright into mine. I know what he wants, but my throat tightens, and a shudder runs through my body.

"Eiara," he says softly, and I nod, swallowing thickly against the pain of the emotions I've kept bottled up for nearly my entire life.

"I-" my breath hitches as a sob threatens to claw its way from my throat, and my body trembles, "I didn't deserve it."

"Again," he demands quietly, still gliding his thumb over my wrist.

"I didn't deserve it." I silently praise myself for keeping my voice steady.

"Again."

I suck in a ragged breath, "I didn't deserve it."

Saying it this final time with move conviction, he nods slightly in approval, and a mixture of pride and relief coats my veins.

It's quiet for a moment as I let it sink in, leaning on and absorbing Zayne's certainty to bolster mine, smothering any doubts that might linger.

"These scars you bear, Eiara," he leans in as he whispers, and my heart gallops in my chest. "From this moment on, we bear them together."

He leans in to brush his lips against mine, and my mind wars between acknowledging the past and embracing the present. Butterflies soar chaotically through my body as I breathe him in, allowing the fear, anger, and sadness of my past to be left behind with each exhale.

Though my emotions are heightened from coming to terms with what happened and acknowledging that I'm not the cause, I know what is between Zayne and me now is much more than anything I could ever convey in words.

This thing between us is life and death, a beginning and an end. My heart thunders in my chest, and I close the distance, pressing my lips to his.

Something in my soul sings as his soft lips move against mine, returning everything I have to give as his hand trails down my waist to my hip.

Gripping the back of my thigh, he drags me on top of him without breaking apart.

My hands snake around his neck as I cling to him, and our tongues dance together.

It's as if the world has faded away, silenced around us into a beautiful sea of nothing as I grind against him, our clothes being the only separation between us. He must realize this as he tugs my shirt over my head before rolling us over once more to remove our pants and tossing the material to the floor.

Pausing, he leans back, and his gaze trails over my nude form as I fight the urge to squirm beneath him.

Unable to read the expression on his face, my brows pull together, "What's wrong?"

"This world doesn't deserve you," he says, leaning forward to capture my lips again. My skin feels as though currents of electricity tingle along it as he hovers over me.

Zayne takes his time. He kisses down my neck, collarbone, chest, and stomach to my inner thighs. I shudder in anticipation as he settles himself between my legs, pressing tender, reverent kisses higher until his breath skates over my pussy. He drags his tongue over and gently flicks his tongue over my clit.

Oh, gods.

My legs twitch as he expertly works my body with his mouth, and he holds me in place. Pleasure builds in my core, and I want this to last forever, but with the way my body craves his...

This yearning for him, for all my men, is all-consuming and unlike anything I've ever experienced.

The moment I left them at Sabinia, my soul ached and has not let up since. Even now, while the very core of my being longs for the others, it calls to him in a way I cannot deny.

"Zayne," I breathe, and he pauses, glancing up at me from between my legs. The look he gives me nearly tips me over the edge, "I need to feel you, please."

I mourn the loss of proximity as he sits up, and his towering form crawls over me, engulfing mine. The soft head of his cock notches in place against the soaking-wet entrance of my pussy before he pushes in gradually, kissing me fervently as he does.

He pauses halfway, only to push in harder, and I break our kiss to breathe through the sting as I struggle to accommodate his size.

When he's nearly in all the way, he withdraws to his tip and brings my hands over my head one at a time.

My heart pounds anxiously in my chest as his magic wraps tightly around my wrists, ankles, and torso.

The warring conflict of acknowledging what happened and allowing myself to feel everything I suppressed comes full circle into my unyielding trust in Zayne, and my breathing steadies.

He searches my face as if searching for any indication to stop.

"You're in full control, Eiara. The moment you want to be free, say so, and I'll unbind them," he says softly, and any lingering trepidation I feel melts away.

I nod, "Okay."

Leaning over me, his gaze not breaking from mine, he presses kisses along my chest before taking my nipple into his mouth and sucking on it hard.

My body arches into him as my arms tug against the restraints, but I feel no pain as he grips the back of my thigh, easing himself in with more force than before.

His magic around my waist squeezes as he uses it to hold me in place against his thrusts, and the restraints tighten around my wrists and ankles as my eyes slide shut.

Everything in me wants to hold him, to pull him into me to satiate this need to have him close, but the restraints keep me still as he thrusts in over and over again. His magic eases me off the bed as he leans back to circle my clit in time with his thrusts, and the angle mixed with his ministrations sends jolts of euphoria through my body.

"Zayne, it's too intense," I breathe. The euphoria in my body overwhelms my mind, and all I can do is ride it out. He slams into me, pulling me tight against my bindings as my orgasm crests, and I'm helpless to do anything as it crashes over me.

I cry out, and my pussy bears down on his dick as he keeps his pace, making my legs twitch and toes curl with each wave of pleasure.

His movements speed up before his dick throbs, and he buries himself as deep as he can.

My head is a whirlwind of pleasure, desire, reverence and adoration as his magic squeezes my body closer, leaning over me as he comes. Our ragged breathing slows as his magic dissipates from my limbs, and the moment my arms go slack, I wrap them around his neck to kiss him deeply.

I never thought coming to terms with what happened in that house would come from a sexual encounter.

Claire sure as hell wouldn't have suggested it.

It finally feels like I've taken back some part of the experience, knowing I could say no at any time, and it would stop. My heart swells in my chest as I clutch him tight with my face nestled into his neck, tears falling from my eyes unbidden.

He must notice them as he rears back, worry etched across his handsome features, and he gently wipes my tears with his thumb as he searches my face.

"Did I hurt you?"

I shake my head.

"Thank you," I whisper, inhaling a ragged breath, "for giving me back control."

Understanding flashes across his face as he leans in to wrap his arms around me, bringing me to his chest, and he rolls onto his back.

"How did you know taking control back would help?"

He averts his eyes as his jaw feathers, and I feel the blood drain from my face—a noxious blend of anger and horror bubbles to the surface as my mind races.

"Samira?" I whisper, giving my brimming rage direction.

"When Caspian returned, it ceased, but prior to that, yes. Cade and I were her," he pauses as he struggles to form the words, "queen consorts."

I swallow down my anger to hold him tighter against me.

Samira's days are numbered, and she should start counting now.

"We will kill her, Zayne," I whisper, a lethal calm taking over my mind as I rest my head on his chest, "If nothing else, I swear this to you."

Chapter 33

Eiara

The snow along the tops of the mountains swirls as the wind howls loudly, and I shiver as the air bites into my skin.

I step closer to the dark stone railing, peering down to the waterfall below, which erupts off the mountain edge into an enormous lake with green, blue, and pink trees stretching as far as the eye can see.

I've no clue where this place is, but it's beautiful, even if the endless darkness in the sky looks like it would devour everything in existence in the blink of an eye.

"You came back," Caspian's voice rings out beside me, and I turn to look at him, "it is not---"

"Safe here, I know," I state, eyeing the horizon again.

I tilt my head to get a better look at him. He's disheveled, his face is pale, and his eyes have dark bags beneath them.

It's startlingly unlike Caspian in every way, and even though he's betrayed me repeatedly, concern washes over me.

"Caspian, what's happening to you? What's wrong?" I ask as the darkness creeps forward slightly.

He shakes his head, "Sometimes when you fight, consequences are severe."

I frown, unsure if he means fighting Zayne or someone else.

There's an air of wrongness around him as he steps closer until his chest is inches from mine, and my skin tingles as goosebumps cover my arms.

"You can't stay here," he says quietly, "I do not have the strength to push you out. If she—"

"Stop-" I say, placing my hand on his chest as something inside of him suddenly rebels under my hand.

My heart thunders, my mind fixating on the odd sensation beneath my palm that feels like an empty void of nothingness writhing inside him.

His chest is hard beneath his shirt, and though nothing moves under his skin, I can still **feel** it.

I retract my hand quickly, glancing at each of his bare fingers before bringing myself to meet his exhausted emerald gaze.

It couldn't be... could it?

"How is Samira---"

The moment her name comes from my lips, he flinches, and the darkness surges forward. Panic overwhelms my mind, and my mind goes blank as instinct takes over.

I raise my arms to protect myself as something inside of me swells, rushing through my limbs like a tidal wave from my body.

When I open my eyes again and look around cautiously, a sheer barrier encircles us, forming a shield around where we stand as the darkness pushes against it.

It won't hold for long, but perhaps long enough.

Now, let's just hope I know how to get out of here.

"How is she keeping you under her control, Caspian? You do not have rings, nor are you wearing any other jewelry. This isn't an illusion or some kind of mind control. I can feel the difference. It's as if you're tied or tethered, but to what I do not know." I frown as the darkness presses against my magic.

Caspian blinks at me with surprise as if I've pieced together the mystery of his captivity faster than he anticipated. He shakes his head slightly before glancing behind me as if he can see past the darkness threatening to swallow us whole.

"I'm afraid I cannot give you that answer," he whispers, and I narrow my eyes at him.

The darkness suddenly crushes against my barrier, but I'm not ready to leave him yet.

Not if my suspicions are correct. I just need time to free him.

"Caspian," I say quietly, and his emerald eyes lock onto mine, looking more hopeful than he did when I arrived, "Fight when you must, but only do so to live." My voice is soft, and I hold his gaze for another moment before pulling myself out.

I wake with a start, sucking in a deep breath.

The soft light filters in from the window as the sun creeps through, and relief coats my veins as my eyes flick to where Zayne lies next to me.

His hair splays against the pillow, the light brightening the indigo hue in his hair as his eyes flutter open, still half-lidded from sleep as he searches my face.

"Everything alright?" Zayne asks softly, rubbing his thumb over my cheek.

I nod.

"Yes, it was just a dream," I say quietly, looking out the window again. "We should head out," I add, leaning in to press my lips to his.

We slowly emerge from bed, snatching some food from downstairs before making our way to the stable. There, we pack our toryian and head north to leave the city.

The ride to Nomentum is long and drawn out. I'm weary as exhaustion weighs on my mind, and sores develop on the inside of my thighs again.

Thankfully, Zayne helps me shift to sit sideways, letting my head rest against his chest while his steady beating heart lulls me to sleep.

When I wake again, it's early morning, and we're no longer riding but perched at the base of a tree. Zayne and his cloak encircle me protectively as our toryian stands not far away, grazing on the low-hanging branch of a nearby tree.

"Are you feeling alright?" Zayne asks quietly, concern etched on his handsome features, "You slept the entire afternoon, evening, and into this morning."

I nod, resigning myself to telling him partially what happened.

Though I know he would not judge me for it, there's still part of me that feels like I don't fully understand why I can dream-weave to Caspian.

I suppose the other part worries about **why** I'm able to, and I'm not sure I want to consider the possibilities.

"I used my magic while I slept when we were in the city, and it appears I needed the rest."

"I see," he says, tilting his head as his gaze slides to me. "Were you practicing, or did you learn anything from it?"

Guilt tremors through me as I wonder why I didn't end up in Val, Kieran, or Darian's dream.

I shake my head.

My gaze scans the treeline, trailing up to the mountains along the horizon in the distance, "Nothing I didn't already know. How far are we from Nomentum?"

His violet eyes flick to the horizon before he stands, extending a hand to help me up, "Half a day's travel or so."

I nod, stretching my stiff limbs before mounting the toryian by myself and grinning triumphantly. Success.

After securing our supply packs to each side of our mount, he slides in behind me, snaking his arms around my waist to hold the reins. My gaze drops to his hands as he steers the toryian onto the road before he relaxes them once more in my lap, and it takes a conscious effort to continue to breathe while my stomach flips nervously.

At this point, I've entirely accepted that something about these men sets them apart from any others I've met.

I don't know what it is, but after what happened between Zayne and me, it's become undeniable in a way I can't explain. The way their presence calms me, their touch sings to my depths of my being that should be impossible or incomprehensible.

Knowing they're there before I can see them, feeling them somehow like they've given a piece of themselves to me.

I'm not fighting it.

But part of me wonders if they feel all this too, or is it just me?

We ride for what feels like an hour through dense forest before the scenery changes. The sound of rushing water fills the air as we approach a wide river that runs south from the base of the giant, snow-capped mountains.

Each deep inhale brings a lungful of the misty air, and I find myself breathing easier, even though the stone bridge that leads over the chaotic waters looks like it's seen better days.

The edges are worn and weathered, with chunks of stone that have fallen to the depths in the time that no one has tended to it.

The mountains in the distance repeatedly capture my attention, pulling my gaze toward them as my mind turns to Caspian, even though the river leading to the mountains doesn't appear to be the same as the one I'd seen the other night.

I find myself continuously wondering if we're anywhere near him or if he's on an entirely different continent.

Would I even be able to free him if he suddenly appeared?

Questions plague my mind as we cross the bridge, and it's not until the dense forest becomes sparse that my focus returns to the present.

What once was lush, green, and vibrant is replaced by cracked and dry ground, with dead trees littering the area. The remnants of the forest do little to stop the wind that howls through the trees, and the crisp air nips at my skin.

As far as the eye can see, dark clouds cover the desolate land, creating an ominous shadow over our trail to Nomentum, and a shudder trembles through me.

Anxiety rises within my chest as I glance up at Zayne who looks fully alert as he surveys the area, "Was this always so barren?"

He shakes his head. "I haven't been this way in years. Last I saw, this was all forestland."

Unease settles within my veins as my father's words again ring through my mind. Deep down, I'm confident this is Samira's doing, but to what end, I do not know.

The desiccated and uninhabited region extends far toward the city of Nomentum, and we continue to travel for another hour with no improvement to the life of the world around us.

Even the air is thick and suffocating as if the very air we breathe yearns to snuff out any life it touches.

The ground rumbles around us for a moment, and I steal a glance at Zayne, trepidation building in my chest as his brows pinch together.

"Are there earthquakes often in Servilia?"

His gaze drops to mine as he raises a brow, "Earthquakes?"

"You know, where the ground shakes and trembles, buildings collapse, and craters form? It's a natural disaster on Earth." I clarify, and my apprehension grows even further when he shakes his head.

"We've never experienced such things here." He whispers, his eyes scanning the horizon.

The ground rumbles again, shuddering for a long moment, and I realize it's not an earthquake.

It's something running.

I twist my head to look around, and my heart nearly stops in my chest as a giant bull-like creature born of darkness barrels toward us. It must be at least twenty feet tall, with six horns jutting forward from its head a few feet. Spikes adorn its body, with longer ones along its spine that have my heart doing flips.

The beast's long tail flicks back and forth like a whip as it races forward with its beady red eyes on our toryian.

"Run!" I scream, and the toryian seems to get the memo, throwing itself into a full sprint down the road.

As we hurtle at top speeds, the creature behind us still closes the distance quickly, and I know it's only a matter of time before it catches up.

My mind races, panic consuming me as Zayne places the reins in my hands. I firmly curl my fingers around the soft leather as my heart thunders.

What is he—?

He shifts behind me, crouching on the saddle as his soft voice cuts through the chaos, "Do not stop, no matter what."

His scythe materializes into his hand as he leaps off the back of our mount, landing on his feet and sprinting towards the creature.

I watch in horror as the creature and Zayne collide head-on, sending a rush of air from where they made impact. The dust and debris fly through the air toward me, and I turn away, covering my eyes with the crook of my arm.

Each lungful of air tickles my throat, and I cough through the dust, waving it away as I squint my eyes through the settling cloud. The rumbling of the creature's sprint has stopped, so I pull back on the reins and search the area where Zayne disappeared.

Suddenly, a roar echoes through the air, and I finally make out the outline of Zayne's form as he stands off against the giant.

Swiping its horns at him, he dodges the attack, and my heart stutters as he slashes his scythe at the beast's side.

His weapon goes through the creature's body like a hot knife through butter, but the injured dark flesh simply reforms after.

He's not able to hurt it.

Terror fills me as the creature's long tail swipes unexpectedly, sending Zayne crashing to the ground and rolling as dust kicks up.

"Zayne!"

Chapter 34

Eiara

My scream echoes in the still air, and the creature's attention shifts to me as it takes a step away from Zayne's form on the ground, obscured by a cloud of dust.

Shit. Shit, shit, shit.

I slide off the toryian, "Get out of here. It's not safe." I say to the gentle giant, slapping her on her hind leg, and she runs off down the road.

The giant creature steps toward me slowly, and a glance at Zayne tells me he still hasn't recovered from the hit he took.

The earth rumbles once as the creature stomps, and I blow out a nervous breath.

It's either I manage to do this or die.

If I can buy Zayne time, maybe we can get through this.

Frantically trying to recall the muscle memory of using my magic purposefully, I square my shoulders as the creature rears onto its back legs, releasing a roar that sends a shiver of dread down my spine before it runs full speed at me.

Oh gods, what the hell am I doing?

My heart gallops within my chest, almost as if in sync with the creature, as it quickly closes the distance.

Just as it rears back and angles its horns toward me, I reactively put my arms up, feeling the familiar surge within me as instinct takes over.

An odd sensation rushes from my chest and through my limbs as I flinch away from the horns that are moments away from impaling me.

When a sudden phantom limb feeling surrounds me, my eyes flick open.

A mixture of shock and relief rifles through me at the shimmering shield mere inches from my arms, concentrated where the dark horns collide with the barrier.

I did it.

The creature roars before bearing its weight down, and the pressure forces me to brace myself on one knee. After the initial crushing pressure of the collision wears off, I manage to push to my feet again, though I can already feel exertion deep in my bones.

Distracted by my success and exhaustion, when the creature suddenly tail-swipes at me, I'm caught off guard. Its tail crashes into my side, sending me flying in the same direction Zayne had fallen.

I hit the hard ground with a thud, and pain radiates through my body as I roll to a stop with a metallic taste that coats my mouth. My gasping breaths echo in the air, and I'm sure the impact from the tail alone shattered my ribs, but somehow, I manage to maintain consciousness, finally spotting Zayne.

He's only mere feet from me, clutching his side, with his free hand grasping his scythe as he coughs. His face twists in pain and something in me screams to get to him.

Excruciating, white-hot pain sears within my chest as I drag myself to him.

My body feels broken.

My lungs struggle to inhale with each movement I make, and my ribs feel as if the bones are sticking in directions they shouldn't, as each shift on the ground jostle them out of place.

Using what strength I have left, desperation fills my veins as I place my hand on his scythe, and a stream of light curves around my fingers, feeding into his weapon.

The dark smoke solidifies into a twist of black and white marble swirling through it, with the blade's sharp edge gleaming against the sun's reflection. The earth rumbles again, and I glance at the menacing creature as it releases another roar from where it stands nearly forty feet away.

Resigning myself to my fate, I place my hands on Zayne's abdomen, picturing his bones and muscles mending together.

I don't even know if it's working.

Setting aside my uncertainties, I urge what is left of my magic to heal his wounds, to prioritize his over mine to keep him alive long enough to flee this place.

The ground shakes as the creature takes another step, and Zayne stirs on the ground.

I need to draw its attention away from him.

Pushing my exhausted, broken body to its feet and staggering to the road, each breath comes in shorter than the last. My strength wanes when I'm finally satisfied with my distance from Zayne as he pushes to his feet.

I suck in a ragged breath that sends white-hot pain into my chest.

"Run, Zayne. Just go." I choke out as the ominous creature breaks into a gallop toward me again.

This is it.

It gets closer, and I try to call forth my magic again, hoping to summon any size shield to defend myself, but the moment the shimmering barrier appears, it flickers out instantly.

Dread pools in my gut as the enormous creature rears back, and I instinctively flinch away, covering my head with my arms as it brings its horns down on me.

But the pain never comes.

My brows pinch together as I peer through my arms, where Zayne's figure stands between me and the creature. His scythe holds its horns at bay before he thrusts them forward, and in one swift slashing movement, the horns fall to the ground.

My head spins as my oxygen-starved lungs fight desperately to suck in air. I watch Zayne masterfully leap into a cloud of smoke as he teleports, reappearing to slice the marble weapon through the neck of the giant creature, and it collapses to the ground in a heap.

It's done.

It's dead.

My trembling legs give out, and I drop to my knees in relief, whimpering as pain shoots up my torso.

"Eiara," Zayne says in a rush as he drops to my side. "What in the gods' names were you thinking?!" he asks, concern etched across his features.

Danger aside, the worry on his face tugs at my heart, and I can't help but be thankful that we both made it through this alive.

My lips twitch.

"I had it covered," I whisper jokingly, "It's not like you to nap on the job." I manage to choke out before I cough in pain.

A steady thud that comes to a stop not far from us makes us both turn our heads to see our toryian standing there. Her antennae shift to the dead creature before turning to us.

Zayne wraps his arms around my body, cradling me protectively to his chest, and I suppress a pained cough.

"Looks like I'm not the only one who is bad at listening," I tease, groaning as the shift into Zayne's arms jostles my injuries.

Zayne's jaw feathers, "You could have died," he whispers as guilt rifles through me.

Dying was out of the question—an afterthought.

Regardless of what happened to me, I wasn't about to let Zayne get killed by that creature.

I frown, eyeing the downed beast as Zayne hoists us into the saddle, "What was that thing? Have you ever seen anything like it?"

He glances at it, shaking his head in response.

"I do not know what it is," he says softly, steering the toryian down the road toward Nomentum, "but I suspect we both know who is responsible for it."

Giving our mount a gentle pat, I clear my throat and wince through the pain in my chest. "We need a name."

Zayne's lips twitch, "A name?"

I nod, rubbing my hand along the wiry fur between her shoulder blades.

"I told her to get out of here, but she came back for us. That is special and deserves a name."

Zayne's features become contemplative for a moment.

"How about Qouirn?"

I blink, and my brows pinch together, "Qouirn?"

Zayne's lips twitch again, and his violet eyes slide to mine, "It means loyalty in Servilian." he says softly.

"I like that," I pat the toryian on the neck, ignoring the pain in my side, "What do you think? Is the name Qouirn okay with you?" I ask, and shock rifles through me as she dips her head.

"I suppose it is," Zayne says quietly, a twinge of amusement in his voice.

Silence passes us, and the path winds north toward the mountains, "Can toryians normally understand what we say?"

His violet eyes slide to me, and the look on his face tells me that the answer is painfully obvious, "Not according to any Servilian knowledge or histories. But perhaps the gods would know."

I fall silent, receding into my thoughts as we continue forward. Sharp pains radiate up my side and into my chest each time Qouirn takes a step, and my breath hitches as I wince.

Definitely broke a rib or two.

"Do you think we'll see any more of those creatures?" I ask nervously, considering our exhaustion as the city comes into view in the distance.

"I hope not. I have to wonder how the citizens of Nomentum have been managing with that thing roaming around," he adds, and part of me already knows the answer.

Anyone who has left the city or tried to visit has likely died or been lucky to avoid it.

We manage to get to the city gates without incident, and my exhaustion weighs so heavily in my bones that it's as if gravity is pulling my body to the foundation of the world itself.

Glancing at Zayne, it's clear that he's struggling to remain vigilant as we get through this last stretch to the city. He's not hurt, but he looks just as drained as I am as his eyes scan the surroundings.

We finally reach the gates, and two guards peer through the slots of the wall, eyeing us with scrutiny. The thick gates groan as they shudder open, and relief washes over me like a warm blanket.

Zayne steers Qouirn past the large gates as the near-empty streets of the city come into view, and a woman's voice rings out into the air down the road.

"You two look like you've been through the underworld itself."

She steps closer to us, crossing her arms over her petite form. Her blonde hair blows in the light breeze as she tilts her head, and her gaze scans over us.

"It's been too long, Vates," Zayne says from behind me as he directs Qouirn over to her, "is there a healer here?"

Her bright blue eyes flick to mine before she inclines her head once.

"She needs rest more than anything, as you both do, but yes, there is a healer here," she says, her voice bearing a twinge of amusement as she guides us to the toryian stables.

Zayne lifts me gently, and I wince as he wearily dismounts before setting me to my feet. He braces to catch or pick me back up at a moment's notice, but I wave him off dismissively.

"I'm okay to walk," I say and take a step. The movement sends a jolt of pain up my spine.

"Ah, just slowly," I add with a pained smile.

Vates moves closer and weaves her arm through mine, supporting some of my weight as she helps me closer to the building attached to the stables.

She pauses a few steps behind as Zayne pushes the door open, and it suddenly swings wide as a body collides with his in a rush. A smile creeps across my face, widening as I recognize the mess of blonde hair of the man holding him.

Their reunion tugs at my heartstrings as Kieran pulls back to cup Zayne's cheeks and presses their foreheads together affectionately.

After a long moment of embrace, Kieran's eyes fall on me, widening as concern etches across his face.

"Lara! Gods, what happened to you?!" he exclaims, rushing over to cup my face with his hand.

The familiar tingle of his magic travels throughout my body as my ribs painfully snap back into place, and I suck in a ragged breath of relief.

"Lara, those wounds were extensive..." He trails off, and his concerned gaze slides to Zayne as he moves to heal him, but Zayne waves him off.

"Eiara already healed me; I was simply unable to return the favor," Zayne says softly. His violet eyes are trained on me, making my heart flutter in my chest.

Kieran looks between us with a frown.

"Eiara? Healing? These injuries? Can someone explain what in the gods' names happened?"

I give Zayne a regretful look before explaining everything from the moment I left them in Sabinia, and there's a long moment of silence before Kieran speaks.

"When Gray returned without you, he said something about you having bigger balls than him. We started planning our search for you, but Sabinia was attacked." His jaw clenches at the memory, "We tried to save as many as we could by getting them on the boats to Aveentia, but many died. Samira wreaked havoc on the city, though Cade seemed to do most of the damage. Caspian was just... there."

"We decided to split up to search for you. I would go to Nomentum and see if Vates could track you. Gray, Val, and Darian would head to Aveentia first before crossing over to Marcellus. When I arrived here, Vates saw that a hylia ilvrost had suddenly appeared in Drusilla. We knew it must be you even though your path to Nomentum was unclear."

My heart stutters in my chest.

They're all okay.

"So where are the others now? Are they safe?"

Vates eyes glaze over before refocusing, "Their paths lead them to Nomentum from what I can see."

I glance at Zayne beside me with a smile of relief.

"As much as I hate to be the bearer of bad news, I have much to say... But not before you all rest," she says, giving me a pointed look, "And I mean rest, vrenlon dyrtia."

As the words leave her lips, my head swivels to shoot her a warning look.

"Why did you just call me that?"

She eyes me warily. "I said it because you are the vrenlon dyrtia," she frowns. "Have you heard the term before?"

I nod.

"Yes. On Earth, someone who worked with Caspian called me that multiple times before-" my voice cracks and I cut off abruptly.

Vates inclines her head.

"I understand and apologize for my ignorance," she says, stepping forward and bowing.

"Allow me to explain. 'Vrenlon dyrtia' means chosen daughter in ancient Servilian. Being the daughter of the god of the Sun and the goddess of the Moon, the title is one I speak in reverence." she says, rising to meet my gaze with a softness in her eyes, "But since it is a point of contention, I ask permission to call you by your name, instead." she asks, tilting her head slightly as she waits.

I blink and nod. "Um, please. Eiara or Lara, either is fine." I say quietly, and she inclines her head again.

"Well, Eiara. I suggest you and your companions get some rest," she says, gesturing to the stairs, "You will need it for what is to come."

The statement leaves a weight of unsettled nerves deep in my core as I follow Zayne and Kieran up the stairs to the room.

"I think you're going to particularly like the bathtub."

Kieran holds the door open for Zayne and me, gesturing to the door across the room where I see the corner of a tub as excitement coats my veins, and I hurry over to it, kneeling to turn the faucet.

I never thought I'd be so excited to get a bath, but here we are.

Water rushes into the enormous tub, and I sigh deeply as a rustle of clothing sounds out beside me. My cheeks flush as a shirtless Kieran opens his palm toward me in a gesture to help me to my feet, and I slide my hand into his.

A wave of nervous desire washes over me, and my heart thunders as Zayne tugs his shirt over his head just a few feet away.

Kieran raises a brow at me as my cheeks burn, turning away to pull my top over my head, tossing it to the side before discarding my pants and eagerly climbing into the bath.

Surprisingly, as my initial nervousness wears off and as both men climb into the water, I find that the comfort of having them close far outweighs any embarrassment of being so openly nude before them.

With the exhaustion settled deep in my bones, the water soothes an ache in my soul as a pang of loneliness hits.

This is the longest I've gone without Darian and Val at my side, and a large part of me yearns for them, even knowing they're safe.

They will come to me, and everything will be okay.

Movement catches my eye as Zayne reaches over to grasp a small bar of soap, lathering it in his hands and along his arms.

The lean muscles of his arms flex with each movement before he dips his head under the water.

Kieran takes the bar from him as he lathers the soap. "Come here, sweetheart."

Zayne's violet eyes are trained on me as water drips from his dark hair, and I shift closer to sit before Kieran as his hands gently glide over my skin.

"What about you?" I whisper as he moves to lather soap along my other arm, but he just shakes his head with a smirk.

"I did not get a near-death experience today. I'm just fine."

He tilts my head back to wet my hair and lathers soap into it before leaning my head onto his shoulder as his fingers massage my scalp.

If heaven existed, it would be in this moment.

I stand wholly corrected as water sloshes beside me, and Zayne's gentle touch against my skin makes me shiver as he begins to massage my shoulders.

Their ministrations make my throat tighten with emotion as I wrap my arms around Kieran, and my eyelids weigh heavy as I squeeze them shut.

This pull towards these men is unlike anything I've ever experienced, and I'm still not convinced that I'm not going crazy with how badly I need to be near them.

To feel their presence next to mine.

Navigating this while still learning about myself is overwhelming, yet I wouldn't change any of it.

It's as though this is how it's always meant to be, as my loneliness and longing ease with their presence.

Just by being near me.

I don't know how long we remain like that, but the bath water has long since gone cold, and I lift my heavy head from Kieran's shoulder. I'm nearly certain I fell asleep as Zayne places a tender kiss on my head.

Kieran tosses me a soft smile and pulls himself out, grabbing a towel for each of us.

I can't help but appreciate the small gestures he and Zayne make as they both take gentle care of me.

By the time we're done drying off, my eyes are fighting to stay open, and we don't even bother with our clothes before we plop into bed for sleep to blissfully take us.

Chapter 35

Caspian

I feel weak.

The lack of strength in my limbs is evident as I unsteadily make my way to the cells to collect the girls for Samira.

It's like something deep inside of me is weighing me down and dragging the very fiber of my existence into the ground.

Being sent to Sabinia with Cade to kill Zayne and Lara drained me of the last of my strength. I've spent days trying to recover, but even my dreams are restless, and I wake up in a cold sweat.

My nightmares are filled with visions of what could have happened.

I used every ounce of strength I had to avoid killing her when she foolishly threw herself between Zayne and me.

Gods, she's going to be my demise.

As long as she's alive and well by the time I'm cold and dead in the ground, that's all that matters.

I have to admit, she's fucking strong, though.

Seeing how she changed Zayne's weapon and the look in her eye when she told Samira her real name...

That was the most fucking satisfying sight in centuries.

This time, I can't take any credit for her strength. This Lara I'm seeing is a product of how she's grown since coming to Servilia, and judging by the look in her eye when she told Samira who she was...

That was more than just giving Samira her name.

It was a promise.

I just hope I'll be there to see her deliver on it.

That's if this magic that holds me doesn't kill me first.

Judging by how weak I am, it very well might.

I turn the corner to the cells as a mixture of surprise and relief washes over me. They're empty, and the key is on the ground next to the open door.

Shoving the key into my pocket, I slowly walk to the hidden door where Samira does her interrogations. By the time I get there, my energy is zapped, and my gut sinks as I spot her waiting, leaning against the doorway with a frown.

"Where the fuck are they?" She asks, and I shrug.

"They weren't in the cells when I went to retrieve them. Want me to go after them?"

She cuts me a glare before her thoughtful look turns. "Hold out your arm," she commands, and my arm jerks between us.

My heart thunders as she slices my arm open and holds a small bucket against the wound to catch the crimson liquid draining from my body, "What are you doing?" I ask, my voice betraying my nerves as she sneers.

"Something I should have done a long time ago. Now leave," she says, and my body turns, heading in the opposite direction from which it came.

She already has control over my body; what the fuck else is she going to do that she hasn't already done?

Trepidation builds in my chest with each step further from the room she disappeared into.

Does she know I let the girls free?

Does she have any idea that I knew who Lara was?

I might as well be dead if she does.

The corners of my vision start to go dark, but my footsteps remain steady.

No, she won't kill me. She's just absolving me of my mind.

Chapter 36

Eiara

Kieran and Zayne's steady breathing eases my mind in a serene sort of peacefulness as I wake with our limbs intertwined.

The heat of Zayne's chest seeps into my back, and my cheek rests on Kieran's shoulder. Every part of me misses the others, and my heart aches as I struggle to fully enjoy the moment.

I'm torn between wishing the others were here and absorbing myself in Zayne and Kieran's embrace.

After Vates warning, I'm unsure when I'll get another chance to just... be.

The close encounter with that creature should have been enough of a message of the dangers in this world.

Still, I can't help but be torn in two.

Part of me never wants to leave this bed, entangled in the best way with both my men. The other part of me knows that Darian, Val, Kieran, Gray, and Zayne will never be safe while Samira lives.

That's not to mention that we still have Caspian and Cade to free from her grasp, too.

Releasing a breath, I open my eyes to see Kieran's silver gaze already on me. "Good morning," I whisper, my voice still groggy from sleep.

"Afternoon," Zayne whispers in my ear, and a shiver runs down my spine.

I frown, "We slept that long?"

The remnants of concern melt away from Kieran's handsome features as he grins.

"You both slept that long," he says pointedly, "you needed the rest after everything that happened," he clarifies, his gaze searching mine. Locks of blonde hair fall forward, shifting against his lashes as he blinks slowly before a hint of a smile graces his features.

He's so fucking handsome.

Honestly, they all are in different ways.

If you had asked me months ago whether this type of relationship was possible, I would have laughed at the prospect.

Now, this dynamic between us is as natural as breathing itself.

It's like my world shifted somehow when I nearly died, and nothing has quite been the same since.

"What are you thinking of?" Kieran whispers, and I realize I've been staring at him.

How do I put this into words?

How could I ever describe the emotions that live within my very being, as if they're somehow woven into the cloth of my existence?

Amusement flickers across his face as if he can see the dilemma painted on it clear as day.

Perhaps he can.

My heart rattles in my chest as he raises his hand, pulling a lock of hair from my face.

"I'm thinking that even if I were to live a thousand lives across hundreds of worlds, I'd still find and choose to be with you all."

My voice comes out no more than a whisper, as if even my voice may betray the emotions welling up within me.

I know it's deeper than I let on.

No piece of me denies that I would lay my life on the line for Darian, Val, Kieran, and Zayne.

Hell, I'd die for them if I had to.

Emotion flashes across Kieran's face, and his hand glides up my side over my breast. His fingers ever so slightly brush over my already hard nipple, and my breath hitches at the contact.

He says nothing, but there's a certainty in his features that reassures me I'm not alone in this feeling.

Like a mirror, his gaze echoes and reflects this unyielding devotion, which once had been overwhelming but now is a blanket of reassurance to my soul.

He turns to face me, holding my gaze as Zayne's hand travels down my thigh and my pulse skyrockets.

Zayne's warm breath cascades over my ear, and his fingers curl around my leg as he tugs them apart, tracing gentle circles along my skin as he gets closer to my clit.

Every place our skin touches feels alight, and even with just their teasing, desire starts to build in my core.

My hand glides down the hard muscles of Kieran's abdomen, tracing the V-line as heat flashes across his face. The look he's giving me sends a thrill down my spine, and I pause at the base of his dick.

Zayne pulls me back into him more, and the searing heat from his chest sends my pulse even higher as my fingers trail along the length of Kieran's cock. I swear he's stopped breathing as my fingers wrap around him, gliding over the smooth skin of his dick from head to base, and his eyes flutter closed.

My clit throbs as Zayne gently circles it, and my breaths come in shorter as pleasure builds in my core.

I feel like I'm already close, and we've hardly started.

The veins that protrude from Kieran's cock are thick, and I swallow as he throbs against my grip. He leans in, placing soft kisses on my collarbone as he cups my breast, trailing kisses to my nipple before taking it into his mouth and sucking hard.

Desire pools in my core as I suck in a ragged breath. My fingers tangle into Kieran's hair as he kisses up my throat, nipping at my skin as he leans his weight in closer, pushing me further into Zayne as he throbs against my ass.

Kieran's hand grips the back of my neck, and his soft lips trail up my jaw, where he pauses. Our lips brush against one another at a feather-light touch that sends my mind into a whirlwind.

My breathing picks up as our eyes meet, and my heart aches at the desire mixed with desperation in them that mirrors what I feel so deeply within me.

He presses his lips to mine, and I fervently return everything he gives.

I may not be able to describe how much they mean to me, but I pour it into every dance of our lips. His tongue glides against the seam, and I open for him as the desire steadily building in my body suddenly rages within my veins.

Zayne slides out from behind me, trailing kisses down my arm to my hip as Kieran shifts to the side, deepening our kiss when Zayne lifts my legs onto his shoulders. My pulse rages as Zayne's hair brushes against my inner thighs, and the warm air of his breath cascades over my exposed skin.

Oh gods. I don't know what I did to deserve these men.

I'm already wet with anticipation and unable to suppress the shiver that ripples through my body.

Zayne's tongue glides along my pussy before swirling around my clit, and Kieran swallows my moan as his fingers tighten in my hair. As my legs begin to tremble from Zayne's expert ministrations, Kieran's kisses become more urgent as pressure builds in my core.

I reach down to glide my hand along his length, pausing distractedly as Zayne's mouth works my body with precision, and I shamelessly grind against his face.

My pulse rages in my ears, and Zayne's tongue is unrelenting as my orgasm nears when suddenly Zayne pulls back at the same time that Kieran sits up.

I look at them from beneath half-lidded eyes with confusion.

"Did I do something wrong?"

Kieran gives me an incredulous look as his arms hook under my body, and I instinctively wrap myself around his neck. His muscles flex as he carries me to the edge of the bed, easing me onto his lap with my legs straddling him.

"I think I speak for Zayne and me both when I say we want to feel you around us when you come, sweetheart."

I feel Zayne at my back, and my gaze locks with Kieran's as my heart thrashes wildly with anticipation. Zayne's dark magic wraps around my wrists and pulls them over my head while a tendril encircles my neck, slightly pressuring the sides.

Another ribbon of smoke glides around my legs, holding them in place as Kieran presses the length of his cock against my clit.

My breath hitches. Even if I wanted to move, there's no way I'd be able to like this.

Kieran notches himself at my entrance, his fingers squeezing my waist as he slowly pushes deeper, and my eyes threaten to roll back. Zayne's arm snakes around my waist and between my legs, circling my clit as his other hand finds its way to my ass. His finger gently pushes in, and the droplets of water swirling over Kieran's skin tell me that he's used his magic to help ease Zayne's fingers into me.

Even with Kieran's magic, I still need to breathe through the pain as the overload of pain and pleasure course through my body.

"Deep breaths, Eiara," Zayne says softly in my ear; his quiet voice holds a note of huskiness as he pumps in and out before stretching me further, and the searing pain lessens as Kieran begins his long strokes.

Zayne withdraws his hand for a moment before I feel the smooth head of his dick, and as he pushes in, I fight the urge to tense against the sensation. His dick stretches me further than he prepared me for, and I let out a whimper, jolting slightly against my restraints at the pain. Zayne slows down to give me more time to adjust to his size, and Kieran pauses his movement below while rubbing my clit, letting a small amount of his magic coax pleasure from my body as Zayne pushes in, inch by painful inch.

I'm panting, suspended upright, as the mixture of pain and pleasure sends pressure deep into my core. My clit throbs and my pussy clenches around Kieran as the orgasm I'd been so close to previously returns with a vengeance.

Finally fully seated, Kieran and Zayne pump into me simultaneously. The pain I once felt is quickly overtaken by ecstasy as they thrust in, throbbing against one another roughly.

I'm unable to move as Zayne's dark tendrils of magic squeeze my throat and limbs while suspending my arms over my head. I don't know how much more of this I can handle.

I'm close. I'm so fucking close.

My breathing becomes as erratic as their thrusts, and I'm pushed over the edge, crying out as both of them throb deep inside me. Kieran moves his hand to my clit as they come, and his magic radiates waves of pleasure through my body, bringing my orgasm crashing over me. My legs twitch and tremble as I ride out my climax.

Zayne is first to withdraw, with his strong arms encircling my body as his magic dissipates. I'm utterly boneless and limp in his grasp as he lifts me off of Kieran and carries me to the washroom.

My thoughts wander to each of my men as the dreaded thought of the future comes into mind. Vates' warning sobers me from my daze, and I close myself off from worry.

Zayne stands next to the large stone tub as Kieran steps forward, turning the faucet to the bath before shifting to stand next to us.

My fingers trace along Zayne's collarbone in contentment.

"No matter what happens in the future or what is to come, you guys are my home, happiness, and where I truly belong. I want you to know that." My voice is hardly a whisper as Zayne kisses my forehead tenderly, my eyes squeeze shut, and Kieran presses his lips against my hair.

"We know, sweetheart, and we feel the same."

My heart swells, but the lingering doubt, the tiny seed of uncertainty that their emotions might not be as all-encompassing as mine, takes root as I swallow thick against it.

Zayne steps into the tub and eases us down, the warm water rising to our chests as Kieran shifts close. He tilts his head to get a better look at me until his head is against Zayne's chest, mirroring mine.

"Everything you feel deep in here," he says, pointing to my heart, "we feel it too. We feel all of the desire, the insatiable longing, the pull that feels like it could drown you."

I blink at him. "You do? All of you?" I can't help the surprise in my voice as I lift my head, my gaze shifting to Zayne, whose violet eyes meet mine.

My heart thunders as his lips twitch slightly, and he nods.

"Do you know what it is?" Kieran shakes his head, but Zayne answers.

"There are old stories of gods having connections with other gods. It's how they'd know if those they cared about were severely hurt or had passed. Without knowing someone who personally experienced it, it's hard to say if this connection is one and the same, but we can only assume it is," he says softly, and my mind whirls.

There's an odd comfort in knowing that I'd be able to if something was wrong with Darian or Val, and my next few breaths come a little bit easier as I let that thought sink in.

Chapter 37

Eiara

We leave the room shortly after, making our way to the living area where Vates sits at a table, and my mouth waters as the fragrant smell of fresh food greets us.

Vates raises her brow at me knowingly, and my cheeks burn as she gestures to the three seats before her, where a plate of food rests for each of us.

Her gaze locks on me, "We have important matters to discuss, and we're running out of time. The deterioration of hylia ilvrost was one of the first signs, ones we should have understood or heeded. Our people losing their ability to wield magic should have opened our eyes, but we've long blamed our allies for a plight they did not cause."

She glances at Zayne and Kieran before her sights finally settle on me.

"There is more evil at work than we've seen, and you all must be prepared to fight it," she says nervously. "It works from the shadows and remains hidden from trained eyes like mine, even going so far as to shield its malicious followers from the watchful eyes of seers and prophets."

Everything she says screams Samira, and as much as I want revenge -as much as I want her to pay for everything- there are still multiple obstacles in our way.

I frown, "So, what do we do?"

Her eyes widen as a grin takes over her face, "Why, you train."

There's a quiet moment between us before Zayne speaks, "How long do we have?"

"A little more than half a fortnight, but Eiara won't need more than a week."

Zayne's lips twitch as he brings a spoonful of his stew to his lips.

Vates' features are painted with confident amusement, and she tosses me a wink before eating a bite of her food, "What's so funny??" I ask, blinking as I glance between them.

Kieran sighs next to me in feigned exasperation, "I'd guess she thinks that you'll beat him within a week, and he seems to think otherwise. My bets are on you, though, sweetheart," he says with a wink, grinning when Zayne rolls his eyes.

He tosses me a wink and grins when Zayne rolls his eyes, "We will see."

Challenge accepted.

"What about the others?" I ask, looking at Vates.

Her eyes glaze over before they refocus, "Their paths and variations still lead them here," she says, "There's a field behind the house you can use, and I'd suggest doing so sooner rather than later. It's never too early to start."

As Kieran leads us through the house to the back door, an intoxicating mixture of excitement and trepidation builds within me.

How the hell am I supposed to beat Zayne?

My eyes track his movements from where he walks in front of me. His shirt shifts as the muscles beneath them flex with each motion.

He's honed to make lethal strikes.

I deduced that much from the moment I met him.

There's no way I can hold my own against him within a week.

The door behind us creaks before it slams shut, and we pad through the remnants of a dwindling garden. Only a handful of various plants' tops, with their brittle and cracked stems as leaves, breach the topsoil.

It's as if the soil itself has lost nutrients, starving the plants these people rely on. It truly seems as though the ground has been drained.

Soon, the sparse landscape gives way to a large, cracked, and dry field. Various wooden weapons lay in a pile on the side, with uneven terrain and structures that look oddly similar to an obstacle course. The wind blows, throwing swirls of dust over the surface of the field, and I suppress a shudder as we make our way to the center.

He crosses his arms, and my pulse hikes as I glance between them in confusion, "What is it?"

A sly grin creeps across Kieran's face, "Normally, Zayne observes to determine the basic skills of recruits before they're assigned to training, but I much prefer the element of surprise for this."

He laughs under his breath as he moves to the outskirts of the field, gesturing inwards, "Go on, Z."

Zayne walks to the edge and reaches down, grasping the wooden weapon before returning to the center, where he outstretches the training sword toward me.

I look at it with a frown, "Where's yours?"

His lips twitch slightly as he suppresses a smile, "If you can hit me with this, I'll get one for myself." he says softly, standing only feet before me.

He honestly doesn't believe I can touch him with it.

Determination courses through my veins as I twirl the wooden sword in my hands, its weight unfamiliar compared to those I'd used in the various classes I'd taken.

"Vates seems to think I'll be able to," I say with more confidence than I feel.

Saying Zayne is a skilled fighter would be an understatement. Doubting his abilities would make me a fool.

Gods, I'm going to look like an idiot if I don't manage to get close to touching him with this freaking stick.

Taking an offensive position, I blow out a breath and wait for him to do the same, but he remains as he is, standing with his arms loosely crossed.

Lunging towards him, he easily dodges my attack and evades to the side as I stumble forward before twisting to face him.

My cheeks burn with embarrassment as his violet eyes burn into mine. His gaze is more anticipation and understanding than judgment, and even though my confidence wavers, there's something about how he's looking at me that makes me want to succeed.

It's as if his confidence in me is bleeding into my own, somehow bolstering it.

Rolling my shoulders, I take up my position again.

It's just a warm-up, that's all.

My next lunge feels like it's in slow motion. Zayne sidesteps me quickly, and I know my attempt was painfully obvious.

I huff, squaring my shoulders again under Zayne's watchful gaze.

I just need to touch him first. If I can do that...

My next lunge is seconds late, and he sees it coming quickly. He dodges to the side once more, his arms remaining crossed as he tilts his head.

Frustration coats my veins as I compare each time he's evaded me.

I'm too slow.

I always aim for the same spot—his left arm—since it's the most comfortable strike from this angle.

If I could just...

"Stop overthinking it, Eiara."

My teeth grit together.

It's not like he's wrong, though.

My next ten attempts fail to bring me closer to touching him. Each attack I make is clear as day.

What's the definition of insanity again?

Repeating the same action in the hope of a different outcome?

I huff in frustration, "This isn't going to work if you dodge everything."

He tilts his head, and a soft smile graces his features. "You will need to learn how to initiate an attack, but you're still overthinking. It's making your movements slow and giving away your path."

I sigh loudly, "Can you please just get a sword and fight me?"

My heart skips a beat as he tilts his head to look at me more clearly.

"Are you certain you wish to skip the introduction and go straight into sparring?"

Again, I nod and bolster more confidence than I have any right to, "I'm positive."

Zayne nods once before walking to the edge of the field, where he grasps a wooden weapon and moves into position before me. As we face off, my heart rattles frantically in anticipation, and he makes the first move within the blink of an eye.

His assault begins so quickly that I just barely avoid his strike as he moves in one fluid motion for another. I just manage to block his second blow at the last second as its vibrations radiate into my palm.

Holy shit.

I swallow thickly as he backs off for a second, and a hint of surprise mixed with pride flashes across his face—only a second passes before he lunges for another series of strikes.

All I can do is fend him off as he relentlessly strikes at me from all angles. I block again.

And again.

And again.

His graceful, deliberate, and intensely powerful strikes come in chains, and it's as though they all meld together, hardly giving me a moment before the next.

I know that he's honed for battle and exceptionally skilled, but if I fight anyone close to his experience, I might as well kiss my ass goodbye.

Soon, my body begins to lag. My muscles ache and tremble as they tense with anticipation before each strike lands.

My eyes dart to each side, tracking his movements, where his eyes travel before he strikes, which direction he leans, and how he shifts his weight.

My years of training slowly resurface like riding a bike. My muscle memory and mental gymnastics in anticipating movements keep me just barely ahead of his attacks. The next strike knocks my training sword from my exhausted hands, numb from the relentlessness of his assault.

My chest heaves, and I lean forward, bracing myself against my thighs as I catch my breath.

Kieran pushes himself to his feet, glancing toward the first moon making its appearance in the sky. "I think that's enough for the day."

Have we truly been sparring that long?

Zayne has hardly broken a sweat as he stands before me, glancing at Kieran before his calculating gaze scans over me.

Does he see me as weak?

As someone who can't defend herself?

My teeth grind together at the thought.

I'll never be that again, not if I can control it.

I know Darian, Val, Kieran, and Zayne would protect me, but I do not want to be the damsel in distress.

I shake my head, "Not yet."

I hardly get the words out before lunging at Zayne. The only indication of his surprise is his eyes widening before he skillfully dodges the strike.

"You're frustrated and tired, Eiara. You need rest," Zayne says quietly, and damn if he isn't right, but I will say when I'm done, and I've never been one to give up.

"Not yet. You can leave if you want, but I'm not done." I say, though my limbs protest my words as they tremble from exertion.

Zayne lunges unexpectedly, knocking the wood from my hand before lunging at my throat. I dodge at the last second, instinctively dropping my head to use his momentum and flip him onto his back.

He lands with a thud as I snatch my wooden sword from the ground and point the tip at him in one fluid movement.

"Leave or stay. Either way, I'm not done," I state between breaths, and he inclines his head.

We train non-stop for days, and I do not best Zayne again.

We spar from morning until night, only stopping to eat at various intervals throughout the day when Kieran calls for it. I've lost count of how many times I've fallen, been shoved to the ground, lost my balance, or just been caught off guard before Zayne's sword has made it to my throat or pointed at my chest.

This morning is no different from any other except that my mood has been sour since I woke up. I rolled out of bed with a short fuse, and nothing has been able to fix that, not even Kieran's lighthearted jokes as we ate breakfast.

Zayne and I face off in the center of the field, each holding wooden swords ready between us.

I grit my teeth.

The callouses on my hands rub against the rough wooden handle, and the half-healed blisters on my palms twinge in pain as I tighten my grip.

It probably doesn't help that I'll hardly let Kieran heal my sores.

They're a reminder of the work I'm putting in, and with all my failed attempts, that's the only thing keeping me grounded.

Everything fucking aches, I've slept like a rock every night, and my frustration has built up to the brim. Multiple times during these sessions, I've almost lost control of my temper and barely kept it reined in.

If this was a real battle with someone half as skilled as Zayne, I might very well be dead. I may be improving per Zayne and Kieran's standards, but it's insufficient by mine.

Today marks day seven of sparring, and while Vates' certainty in my abilities initially boosted my confidence, it's definitely waned as the slight breeze slicks over my skin.

Zayne nods almost imperceptibly before he's in action, and I manage to block his overhead strike, twirling in place before blocking a continual blow that would have hit my ribs.

Instead of stopping after two blows, Zayne strikes a third time unexpectedly, his weapon colliding with the tender skin over my ribs, and I cough involuntarily, clutching my side.

He moves to check my injury, and anger wells up within me as he speaks, "You must be ready for any—"

The world turns red, and time seems to slow as I lunge at him. His eyes widen as he jumps back, blocking the attack at the last second, but I do not stop.

I strike again, again and again.

My assault is unrelenting as my frustration and anger build, and Zayne's surprised expression quickly turns to concentration as he focuses on blocking my quick succession of blows.

Finally, with his movements lagging behind mine, my last strike catches across his side as a crack echoes into the air, and I aim the tip of my weapon at the crook of his neck. His violet eyes flash as they flick to mine, and Kieran's slow clap catches my attention at the edge of the field.

"Fascinating," he says, glancing between Zayne and me. "Now, we just need to achieve that to start, and we should be in good form."

His clapping stops as Zayne shakes his head.

"Anger is a tool you should rarely rely on, Eiara. It may give you the temporary boost you need, but with both physical and magical attacks, it will drain you," Zayne says, tilting head thoughtfully, "But now that we have the basics down for sparring, it's time to practice magic. Physical skills and reflexes are one thing. Magical abilities are another, and you've only used yours a handful of times using what I assume to be your natural reserves of magic. We've yet to see the true potential of your powers."

"How can I tell if it's my reserve of power?" I ask, frowning at my hands.

"You would have felt if it wasn't." Zayne says quietly, placing our training swords on the ground.

My heart thunders in my chest as my nerves come to the surface.

"What if all I'm capable of is small bursts of power?" I ask, glancing between both men as their gazes soften.

Kieran's hand falls onto my shoulder with a slight squeeze, "We'll never know unless we try."

I nod once, uncertainty settling deep in my mind as I move to stand in front of Zayne.

"So, what do I do?"

Zayne tilts his head thoughtfully, studying me before he answers, "Think back to the other times you used magic. What was the commonality between each?"

I take a long moment to reflect, and silence hangs thick in the air until I finally answer.

"Outside of dream-weaving, it was mostly instinct, I suppose."

Zayne nods once, taking a seat before me, "So it seems, most of the time, when stakes are high, you can wield it."

"That is a good problem to have," Kieran interjects in a supportive tone, and I toss him a grateful smile.

"Our training will focus on calling it forth without these risks," Zayne says quietly, motioning for me to sit.

I swallow, sinking to my knees in front of him.

Why is this more daunting than sparring with him?

"I want you to focus on your breathing, empty your mind to open yourself up to your power. When you summon your magic this way, it is normal to feel overwhelmed. Without the adrenaline of a dangerous situation to help you in bursts, channeling your power will feel like reining in a storm itself."

Great, that sounds fun.

I inhale deeply through my nose and blow out my breath.

"Good. Close your eyes and focus on each breath," he says softly, "As your thoughts come, acknowledge them and let them go. Once your mind is empty, you should feel the door to your magic, and you'll be able to open yourself up to it."

After what feels like an eternity passes, my mind struggles to remain focused, and I release an exasperated sigh.

"I feel nothing. This isn't working." I huff, opening my eyes to see both men looking at me with pure amusement.

"What is it?" I ask, not bothering to suppress the annoyance in my tone.

"That took all of thirty seconds," Kieran's laugh reaches his eyes as he covers his mouth with his hand, and I glare at him.

Don't use anger. Don't use anger.

Zayne clears his throat, tearing my attention off of Kieran.

"Managing your well of power will not be easy and will require all of your focus. Should your magic make you lose control, you could very well die and take everyone nearby with you. Try again. Open yourself to your magic, Eiara," he says, our gaze locking for a moment before I concede, shutting my eyes again.

His warning lingers in my mind over the next few hours, and my attempts to meditate are thankfully longer, but they play out the same way.

My frustration mounts until finally, I sigh loudly, throwing myself backward with a thud.

Zayne pushes himself to his feet and extends a hand toward me.

"Frustration and anger may work with sparring but will get us nowhere with magic. Let's pause for tonight and come back fresh to it tomorrow."

Chapter 38

Eiara

Glancing at the first moon's edge cresting over the horizon, the strain of the day's training weighs heavily in my limbs as I follow closely behind Zayne and Kieran.

By the time we get through the backdoor of the house, the intoxicating herbal scent of food greets us, and my mouth waters as we make our way to the dining area.

Two full bowls are set on the table, and Vates approaches me with a third bowl. Her gaze scans over my body as she holds the food between us.

"I ran a bath for you, figured you may want some time to yourself while you eat and clean up," she whispers, tossing me an empathetic look.

Thank goodness for Vates.

I take the bowl faster than even I expected and give her a grateful smile, "Thank you, Vates. I desperately need it."

Pausing in the bedroom to spoon a bite of stew into my mouth, I glance out the big picture window that's ajar, assuming Vates opened it for airflow.

The training field in the distance and barren trees that litter the horizon may give the night an eerie aura, but as the full shape of the first moon finally comes into view, I can't help but feel a sense of renewed awe.

This place is so different from Earth in so many ways. The call of birds in the distance, echoing in the air, distracts me from my thoughts as I hurry to the prepared bath.

Setting my bowl along the side of the tub, I strip down and tentatively put one foot in to test the water.

It's hot, nearly too hot, but manageable.

I slowly sink beneath the water's surface, leaning back to let the heat reach as much of my body as possible as it seeps into my sore and strained muscles.

Ribbons of steam rise from the water, and I find myself in a daze as my thoughts wander lazily. Slowly becoming less conscious of the cool air against my exposed skin as my chest rises and falls with every breath, my mind goes quiet.

It's a brief, albeit tentative peace.

I suppose this was the state of calm Zayne wished for me to achieve all that time.

It's a wonder anyone can focus that way under pressure.

Perhaps that is the point.

My attention snags to the bowl on the side of the bathtub as my stomach growls angrily, and I slide forward to pull it closer, taking mouthfuls of the flavorful stew with various vegetables and meat.

Once emptied, I place the bowl along the side again and lean backward, letting the warmth of the water soothe my body and mind as I lay there with my eyes closed.

~

When I open my eyes again, it's to the strangely familiar dark stone castle watchtower.

Caspian.

Quickly scanning my immediate surroundings, a mixture of worry and confusion sets in when I don't find him already here.

Could this be a trap?

He said it wasn't safe here.

Keeping his warning in mind, I step forward with caution.

Mindful of my footfalls, I lean forward against the cold stone rail and slowly peer over the ledge to the snow-capped forest canopy, with the ominous empty darkness looming far in the distance.

It's a dread-inducing abyss amidst the backdrop of what would be an otherwise beautiful scene—enormous mountains towering above an endless forest bordering the crystal blue lake fed from the waterfall nearby.

Do I wait here for him?

Is there anywhere else I can go?

Could I run into others here?

I shake my head in an attempt to clear my thoughts.

You're dream-weaving, clearly. Unless you pull anyone else in, it should just be Caspian here.

...Key word, 'should'.

Turning to the open doorway that leads into the castle, I square my shoulders and cautiously walk through it. The sconces along the walls flicker against the dark stone, and the chill in the air sets into my very bones as I navigate further into the castle.

My heart thunders in my chest, and my pulse rages in my ears with each step. I'm fully aware that I'm in uncharted territory as I pace down the tall corridor, but something feels **off**.

He should be here, and I refuse to leave until I find him.

As I approach another open doorway, my soft footfalls echo in the space, and my heart rate spikes as I peer in.

The large room has wooden cabinets along one side, leading to a wardrobe with beautifully crafted art all over it.

The dark wood is complimented by an equally dark wood bed frame, with plush gray bedding, and in the center of it is Caspian.

My relief at seeing him quickly diminishes when my gaze lands on his now ashen skin, marred with dark veins that web along his body.

No, this can't be happening.

I rush to his side, and panic sends my mind into chaos as his chest rises and falls with each of his shallow, labored breaths.

"Caspian," I whisper, placing my hand on his arm.

The chill of his skin seeps into mine, and I shiver as I search his face. His breath hitches, and my heart leaps eagerly, but my excitement is short-lived as he shows no signs of waking.

Fuck.

What do I do?

Crawling further onto the bed and leaning over him, the battered state he's in becomes abundantly clear.

My mind races.

I don't know how to help him, but there's a nagging certainty deep inside me that is desperate to find a way.

Glancing around the room with no signs of darkness creeping in, I place my hands over his chest. I feel silly, like there's no way this will work, but I have to try.

I have to do something.

Willing myself to stay calm, I focus on my breathing while keeping one thought in mind to recreate how I helped Qouirn.

Heal him.

I repeat it over and over like a prayer, with the image of a healthy Caspian within my mind.

Please, please, please. This has to work.

When he remains unchanged, I panic, and it takes a conscious effort to calm my breathing again.

I remember the serene state I was in during my bath, and I exhale deeply, rolling my shoulders to release the tension in them. My throat tightens as I squeeze my eyes shut, quietly urging the frantic thoughts in my mind to cease.

My trembling hands hover above his chest as it rises and falls, and Zayne's words echo in the back of my mind.

Open yourself up to your magic, Eiara.

It can't be that simple, could it?

Frowning, I close my eyes and look within.

After a few quiet moments, I find myself in an empty, dark room with winding stairs that spiral upwards. My feet tentatively move forward, climbing the staircase cautiously, taking in the deep red aura at the top of the stairs that grows more imposing the higher I get.

Once at the top, the soft, velvet-like walls stretch as high as the eye can see, with a large white marble door in the center of the room.

As a ribbon of light seeps through the handle, gliding around the door gracefully before dissipating, it's clear this is what I've been looking for.

My fingers wrap around the door handle, energy radiates into my palm, and I hesitate.

Is this the right thing to do?

The image of Caspian's lifeless body makes my chest tighten and throwing caution to the wind, I twist the handle before throwing the door open.

My entire body pulsates as electric energy radiates through my limbs and swirls within my veins. My mind whirls like water down a drain, and I'm merely paddling to stay afloat amongst the pull of the chaotic waves.

My eyes snap open as I struggle to contain the power coursing through my body and into limbs that leave a searing trail of pain in its wake.

Zayne wasn't lying about it feeling like reining in a storm.

Looking at Caspian, the turmoil and pain within me are temporarily forgotten as the dark webbed veins under his skin pulsate in response to my power. The dark magic inside him rebels beneath me as if deflecting against the ribbons of light that swirl over my arms and into my palms.

Hovering my hands over his chest again, I allow my magic to seep out slightly and ease into his chest. A tiny thread of light disappears into his skin, and though I can't see it with my eyes, I can feel it as it tracks the webs of darkness within him.

Using the magic within his body as a guide to hunt for the source, I wait impatiently as my tendril of power tracks the ominous darkness, easing itself deeper within him until it finally stops.

Deep within the center of Caspian's chest is the source of whatever power holds him hostage. A gaping abyss of darkness the size of a baseball pulses with magic so sinister that it sends fear into my heart.

My power whirls within me like a tidal wave crashing over my body, and my chest heaves as I gasp for air, struggling to maintain control of the chaotic energy.

Another wave of power just as strong as the last rams into my very being, and a renewed sense of urgency takes over.

I need to help him before I lose control.

Sending more tendrils of magic into Caspian's chest, they crash against the magic that has taken over his body, pushing back the darkness that has spread throughout his chest and limbs.

The inky veins that web over the surface of his skin slowly recede as my magic pushes further into his body.

Beads of sweat drip down my body as I ignore my triumph and soon manage to confine the dark power within him to that small baseball-sized chasm. My magic churns chaotically within me, and my heart thunders as I flood the abyss within Caspian.

It surges and rebels in force as I flood my power into it, but it's useless. My magic simply crushes against the core of power within him to no avail.

Caspian remains motionless in the bed, though his color has begun to return, and my pulse rages in my ears.

Fuck.

What do I do now?

I can't cleanse whatever this is…

Can I contain it?

Is that even possible?

Given no other choice, I weave ribbons of my power over the chasm, entwining it within itself to ensure that none of this dark power can seep out. As I continue to cover gaps in the weaving, the healthy, warm glow has fully returned to Caspian's skin, and he begins to stir below me.

Covering the last hole of dark magic, my power weaves into a tight ball, encasing it like a layered vault. I pull the remnants of my power out from him so that only my magic encasing it remains, and the energy coursing through my veins surges once more, burning through my limbs.

His eyes snap open as I pull my unused power back to my own body through desperate gulps of air.

Thank the gods.

It worked.

"Lara?" He whispers in astonishment, his wide eyes bewildered as he tracks the ribbons of light that swirl over my arms.

My power whirls once more as if threatening to explode from my body, and I gasp, clutching my chest as if that would help contain it.

"You must sever the connection to your magic," he states quickly, sitting upright before clasping my head between his hands.

His emerald gaze searches mine as another pulse of power radiates pain within my body, and all my nerves feel as though they're on fire.

It's like my magic is branding each one, staking its claim on me.

"Cut it off, Lara. Close whatever window or door you opened. Cover it with a lid. Just do something. Anything." His commanding plea echoes in my mind, cutting through the chaos.

The door.

Squeezing my eyes shut, I frantically picture the staircase once more. The stairs look taller, the steps wider as I drag myself up them, nearly stumbling as another wave of pulsing energy crashes over me again and again before finally I'm in the red, velvet-like room.

The open door in the center seems intimidatingly larger than before, wider than I remember as I push myself to my feet and stumble to it. Bright white light flashes from the doorway, and it's so blinding that it nearly overtakes my vision as I reach out to grasp the handle.

My fingers burn as they wrap around the metal, and I heave it closed with all my might.

It takes every last ounce of strength I have to pull it shut, instantly dissipating the searing pain within my body, and I suck in a ragged breath.

My eyes open, blurred from the tears streaming down my cheeks as my gaze finds a pair of bright emerald eyes.

"It worked," I whisper, relief coating my veins as he pulls me into his arms, "You're okay."

A shudder works its way through his body as his arms encircle my shoulders. The exhaustion has already set in my bones as my chest heaves, and I catch my breath.

"You're okay," I whisper again as if just to reassure myself.

My tears continue to fall unbidden as he tightens his hold and squeezes me into his chest.

"I am because of you." he says, and emotion clogs my throat.

A long moment passes between us before I lean back to look at him.

"What happened to you, Caspian?" I ask as he eases my exhausted body onto the bed with him, rolling us onto our side while keeping me clutched to his chest.

He's holding me to him like he's afraid I will disappear or vanish into thin air any second.

If I didn't know better, I'd say he's actually worried that I might.

He shakes his head, "I wish I could tell you, little one."

My brows pinch together, and I bring my hand to his chest, sensing my orb of magic still woven tightly within him.

Even after all of that, he's still tethered to something.

After a long moment, Caspian's hand covers mine, "I can feel it," he says, searching my face, "but why? After all that happened, why save me?"

My gaze drops to his chest where my magic is, "I am not the same woman I was when all of that happened, but I suspect, nor are you the same man," I whisper, and as his grip on my hand tightens, his gaze drops to my mouth.

Suddenly, the darkness within him surges against my bundle of power, and instinctually, I throw a shield over us as darkness collides violently against it from all sides of the room, causing the surface to tremor as my already exhausted body struggles to maintain it.

My magic reserves are quickly draining to shield us, and dread fills me as I consider leaving him here.

"You need to go," he states quickly, bringing his free hand to my cheek as my heart thunders erratically, "I cannot say much, but some... thing is coming for you, Lara," he manages to chew the words out just as the pressure on the shield bears down.

I have no choice but to throw myself from the dream as I surge forward, sitting in the tub and gasping for air.

Chapter 39

Eiara

Water sloshes against the tub's sides, echoing within the silence surrounding me as I collect my bearings. The water has since gone cold, and it's a wonder that the guys haven't checked on me yet.

Curious, I weakly push to my feet. My already tired body from training now only more exhausted with the added strain of using so much magic in such a short time.

The exertion has definitely taken its toll.

My body sways unsteadily as the water sluices off my skin, and the brisk air gives me goosebumps over my quivering limbs. I climb out of the tub and grab a robe from the counter, gingerly wrapping it around my body.

My hair still drips as I slowly go to the door, wincing at the tenderness in my limbs as I pull it open.

A wave of unease washes over me, and though I consciously try to shake it off, Caspian's warning lingers in the back of my mind as I pace a few steps into the bedroom.

I stop abruptly.

The silence is deafening.

The brisk air from the window kisses my still-wet skin, making my hair stand on end as I slowly enter the dining room where Kieran, Vates, and Zayne had been.

Their bowls have been put away, and the table is clean, but there's no sign of them.

Concern growing, I tighten the robe around my chest, cautiously venturing out the back door towards the training area, straining to hear any sign of chatter or training.

But there is none.

Where the hell are they?

Caspian's warning sounds out in my mind like an alarm, heightening my anxiety to peaks I hadn't known before as my heart thunders like a war drum in my chest.

I slowly pace down the path to the training area, jolting at each shadow that dances in the corner of my eyes as I near the edge of the field.

Finding no one here either, I continue forward until I'm standing in the center of the field, turning in a full circle before sighing loudly.

"Where are they?" I murmur to myself.

A sudden shuffling behind me catches my attention, and I whirl around to see Kieran out of breath as he stops with relief on his face.

"Lara! We've been looking for you," He says with a smile, but he suddenly stops.

His face falls, and his eyes turn into saucers as his gaze flicks behind me. Panic flashes across his face as he steps forward, and drops of water rise from the ground.

What's going-

A pit of dread fills my stomach as the cold bite of a sharp blade digs into the side of my neck, directly in line with my carotid artery.

"Cade, let her go," Kieran warns, but the blade digs into my neck more.

"She must die," he whispers, almost inaudibly behind me.

My heart jumps at the possibility of freeing Cade.

He's so close… if only we could just-

My thoughts are interrupted as time seems to slow. Cade's blade moves, and I know by the horror on Kieran's face that it will end my life, but just as the blade bites into my skin, it suddenly stops before dropping to the ground.

Kieran's features twist in pain as Cade begins to sputter and cough behind me. I turn around, and my gaze lands on Cade, his white-silver hair a stark contrast to his dark robe, and his lifeless purple eyes widen as he stares at me with blood sputtering from his mouth.

My gaze drops to his chest, where the smoky tip of a dark scythe protrudes before it suddenly dissipates, and blood spurts from the wound.

No. No, no, no, no. No!

As blood streams down his chest, he drops to his knees.

Kieran rushes to Cade's side, catching him in his arms and easing him down. As I kneel next to him, a line of blood spurts from the wound, splattering Kieran and me.

I flinch away instinctively, and Zayne's figure catches my eye.

He attacked his brother to protect me.

His shadowed eyes gaze at his brother on the ground, but the feathering in his jaw tells me everything I need to know as I reach Cade's arm. I feel along his hand, looking for the object keeping him under control, but I find nothing.

Why isn't Kieran healing him?

He coughs again, and my heart stutters in my chest as I frantically reach for his other hand. My fingers graze the cold metal on his third finger, and I wrap my hand around it, willing my magic to the surface.

When nothing happens, my heart feels as if it may very well shatter.

No! Please just let me be strong enough to do this.

Panicked with my chest tight and my pulse raging in my ears, I clamp my eyes shut and try again, tears brimming beneath my eyelids.

"Come on," My desperate plea rings out as Kieran's hand falls to my shoulder.

"It's alright, Eiara," Zayne whispers beside me, and something inside me cracks.

"No," I shake my head defiantly as Cade's breathing becomes labored.

I picture the winding staircase, the velvet room, and the doors. I shove them open, and my magic responds in force, whirling before it sputters out. The consistency is volatile, and I know I only have seconds to break this hold before I'm useless.

Mustering all my strength, I channel my residual energies into the ring. Thin ribbons of light surge over my skin into the metal, suffocating the dark residing in it as the metal shatters, and with it, my magic sputters out once more.

"Th-thank you," Cade's voice fills the air as my gaze meets his now bright, violet eyes.

Hope surges through me, and I quickly move my hands over his chest, praying I have enough power to help.

"Lara," Kieran begins solemnly, and I shake my head.

"No, this can't be it. Kieran, heal him!"

"Sweetheart, I can't heal what Zayne's magic has..." he trails off, but I understand what he's trying to say.

He's as powerless as I am.

Emotion tightens my throat at the realization, and the heartbreak on Kieran's face fractures something inside of me. Cade's hand covers mine on his chest, and I feel the warmth of his blood as it pools beneath my fingers.

"She must die," he repeats before glancing at Zayne, "Samira must..." The three of us watch his chest fall for the last time before the light leaves his eyes.

No...

Gods, please.

Bring him home to me.

He belongs with me, with us. He's supposed to be here.

Please don't let this be it for him.

Tears silently fall to the ground as I stare at his lifeless body, waiting for any indication of movement.

But there is none.

He's gone.

This can't be.

I lean forward, pressing my lips to his blood spattered forehead as tears stream down my cheeks.

This wasn't supposed to happen.

Still half in shock, I hardly register the movement as Kieran wraps his arms around my shoulders, tugging me into his chest as tears stream onto the top of my head.

I'm not sure how long it's been when the shock wears off, but I'm still dazed when I realize Zayne is no longer beside us.

Kieran follows my gaze as tears stream down his face, answering my unspoken question, "He will come back. Give him time, Lara."

Quick footsteps behind us have Kieran on alert, twisting to look over his shoulder as Darian, Val, Gray, and Vates approach.

A mixture of relief and sadness overwhelms me as my gaze locks with Darian's. His mismatched eyes slide to Cade before they burn into mine, and even if I could speak, I don't think I could find the words to comfort him.

Val curses beneath his breath as he and Gray exchange looks before moving to Cade's side.

But I know they won't be able to help.

If anyone should have been able to help, it was me.

What is the point of having these powers if I can't even be strong enough to save those I love? To save those that they love?

Kieran's arms tighten around my shoulders, and he leans his head against mine as my chest shudders. A fresh wave of tears streams down my face, and the ache in my soul feels like it could shred me to pieces.

A sudden shout jolts me as Gray's guttural cry echoes into the night, the sound only rivaled by his fist pounding against the earth below him.

Val leans forward to cover Cade's forehead with his hand, whispering beneath his breath as his shoulders shake. He trembles as tears fall from his cheeks onto Cade's shoulder, and something inside of me feels as if it's shattering anew.

"Fuck!" The pain in Gray's voice as he rests his forehead against the beaten ground breaks my heart all over again, and it isn't until he places his hands flat on the ground that I notice his knuckles are bleeding.

This is all my fault.

If I hadn't left the house, maybe it would have given them more time...

My eyes shift to Vates as she kneels next to Cade's body, her eyes sliding shut as she rests her hands on the arm of their fallen brother.

"We should have been here sooner," Gray says in a low voice. "We could have avoided this if we had just gotten here faster."

"There was no way of knowing this would happen," Kieran says quietly, "Even Vates hadn't foreseen Samira sending him here."

Guilt coats my veins as Caspian's warning echoes in my mind. "We would have known because we would have been here," Gray snarls, his golden eyes burning as bright as molten lava as he glares at Kieran before his eyes shift to Val, "If we had just flown in, this would have never happened."

Val sighs deeply, the weight of his sadness etched deep into his face as he shakes his head.

"We had no way to know it was safe to do that, Gray," he says, touching the ground as the earth trembles. Gray's mouth opens to retort but snaps shut as his gaze locks with Darian's.

The ground shifts and tremors as Cade's body slowly eases toward a newly created cavern. The vines Val has summoned slowly ease his limp form underground, and his silver hair disappears into the shadows as the earth swallows his body.

Shifting out of Kieran's grasp, I lean forward to place both palms on the ground. Digging my fingers into the blood-soaked dirt, I shut my eyes and say a silent prayer for Cade wherever his soul now resides.

My heart knows he's no longer burdened by Samira's control and free from the pain he likely endured while in her clutches, but the pain on Kieran's face still flashes through my mind, and imagining the burden Zayne must carry, having slain his own family is almost too much to bear.

This is my fault, and I wish it weren't the end for him.

I wish they hadn't lost their brother.

Behind the stillness of my closed eyes, an image of my parents fabricates as if they were standing before me in a field filled with hylia ilvrost.

They stand tall, proud amidst the trees, with a beautiful gold and white marble castle behind them. Another woman, with eyes like fire, sits atop a horse beside them with a smaller horse or donkey-like animal, gazing toward me as if she can see me kneeling before her.

Their smiling expressions turn solemn as they step aside, revealing Cade's form between them. They look at me with a hopeful sadness painted across their features as they gesture to him, and he steps forward.

His wound has disappeared, and his violet eyes shine bright as he inclines his head once before the vision fades.

I open my eyes, and my breath hitches at the tall hylia ilvrost before me. Its golden bark is imbued with swirls of silver and white that travel along each long branch, reaching in every direction.

The bright golden leaves are already beginning to bud in front of my eyes as tears spring to my eyes anew.

"Fascinating," Vates's soft voice rings out as she stares at the tree in awe. "They've welcomed him in," she murmurs before her gaze locks with mine, and she inclines her head once.

Does that mean she-

My heart thrashes in my chest as I realize that the vision in my mind is not just a figment of my imagination. I look at the tree wide-eyed as the others glance around in confusion.

"They've welcomed whom?" Kieran asks quietly behind me.

Gray crosses his arms over his broad chest while glancing between Vates and me, "And who is 'they'?"

I resist the urge to squirm beneath his gaze and sigh, resigning to answer.

"My parents," I say softly, my gaze sliding to the tree once more as the wind rustles through the now fully grown leaves, "Cade is with them."

My voice is no more than a whisper, "What does this mean, Vates?"

She shakes her head, "I don't know for certain, but the gods usually have their reasons."

A long moment of silence passes before Kieran speaks up, "So, what do we do now?" he asks, and everyone glances around before their gaze lands on Darian.

His silence as he gazes at the tree only serves to heighten the tension in the air, and it isn't long before Gray pushes himself to his feet.

"I say we burn that bitch in her castle and be done with it," he growls, his attention shifting as Val huffs under his breath, "What, do you have a better idea?"

"I could come up with better ideas in my sleep," Val laughs but there's no humor in it. "Burning Darian's rightful home won't do any good if we're not sure she's inside of it. Or did you forget that we don't know where she is?" he adds, his voice thick with sarcasm, which only serves to rile Gray up more.

"Oh yeah? Do you have a better plan, then? Name one," he roars. "That's what I thought," he says wildly when Val doesn't respond.

Kieran's eyes roll as he sighs, "We're not burning entire castles without knowing for certain she's in it, Gray."

"Well, who has a better suggestion?" he asks loudly, his eyes wild as he looks between each of his brothers, "Cade is dead, Zayne is gone, and the rest of us will just sit here and do nothing?" he shouts angrily, the muscle in his jaw working as he snaps his mouth shut.

"Perhaps," Vates says, stepping forward to stand next to Val, "Eiara may have some insight as to our next move," she says cautiously, my eyes widen and heart thunders as all the men look in my direction.

Me?

She thinks I have a better idea?

Nodding once in acknowledgment, my mind races to find the best possible decision. Though a large part of me wants to hunt down Samira to make her pay for her crimes, there's no guarantee we will find her anytime soon.

There's one other possibility, though, that could prove fruitful.

"I say we spend our time preparing to fight -however that may look- while we search for the location of Caspian's tether." I offer apprehensively, and as his name leaves my lips, their brows furrow in confusion or disdain.

Gray scoffs and shakes his head but stays quiet as Val shoots him a look.

"Caspian's tether?" Darian asks, frowning. "What do you mean by his tether?"

I swallow audibly.

"Caspian is not working with Samira by his own will, I believe." I say, glancing at each of them before continuing, "When I first dream-weaved into Caspian's mind, there was a darkness surrounding his consciousness. He was not wearing any jewelry like Cade and Zayne did, nor was he under any illusion, such as Gray or Kieran. Instead, it was almost as if something within him had dark magic tethered to him. As if Samira weaved into his very being."

Darian's face pales as he blinks at me, but Gray pushes to his feet angrily, "What else do you know that you've been keeping from us?"

"Gray," Kieran and Darian warn at the same time.

He's right, though.

I hadn't told them about most of this because I wasn't even sure of it.

I should have told them, as much as I shouldn't have left the house tonight.

Guilt tremors through me, and emotion tightens my chest.

"When I dream-weaved into his mind, I was standing atop a watch tower on the side of a mountain. The stone was dark, and the tower overlooked a large forest of varying colors. There was a waterfall that came from the mountain itself and fed into a large lake," I say, and Gray's eyes light up.

"When I asked Caspian how I could free him, he could not tell me verbally, but I believe the key to freeing him is somewhere near there."

"Caesarea," Gray says with a wild expression of excitement, "the lake you just described is behind Caesarea."

"Then we begin with Caesarea. We find Caspian's tether, break Samira's hold on him, and use the information he has to find and beat her," I state confidently.

"Caspian? Helping us? We must be mad," Darian says under his breath before shaking his head, "How do you know he will help us beat her?" he asks, glancing up at me.

"He has a point," Gray mutters, "Caspian could just as easily kill us to take the throne without competition."

"I believe he's been actively trying to help us," I say quietly, and Val curses beneath his breath.

"Of course," Val says, locking eyes with Darian, "In Sabinia, Caspian didn't attack anyone unless he was attacked first. He was just there."

I nod, relieved that Val can support my observations, "And when I saw him soon after while dream-weaving, he looked as though he'd paid a terrible price as a result."

Darian's head rests in his hands as he absorbs the information.

"If what you say is true, how long has he....?" he mutters, and my heart breaks all over again for him.

"I don't know how long. Only Caspian will be able to answer that." I whisper, pushing to my feet and swaying unsteadily as Vates hooks her arm into mine.

"You must rest, Eiara. You stretched yourself thin tonight, and there is much to prepare for," she says, her eyes softening as she smiles warmly at me.

Chapter 40

Eiara

Darian's arm wraps around my shoulder as we approach the house before he lifts me into his arms.

There's tension in his neck as he holds me close, and I'd be a fool to think he wasn't affected by losing Cade.

No.

If anyone knows about bottling up emotions and avoidance coping mechanisms, it's me.

"Lara," he whispers, opening the door to the house and carrying me through the dining area, "Are you alright?"

Am I alright?

He just lost his brother, and he asks me if I'm alright?

I shake my head, "No, but I imagine you aren't either."

The muscle in his jaw feathers as his mismatched eyes slide to mine as we enter the bedroom, but he doesn't stop there and instead continues to the bath.

He eases me to my feet and twists the faucet, snagging a small cloth from the cupboard nearby before placing it under the running water.

I watch as he methodically strains it before bringing it to my face and wiping my cheek.

Cade's blood.

He's cleaning his brother's blood from my face.

Emotion clogs my throat, and I swallow thickly against it.

"I'll be honest, Lara. I'm not entirely certain how I feel."

I frown.

"There's something you should know. You deserve to know." he says tentatively, and for once, he seems lost for words as he rinses the cloth and sets it aside.

My heart thunders in my chest.

Is this it?

Is this when the other shoe drops?

A million scenarios run through my mind in the brief silence, but he just shakes his head.

"Darian, you're scaring me," I whisper, and his gaze softens as a hint of a sad smile tugs at his lips.

"Not my intention, Sunshine," he says, glancing to the bedroom before lifting me into his arms again.

The smell of forest rain brings comfort to my raging mind until he sets me into the bed, kneeling in front of me. He looks as though he's uncertain or afraid, which is a stark contrast to the confidence and surety that he usually carries himself with.

My hands tremble against my thighs as I search his face, "This is torture, Darian. Just say it."

He sighs deeply in resignation, and as his mismatched gaze burns into mine, it's as if a floodgate has opened.

Sadness, anger, worry, relief, and happiness all crash over me all at once, mingling and intertwining with my thoughts until I don't know up from down.

"Darian, what-"

Worry suddenly takes over, smothering everything else before dissipating completely, and I stare at him with wide eyes.

What the hell was that?

Where those... his emotions?

"Is this what Kieran meant when he said he and the others could feel everything like I do? Zayne said that he thinks it has something to do with the connection between us all."

A flicker of relief washes over me as I blink at him.

"We have been doing our best to shield you from ours once we felt your emotions, but I'm afraid that's not everything, Sunshine. Do you remember when I told you Lor used a rather unconventional spell to save you...?" he asks, and my pulse rages, but I tamp down my questions as I nod.

He swallows audibly but continues, "The spell Lor used tied my essence to yours to keep you alive and heal you. It's only been used a handful of times throughout the millennia because of the risk it poses."

I feel the blood drain from my face as the weight of his words sinks in.

Ties our essence together.

Essence as in lives?

If our lives are tied together, that means...

"If I die—" I whisper, and he nods slightly.

"It means there will never be a time where I will have to live a life without you, and that would not be a life I would want to live at all."

He says it like the pros far outweigh the cons of this scenario.

My heart thunders, but the weight of freeing Gray and risking my own life, now knowing that I was risking his, comes crashing down like a thousand bricks.

I could have gotten him killed.

"Why didn't you tell me?" I ask in a shrill voice, and he winces.

"I didn't want to put that decision on you. Would you have made the same decisions had you known?" Darian looks at me pointedly, and damn him for being right.

I wouldn't have made the choices I did if I had known.

The safest route would have been taken solely to keep him from harm, which means I never would have freed Zayne or met my parents.

At the thought, Darian's lack of surprise when Cade was welcomed into the realm of the gods comes to mind, and suspicion coats my veins.

"When did you know?" I whisper, and his eyes flick to mine before understanding takes over. A wave of guilt that's not mine washes over me, and dread pools in my gut that this is yet another thing that was kept hidden.

"It was clear that you were not human at first, and once I knew you were the key to finding the amulets, I suspected. When I got wind of the prophecy, my suspicion grew even more, and it was all but confirmed once Lor used the spell to heal you. I could sense your magic when the initial transfer happened during the spell. It was deep and hidden, but it was there, which further solidified my suspicions."

The door opens to the room, and Val steps inside with Kieran, both pausing as they glance between Darian and me.

Was this the best-kept secret of the century?

"Did they know all this time too?" I ask, and they look at one another before stepping further into the room.

"Know what, sweetheart?" Kieran asks quietly, sitting in bed next to us. "That I was the daughter of two gods, and if I died, I'd take Darian with me?"

Kieran drags his hand through his blonde hair, "I only found out for sure when you arrived in Nomentum with Zayne, and Vates stated your direct bloodline," he says, leaning further onto the bed beside me.

My momentary relief stutters as my gaze shifts to Val, standing in the center of the room with his arms over his head.

He stretches before tossing me a boyish grin. "I had read that your magic typically was only derived from being direct descendants of the gods, but since there was no confirmation of who your parents were, I felt it best not to say until we knew more."

"And? What about the part where if I die, he dies?"

Guilt flickers across their faces, telling me everything I need to know.

I sigh loudly and throw myself backward onto the bed, "I can't deal with secrets anymore. I could have killed you without even knowing. I'm so sorry," I mutter as the bed shifts from Val lying above my head.

"No need to apologize, Sunshine. It ended up working out," Darian's voice reverberates through the room as the ground trembles, followed by a roar outside. The roar is followed by the heavy beating of wings, and it's clear that Gray shifted and took to the air.

"Will he be alright on his own?" I ask, glancing at each of the men on the bed with me as their faces fall. The grief bleeding out from them is like a thick fog.

It's muted beneath an unseen veil, but it's there all the same.

I don't know how I didn't realize it this whole time.

Kieran nods, "Gray will fly to take the edge off, maybe let off some steam, but I doubt he'll do anything too rash or stupid."

"We hope," Val adds sarcastically, and Kieran rolls his eyes before smirking.

"How can I keep my emotions from bleeding out like you are?"

Darian's eyes flash like he doesn't enjoy the thought of being cut off from my emotions, but he still answers, "It's like pulling a blanket over your body and wrapping it tight. The more you cover the less emotions that leak out."

Val and Kieran crawl into bed alongside us, as Val runs his fingers through my hair, "The more you do it the more second nature it is, but don't cut us out for too long."

"Get some sleep, Lara," Darian says quietly, pulling the blanket over my body before brushing his lips against my head as Kieran and Val do the same.

It's not long before the calm darkness of night claims my exhausted body.

Chapter 41

Eiara

Surprisingly, though exhausted, I managed to wake up with the others.

It's relatively quiet as Val, Darian, and I gather in the center of the field in the brisk, early hours of morning. Goosebumps break out over my bare arms with the breeze, and I suppress a shiver.

I'm not sure what the seasons are like in Nomentum, but here it's usually warmer during the day, with the nights having a bitter chill that sets in.

Unlike the rest, today doesn't seem to have warmed as clouds cover the sky, blotting out the sun.

It's fitting, considering everything that's happened.

Sucking in a deep breath, the crisp air in my lungs is welcome for now as it chases away the last weariness of morning. My eyes track the movement as Darian crosses his arms before me, tilting his head to the side where a few strands of long black hair fall. "We'll work on hand-to-hand this morning and end with calling forth your magic."

A heavy ball of nervousness settles in as Darian steps to the side, awkwardly leaving me standing before Val.

"Well, **Eiara**," Val grins, "Time to show me what you're made of."

My nerves fray further as my heart thumps steadily in my chest.

Do I think I'll be able to beat any of them in hand-to-hand combat?

Absolutely not.

Am I still going to try?

My gaze slides to Darian near the edge of the field. His arms are crossed over his broad chest where his tattoos peek out from the edges of his clothes.

His life relies on my ability to avoid death, so I have no choice but to give it everything I have.

I refuse to be the catalyst for his demise.

My gaze returns to Val, and he glances between Darian and me before giving me a nod.

Whether he had the same line of thought, I'll never know as I widen my stance and ready myself for his assault.

Val's skills in battle rival Zayne's in all areas, including gracefulness.

Amidst the blows, the blocks, and dodges, there's an art to how he moves. Each attack is well-thought-out seconds before it happens, and each counter is masterfully planned, seemingly well in advance.

He knows my next move and anticipates it with ease as we fall into a steady rhythm of chess until my limbs tremble with exhaustion, feeling like they're made of lead.

I've begun to spot weaknesses in his movements, though.

His ribs are exposed when he throws his hand up to block my jab. When he knocks my right hook away, it takes him .8 seconds to return to his defensive position, and he usually hesitates there.

Val could easily take me down and break me, but he's holding back just to allow me to learn his movements. The notion is endearing but also frustrating.

In a real scenario, I will not get this luxury.

He watches my body movement for change, his bright hazel eyes tracking my stance, hand placement, and posture.

But my body is exhausted from the endless dance of limbs and can't physically go on as we work through another set of blows.

I just need a moment to breathe.

My arms drop as his counter jab comes directly at my face. His eyes widen as he realizes at the last second that I'm not moving to block, and he averts his blow just enough to graze my cheek.

"Gods, Eiara," he curses under his breath as he steps in close, grasping me with both hands. "I could have hurt you."

I manage a laugh between deep breaths. "Is that not the point?" I ask pointedly, and he blinks.

"Are you saying you want me to hurt you?"

"I want you to try, actually try, and if you do, fine."

"Lara," Darian warns from the sidelines, but I shake my head.

Going easy on me will not benefit anyone.

"In a real fight, I will not be given chances!" I shout, my frustration brimming as a chuckle sounds out from behind me.

I twist to see Gray on the edge of the field, sitting and bracing himself on his knee as his golden eyes burn bright.

"Gray..." Val says, but I hold my hand out to silence him while I hold Gray's gaze.

"Do you disagree?"

A malicious grin spreads across his face, sending my heart into my stomach.

"Absolutely not," he says, "In fact, I think it's quite a good idea. I'd rather not lose any more of my brothers to ignorance."

"Gray," Darian scolds, but the jab hits its mark as guilt washes over me. Anger flickers from both men before I pull a mental blanket around my mind, hoping that works.

"I mean, really, who ventures off by themselves in the middle of the night?" His jaw works as his teeth grind, "Maybe that's a lesson Val can teach you before we leave here, too." he adds, glancing at each of his brothers before grinning again.

"Leave us, Gray," Val says with an intensity I haven't heard from him before.

Gray's grin widens, "I think I'll stay."

Val's gaze slides to me. The apology is clear on his face, but I just shake my head.

I know Val and Darian would make him leave if I really wanted, but it's better if he stays.

As much as I hate it, Gray is right.

Cade's death should have been avoidable, especially considering Caspian's warning.

Zayne didn't kill Cade.

I did.

My resolve hardens as my gaze meets Val's once more, and he gives me a single nod.

"Let's move on to opening yourself up to magic for now," he says, sitting on the ground before me.

It doesn't take much to sit my exhausted body in front of him as Gray scoffs behind us.

Little does he know, the guilt of knowing the truth of Cade's death only fuels me, and his commentary only adds tinder to the fire.

Val's voice is quiet as he wraps his hands around mine. "Did Zayne explain how to open yourself up to your magic?"

I hadn't realized they were trembling, and I nod, not bothering to mention the events with Caspian or go into detail.

Gray would likely blame me even more for not being able to save Cade if I did.

My teeth grind together as I shut my eyes, picturing the winding staircase that leads to the red satin room. I can still feel the remnants of exhaustion from using my magic last night, so it's clear I'm not fully recovered, but real life won't care if I'm fully rested.

Now is a better time than any other.

Within a few moments, I'm standing in front of the doorway in the center of the room, my fingers wrapped around the door handle before I twist and throw the door open.

My magic surges through the doorway, and my eyes snap open as power fills my limbs, making the hairs along my arms stand on end.

It whirls and soars within me, and I struggle to contain it within my body. The internal battle is like catching rain through a net in the middle of a hurricane, and with each passing second, I'm losing.

Unable to withhold it anymore, my magic bursts forth from my body in streams, and the air gets thick as I fight to rein in my power. It's elusive and slips through as I try to pull it back.

The feeling is akin to grasping oil after pouring it into a tub of water as it evades your grip, escaping my palm as I close my hand.

"Gods," Val whispers with his eyes wide as ribbons of light swirl over my body chaotically, extending down his arms and around his body.

Sweat licks down my spine as my power surges again, and I cry out, as white-hot pain shoots down my arms.

"You're open to too much power, Lara," Darian says, his baritone voice cutting through the chaos.

"You don't say," I choke out as my power whirls again, and I tighten my grip on Val's hands.

"Close it off, Eiara," Val says quickly, watching the ribbons dancing along our arms nervously, "Close yourself off to your power."

My eyes squeeze shut, and I picture the staircase as another wave of power crashes over me, and I gasp.

The red velvet room comes into view, and I again drag myself to the imposing door. Caspian's face flickers in my mind as I pull the doors shut, panting as the overflowing torrent of magic ceases.

The remnants of power ebb and flow, and I open my eyes as I catch my breath.

Val's eyes are on me, and he stares at me as if he's never seen me before. My heart stutters as the ribbons of light twist around us.

"We need to expend the excess power. Do you know what you can do so far with it?" Val asks and I nod.

"Shielding, healing, dispelling illusions, and I changed Zayne's scythe." Heavy footsteps to my right sound out as I hear Darian call Gray's name in warning.

Within a second, the area around us brightens before the heat hits me. Val's eyes widen in shock, and instinct takes over as the heat intensifies.

He's going to burn us alive.

The shield around us shimmers as red and white flames collide against it. The assault is unrelenting as my power drains, and it's not long until it gets dangerously low, but his flames don't let up.

I focus my shield on the impact area, freeing up some power as my reserves deplete.

But he doesn't stop.

Panic builds in me as I frown, my gaze meeting Val's before he glares through the flames at Gray.

As my power nearly bottoms out, I panic and throw the doors to my power open, my adrenaline and nerves skipping the mental journey to the velvet room altogether.

My magic surges in force against his flames, solidifying the shield that had begun to dissipate against his attack. My power swirls once again, the overwhelming force threatening to overtake my exhausted body as I channel it into the outlet, driving it to bend to my will.

"That's enough, Gray," Darian's voice says as another wave of power crashes over me.

At this rate, I'll take them all with me when my power explodes from my body.

Panic wells within me as I realize what he's doing.

He's testing me.

He's pushing me to my limits to see what I will decide to do: die to an attack or explode and kill myself, those around me, and Darian.

I grit my teeth as frustration coats my veins, likely bleeding into Darian and Val.

I won't let him win this.

Molding my power, I curve the shield away from Val and me as I push it further from us.

"Holy shit," Val breathes, but I keep my focus.

I can see him now behind the flames, hands outstretched, his dark hair sticks to his forehead as my magic pushes his flames back inch by inch. Another wave of power swells within me, but instead of fighting it, I allow it through, channeling it in full force at him as the shield suddenly lurches.

He only gets a second warning before his flames surround him, and they sputter out as my power wraps around his limbs.

His hands drop to his sides as he pants in exertion, and I shut the door to my power again, feeling my energy bottom out with it.

I'm gasping for breath as Val pushes to his feet before me, "Did I pass your fucking test?" I manage to chew out.

Within seconds, Val's lunged at Gray, and his fist collides with his cheek. "You asshole," Val growls as he throws another punch at Gray, who just smiles.

"Passed with flying colors," he laughs, catching Val's hand as his eyes dance with amusement.

This guy is fucking insane.

"I think that's enough for today," Darian says, his voice closer than expected, and I turn to see him stepping closer. He offers to help me up as he watches Gray and Val.

The moment I take his hand, his gaze shifts to meet mine, and relief that's not my own floods my mind.

Surprisingly, not a hint of anger or frustration bleeds through, and I can't help but wonder if he's relieved that I passed Gray's test, too.

Chapter 42

Eiara

The next few days are relatively quiet, and we fall into the grueling hand-to-hand combat training routine before swords and bows come into the mix. The latter half of the day ends with calling forth my magic, opening the doors within, and allowing it to flow through me over and over again.

By last night, I could quickly open myself to my magic without picturing the doors within my mind being pushed open, though harnessing the flood of power for longer than a few minutes is still a challenge I've yet to overcome.

Dragging myself from the kitchen to the field is a task as I dread another day of training.

Gray's scrutinizing gaze has burned holes in the back of my head all week as I train with Val, Kieran, and Darian. His low-blow remarks have boiled my blood and riled me up much more than I'd ever let on.

*It's as though he's **trying** to get a rise out of me.*

Every time I was struck down, or my magic failed me, Gray's snide commentary was never close behind.

"We'll never win if that's the best you can do."

"She can't even defend against one obvious strike."

"Maybe we're all better off just hiding until Samira gives up."

I've had enough.

My feet carry me to the field on autopilot, where Val is waiting in the center as usual. Surprise rifles through me when Darian and Kieran are nowhere to be seen.

"Where are—?"

I jolt as Gray's voice sounds out, twisting to look at him with wide eyes, "They're helping Vates," he says with a sigh, "Do you ever pay attention to your surroundings?"

I roll my eyes, ignoring him as I move closer to the center of the field. Val grins at me, "Ready, Eiara?"

I nod once, and he lunges when I'm hardly in position before he knocks me on my ass, and I cough.

"Sorry. You said you were ready," he says, offering his hand between us, but I knock it away as Gray snickers.

Val must sense my frustration as he steps back, "Your turn."

He hardly gets the words out before I'm in motion, throwing my fists at him in a series of moves.

No matter how fast I am or where I attack, he manages to block them all. My frustration builds as I spot openings in his defenses, but by the time I'm in a position to hit them, my opening is gone.

Distracted by my emotions, Val takes advantage of an opening, gripping my arm and twisting me around until my back is flush with his hard chest. His free hand slides across my waist, keeping me steady as I wobble to the side awkwardly, and my gaze collides with bright golden eyes across the field.

"Do you see how happy he is to see you lose focus?" Val whispers in my ear, and I grind my teeth.

Val's hand rests against my abdomen as he leans in, his lips brushing my ear, "Don't give him the satisfaction, Eiara."

He releases me abruptly, and I twist, hoping to catch Val off guard. Once again, my opening is lost a millisecond too late, and Val's counter sends me to the ground with a thud as the air gets knocked out of my lungs.

"Great. By this time next year, maybe Zayne will be able to kill Samira by himself because, at the rate this is going, we'll all be dead," Gray says sarcastically, "But hey, at least we'll be with Cade again."

Something inside me feels like it's snapped, and a sudden surge of rage washes over me as Val's weight lifts off my body. Within seconds he's lunging at Gray.

"Stop," I say, and Val pauses just feet from Gray, who has a wide grin spread across his face, "Step aside, Val."

Concern and anger radiate from him, but he steps aside as I push to my feet.

If he thinks he can just berate me constantly with no repercussions, he's in for something else.

"You want to blame me for Cade's death? Fine. Go ahead. Anything you can think to insult me or blame me for his death, I have already done ten times over, but I refuse to be the reason anyone else loses their lives," I say quietly.

Pure, unadulterated rage flows through my veins as I glare at him, "Come here."

His eyes flash with the challenge, "Are you sure you don't want Val, I won't go ea-"

"Now, Gray."

His mouth snaps shut as he steps closer, and I tilt my head to hold his gaze.

The moment he's close enough, I lunge at him. Fuelled by years of anger, my movements are faster and more forceful than my training with Val, and Gray's amusement melts into focus as he quickly reacts to my attacks.

What he doesn't expect is for me to use my magic to block his blows.

He deflects my jab before gracefully countering with his own, grinning as I make no move to defend against it. His fist suddenly collides with the now shimmering barrier inches from my face as I duck down to take advantage of the opening, putting more force than necessary into my strike as my fist collides with his rib cage.

The strike sends him staggering backward, coughing and sputtering with wild eyes as pain radiates from my fist.

"Holy shit," Val breathes from the side of the field as a broad smile spreads across Gray's face.

"There she is. My turn to play, Eiara the Goddess."

Rage still coats my veins as he lunges in my direction, colliding with force against my shield.

"Are you sure you want to do this, Gray? I won't go easy on you."

His eyes flash with anger and excitement at my taunt as he lunges again. My heart races with a heady concoction of confidence as I drop down, using his height to my advantage.

Bringing my fist up into his ribs, I curve my shield over it, using it to take the brunt of the damage rather than my fist as I use my full momentum with the strike. He coughs, bringing his knee up into what otherwise would have been my exposed stomach. My shield shimmers against his attack, and he steps back as flames burst forth from his skin.

"Let's even the playing field then and see how well you do."

After half an hour of Gray laying into my shields with counter strikes knocking him back a pace, my magic is spent, and I'm gulping air as he braces himself against his thighs.

I felt the moment my magic failed me with that last strike, and I nearly took the full blow to my cheek. Val's concern radiates from the side of the field where Kieran has joined him, echoing the concern as they watch us spar.

"How much longer will our Goddess last, I wonder."

My teeth grind together, and my fists clench.

There's no way he could know I bottomed out.

One more. Just one more shield. One more strike is all I need.

It has to be perfect.

My chest is still heaving as he lunges forward, and I manage to dodge at the last second. My limbs slow from exhaustion, and my window to counter begins to close as I twist.

"Eiara!" Val and Kieran shout, but it's too late.

A burst of flame suddenly hits me from behind, and I cry out as it sends me flying forward to the ground with a thud.

The air gets knocked from my lungs as I use my arms to protect my head, feeling my clothes burning at my back. The searing heat licks my skin and the smell of burning hair invades my senses, but I can do nothing as I gasp against the dry ground, desperate to fill my lungs.

Just as I feel my skin bare against the searing flame, cool water washes over my back, and I weakly push my chest off the ground with one arm. Sucking in a deep breath, I hold the remnants of my shirt on as I sit up, with my mostly untouched hair falling forward in front of my face.

Fuck that was close.

A mixture of anger and something else I can't quite make out radiates from Kieran and Val as silence falls over the field.

Finally, after catching my breath, I glance at them, but their eyes are fixed on Gray, and I follow their gaze.

I look over my shoulder at him as he stares at my back, the muscle in his jaw working, and all the amusement has disappeared from his features.

His eyes flick to mine before he suddenly shifts, his body morphing and changing as scales cover his body. It's only seconds before he towers over us all, releasing a roar before launching himself into the air.

I glance at Val and Kieran, "Did I do something?"

Val steps closer, pulling his shirt overhead before handing it to me.

"Not at all, sweetheart," Kieran says, tracking Gray's form high in the sky as he disappears into the clouds.

I tug Val's shirt over my head, letting the remnants of mine drop to the ground, partially seared.

"Let's go clean up and get some food. You've damn well earned it." Val says, placing a kiss on the top of my head.

Chapter 43

Eiara

After eating, I climb into the hot bath with a breath of relief.

The heat seeps into my muscles, burning my blisters and sores as I relax against the back of the tub. Despite my exhaustion, an echo of pride over-shadowed my evening with how good it felt to get small victories during our sparring session.

I'm not a fool to think that my success during training with Gray was solely my doing.

He pushed my buttons to rile me up enough that I would snap, and I did.

I just don't think he had any idea that I would snap in the manner I had. After bathing, I pull my robe on and climb into the giant, empty bed.

Vates requested Kieran, Val, Darian, and Gray to help with some tasks for the evening, giving me some time to myself.

I find myself breathing easier now that I'm on my own.

The last time I was left to my own devices, I helped Caspian but, in the same breath, got Cade killed.

I breathe deeply and melt further into the blankets.

Thinking back, this is one of the few times I've been alone since this entire ordeal started.

It's sobering to believe that it's only been what I'm assuming is a hand-ful of months since I saw Caspian in that bar on my birthday.

I don't even know if time goes by the same here as it does on Earth.

The moonlight slowly trickles in from the open window as my mind wanders, and three moons shine bright in the distant sky. Reflecting on that night in Drusilla, my heart fractures as I consider the weight Zayne bears after all that has happened.

Restless from reminiscing, I sigh deeply and resign to staying awake as I kick off the blankets.

My feet absentmindedly carry me to the tall, marbled hylia ilvrost tree in the training field. The wind howls eerily as my soft footfalls sound into the stillness of night, and I gaze up at the tree's towering height.

Putting one foot in front of the other until I'm at the base of the trunk, I can't help but wonder if my parents decided to let Cade in or if he even wanted to be there.

Is it rare for them to welcome people in?

Why would they have even done so in the first place?

What are the repercussions?

Remembering the peaceful smile on his face as he stood beside them, I let all uncertainties and worries melt away.

I ease to the ground, leaning against the shimmering bark as a cold breeze passes through the field, and my eyes slide shut.

~

I'm faintly aware of the warmth surrounding me as my eyes adjust to the dark.

My hands press against the hard ground as my vision focuses on the smooth, dark surface riddled with vein-like membranes. My body sways, and I realize I'm no longer leaning against the tree; instead, my back and head rest against a dark-scaled body.

Gray...?

Disbelief rifles through me as my eyes trace the span of his wing, keeping me nestled into him. I lean forward, and his wing stretches, allowing the bright morning light to assault my sensitive eyes.

I squint as they adjust to the change before his wing returns to his side.

His body moves as he cranes his neck, and his molten eyes turn to look at me before his body morphs. I lean forward more as he returns to his regular form and steps to the side.

It takes a conscious effort to remain focused on his face, not his fully nude form, as his gaze slides to mine.

"Maybe next time, don't fall asleep outside alone when you're being hunted," he says, and my shame melts into annoyance.

"Clearly, I wasn't alone," I state pointedly, and he sneers before stalking toward the house.

Shaking my head, I shift in place, leaning back against the tree with a sigh.

Why is he so hot and cold?

Did I manage to piss him off from something I did?

Is this all because I got Cade killed?

How can I get through to him?

"Eiara." Zayne's soft voice cuts through my flurry of thoughts, and I twist in the direction in which it came.

His mussed, dark indigo hair looks like he has not stopped for days, and the dark bags contrast his violet eyes. He looks exhausted, but thankfully, he appears unharmed.

A wave of relief washes over me as I scramble to my feet, stopping myself just before him.

I search his face for any indication of disapproval, "Uh, may I?"

His features soften as he inclines his head.

"You never need t-" he manages to say before I throw my arms around his neck, clutching him tightly.

Without missing a beat, his arms wrap around my waist, and I feel the tension leave his body. As his shoulders relax, I know he needs this as much as I do, and he inhales deeply into the crook of my neck.

"I was worried about you."

His arms tighten around my body, "Forgive me. I had to try to find Samira."

His words make my heart stutter.

"You found her?" I pull back, searching his violet eyes in disbelief as he shakes his head.

"I can't be certain. Caesarea has rumors of creatures of unknown origin in the mountains. Their numbers haven't been determined since anyone who ventures deep enough doesn't return, but there is a good chance she is there or has some sort of operation within the mountain."

"I suspect Caspian's tether may be there, though there's no way to know for certain."

"We go to Caesarea then," He says quietly before glancing at the tree behind us, "This was your doing, I assume?"

Following his gaze, I smile sadly, "Mine and my parents, actually."

I say, clarifying when his attention turns to me with a raised brow, "Vates and I both saw Cade with my parents when we buried his body."

A small smile graces his features before he looks back to the tree, "It's beautiful."

"It is," I agree, leaning against him as we stand in comfortable silence.

Clattering from the house sounds out, and we exchange a look before slowly returning.

"Is everything alright between you and Gray?" Sensing my hesitation, he adds, "There seemed to be some tension earlier."

Tension is putting it lightly.

I chuckle, "I think everything will be fine."

As we near the house, a handful of bags sit next to the door, and Kieran carries them around the side of the house toward the front road. Zayne and I exchange looks before following to the front, where Gray stands, leaning against the side of the house.

Kieran's hands are full of bags as his glance turns into a double-take.

The moment his gaze lands on Zayne, he drops everything he's carrying and sprints toward us, colliding into a tight embrace with Zayne.

"We were worried about you," Kieran says quietly, pulling away from Zayne and leaning over to brush his lips against mine.

He pulls back with a soft smile before whispering to Zayne, and I feel Gray's burning gaze.

My heart gallops as my eyes slides to his, and my cheeks burn.

With the look he's giving me, I don't know whether he wants to kill, eat or fuck me.

"What's with all the bags?" I ask, glancing at the sacks next to Gray as Darian and Val come out the door, each carrying another bag.

Kieran opens his mouth to answer, but Vates' voice sounds behind us.

"Now that we're all here and have a location, we must move quickly. While you two were getting reacquainted, I had the others preparing to leave. I cannot see your paths once you near Caesarean mountains, which means our assumptions about it are likely correct."

She ushers us aside and gestures to Gray, standing near the door, "Gray. If you could please."

Gray pushes off the wall and stalks to the center of the road.

Vates steps up closer to me, "You'll have to enter the mountains; how you manage to do that, I leave up to you."

Surprise rifles through me as Gray tosses me a wink before shifting into his dragon form. As his body morphs, he adjusts his footing, and I swallow nervously as the earth around us trembles.

Holy shit.

We're going to ride him?

Glancing around at nearby buildings to see if any debris has fallen from the tremors around us, I hear a loud huff of air. I turn, my gaze colliding with Gray's golden eyes as he watches me with rapt attention.

If I didn't know any better, I'd think he found my reaction amusing. Shaking off my initial anxiety, I stomp past Kieran to grab one of the bags on the ground before moving to Gray's side.

My gaze travels up his front leg to his shoulder, standing at least five feet above my head.

How the hell did I ever crawl on his back?

Another huff of air snaps me from my trance, and I glare in his direction. Slinging the bag onto his large torso, I silently thank the gods as it settles in the center of his shoulders, hooking around a spike.

I survey his front leg with trepidation. The spikes on it are too high to climb up, so I slowly move down his side. Mindlessly tracing my fingers along his wing, I freeze when his entire body visibly shudders before glancing at Kieran.

"Is he okay?" I ask, blinking in confusion as both Kieran and Val chuckle.

Thankfully, Darian answers, "He's fine, Sunshine. You just... tickled him a bit." He fights back a laugh of his own.

Frowning, I look at Gray once more, realization setting in as he stares at me with his once slit pupils now dilated wide as he huffs, shaking his head and long neck in annoyance.

"Right, avoid the wings. Got it," I say, getting his message loud and clear as I approach his hind leg, where the spikes are at eye level.

Using them as leverage, I pull myself up his body, crawling to sit between his enormous wings. The others climb on Gray's back one at a time, and the realization sets in that we're about to be airborne soon, bringing a heady mix of anxiety with it.

Gray shudders again, his entire body trembling, and I freeze in place, noticing my thumb on the connection where his wing meets his body.

In an attempt to self-soothe my anxiety, what usually would be my skin was inadvertently Gray's wing once again.

"Fuck. I'm so sorry," I retract my hands to my body as if I'd just burned them, "I've never flown like this before. I'm just really nervous."

Val chuckles behind me as he climbs onto Gray, "I'm really sure he doesn't mind, Eiara," he drawls teasingly, and my cheeks flush in embarrassment.

"Don't worry, Eiara. Gray will be cautious. Barring any unforeseen circumstances, the skies should be clear. Dragons don't typically have any predators above them on the food chain." Zayne says softly, sitting beside me.

Swallowing my anxieties, they melt away further as Kieran sits in front of me, Val takes a spot to my left, and Darian sits close behind me.

Wasting no time now that we're settled, Gray's large form takes earth-shaking steps down the wide road, spreading his wings on either side before launching himself into the air masterfully.

Gravity pulls me further into Gray's back as we take off south, each beat of his wings working us higher into the air, and slowly the city of Nomentum becomes no more than a small, distant cluster of buildings.

My stomach turns over repeatedly as the wind whips against my face.

Now I understand why people wear goggles in wind tunnels and skydiving.

The air gradually thins as we reach an altitude where we can avoid being immediately noticed while still managing to breathe. Gray's wings extend on each side as he coasts along the wind, allowing it to carry us to our destination, occasionally beating to keep altitude.

The wind lashes against my skin, and my hair flicks across my face, but without the initial fear and anxieties of flying, the feeling is rather freeing.

Gathering some courage I didn't know I had, I peer between each of the men beside me, trying to catch a glimpse of Servilia from a dragon's-eye view.

On our right, the desolate forest around Nomentum stretches for miles below us until, finally, lush green colors scatter the ground, thickening the further away from Nomentum we get.

The contrast is a painful reminder of what is at stake if we fail to stop Samira.

Gray banks hard, keeping the mountain ranges to our left as he soars through the air. A river comes into view in the distance, and Zayne's hand on mine snags my attention as he leans toward my ear, sending shivers down my spine.

"It might be hard to see, but over there is Marcellus," he says, leaning to the side and pointing to his right.

Off in the distance, I can barely make out a group of buildings that must be Marcellus, with towering trees on either side. Memories from our stay there flood back, and I can only hope everyone we met has stayed safe so far.

It's not long before we reach the coast, and my anxieties begin anew as the solid ground beneath us disappears into a blur of blue, and we coast over the vast ocean.

I hardly realize the extent of my nervousness until Darian hooks his arm around my waist, holding me to him tightly as his lips brush against my ear.

"Easy, Sunshine. We're safe with Gray." His warm breath sends shivers down my spine, and I nod lightly.

Thankfully, he doesn't loosen his grip on my waist until we reach the coast again, and my nerves settle, knowing we're nearly over solid ground.

Though at this height -regardless of what's beneath us- if we fall, we die. I notice Zayne staring off to the left and follow his gaze to a crossroads city in the distance, hardly visible against the sea of forest that encircles it. A golden hue catches my eye, and the realization hits me that that must be where Cato died as my chest tightens.

My hand slides beneath his, and he automatically lifts his palm as I weave our fingers together, giving them a slight squeeze. Zayne's violet gaze is shadowed as his eyes slide to mine, and I know there's nothing I can do to erase the past.

But the past is gone.

Those ghosts are simply there to remind us how we can do better.

Be better.

We cannot dwell on the events that led us here; all we can do is ensure a better future for those who remain.

My heart clenches at the sadness in his features, and Darian's hand on my waist tightens before he kisses my shoulder tenderly.

It's hard to imagine what kind of future we may have after this, but it starts with us stopping Samira so that there is a future for us at all.

We follow the winding river, and Gray descends, using the towering trees on either side of us as cover. It isn't long before we veer to the side of the river bed, which has towering mountain ranges in the distance.

My heart pounds frantically as the familiarity of the peaks brings flashes of dream-weaving to Caspian into my mind.

We're coming, monster.

Gray's large wings beat against our momentum, slowing us to a near stop before his feet collide with solid ground, and the trees around us shake at the movement. The movement tremors everything around us, and I swallow audibly.

Anyone in close vicinity would know we're here now. One at a time, we ease ourselves off Gray's back and onto solid ground before he shifts. His giant body morphs, and his dark, webbed wings and tail meld into his body as the iridescent scales lighten into the color of his skin.

It takes mere seconds for him to return to his other form, standing tall and bare before all of us, and this riverside area seems much larger without his imposing dragon form filling it.

Realizing that I'm staring at him, I avert my eyes as my cheeks warm, and Kieran passes him fresh clothes before my attention turns to Darian.

"I thought we were entering the mountain?"

Securing his sword to his side, Darian nods once, "There is a cave system nearby at the base of this mountain," he says, pointing to a large snow-capped mountain not far away, "We'll enter through there and hopefully remain undetected for as long as possible."

A mixture of apprehension and excitement builds in me as I secure my short sword to my hip.

My nervousness only builds as we lift our hoods over our heads and step into the woods toward the mountain.

Hope you're ready, Caspian.

Chapter 44

Eiara

It doesn't take long for us to reach the mouth of the caverns Darian spoke about as the sun peaks, with the quiet forest at our back.

The darkness inside is eerie and almost seems to expand as we peer inwards. My heart thumps steadily in my chest, but something has my nerves fraying as we step closer and closer.

Knowing we're approaching one of Samira's main bases without any clue about what awaits us is likely the main contributing factor to the clamminess of my palms, the sweat slicking down my spine, and the blood that rages in my ears.

It doesn't help that I've been overthinking every way things could go wrong with each passing moment.

What if we find her here?

What if she's nowhere to be found at all?

What if something worse than Samira awaits us?

What if Caspian's tether isn't here either?

I shake my head against the numerous hypothetical scenarios that flutter through my mind unbidden.

Nothing good will come from being more anxious than prepared.

My eyes track the movement as Zayne and Val lead us into the seemingly empty cavern. The musty air thickens with each step until it's oppressive and only worsens as we venture deeper.

A putrid scent invades my senses with each inhale. The acrid smell turns my stomach, like meat left in a hot garbage bin for far too long because you missed trash day for ten weeks. My stomach flips as I swallow against the bile rising in my throat.

Finally, I cover my mouth with a cloth that hardly muffles the smell, if only a little bit.

"What is that?" I ask, squeezing the cloth against my mouth and nose.

"Rot." Val says, his face pinched in disgust, "I'm assuming it's carcasses by the scent."

The stench becomes nearly unbearable as we close in on the source—a heap of decaying bodies lies on the side of the tunnel as if tossed onto one another like the remnants of a meal.

It's like a bad train wreck that you want to look away from but can't, at least not until I'm staring into what used to be an eye socket, with half of a blue-hazed eye remaining and various tiny insects eating them.

My next step makes a squishing sound, and I glance down to the pool of thick ooze around my foot, following the trail to the bodies as my stomach flips.

Bile springs up my throat once more, and I nearly gag as I quickly step to higher ground, pushing forward to escape the gut-twisting smell as fast as possible.

In front of us, metal sings into the air as Val unsheathes his sword, and my pulse hikes when Zayne's scythe materializes in his hand, blending into the cave's shadows.

I squint against the dark, hardly illuminated by the low light behind us, keeping my hand pressed firmly to my face against the invasive smell.

It starts as a low skittering in the distance. The sound gets louder as it echoes towards us, and dread pools in my stomach. The abyss of dark before us feels as if it extends infinitely as each second passes, and I slowly draw my sword at the exact moment that Kieran, Darian, and Gray do.

That's when the skittering becomes more prominent, and only once they're mere feet away they come into view. Two large insect-like creatures the size of a horse come barreling toward us out of the shadows, their giant beady eyes fixed on Val and Zayne as they scurry closer.

Zayne strikes first, his scythe slicing the head off one of the creatures just as a loud crack sounds out, and Val's sword cuts into the body of the second beast.

As both of them crumple to the ground with their legs still twitching, stillness returns to the putrid air around us, and relief floods my veins.

Please don't let them be hive creatures.

"This place is—" Darian starts with a grimace.

"Yeah," Val agrees, using his sword to prod the lifeless creature on the ground. "We should go just in case there are more of them."

My heart thumps steadily in my chest as Gray keeps a flicker of fire in his palm, and we slowly move deeper into the cave system.

"What were those things?" I ask, choking on pungent air with my next breath. It's thankfully gotten better as we've gotten farther, but every now and then, it still manages to make me gag.

"I'm not sure," Kieran says, "I've never seen them before, though admittedly, I haven't made a habit of venturing into caves, never mind the ones in the mountains."

Gray twists to look at Kieran, raising his brow at him, which results in a half-scoff, half-laugh from Zayne.

Kieran rolls his eyes, "Well, the time spent caged by whatever magic Samira used on me doesn't count."

We fall silent as we continue deeper into the cave for what feels like an hour. Val and Zayne guide us through the winding darkness until the area around us expands wide. We find ourselves at the entrance of a larger cave, but its actual size is unknown beyond the expanding darkness.

The faint outline of pillars against the shadows are barely visible as Val holds his hand up, halting us.

"Something's not—" he whispers before more skittering sounds out again.

It echoes above, beside, and behind us before sounding out over our heads again.

Each of us tracks the sounds, heads turning in the direction and peering into the darkness as it draws nearer.

"It's crawling along the walls," Darian growls, holding his sword higher as he tracks the movement.

Within seconds, a giant insect more than twice the size of the last ones leaps toward us, landing on its eight giant spider-like legs. It lurches in our direction, but before we can do anything, a burst of red and white flame sears past where we stand.

The flames spout from Gray's hands, and the creature jerks backward before the flames reach it.

For being such a large creature, it moves fast, and even the surprise attack only delays the beast for a moment before it lunges at Darian once more.

As the light from Gray's flames dissipates, movement in my peripherals catches my attention, and I twist to face it.

"There's another one coming," I say, lifting my sword. "Kieran!"

He quickly evades the attack while Zayne and I are already in motion, driving our weapons into the beast's torso. The tip of my sword pierces the hard outer surface of the creature's body with a crunch before it buries into the softer flesh beneath.

The creature releases a loud, shrill cry. Its legs begin to thrash frantically, and I just manage to withdraw my sword as it twists abruptly and collapses.

One of the long legs crashes into me, knocking me away from the group as I collapse to the ground and roll to a stop, ignoring the throbbing pain as I quickly scramble to push to my feet.

Getting caught unaware right now would be very, very bad news.

Turning toward the others, Darian finishes the creature in front of him, and I only have seconds' notice as I hear the movement directly above my head.

Without thinking, I act on impulse and instinct, diving to the side as another beast comes crashing down where I stood moments before. I roll along the cold, hard cave floor before scrambling to my feet, desperate to put space between myself and the massive creature as my heart thrashes wildly in my chest.

Suddenly, on either side of me, a burst of water surges forward in the shape of two long spears, and they impale either side of the creature's body with a loud crack. The attack sends the beast into a frenzy, squirming and flailing as Zayne decapitates it with one swift slice of his weapon.

The enormous head falls to the ground with a sickening crunch before the rest of the body falls with it, and an intoxicating mix of relief and adrenaline pumps steadily through my veins as I catch my breath.

That was close.

Way too damn close.

I push to my feet, listening intently for any sign of danger as I return to the group.

"I never want to see another one of those things again," I mutter as Kieran and Val nod in agreement.

"We need to conserve our magic, so only use it if absolutely necessary," Zayne says softly, glancing at Gray and Kieran.

Val and Zayne lead the way once again, expertly finding the tunnel that leads deeper into the mountain. We stay quiet as we listen for more of those bug-like creatures, but thankfully, after walking for what feels like an eternity without running into any more beasts.

It's quiet until my stomach growls loudly into the stillness around us, and Val snickers.

"We should eat. If we don't get food in her, we're just as likely to perish at her hands as we are to those things down here," Val teases, reaching into his bag as I stick my tongue out at him, which only results in a heartier laugh.

He hands over some dried fruit and bread before we continue through the tunnels at a slow pace.

Thankfully, our journey goes eerily well.

We don't run into any more of those beasts, and I nearly start to hope for smooth sailing when my foot presses to the ground with my next step, and a click sounds out into the air.

I look up, and within a fraction of a second, Zayne has teleported to me. At that exact moment, Gray grasps my shoulder, and Zayne teleports the three of us a few feet away. The momentum of our sudden evasion sends me hurtling backward, and we collide against the cave wall.

Zayne's weight presses me further into Gray's chest, with his arm wrapped around my collar as he holds my back against him. Being the center of this man-wich is nearly forgotten as my gaze falls upon the spear jutting out from the ground.

I was nearly impaled.

My pulse rages, and blood roars in my ears as I realize how close of a call that was.

Booby traps?

"That was..." I begin to say, but Gray finishes the sentence with his warm breath skating over my ear.

"Far too close for comfort."

There's no malice or annoyance in his tone, only pure relief.

Though, I'd be a fool to think his relief is that I'm alive rather than knowing that Darian came that close to death without being the target.

Zayne extricates himself first, offering a hand to steady me on my feet as Gray straightens. We return cautiously to the others who -to their credit- haven't moved an inch from where they were.

"I recommend we walk in one or two lines and do our best to follow in each other's footsteps," Zayne says softly. "Eiara, Gray, you're behind me. Darian, Kieran, you're behind Val."

Zayne's calculating gaze lingers on me as everyone nods in agreement.

Is he looking at me because I need more protection or because I nearly got Darian killed accidentally?

I guess perhaps it's both.

Or maybe I'm just overthinking it.

The tunnel finally ascends as we push forward, cautiously following each other's steps. Without the sun to tell how much daylight is left, it's hard to know how long we've been venturing through the tunnels, but judging by how exhausted my body is, I can confidently say it's been hours.

We pause in the broader part of the tunnel, with Val and Zayne scouting the area for more traps before settling down for much-needed rest.

"I'll take watch," Zayne says, glancing down either side of the corridor, "Get some rest, and we can continue in a few hours."

"No," Darian's baritone voice echoes as everyone's head turns to him, "You haven't rested since Nomentum. You rest. I will keep watch."

They lock eyes for a moment, and I nearly think they'll argue, but Zayne inclines his head before settling down next to me.

He leans his head against the cave wall, sliding his eyes shut.

After a long moment, his eyes snap open, darting toward every sound.

He won't be able to rest the way he is, and I sigh deeply. Leaning against the cave wall, I gently wrap my fingers around his forearm.

His gaze flicks to me as I pull on his arm, and he half-leans toward me, expecting me to whisper to him.

"Lay down," I instruct, rolling my eyes when his brows furrow in confusion. "Zayne, please."

He searches my face before reluctantly complying, and I guide him to lie on his back with his head resting on my thighs. His body relaxes against me. The tension in his shoulders and neck melts away as I slowly run my fingers along his scalp, using the tips of my nails to keep his focus with each stroke.

Within minutes, his breathing evens out as he falls asleep. Leaning my head back against the wall once more, I also manage to fall asleep.

I'm uncertain how much time has passed when Darian quietly wakes everyone. His large hand cups my cheek as he pulls me from my slumber. As my eyes adjust to the dark once more, my chest tightens when Zayne is still fast asleep with his head in my lap.

Darian's mismatched gaze slides to him, and even in with the minimal light from Gray's magic, I can make out the softness in his features before he glances back at me with a thankful smile.

I would do anything for that look of peace on all their faces.

My hand gently grazes Zayne's shoulder, and his eyes snap open, looking brighter even against the tunnel's darkness as he sits up.

He pushes to his feet, extending a hand to help me up as he whispers, "Thank you, Eiara."

"No thanks needed. You deserved the rest," I whisper as my fingers slide into his palm, and he eases me to my feet.

He steps forward, crowding me against the cavern wall, and my entire body flushes as he searches my face. Even in the shadows, I can see the violet of his eyes as they search my face, and he leans in.

As his forehead brushes against mine, my heart races fast enough that I'm confident it could explode from my chest.

Hell, with how close he is, I'm positive he can feel my heartbeat himself as he leans in.

"This world does not deserve you," he whispers against my lips before closing the distance. His kiss ignites like gasoline in my veins, and as his hands cup my face, Val clears his throat.

Zayne pauses at the sound, his lips still lightly brushing mine as his lips twitch, and he retreats a step, leaving me breathless.

"That's one hell of a way to say thank you," Kieran says teasingly. "How come I never get thank you's like that?"

Darian laughs under his breath, and Gray responds, "I can thank you like that if you'd like," he says, grinning wildly as Kieran puts his hands up in surrender.

"No, no. On second thought, I think I'm alright, actually," Kieran says, shaking his head with a nervous laugh.

Val flashes a grin from the shadows, and we reform our two lines to continue through the tunnels. With one foot in front of the other, our pace is not fast by any means, but certainly quicker than before resting.

"Any guesses on what we'll find at the end of this tunnel?" Kieran whispers, and Gray laughs behind me.

"If we're lucky, we'll find Samira," Darian's response is grim, and I can't say I disagree with him.

Although, the pit of dread at the bottom of my stomach has me worried that we'll find something much worse than Samira.

"Yeah, maybe lucky if we find her already dead," Val whispers as he takes another step forward. A click sounds out into the air, and my heart drops as the floor beneath him opens up.

As Val plummets into the gaping hole, Darian lunges toward him. Val's hand finds purchase on the ledge of stone that hadn't shifted from the trap as the rest of his body dangles.

My heart gallops in my chest, and the seconds it takes for Darian to reach Val's hand feels like they've stretched into minutes as he wraps his hand around Val's wrist.

Within a moment, Kieran is next to them as they work to hoist Val onto the solid ground once more, and we all gaze in shock at the giant hole in the ground. The three of them look at one another before pushing to their feet.

Val nervously leans over the ledge to get a better look, "That was another close one."

Part of me wants to yell at him for even getting close to it after what just happened, but after my own experience with the booby traps, I can't say much.

"I wonder what's at the bottom," Kieran says thoughtfully before shaking his head, "Actually, scratch that. After seeing those creatures earlier, maybe I don't want to know."

With my nerves on edge, my heart thumps steadily as we ease further down the tunnel until carved stone archways decorate the tunnel up ahead, and relief washes over me like a warm blanket.

The semblance of craftsmanship with sconces along the walls cast an eerie, flickering glow in the distance as we quiet our footsteps.

We've just begun to navigate the dimly lit halls when footsteps halt us in place, and my heart leaps into my throat. My blood rages as what looks to be a formation of soldiers paces the long hallway in sync.

My foot catches on a loose stone, which hurtles against the wall with a loud crack.

Oh, fuck.

They suddenly stop simultaneously, and my heart stutters in my chest. An ominous silence takes over, and dread settles in my gut.

My worst fears are confirmed when they turn in our direction, shouting as they notice our presence.

"Shit," Val says under his breath, "If they don't stop, the whole mountain will know we're coming."

Within the blink of an eye, Zayne and Val rush toward the group of guards with their weapons drawn, and my feet carry me forward without a second thought.

Whoever said that death is slow has never seen a battle with these men.

Val and Zayne make quick work of the first two soldiers they reach before Darian surges past them. With one graceful movement, his sword decapitates a third soldier. Rhythmic footsteps in the distance create a pool of dread in my stomach.

Reinforcements.

Countless soldiers come around the corner as Val takes the right side, with Zayne on the left and a handful of guards covered in black garb break through the doorway, sprinting toward us.

My heart thunders as a man hurtles toward me with his weapon raised overhead. With nerves frayed from adrenaline as his weapon drops toward my head, and I narrowly avoid it before countering with a strike of my own.

The tip of my blade buries into the weak point in his meager armor under his arm, and my hands tremble as I thrust it deeper. Crimson pours from the wound as I withdraw my sword, flinching as a flash of movement at my side catches my eye.

Gray's sword is the only thing stopping the heavy mace of another soldier that otherwise would have collided with my skull.

Shit.

He thrusts the length of his sword toward the soldier, forcing him backward before landing a kick to the man's body, and the soldier lands with a thud.

Gray's molten lava gaze slides to mine, lingering for a moment before he turns his attention to the man again.

He steps forward, and drives his sword into his chest forcefully.

Holy fuck.

I shouldn't be attracted to this.

We throw ourselves into the fray once again as more soldiers begin to trickle in, many of whom are quickly disposed of as we continue to fight our way through the halls.

With each man we strike down, it's as if the next soldier to take their place is larger, stronger, and more brutally skilled than the last.

After what feels like an eternity of constant fighting, three monstrous soldiers enter the hall from a nearby doorway and charge directly at us.

The brutes go after Gray, Darian, and Zayne as Kieran, Val, and I work to clear more of the lower-skilled soldiers.

Between slashes, I manage to keep Gray, Darian, and Zayne in my peripherals, watching in dreaded anticipation as the brutes swing giant clubs with black spikes that each of the men masterfully dodges.

The urge to want to shield them is overwhelming, but I refrain from it.

Who knows how much of my strength will be needed for Caspian's tether.

I don't even know if I'll be strong enough.

I'll have to be.

A soldier shrieks as he runs at me with his sword held high. I manage to evade the swing of his sword, slashing his torso open as he staggers a few steps before collapsing to the ground in a bloody mess.

Without another enemy near, I pause to catch my breath.

My attention turns to Gray as a spike of the brute's club grazes his cheek, and Gray grins for a moment before panic fills his eyes.

The next few seconds play out in slow motion as Gray falls to his knees, and his sword drops to the ground with a clatter.

My body moves without thinking, and I'm fuelled by pure instinct as the brute winds up another heavy swing aimed directly in line with Gray's head.

With no time to spare, I place myself between the brute and Gray.

It takes all my strength to deflect the blow to the side, and I use my momentum to slice through the gap in the soldier's armor at his wrist.

With the tendons in his wrist severed, the mace drops the short distance to the ground with a reverberating thud, the metal against stone grinding in my ears.

The bitter taste of rage lingers on my tongue as I swirl my sword in my palm once before driving it through the soldier's eye socket.

The brute falls to the ground with a thud, grasping at his head before going limp in a pool of his own blood.

Chapter 45

Eiara

My relief is short-lived when more footsteps sound off in the halls nearby.

Is there no end to their numbers?

How many soldiers did Samira raise for her army?

My gaze falls to Gray, still lying on the ground as Kieran kneels at his side, his face filled with panic. He holds his trembling hand over Gray's chest, looking over his body.

"Guys, we need help here."

The last two brutes fall lifelessly to the ground as Darian and Zayne move closer, and the thunderous footsteps of reinforcements draw near. Val downs one soldier that comes through a nearby doorway, then two, and Kieran's hands shake as they cover Gray's legs.

He begins to assess the damage, and his brows pinch together as he focuses, ignoring the chaos around us.

As Val fends off the handful of soldiers in the hall, more continue to pour in, and I watch Darian and Zayne position themselves alongside Val to hold back the incoming horde.

Darian adjusts his grip on his sword, and his knuckles turn white, "Figure it out, just do it quickly. We'll hold them off."

Kieran's hands move to Gray's stomach and chest before he shakes his head, "I don't understand."

Gray's eyes are wide, darting around frantically as he looks beside me and into my eyes.

He repeats the action, and again.

He's not looking, he's pointing.

Without a second thought, I turn quickly, my grip on my sword tightening in case of any attack, but relief washes over me when there's no one there except the brute's severed hand.

"What are you pointing to?" The words hardly leave my lips before the realization hits me.

The mace.

Pointing at the mace, I turn to Kieran with my pulse roaring in my ears, competing with the chaos of the battle around me.

"Could the mace have caused paralysis?"

My voice is hardly audible over the clash of metal in the air, and panic begins to set in as more soldiers push through the doorway. I tear my eyes from them, trusting the others to keep the horde at bay.

Kieran's movements are just as frantic as his voice now as he combs over Gray's injuries.

"Yes, if there was a toxin. That's it, Eiara! Look for a cut or a scrape of some sort."

I don't need more than a second.

The memory is fresh in my mind as I point towards his face, "There, on his cheek."

Kieran moves quickly, placing his hands over the shallow cut along Gray's cheekbone. A long moment passes before Kieran's brows furrow deeply, and he pulls his hands back.

"My magic isn't able to isolate the toxins in his blood. Eiara, can you try?"

My anxiety skyrockets as he guides my hands over the wound. He expects me to be able to do something?

How can I possibly help when he's unable to?

I shift closer, placing my unsteady hands over his cheek, and call forth my magic. The noxious mixture of nerves and adrenalin coursing through my veins, combined with the overwhelming surge of power filling my limbs, has my hands trembling like leaves in the wind.

The panicked voice in the back of my mind reminds me of what's at stake if I don't keep my magic reigned in, adding a new sense of worry to my already burdened mind.

But I can't bring myself to consider that possibility, even if it exists.

There is no choice here but to succeed.

For me, for Darian, for Gray. For our entire group.

I won't fail them.

I won't fail him.

Not now.

Gray's eyes widen as my power surges, and ribbons of light swirl around my arms as I manage to contain it. My magic seeps into the cut within his cheek and traces along his veins, but I don't detect anything out of the normal.

There has to be something.

Anything.

My power stretches across his limbs like a web of light beneath his skin until it covers his entire body. After scanning through him for a minute, I'm about to give up when I feel it.

It's everywhere.

Tiny, miniscule tendrils of dark magic so small they could be easily missed assault his system all over, rendering him paralyzed.

Relief sweeps over me as I suffocate the countless microscopic echoes of dark power within him while using my magic to mend the scratch on his cheek.

Finally, confident that the darkness is gone, I withdraw my hands and cut off the supply of my magic.

My body weighs heavy as my power fades, and I search Gray's face for any change.

His neck muscles tense, and a long moment passes before he blinks, turning his head slightly toward me.

"Thank the gods," Kieran's relieved voice trembles, and I hear his sword rattle beside me.

Gray's golden eyes are wild as he looks at me, his features a mixture of reverence and surprise, "Not the gods, just one."

In my peripherals, Val thrusts his sword through a soldier's stomach, his movements slower than usual as sweat drips down his brow. "A little help over here?"

Gray sits up, and our eyes lock for a moment.

Whatever once stood between Gray and me has disappeared entirely as my heart thunders.

His wild, dark hair shifts as his head tilts toward the others, and he grins at me.

"I bet I can kill more of them than you can."

My fingers find the cool leather-wrapped metal hilt of my sword as the weariness of using my magic settles in, and a smile tugs at my lips.

"We'll see about that."

After what feels like an hour of battle while slowly descending the long, winding tunnel, we finally put down the last reinforcements before entering a large room with vaulted ceilings.

Strange crimson markings adorn the walls, sending a troubling shiver down my spine. They look like ancient runes of some forgotten language that just spells bad news for anyone they're the target of.

The room is ominous, and my gaze falls upon the center, where a single symbol is drawn. In the center is an altar coated in such a deep shade of red that it's nearly black.

It's blood.

Bile rises in my throat as the area pulsates with dark energy as if alerted to our presence, telling me without a shadow of a doubt that this is precisely where we need to be.

The magic emanating from the altar is volatile.

When Zayne goes to step forward, I put my hand out, instinctively shielding him with my magic as dark energy rushes forward, crashing into the shield and forcing him back.

The sheer magnitude of the attack against my shield is enough to make me swallow, "I will do this."

"Eiara," Zayne's voice has an edge of warning to it, "Do not push yourself."

I shake my head.

We've come this far; this may be our only chance to free Caspian. I can't fail here.

I won't.

Resolve and determination settle into my very being, and I take a tentative step forward, shielding myself against the surge of energy emanating from the altar.

The force of it staggers me back a step, and I hear Val curse under his breath behind me.

Darian's reassuring voice fills the air, "You're doing just fine, Sunshine. One step at a time."

My pulse rages in my ears as I step forward once more. The blast of dark energy sends me back to where I started, and I grit my teeth.

I'm just expending energy uselessly.

There's no way I'll be able to get close.

"Use that beautiful mind of yours, Goddess!"

I blink, my frustration forgotten, and turn to look at Gray, who's grinning from ear to ear.

Stepping forward again, the burst of energy thrusts me backward.

There's that definition of insanity again.

Change the approach, change the results.

The realization hits me like a tonne of bricks, and I suddenly allow more of my magic to flow through me, channeling more and more of it until the entire room is a cacophony of chaotic light and dark energies.

Sending my magic to the room's edges, I create a bubble encircling the dark aura before gradually shrinking its size.

With each inch I gain, the altar contained within pulsates erratically, surging violently against my control. Each forceful blow of dark energy is like containing the damage of a bomb, as sweat forms on my temple.

My next steps forward are more sure, more certain, knowing that the real fight is yet to come as I slowly approach the altar.

By the time I reach the top of the altar, my gaze falls on a stone bowl filled with a red viscous substance that leaves a metallic tang to the air around it, and I can only assume its blood.

This is it.

Everything inside my body is screaming, like some innate part of my being tells the rest of me to pour all I have into the altar to expel the sinister magic within it.

Unable and unwilling to delay any longer, I open myself even further. There's no longer a door within me for my power to come through, but rather, my entire body is an open passage.

Without the bottleneck effect hampering the flow of magic, I channel it directly into the bowl as the room brightens. My nerves have been set afire, searing pain throughout my body as the darkness resists, surging in response and rioting against the pressure as I squeeze my magic against it.

My chest heaves as my power suffocates the darkness until it finally collapses into itself. Suddenly, the altar cracks to the floor before a rush of air surges outward, forcing me back a step as I brace against it.

Panic begins to set in when nothing but my power circles the room, radiating from every part of my body and creating streams of light that churn chaotically.

I can't cut myself off from the source.

Oh my god.

I could kill everyone.

A powerful surge of unbridled energy forces me to my knees, and I brace against the altar as the corners of my vision begin to turn white.

"Contain it, Eiara." Zayne's voice cuts through the raging in my ears, and I look around frantically for the source.

It feels like there's a cord inside of me that's the only thing not burning, not in pain, not complete agony, and I hold onto it like a lifeline.

Some part of me knows it's the only thing that will save me, keep me grounded, and stop me from destroying everything I hold dear.

When I finally spot him, I can't help the whimper of relief that escapes my throat. His magic surrounds his body in a swirl of smoke, whipping against the streams of chaotic light that crash against him as he moves closer toward me.

"I can't control it. I don't know how."

My words come out strangled, and my magic surges painfully once more, the pressure in my chest building now that it doesn't have an outlet. "Yes, you do." His voice is steady, and his movements are purposeful as he steps alongside me.

Our magic dances alongside one another as he grasps my arm, pulling me into his chest, and the cord I'd held onto desperately keeping me grounded tightens.

I know it's him.

My magic surges once more, and his arms wrap around me, squeezing me closer to him.

"You opened yourself to it and knew how to do that. You can shut it off. You simply need to believe that you can." His breath skates over the skin of my cheek as he pulls back to look at me, and as I search his intense violet gaze with my vision beginning to dim, I focus all my attention on my magic.

It swirls once more, and the pressure within me reaches the tipping point as I frantically let his words soak in.

I can do this.

I'm in control.

This is my power.

*It answers to **me**.*

Starting with my head and feet, I narrow the flow of power within my body almost as if pulling a curtain over my skin, restricting the magic from that entry point. Tentative relief washes over me as the power coursing into my body slows. The pressure of it threatens to open the entryway, pushing against the meager veil I've created.

Finally, the last sliver closes off, and the pressure within my chest dissipates, leaving only relief and exhaustion in its wake.

Thank the gods.

My vision blurs and tears stream down my face as I look up at Zayne's violet eyes before glancing at Gray, Darian, Val, and Kieran. Each of them has a look of tentative relief as I laugh, with more tears leaking from my eyes.

"We did it." Glancing at the cracked altar, which no longer has any hint of dark magic tied to it, my throat tightens.

"You did it, Eiara," Zayne squeezes me tightly into his chest and leans his forehead against my hair.

The relief radiating from each of them is palpable, and it bleeds into my own as tears spring to my eyes anew.

Darian kneels beside us, running his fingers through my hair before embracing us tightly.

"You did it, Sunshine."

My chest tightens as he kisses the top of my head at the same moment that Zayne does the same to my cheek.

"Not to interrupt, but we should really get out of here," Val quickly steps up alongside Darian with Gray and Kieran, "I'm picking up a lot of movement, and I don't think we want to be here when they realize what we've done."

Zayne cradles me against him as he stands, and I welcome the rest as Kieran, Val, and Gray huddle in closer.

With the exhaustion radiating through my bones right now, I don't think I could move if I wanted to.

"Come," Darian says, placing his hand on Zayne's shoulder before glancing at the others. "I'll teleport us to the river."

As the world around us blurs, Zayne squeezes me tightly as if I'm about to fall apart in his arms until the area becomes focused again.

I guess I can't say I blame him after what just happened.

Gray quickly shifts into his dragon form, lowering his shoulder to let Zayne climb on top more easily as he carries me. He settles me in his lap, and I lazily glide my finger along Gray's wing where it connects to his shoulder, earning a full-bodied shudder.

"You could have leaned down for me earlier, ya know."

My tease earns an amused huff of air from Gray as the others settle in alongside us.

Chapter 46

Caspian

Hundreds of soldiers file onto the boats not far in the distance, headed to Maximillia to lay siege on the city.

My feet carry me forward of their own volition down the crowded road as a handful of men scurry out of my way.

I shouldn't be here.

Hell, I shouldn't even be aware of where 'here' is right now.

Thank fuck I am because otherwise, I wouldn't have known what Samira's plan was.

Not that I can do anything to stop her.

No.

Maximillia will fall unless a fucking miracle happens.

That city was done for the moment Samira knew what artifact they had uncovered. The wind blows hard, the bitter chill of the ocean biting into my skin as I turn the corner toward the docks.

That's when I feel it.

My footsteps slow to an uneasy stop, and I frown, lifting my palms as my hands shake.

This can't be possible.

I take another hesitant step.

A noxious mixture of surprise, relief, and confusion rifling through me as the physical drive that propelled me forward is gone.

This body that has been my cage for so long is now... free.

A nervous excitement tremors through my veins as I glance around, blinking as if seeing from my eyes for the first time in centuries.

For the first time in centuries, I'm fucking free.

Samira's soldiers continue to board the ships, and cold, hard reality sets in as two winged beasts screech overhead. Their large wings beat loudly as they surge towards Caesarea at breakneck speeds.

Some soldiers pause their idle chatter as I take another few steps to the docks.

Samira's army doesn't know what's going to hit them.

With my sword at my hip, my footsteps feel more sure and confident than ever.

I get halfway down the dock when the realization hits me.

If I'm free, that means Lara's at Caesarea.

Fuck.

My gaze scans the thousands of soldiers boarding the ship in front me before scanning the handful of boats already on the horizon.

Staying on this ship could save the entire city of Maximillia.

I'm losing precious time.

Turning quickly, I sprint in the other direction as fast as my legs carry me.

Fuck the army, and fuck the city.

I won't lose her.

Chapter 47

Eiara

The earth rumbles as Gray beats his enormous wings, launching us into the air and giving me some semblance of relief as we gain distance from the cave.

Glancing around at each of my companions, it's clear that we only just made it out. Each of them breathes hard, with blood, dirt, and various other substances caked onto their hair and skin, also marred with bruises, minor cuts, and scrapes.

We're lucky to be so fortunate.

Sucking in a deep breath, I have to fight the urge to keep my eyes closed, my body desperate to recover from my excessive use of magic.

Gray keeps low to the trees, his wings nearly touching their tips as a shrill roar in the distance jolts me in Zayne's arms.

My heart thunders as I scan the horizon ahead of us, "What was that?"

I glance at Darian, whose mismatched gaze is already scanning the direction of the roar, and he shakes his head. "I don't know."

Kieran points in the opposite direction from where we're all looking, "What in the gods' names is that?"

On the horizon, flying toward us is an enormous red-scaled creature with four horned heads and enough teeth to tear us all to shreds in a second. Its vast wings pick up tempo as it gains on us, and the serpentine beast lets out another roar that sends a cold note of dread into my bones.

Another roar sounds out much closer, and my head snaps in its direction only to find another one of the creatures flying straight for us at break-neck speeds.

Val's grip on Gray's spiked scales tightens until his knuckles turn white, "Gray, we're gonna need evasive maneuvers."

The giant beast inches closer, and my heart is pounding so hard that I'm sure it will rattle out of my chest as Gray's wings beat fast. The wind whips at my face as he tilts his wings from side to side, nearly missing the creature's teeth as it snaps at his wings.

The second beast dives at us, and Gray just narrowly turns, avoiding what would have been a direct blow to his left wing. Gravity squeezes us against Gray's back until he straightens out, and Zayne eases me out of his arms.

"We need to split them up," Zayne's violet eyes slide to mine, and I feel the weight of that decision as if it were my own.

The last thing we want is to split up right now, but he's right.

Gray can't evade both of these beasts.

We brace against another evasive turn, and as we level out, Darian looks at Zayne, "You go with Kieran and Val. With your combined strength, you should be able to take one down. We'll circle the area, and whoever downs theirs first wins." he grins, but there's almost no humor behind it, and we all brace against a turn as Gray just narrowly avoids another attack.

"Go, now!" Darian's command hangs in the air as Zayne grabs Val and Kieran, smoke engulfing them as they teleport out.

I'm torn between looking for them and watching the giant creatures as a spear of water strikes the wing of one beast, capturing its attention as it veers off.

Gray suddenly bellows, the sound vibrating through his body below us as Darian's arm secures around my waist, holding us to Gray's back as he tucks his wings and rolls in the air.

My head spins, and my stomach flips as the world circles.

By the time we straighten out, I don't know up from down as my vision spins on its own. When my vision settles, I turn quickly to find the second beast banking as it continues to chase us.

Darian pushes to his feet, looking more comfortable than expected to be ready to fight on top of a flying dragon.

He sends spears and ice bullets at the creature, who surprisingly evades the attacks. Gray evades another bite from one of the heads and turns slowly to avoid straying too far from the others.

As a commotion in the distance of smoke and water catches my attention, I can't help but feel useless.

I don't have any attacks I can use to help Darian and the others, but as the beast snaps once more at Gray's wing, I watch in horror.

The jagged teeth are seconds from closing on the sensitive flesh of his wing, and my heart stutters.

No. No!

My magic surges through me once more, and although I'm nearly at my end, I manage to shield his wing just enough as the creature's teeth close onto it.

My shield shimmers against the bite before a tooth breaks off, and it jerks back with a sudden shriek as my magic bottoms out.

The next few moments feel as if they happen in slow motion, as Gray's body jolts upwards, followed by a blood-curdling screech from him that I feel like a dagger in my own heart.

Darian's voice sounds out behind me, mirroring my sheer panic and terror, "Gray!"

Working against gravity, I twist toward the sound, only to see a different creature with Gray by the throat. Its black, razor-sharp teeth draw blood through Gray's thick black scales as he releases another screech.

That's when our momentum shifts, and Gray lowers his body to the tree line. The trees pelt the creature against his enormous chest as he tries desperately to free himself.

Crimson sprays into the air from the wound as Darian dives forward with his sword in hand to get to the beast still lodged in Gray's throat.

At that very moment, the other winged creature swipes again at Gray's wing, and somehow, he still manages to avoid it.

The evasion costs us as a tree collides with Gray's other wing, folding it with a sickening crunch before Darian and I are thrown from his back into the air above the trees.

A moment of weightlessness takes over before gravity works again, and I'm hurdling dangerously through the top of the forest line. The small branches whip painfully against my body, and I do everything I can to grasp them and slow my descent.

I drop lower into the forest, and my momentum is stuttered as a thick branch collides with my rib cage, forcing the air from my desperate lungs.

Finally, still more than twenty feet from the ground, I grasp the branch of a large tree as it creaks against my weight and the speed of my fall. The inside of my hands and arms scrape painfully against it as I hold on for dear life.

I don't give myself time to think.

If I do that, the pain will follow, and I'm not out of danger yet.

So I don't think I just move.

I gulp down quick, shallow breaths. Adrenaline and shock take over as another roar close by sounds out into the forest. Everything in me screams in protest as I ease myself down the length of the tree.

Each breath and movement as I climb down radiates pain throughout my limbs and torso, but I finally reach solid ground. The sob of relief and pain gets caught in my throat as another roar echoes nearby, sounding closer than the last, and instinct sends me into overdrive as I limp through the forest.

I don't get very far as trees behind me crack, and I turn to see the four-headed, winged creature breaking entire trees as they groan and collapse to the side under the weight of its body as it triumphantly eases itself to the ground.

Dread, like ice-cold water, coats my veins as I meet its gaze. It stalks closer as the ground tremors and uses its weight to knock another tree to the side as the roots are upended with it.

I suppress the whimper in my throat as it nears, my eyes darting to each of its heads, snapping at the air as it sniffs with streams of saliva dropping to the ground.

My head feels light, and it's a struggle to remain standing as I clutch my ribs, still sucking in short breaths into my oxygen-starved lungs.

The creature roars again, taking a step closer as another of its heads snaps at me, and I jerk backward to avoid the bite as I fall to the ground.

Pain radiates through my heavy arms as I scurry another few inches back, but my arms threaten to give out.

This is it.

Staring into the endless rows of teeth before me, I have no choice but to accept my fate.

My body is broken.

My magic is drained.

I can only hope the others managed to make it out safely, and I shut my eyes, praying that my death, and Darian's are quick.

A moment passes, and when nothing happens, my eyes snap open to see a figure before me. The smoke dissipating around him is Zayne's, but his shorter, jet-black hair and long sword in his hands make my heart stutter in my chest.

"Caspian?"

The creature rears back with another roar before lunging at him, and he surges forward. He brings his sword across its giant-scaled body, slicing the beast's chest open, and it staggers back with a screech.

My vision blurs as he teleports onto its shoulders, and in a quick sequence of moves, he decapitates each head before landing on the ground. The body shudders before collapsing with a thud, sending tremors through the forest around us.

Holy shit.

The efficiency with which he just brought the giant creature down is terrifying, especially if I was unsuccessful in freeing him from Samira's control.

He still looks like the cold, calculating, and indifferent Caspian as he secures his sword at his hip before taking a step closer.

His emerald eyes meet mine, and he hesitates, as if unsure whether to come any closer.

"How," my voice cracks, and I suck in another shallow breath, "How did you find me?"

My chest tightens as his gaze softens, "You ask that as though I ever lost you."

I swallow against the lump in my throat as his eyes trail my body, "You look like shit, Lara."

My laugh comes out strangled as pain radiates from my more-than-likely broken ribs.

"Fuck," he glances back the way I came, "Let's get you to the others."

He steps closer, gingerly placing his arms beneath me and cradling me to his chest. His touch is more gentle than ever before, and I'm thrown back to that cabin in the woods when he carried me out the door.

Things are different now, though.

That feels like it was an entirely different life I had led.

Yet the gentle nature of his touch at this moment is one and the same.

Something in this moment, some part of me, even knowing his history, capabilities, and past...

Somehow, I know I'm safe with him.

Perhaps that's the most surprising revelation of all.

Exhausted, I lean my head into him. Surprise rifles through me at my weaved ball magic deep within him, still curled protectively around the center of his chest.

Smoke swirls around him, and I frown. "You still have Zayne's power?"

His emerald gaze slides to meet mine, and the muscle works in his jaw.

"She—" he starts but catches himself, "Samira always ensured I had a vial of his blood. When I was free of her influence, I used it and came straight here."

The smoke engulfs us as the world blurs, and we reappear amidst broken trees with Gray's limp human form on the ground.

"No, no. No!"

Anxiety builds in my chest as I squirm in Caspian's arms, ignoring the agony radiating through my body, "No, this can't be happening."

He steps closer to Gray, and I stop struggling as much.

"Easy, little one. He is breathing, and though he needs a healer, I'm sure he will live."

Caspian sets me down alongside Gray's body and turns him over to face us. My meager attempts to assist in rolling him over send radiating pain through my torso, and I wince as I place my hands over his chest.

My pulse rages as I feel Caspian's gaze burning on me, and I try to summon my magic forth. Even picturing the doors flying open sends a burst through my body before it fizzles out, and my breath hitches.

My hands tremble over Gray's bloody and torn skin as desperation tightens my throat.

"It's no use," my voice is no more than a whisper as I glance at Caspian.

"But you, you could." I place my wrist between us, "Use my magic and heal him."

Caspian looks at me with eyes as wide as saucers as I gesture my wrist between us again.

"You can't be serious," he presses the back of his hand on my forehead, "You don't have a fever, but your actions clearly indicate you are unwell." "Caspian, I'm serious. I cannot summon my magic to heal him, and his neck is still bleeding. It hasn't stopped. Please." my voice cracks as I glance once more at Gray's blood-soaked body.

His jaw clenches as he glances around apprehensively.

"I do not want to do this, Lara." His voice wavers as he locks eyes with me, and I can see the resignation on his face as he holds my gaze. "But if you wish."

His touch is gentle as he takes my battered arm in his hands and lifts it to his lips. My heart threatens to beat out of my chest as he holds my gaze, and I wince when his sharp canine tooth reopens my wrist wound.

His lips encircle my wrist, covering the small area as he drinks me in. The sensation is odd but not unwelcome.

It's a dull, burning feeling that radiates from the movement as he swallows my blood.

It feels oddly intimate, but I can't look away as his throat bobs with each gulp.

A moment later, he pulls away from my wrist, and his eyes burn bright as his hand covers the small incision and the skin stitches together.

Before I know what's happening, his hand glides over my ribs, and I cry out as something snaps painfully back into place.

"Gray," I gasp, waving Caspian off dismissively as if it would ease the pain, "Heal Gray, please." Caspian pauses, glancing in the distance before hovering his hands over Gray's neck. His brows furrow in concentration as the gaping holes in Gray's neck slowly begin to close, and his breathing evens out.

After a long minute, Caspian straightens his back, sweat beading down his temples as he shakes his head. "That's about as much as I can do, little one."

Footsteps sound out behind us just before the sound of steel rings into the air, and pain shoots through my body as we both twist in the direction of the sound.

At the edge of the treeline, Darian stares at us both with wide eyes and a clear expression of alarm.

It dawns on me that between my battered state, the blood on Caspian's mouth, and Gray being unconscious after multiple creatures they've never seen before attack us, this doesn't look good.

His mismatched gaze flicks between us, and his eyes darken. "Caspian, get away from her. You've done enough."

Darian raises the tip of his sword toward his brother, and Caspian sighs. He goes to step aside, but my arm shoots out, grasping his wrist as he stops abruptly.

He looks at me in surprise before glancing at Darian with a shrug.

"Darian, Caspian saved me and has now saved Gray. He's the reason we're still alive." I can only hope he realizes the double meaning behind my words as his eyes shift between us and he sheathes his sword.

"This doesn't mean it's over," his lethally calm voice says as he stalks over to us and kneels between Gray and me.

My hands tremble, and I wring them together anxiously, "We need to find the others, assuming they're better off than we are."

"Not before we find you first," Val grins.

Zayne's smoke slowly dissipates as they take a few steps closer. Kieran glances between Caspian and Darian, and he clears his throat.

"Is there going to be an issue?" Zayne asks quietly, clearly noticing the tension in the air.

"No," Darian, Caspian, and I answer simultaneously.

"Great," Val's voice is thick with amusement as he tosses me a knowing grin, "So what do we do now?"

Kieran steps closer toward us, "I'll heal Gray." He stops when I shake my head, "No need, Caspian already healed him."

Sighing, I push to my feet, "I doubt we're safe here, so we need to get somewhere to rest up before we head back to Nomentum."

I sway unsteadily as my knees threaten to buckle beneath my weight. My head feels light, and exhaustion has settled deep in my bones.

If I could just rest my head...

Caspian places a supportive hand on my elbow, and I toss him a grateful smile.

"We could go to Aveentia," Kieran suggests, "It's not far from here."

Caspian shakes his head, "I wouldn't recommend it; Samira controls Aveentia and has a host of soldiers there for now." his gaze drops to the ground, "I was there when her control over me was broken."

"Right," I say, feeling increasingly lightheaded, "Aveentia is off the table then. Where else could we go?"

Concern paints across Kieran's features as he looks at me, "We could go to Trebonia, though it is farther north. Unless that is under Samira's control as well."

Caspian shakes his head, "Trebonia is a rebel city to Samira. They killed all the guards who refused to turn against her. They're allies."

Zayne steps closer as I sway again, "Then it's settled. We join the rebels."

Arms encircle my body as Zayne lifts me into his chest, and I've never been so relieved to be off of my feet as my head melts into him.

His lips press against my hair, "Rest, Eiara."

My eyes slide shut as the world begins to fade, and I finally succumb to the exhaustion.

Chapter 48

Caspian

I watch as Zayne scoops Lara's limp form into his arms before I let relief finally wash over me.

I've never been so fucking terrified as the moment I teleported in to see that creature seconds away from killing her.

A few seconds later, and she'd be dead.

I was that fucking close to losing her forever.

My eyes track the movement as Zayne settles her against his chest. I know she's safe with him, but fuck if every fiber of my being wants to be close to her right now.

Sudden movement in the corner of my eye catches me off guard as a fist collides with my cheek, and my head snaps to the side.

I should have seen this one coming.

I manage to dodge the second fist as Darian's face contorts into rage.

"You piece of shit. Do you think you can just swoop in, and everything is forgiven? Like the last two hundred and sixty years didn't happen?"

His jaw ticks as he lunges forward to grab my collar...

And I let him.

He grips my clothes tightly and searches my face, his features incredulous.

"You think that just because you came in at the eleventh hour, it would be water under the bridge?" he seethes, and my blood pressure rises.

He's angry that I showed up?

The notion is nearly laughable.

I scoff, "Would you have rather she died?" I'm unable to mask my own emotions as the anger leaks out into my voice, "Because where were you when she was staring down the gullet of a beast with her broken body?"

Darian's face flashes and that's the only warning I get before his fist collides with my cheek again.

"You think that changes everything?" He gets one last strike in before Zayne's smoke wraps around his recoiled arm, and he struggles against it.

A metallic taste fills my mouth, mixing with the taste of Lara's, and I turn to spit my blood on the ground, leveling him with a deadpan stare.

"I wonder what you would have done, what you would have become, had you been in my shoes, brother. Suppose your body worked and moved of its own volition when the subject of its command is nearby. If your very being was used against your will, would you have become the righteous King you are today or a monster like me?"

The muscle in his jaw feathers and the vein on his temple pulsates, telling me all I need to know.

"You may not trust me, Darian. Hell, I hardly blame you. But there is one person we both wish to survive this above all else and if that isn't enough for you to stomach me, then you might as well kill me now, brother. Because, like it or not, I am not letting her out of my sight, and I would kill all of you if it meant keeping her alive."

He leans in, his hair grazing my skin as he searches my eyes, "Are you telling me that I should just forget it all because you saved Lara once? Do you even know what happened to her while she was 'under your protection' in foster care?"

In the corner of my eye, Val crosses his arms.

I didn't know.

I fucking hate that I didn't know.

As much as I paid Claire, she was only tied to telling me about the keys or anything that could be one. She didn't say shit about what happened, and I had to fucking learn about it from Lara herself.

Tamara didn't tell me shit, probably because she didn't trust me and thought I was behind all of it.

Darian's grip on my collar tightens, and his mouth twitches in anger as he searches my face.

"Everything you can possibly imagine that shouldn't be done to a child was done to her, Caspian. And now you suddenly care? She was whipped, beaten, raped, starved."

Valerian's voice chimes out, "Burned."

A shiver of guilt creeps up my spine, but I stand firm, "Frank Mores paid the price for what he did to her."

Darian scoffs, "Yeah, by what? Killing him-"

"He's not dead."

He frowns at me, and I click my teeth.

"He's alive, surprisingly. My men have starved him, dehydrated him, burned him, cut him, whipped him, electrocuted him, and nearly drowned him. I thought his heart would have given out by now, and maybe by now it has, but before I left, my men had spent over a month making him regret his actions."

Surprise flashes across his features, and Zayne's dark magic releases his limbs as he steps back.

"It was more than just Frank, Caspian. It was every fucking foster family she had."

My eyes widen, and I search his face for any hint of lies.

"Every—?"

"Yes."

My teeth grind together, and I ignore the pain from Darian's punches as I avert my gaze.

He must realize that knowledge is enough as he takes another step back, "I still do not forgive you."

I nod once, still absorbing the information and mentally filing through the names of every fucking foster family Lara had.

"I wouldn't believe you if you said you did, nor do I deserve it."

My gaze shifts to each of them before landing on Lara's limp form, and the bitter taste of guilt ripples through me as I consider the years of trauma she endured.

Zayne shifts Lara in his arms as Kieran heals her, "We should get going. I'd hate to be caught out by more of these creatures while Eiara and Gray are unconscious."

Darian nods, glancing at the others, "Let's go then."

~

We walk for a full day and a half before we finally come across a small town with enough toryians for each of us. I've kept to myself most of the journey, scanning the trees for any sign of danger, but thankfully, there's been none.

Thank fuck, too, because judging by the exhaustion on everyone's faces, they just barely made it out of this alive, and while they might be able to lend a hand, keeping them alive for Lara's sake would fall mainly in my hands.

And I wasn't lying when I said I would kill them all to save her.

The small community of homes and shops is tucked into a hidden glade, and surprisingly, as we approach the first few buildings, the town has mostly remained untouched by Samira's corruption.

The civilians here watch curiously as we file into the stables while Val grabs food from the nearby farmhouse. Darian holds the first toryian's reins, and I glance around for the saddles, spotting them along the wall near the entrance.

By the time I make it there, I'm face to face with a middle-aged Servilian who stares at me with wide eyes. The panic in them is typical of what I usually see, so it doesn't surprise me when he staggers back a step, his chest heaving as the wild look on his face grows more animated.

I sigh deeply.

Here we go.

His face twists into anger, and he hurls his fist forward, shouting incoherently as my hand snatches his arm midair. He cries out in surprise as I twist his arm behind his back painfully.

The move is reminiscent of how Lara pinned me at the house that one night after her nightmare, so much so that I can't help but laugh under my breath.

Distracted, hands grab my shoulders and pull me away from the man roughly as he gasps in pain, his arm hanging limp at his side.

Oh.

I broke his arm.

Darian glares at me before calling Kieran to heal the man, and my eyes roll.

It's not my fault he made a stupid decision.

Grabbing the saddle, I place it atop a black toryian to the side, and it eyes me warily before I hoist myself onto its back. Like a magnet, I track the movement as Zayne pulls Lara onto his mount, shifting it closer to mine as he tosses me a cloak before tugging one over himself.

I guess that's one way to solve the public's reaction to me.

The others return from helping Darian and Kieran settle things down before lifting Gray onto a toryian as Kieran settles in behind his prone body.

Darian casts me a long look before guiding his mount alongside Val's. The two pull themselves onto their toryians before we finally leave the lingering gazes of the townspeople behind.

As night falls and the first moon rises, we veer off the road into the nearby trees to finally get some rest. I'm tying my reins to a low-hanging branch as Val shifts, his dark fur blending into the forest's shadows as he patrols the area.

Surprisingly, I'm relieved they decided to rest.

I'd rather not be the primary fucking defense if we get attacked.

As Darian approaches them, I watch Kieran and Zayne settle beside Lara and Gray.

Darian's voice is quiet as he rests his hand on Kieran's shoulder, "How long do you think they'll be out?"

Kieran shakes his head, "Could be days, could be weeks. It's hard to say."

Zayne murmurs something, and I'm too far away to hear, so rather than joining the conversation, I move deeper into the trees.

I'd be surprised if Lara didn't wake up in the next day or two, but it's hard to say how much energy she expended releasing me from Samira's grasp without knowing her limits.

Released. Free. Unbound.

The words feel foreign.

All thanks to the actions of the unconscious goddess not far away.

Incredible.

A crest of moonlight illuminates a tree not far away, and I move closer before taking a seat against its trunk.

I never thought I'd see the day when my will is my own.

The crunch of footsteps sounds out against the stillness before his scent reaches me, and Darian stops once he reaches my side. He squats down awkwardly, relaxing his back against the tree, and my gaze slides to him.

He's staring into the treetops, but his expression clearly indicates something is weighing on him.

Honestly, I couldn't care less.

As long as he doesn't throw another fucking punch.

"I've been thinking..." he says quietly, and I nearly roll my eyes.

"Glad to hear the rightful King has the capacity to do so. Is this a new development?"

He sighs and ignores my jab. "What you said about not controlling your own body. Was it the entire time?" he asks, his gaze flicking closer but not fully to mine, as if he can't bring himself to make eye contact.

I know what he's asking.

He wants to know if it was my idea, my will, my desire to kill our parents.

He wants to know if I'm truly the monster everyone already thinks and knows I am.

"Not the entire time," my voice is low, and his gaze flicks to mine. "But that night, I was not in control."

His eyes widen before he looks into the forest again, and I resign myself to letting him in on the details.

I owe him that much, at least.

"When I nearly killed Cade that once, Samira tested my ability to temporarily take others' forms with their magic. When that proved successful, she created this plan to take the throne, and up until that day, to my knowledge, it was a plan that didn't involve killing them."

Darian's hands flex beside me, but he says nothing.

"That morning, she handed me a vial of someone's blood. I didn't know who at the time, but she told me to drink it and use it to get into the castle. She had specifically stated, 'Murder your parents, Caspian. Kill the King and Queen, and take down anyone who stands in your way.' which left no room for avoiding the command. It was like a bad dream, and when it was done, you walked in..."

My hands ball into fists, "I didn't know it at the time, but it was Lara's friend Tamara's power that she had given me."

Darian's head snaps to the side as he looks at me wide-eyed.

"Yeah, I know. Her magic literally makes her disappear into thin air, and had I kept her power any longer, I might have killed you, too."

"That's why you bit me first," a mixture of shock and disbelief paints his features as his brows pinch together, "but how did you control that?"

I laugh dryly, "It came down to timing and sheer fucking luck, in all honesty. You weren't considered 'in the way' until I was nearly drained of Tamara's power. Had you struck any sooner, we may not even be having this conversation."

He drags a hand down his face, "Fuck."

After a long pause, letting him absorb the reality of that day until I finally break the silence.

"This doesn't change anything, though, brother."

He frowns at me, the question clear in his expression.

"I'm still very much a monster."

Chapter 49

Eiara

I'm faintly aware of the swaying movement of a toryian beneath me and a pair of strong arms wrapped around my body. As my eyes open, I squint painfully against the light invading my senses as I stretch my stiff limbs.

The arms around me tighten, and Val's hair tickles my nose as he kisses the top of my head.

"I was starting to wonder if you'd ever wake up." Although I can't see him, the smile on his face is evident from his tone, and I yawn, rolling my stiff shoulders to loosen them as they crack loudly.

"How long was I out?"

"Two and a half days," Zayne answers quietly from the toryian beside us, and I twist to look at him, my brows pinching together.

"You're joking." My eyes flick to his piercing violet gaze, "None of you thought to wake me?"

He simply shakes his head, "You needed the rest, Eiara. You expended more energy and power than ever before. It is a surprise that you've recovered enough to be awake this quickly as it is. By all rights, the amount of power it took to free Caspian and survive the battle afterward, any normal Servilian would have taken weeks to recover."

He pauses as Caspian's voice cuts in, "But she is not any normal Servilian. She is the daughter of two gods and a goddess by all rights."

My heart stutters as I turn in the direction of his voice.

He's here.

As my gaze meets his, an odd mix of relief and excitement rifles through me.

The way he emphasizes the term 'goddess' makes heat rise to my cheeks at the acknowledgment. Although we all know the truth, hearing him say it out loud in such a serious way, with no room for argument, makes my stomach flip.

Caspian's emerald gaze burns into mine for another long moment before he inclines his head respectively, and it's only when our eyes break apart that I notice the healing bruises on his face.

Bruises that weren't there when I fell asleep.

I frown, glancing at the others, including Gray's limp form in front of Kieran. "What happened to you?"

"We had a disagreement," Darian says, snagging my attention as I note the bruises on his face and knuckles, "Of sorts."

His lips twitch when I raise an eyebrow at him.

I sigh deeply, rubbing my temples at the headache behind my eyes. "Men..."

Val laughs, and I feel it rumble in his chest as Kieran joins in.

I glance down the road as it bends out of sight, "So, how far are we?"

"We're roughly a half day's ride from Trebonia."

Zayne's voice wavers, snagging my attention, but his face remains unreadable as he scans the treeline.

I frown, following his line of sight without any answer.

It doesn't take me long to understand what's causing him distress as the town where we met with Cato comes into view. The top of the tall hylia ilvrost stands like a sentinel in the center of the crossroad, with its branches hanging over the surrounding buildings.

Memories of that night wash over me like a bitter note of sadness, and I know it's hardly a fraction of what Zayne feels. No amount of reassuring words will ever make him feel better about it.

No, only time will.

As we get closer, there's movement between the buildings which has Darian and Caspian pulling their hoods over their heads. Seconds later, a small girl peers at us from the side of a house before disappearing around the corner.

Usually, this wouldn't worry me, but given the history of this town and how we left it...

Unease settles in my stomach, whether due to the memory of what happened here or nervousness, I do not know.

My gaze trails up the length of the golden tree, "I wish we had flowers."

Kieran steers his toryian closer as we near the center of the town, "Why flowers?"

"On Earth, it is customary for families to bring flowers to the resting places of loved ones to mourn their loss or honor their lives."

Kieran rubs his chin thoughtfully, "I see. We don't have that custom, but we do celebrations of life for those who have passed on."

Our toryians stop at the foot of the tree, and I have to tilt my head back, leaning it fully onto Val's chest to look up at its imposing form above us.

I feel him lean in as his lips brush my ear, "What kind of flowers would you usually bring if we were on Earth?"

"Personally, I love white lilies and roses."

"Here." He places his palm upright alongside mine as a vine encircles his arm before twisting into my hand. One vine becomes two, then four, and soon, a whole bouquet of roses and lilies emerges.

The petals bloom as I bring my second hand up to support their weight with my eyes wide as his magic dissipates and the vines crumble to dust before falling to the ground.

The lilies are just how I remember. Pristine white petals that remind me of a star in the night sky, and the roses are deep red, creating a beautiful contrast. As I survey the roses, I notice they have no thorns, and my chest tightens.

Glancing up at Val with emotions thick in my throat, he gives me a sad, knowing smile from before pressing a tender kiss to my temple.

His voice is low as his thumbs rub my forearms soothingly, "I remember what happened the last time you fought with a rose bush."

We both chuckle, "I totally won."

His chest rumbles as a boyish grin creeps across his face, "Is that what that was?" He eases off the toryian and helps me down, gently setting me on my feet.

I know, like a sixth sense, that he's staying close as I approach the base of the tree, clutching the bouquet to my chest.

Each step I take is cautious as I avoid the large roots jutting from the ground in all directions. Feeling another presence at my side, I pause as Zayne joins us, his face shadowed as he gazes at the base of the tree.

My chest tightens, and I carefully split the bundle of flowers into two, offering him half as he blinks at me.

His confusion bleeds into understanding as he gently takes the bouquet between us. I can see the hesitation, nervousness, and grief in his eyes, so I slide my free arm around his, guiding him closer a few steps.

Being this close to him, his sadness is a living, breathing thing. The regret is nearly overwhelming as tears spring to my eyes.

My breath hitches as I slide to my knees, resting the bouquet at the base as Zayne sets his alongside mine.

I don't miss the trembling in his hand as he places it down, and while I don't trust my voice at this moment, my hand slides into his palm as our fingers lace together.

"I wish I could make amends to them all," his voice is soft, though my heart wrenches in my chest as he continues, "Perhaps in another life, I may."

My gaze slides to his, and a tear falls down my cheek as he tracks the movement, "You have nothing to make amends for. Samira is responsible and will have to answer for their deaths, not you."

He inclines his head once.

I can only hope my words sink in as he stands and looks around, surprise flashing across his face as he does. Following his gaze as I push to my feet, seeing a crowd of people peer at our group curiously, but the majority have their wide eyes on Val.

The young girl steps toward us from a nearby house, looking anxious as she looks up at him with a finger pointed at the flowers, "Can I have one?"

Val kneels at eye level with her and tilts his head as she pulls her hands to her chest, "Which kind would you like?"

He summons his magic on either side of him to create one lily and one rose, and she excitedly points to the rose.

Val grins, "Or, do you want a whole bush of them to take care of?" Her eyes widen, and she jumps up and down in excitement, "A whole bush?"

Val laughs under his breath and presses his palm to the ground. A handful of vines breach the surface, and before our eyes, a vibrant display of green and red encircles the tree, leaving a small barren area to approach the base where the bouquets were laid.

He ruffles her hair with his hand, and she giggles, "Do you think you can keep them in good shape while I'm gone?"

She nods eagerly, and a woman standing behind her, who I presume to be the girl's mother, glances at each of us.

"Who are you people?"

Val glances at Darian, who subtly shakes his head.

"We're traveling mercenaries for hire." Val offers her a charming smile that sends even my heart fluttering in my chest, but she doesn't look like she's taking the bait.

A frown creases on her forehead as she scrutinizes us, and I decide to speak up before she can press further.

"Is it true that Trebonia is rebelling against the queen?"

My diversion seems to have worked, as her attention turns to me, and she assesses me for a moment before she answers.

"That's right. We all came from Trebonia to see family who lived here, but when we arrived, our families were no longer there, and instead, we found this." She gestures to the tree, and my heart squeezes painfully.

Bile rises in my throat at the memory of the bodies littering the ground. I nod once in response, and my voice comes out in a whisper as I fight against the lump in my throat.

"We are heading to Trebonia. We only stopped to pay respects."

She scoffs, "Pay respects to whom? The gods?" She laughs, pointing to the tree, "The gods are the ones responsible for this mess and aren't worthy of our respect." She crosses her arms, and the muscle in Val's jaw feathers as another woman in the crowd steps forward.

"Yeah, if the gods cared, they'd be here. They'd be helping!"

As others murmur in agreement, my father's words about intervening echo in my mind, and I can't help the guilt I feel at their inability to help with the mess they created by bringing Samira into their home.

That said, in the same breath, there's no way they could have known she would have been responsible for all of this...

Someone in the crowd angrily raises their fist, "I say we chop down this tree and be done with 'em."

Before I can say or do anything, Caspian slides off his toryian in one swift movement. His hood falls back as he stalks toward them with a lethal glint in his eyes.

"Is that...?" A woman in the back asks, her shrill voice wavering as heads turn in Caspian's direction.

Kieran adjusts the reins in his hands from where he sits on top of his toryian, "Oh boy."

The crowd takes back a healthy step from Caspian, and their eyes widen with a mixture of fear and confusion.

The hostility in the air rises around us, and Val glances at the crowd, "D..."

"Enough, Caspian," Darian's baritone voice rings out, and to my surprise, Caspian stops abruptly. His head tilts back to look at Darian with a raised brow.

"You would allow them to disrespect her so openly?" His emerald eyes burn bright with rage as he surveys the crowd before turning his attention back to Darian.

Her?

He's upset at their disrespect of... me?

My pulse hikes up as heat rises to my cheeks.

"Their frustrations are sound, brother, but yes, they are misplaced. They do not know who is to blame, nor do they understand who they insult."

The crossroads has gone deathly silent, and Darian's calm voice echoes through the still air as all eyes have turned to him.

He sighs deeply before removing his hood, "We did not mean to cause strife by paying respect to those who fell when this town was attacked. We will be on our way shortly." He scans the faces of the people, murmuring to one another, "I suggest you make your way to Trebonia as well. It is not safe here."

A collection of voices speak up at once, some demanding to understand why Caspian is here and not answering for his crimes, some begging for Darian to help the cities fight back against the queen, and others just yelling his name to get his attention.

Zayne moves ever so slightly to my side, angling himself protectively between me and the crowd as Caspian stalks towards me.

He stops, and my head tilts to look at him as he reaches between us, holding his palm up.

I blink in confusion but slide my hand gently into his.

Surprise flickers across his features as soon as our hands touch but vanishes when he glances at Zayne. His hand curls around mine, and he wordlessly scans the crowd as he turns, bringing me with him while the commotion around us grows louder.

Nearing the mount, I hesitate when he doesn't move to lift me up but instead raises our connected hands slightly as if waiting for me to climb atop the giant creature. Managing to hoist myself up in one swift motion, I silently praise myself as Caspian settles in behind me.

His arms snake around my waist to the reins, and my entire body flushes as the heat of his chest seeps into my back. He eases the toryian into motion, moving closer to where Gray and Kieran are as Darian, Val, and Zayne join us.

The chaotic shouting quiets down as Darian moves past the crowd, and as we slowly gain distance from the crossroads of town, my eyes linger on Gray's body.

"Why hasn't he woken up yet?" My voice is quiet, and although my question gets Kieran's and Zayne's attention, Caspian answers.

His words reverberate in his chest behind me, "His wounds were... extensive. Those creatures have toxins in their saliva, which stops the body's natural healing process, and their prey usually bleed out. He will likely need another few days to recover."

I nod as anxiety builds in my chest. My attempt to focus on the road ahead fails as my brain replays how close we were to losing Gray over and over.

The further down this journey we get, the greater the risk.

We already lost Cade.

I don't think we could stand to lose another.

Lost in my thoughts, a brisk wind picks up and blows locks of hair into my face.

...Eiara...

The wind howls loudly through the trees, and I wonder if I imagined the whisper of my name as I twist from one side to the other, scanning the treeline in confusion.

Caspian's grip on me tightens, "What is it?"

I glance at him with furrowed brows before shaking my head. "Nothing, it was just the wind."

His eyes are clear with concern, but he doesn't press for answers before he scans the treeline cautiously.

I brush it off as nothing when it doesn't happen again, and as we break past the treeline on the road to Trebonia, it's clear that things have changed since we last visited this city.

A horn blows in the distance as I survey the large walls erected around what once was a lively, open-entry town. The smiling families and busy merchants selling wares from their tents are gone.

Various sentry towers scatter along the walls, and I spot at least one archer positioned within each, their arrows trained on us as we cautiously approach the gate.

Darian positions himself at the front, flanked by Val and Zayne, with the rest of us closely behind. We slow to a stop before a large gate, and my hands tremble nervously as I consider the number of attacks we could be vulnerable to.

Will they trust newcomers?

What if they don't recognize Darian or decide to let him in but leave the rest of us behind and shoot us down?

Caspian's arms shift and I glance up at him, finding his emerald eyes already on me, "Easy, little one. They would not be wise to attack the one they are loyal to." His voice is thick with amusement as he adds, "Though, they could certainly try. I doubt they'd get a single arrow through."

A man with short brown hair peers down from atop the gate, scrutinizing each of us. When his gaze lands on Darian, his eyes widen, and he turns to shout something as the arrows that point at us lower.

The large gate creaks as it's pulled open, and Caspian takes my still-trembling hands firmly into his hand while he steers the toryian through the gate.

"See? Nothing to worry about at all."

The inside of the city remains nearly identical to how we left it, minus the presence of Samira's guards patrolling the streets.

We've not gone further than ten feet when the brown-haired man from the gate appears on the side of the road, accompanied by two others at his flank.

They take a couple of steps closer before dropping to their knees with their heads bowed.

I watch with rapt attention as the others on the street quickly follow suit until all around us are the crowns of civilians' heads as they face the ground in respect.

Darian's voice carries as he grins at them, "Rise, my friends. I'm thankful to find you all in good health. Could we trouble you for a room for the night?"

My chest squeezes as they rise with their cheeks glistening, flashing him smiles and laughter as they push to their feet. Darian slides off his toryian as the crowd grows, and I watch as he clasps arms with some, hugging others fondly.

He treats them as you would any brother, sister, mother or father, aunt or uncle after years of being abroad. Caspian dismounts first, holding his hand out to help me slide down the side of the giant creature.

My feet have hardly touched the hard ground when I hear it again.

...Eiara...

I go still.

My entire body is on high alert as the echo sounds out amidst the chattering crowds, and I glance around wildly.

Caspian's concerned features are mere inches from mine as he leans in to search my face.

"Lara? What is—?"

He hardly gets the question out before he's yanked away and shoved against the toryian's leg roughly by a stranger.

I act without thinking, using my leg to sweep under the broad man before gripping his arm with all my strength and using his momentum to throw him to the ground. My free hand moves to the dagger at my hip, and within an instant, I'm kneeling on his chest with the blade angled against his throat.

Pulse raging in my ears, everyone around us has gone silent as I stare down at the broad-shouldered older man as he seethes below me.

"You would defend him?"

As if to emphasize his disgust, he spits a mouthful of saliva at my chest. Movement behind me catches my attention, and I glance behind me to see Caspian restrained by Zayne, and though his advance halts as Zayne whispers to him, the burning rage in his eyes remains.

This isn't going well.

At this rate, Caspian is going to kill them all.

Darian steps forward and reaches a hand down to help me up, "Perhaps you should consider that he was accompanying me and think twice before attempting to assault my brother."

The man goes to argue but stops abruptly as Darian holds his hand up, "Not everything has been as it seems. My brother is not a prisoner, nor is he the one responsible for the death of our parents."

He emphasizes the word 'our' as he crosses his arms, and my heart nearly stops in my chest.

If Caspian didn't kill them, then that means...

My gaze slides to Caspian's, and though guarded, the pain and anger behind them all but confirms it.

Silence hangs heavy in the air as I push to my feet, my steps echoing as I move to stand next to Caspian and Zayne, ignoring the glare from the man still lying on the ground.

A man in the crowd steps forward, his face contorted in anger, "We're to believe that after hundreds of years?"

"Who is responsible, then?" A young woman asks, her voice carrying loudly amidst the others as they all fall quiet.

Darian scans the crowd, and his gaze settles on Caspian as he answers.

"Samira, the false queen."

Chapter 50

Eiara

We finally manage to get to the nearby inn without incident.

Kieran and Zayne are settling Gray into the bed as the rest of us file into the dining area. The tables have been moved together to create one long seating arrangement, and I follow close behind Val, with Caspian at my back as we take a seat.

Various hosts bring filled cups to each of us, setting down trays of bread and fruits in the center of the table as idle chatter fills the air.

Darian takes a long sip of his drink, setting it down as he looks at the brown-haired man at the end of the table. "What happened after we left?"

The man sets his cup down and wipes his mouth with his hand, "The guards were given two choices. Kneel or die. They did not kneel."

I swallow hard, the image of even more needless death bringing bile up my throat. The overarching thought of whether all this death is necessary weighs heavy on my mind.

I wish there were a way just to end it all.

Swift.

Efficient.

Darian graciously changes the subject, "What do we know of the false queen's movements?"

"Aveentia's status is unknown. Sabinia has some civilians within it; while weary, they appear loyal to the crown. Drusilla recently expelled all the false queen's presence from their borders. Nomentum and Marcellus are both allies, which leaves Lavinium as the main base of operations. We received word that there was commotion between Caesarea and Aveentia, but Caesarea remains generally a secondary base of operations for her soldiers."

Darian's knuckles turn white as he grips the handle of his cup, "And what of Maximillia?"

The man shakes his head, but Caspian responds. "Maximillia is under a full-scale assault," he says, and every head at the table turns in his direction.

Every head at the table turns in his direction as the brown-haired man jerks back, "You know this? How?"

Caspian's gaze remains trained on Darian: "When I was freed, and two of those creatures were being sent to kill her," he tilts his head in my direction, "Samira simultaneously was taking a portion of her army to their shores."

The muscle in Darian's jaw works, "What are the odds they survived?"

There's a long pause as Caspian winces, "Maximillia may have held off the initial assault, but I doubt they will last long."

I frown, "What is in Maximillia that she would want?"

The answering silence only furthers the tension in the air as I glance at Darian, and he sighs deeply, leaning back in his chair.

"It is said that there is a weapon buried deep in the frozen wastelands in the north. For centuries, relic hunters and various historians have searched for it to no avail. If she has sent even a fraction of her army there, I can only imagine it has something to do with that."

The brown-haired man raises his hand, with a single finger pointed in the air, as if suddenly remembering something.

"Until recently. The last we heard from Maximillia, one of the scholars there had uncovered a tome that spoke of a relic deep underground beneath the frozen lake. The script spoke of an object with powers of unknown origin."

He pauses, his upper lip curling as if disgusted that he didn't consider what dangers the city was under sooner, "That was the last we heard from Maximillia half a fortnight ago."

Val curses under his breath as the room murmurs to one another nervously.

My gaze falls on Caspian, and I nearly forget my question when he's already looking at me, "What are the chances she could have it in her possession already?"

He holds my gaze for a long moment. "The likelihood of her already having it is slim. Should she have extracted the information from the scholar, she still needs to get past the city in order to get to the lake before she excavates the area."

A woman sitting across from Val turns to look at the brown-haired man, "So we may still have time. Tiul, do we have enough resources to reinforce the city?"

He shakes his head solemnly, "We hardly have the resources to remain here as we are. With crops withering in our farmlands, the traders that have come through have had lackluster wares..." he shakes his head, leaning forward to rest his forearms on the table.

"We will go," Darian's voice rings out, and it feels like every person in the room save our companions holds their breath.

Tiul blinks as he glances at us nervously, "You can't be serious. We can send others to fight, your majesty."

Another woman at the table chimes in, holding her hands to her chest, "You've just returned. Your people need you."

Murmuring in the room gets louder, and his knuckles turn white again, "This is precisely why we will go."

Their mouths snap shut as he turns to Zayne, "Find a ship just large enough for us and a place to make landfall where we can avoid her army if they've taken over the city, but close enough we can lend aid if they haven't."

Zayne nods before his smoke engulfs his form, and he disappears into the darkness.

Darian looks at Kieran and Val next, "We will need Gray for this, so the sooner he is awake, the better." Val and Kieran grin before pushing to their feet and disappearing from the room, leaving just Darian, Caspian, and I.

Tiul wrings his hands together. "Your majesty, I cannot in good conscience let you go head-first into the enemy alone."

He nervously glances between Caspian and me as Darian smirks.

"It's a good thing I'm not alone then."

Darian's gaze shifts to his brother. "We will need food. Val can provide some, but we will need to replenish the meat we're going to take."

Caspian's jaw feathers, but he nods once before leaving out the door, and Darian's mismatched gaze turns to me.

He gives me a pained smile as if torn in his decision, "Go with my brother. As much as I would prefer you to remain with me, we need him, and you are the only one he seems to trust."

My chest tightens as he searches my eyes for a moment before tugging me into him, and I wrap my arms around his body as he encircles my shoulders.

Ignoring everyone else in the room and the handful of eyes that I can feel burning holes in the back of my head, I bury my face into the crook of his neck, breathing in his familiar scent.

Releasing him is almost painful as he leans his forehead against mine for a long moment.

He places a lingering kiss on my lips before I pull away to find Caspian.

It doesn't take me long to spot him when a handful of people stare down the road in the same direction with disapproval on their faces. My pace quickens to a jog as I spot him turning into a shop with the door swinging closed behind him.

I ignore the hushed murmurs as I approach the door, pushing it open to see Caspian only feet away inspecting a bow.

His gaze doesn't leave the bow as he traces the string, "Come to chaperone?"

I scoff, gesturing to the bow, "Clearly, you require adult supervision."

He chuckles at my sarcasm before holding the bow in my direction, "Pull back on the bowstring and test how it feels."

He moves closer as I take it from him, pulling the string to my shoulder with my right hand. The strain is painful in my shoulders and back as I hold it in place before releasing it with a twang.

I release an awkward sigh, "It's good."

Caspian lets out a laugh so genuine that I find myself unable to look away from his smile until he composes himself again.

"If your face wasn't so red, I might have believed that." His lips twitch as he suppresses a smirk, handing me a different bow in place of the one I just tested, "Try this one."

I frown, "Aren't you doing the hunting? Why do I need to test it?"

"If you're coming with me, little one, you're using the opportunity for target practice."

He leaves no room for argument, and I groan, taking the bow in hand and pulling the string taut.

"This one is much easier but still has some snap to it."

Caspian nods in agreement, brings the bow to the counter, and quietly exchanges words with an older-looking man who waves him off.

With bow and arrows in hand, we get to the door, and my brows pinch together, "We don't have to pay for this stuff?"

He shakes his head, "I offered, but he refused payment since these are used for the city's defense and replenishing food stocks."

The moment exit the shop, I'm immediately aware of the countless eyes on us as we turn down the road.

Murmurs trail behind us as we slowly make our way to the city's edge.

"If it bothers you, you do not need to come with me."

I tilt my head, "If what bothers me?"

He glances around at the handful of people watching us as we pass by, "Having defended me earlier, whether intentional or not, and now being seen accompanying me, will cause you to be stained as I am."

Laughing softly, I shake my head, "None of that bothers me. Besides, everyone deserves a second chance."

His expression becomes cold and distant, "Not everyone."

I don't have the heart to ask if he means himself or Samira, and the rest of our journey to the city's edge is quiet, save the sound of our footsteps.

The side door out of the town is heavily guarded, with sentries overlooking the entrance from towers nearby and four armed guards standing watch, two on either side.

They eye us warily as they step aside, allowing us to leave, and their eyes burn into my back as we cross the fields before slipping into the eerie shadows of dusk as night creeps closer.

The light of the first moon peers through the canopy above, with the stillness only broken by our quiet footfalls on the mossy ground. Caspian slows to a stop, scanning the area before pointing to a tree with some lower-hanging branches.

"We'll wait here, facing upwind. There's quite a few tracks passing through here, so this seems as good of a place as any."

I blink, squinting into the dark to try to see the tracks he's referring to. My confusion must be clearly written on my face as he chuckles before moving to the tree.

With the bow hung over my shoulder, I watch as he pulls himself onto the first branch and the moonlight peering through the canopy dances along his skin. My heart stutters as he settles comfortably, and his attention fully turns on me.

Amusement paints his features as he raises his brow, "Do you need help, little one?"

I scoff and step closer. "I could climb this in my sleep." My head tilts as I near the tree.

The branch is a full two feet higher than me, and it's clear that I might need his help.

Not that I would ask for it.

I remove the bow from my shoulder and toss it up a few inches for him to catch, allowing me to focus on climbing rather than snagging on a random branch.

Wringing my hands together, I step away a few paces before sprinting to the tree, using my momentum to run up the trunk.

The tactic works, but I'm not accounting for how well it succeeds, as my head hits the branch unexpectedly, and I lose balance before falling to the ground with a thud.

Caspian's choked laughter breaks the stillness in the air, and I cut him a glare before pushing to my feet.

My second attempt is better, and I manage to get my hands around the branch before losing grip and falling to the ground again.

The amusement is thick in his voice as he fights back another laughing fit, "Are you sure you don't want my help, little one?"

A heady mix of embarrassment and stubborn frustration coats my veins as I shake my head.

"Nope, third time is the charm."

Gods, I hope it is.

I launch toward the tree once more and hurl myself to the branch, hugging my arms around it with a wave of relief. Pulling myself over takes another minute, and I finally settle down on a branch next to Caspian's with a sigh.

I shoot him a triumphant grin, "Told you."

His lips twitch as he holds the bow between us, "Good girl."

And just like that, the smug feeling coursing through my body turns molten. I blink, placing my feet on another nearby branch before scanning the dimly lit forest floor in a meager attempt to clear my mind.

A few minutes of silence pass, and I glance at Caspian, whose gaze is locked in the distance, clearly surveying places I cannot see.

Even in the low moonlight, his high cheekbones and defined jawline stand out as much as his eyes.

I wonder what he's thinking right now.

Is he focused on looking for food?

Does his past ever plague his thoughts, or is he entirely in the present now that he's free?

Would he ever be willing to share what happened, or is he a vault with his traumas like I have been?

Does he remember how it all started, or is it a blank space like Kieran's memory?

Setting aside the influx of questions, I give the forest another lingering once-over. When my gaze slides to Caspian again, my cheeks burn as our eyes meet.

"What is it?"

My heart rattles in my chest as I prepare to reopen old wounds that I have no right to open.

"How did she do it, Caspian?"

I can't bring myself to clarify who or say her name, not when the question is already so deeply personal and tied to so many tragedies.

A long moment of tense silence passes between us, and guilt coats my veins for even asking.

If I were in his shoes, I'd simply shut it down, lock it up, and pretend it never happened.

I swallow against the lump in my throat, "Never mind, I—"

"No," He interrupts me abruptly with a sigh, "I.. If I were to tell anyone this finally, I would only want it to be you. It happened so long ago, and I never thought I'd be free from her to talk about it, so knowing how or when to start is..." He shakes his head and laughs under his breath as if the fact that he's struggling this much is funny to him.

"When Darian and I were young, we were difficult together. I often foolishly acted out because my magic never surfaced, and I saw Darian as the perfect son and brother I could never be. So I decided to go off alone and ran into Dolly in a town just outside of Caesarea. She told me she knew someone who could awaken my magic, and I, being the fool I was, desperate to measure up to my brother... I took the bait. She brought me into the mountains where I met Samira; the rest is history."

He opens his palms and looks into his hands as if they hold the words he's trying to say, "Dolly hadn't even been under Samira's control, and she willingly delivered me on a silver fucking platter. The next thing I knew, I was myself, but any commands she gave me had my body controlled by a force I couldn't see."

He hesitates, his throat bobbing as his hand curls into a fist.

So, his revenge on Dolly was quite literally hundreds of years in the making.

My chest tightens, and I reach over to slide my hand into his with a squeeze. "So, that's why you hunted Dolly all that time... What did you do to her?"

"I did everything I could to inflict the most pain possible before I ended her life." He glances away to the forest floor, and I frown.

Does he think I'm judging him for it?

"Good," His attention snaps to me again as I nod, "She deserved that and much worse."

His lips twitch, "Are you sure you're a goddess?"

I bring my hands to my chest as if wounded, "As sure as I am that you are not."

We both laugh under our breath as a branch snaps in the distance, and my pulse jumps. Caspian points subtly in the direction of the sound, and I squint into the dark, seeing the silhouette of a creature grazing not more than fifty yards away.

Swallowing my nerves and taking a centering breath, I slowly nock an arrow, keeping my movements sure as I pull the bowstring back to my shoulder. The muscles along my arms, shoulder, and back all strain as I take aim and suck in a breath, holding it as my hand releases the arrow.

The string snaps forward, sending the arrow hurtling towards the animal.

A shrill, strangled cry sounds out before a thud, and the stillness that follows tells me that my aim is true as Caspian takes the bow from my hands to sling it across his back.

"Nice shot, little one." My chest swells with pride as he maneuvers off the branch to the ground, and I follow his movements until we reach the downed animal.

Its brown fur is short and curled, with tufts of white giving it a spotted appearance. My arrow protrudes from the middle of its neck, where a trail of orange flows from the wound onto the ground in a puddle.

Caspian appraisingly lifts the creature's large head before gripping its front legs and hoisting it over his shoulders.

My gaze lingers on the orange blood for a moment before I follow him in the direction we came.

"What kind of animal is this?"

"It's called a prelyorin. They're harmless creatures that graze on the bark of trees, various bushes, nuts, and seeds. Their meat is regularly used for stews." He follows my gaze to the blood now covering his hands against his chest and chuckles, "Yes, they bleed orange."

I blink at him in confusion, which only makes him laugh more.

Chapter 51

Eiara

All four moons have peaked in the sky as the side entrance to the city comes into view. I yawn deeply as the long day starts to catch up with me.

Somehow, it hasn't felt like much has happened to warrant this level of exhaustion, but I brush it off.

We step up to the door as the observation holes slide open. Two pairs of eyes gaze out at us before disappearing, and the door groans as the guards grant us entry.

The streets are mostly empty, with raucous laughter erupting from some houses along the way. Caspian hardly gives each house more than a glance, and I can't help it when my chest tightens.

There's a very good chance that he didn't think he'd ever be free to have that kind of experience without the overarching dread of not having control over himself.

We approach a shop with dim lights shining through the window and venture inside. It's a homely shop with dried vegetables and fruits on one side and drying meats on the other, with a door leading to the back where the light is coming from.

Caspian thumps the large carcass onto the table as a shorter woman steps out from the back, wiping her hands with a cloth covered in orange stains before flicking her long, brunette braid behind her shoulder.

Before tonight, I never would have thought that was remnants of blood.

She glances between us, her eyes lingering warily on Caspian before sliding to the creature's body on the table.

She blinks and crosses her arms, "Ah, looking to have that cut up or prepared?"

"It's to replenish inventory. In exchange, we would like to take whatever you have readily available."

She grins, nodding in our direction, "I can do that. Give me a moment." She quickly disappears into the back before I hear cupboards and drawers opening and closing.

It's not long before she reemerges with a large sack over her shoulder, hauling it onto the table in front of us.

"That should be good," she says, rattling off a series of cuts and weights in dried meat.

Caspian nods, taking the large sack from the table and slinging it over his shoulder as he stalks out without so much as a goodbye.

"A man of few words, huh?"

Our gazes meet, and I throw her an awkward smile, "Something like that." I chuckle, giving the woman a small wave before hurrying after him.

When I catch up, another deep yawn crawls out, and Caspian glances at me with his brows pulled together.

"Did you use magic today?" His tone sounds nonchalant, but I don't miss the hint of concern behind it, and I shake my head.

"No. I think I might still be recovering from the other day."

His gaze lingers on me for a long moment, but he doesn't press further. By the time we finally reach the inn, I've let out yet another deep-seated yawn, and all I can think about is resting my head on a soft pillow as we push through the doors.

My gaze hops from Darian, Val, and Kieran as they sit around a table of empty plates. Their conversation comes to a stop as we pause in the doorway. When my gaze lands on Gray, relief washes over me, and I step toward them as my head spins.

...Eiara...

Gray tears his gaze from Caspian to look at me, and my heart rate spikes for a moment, but I know I'm not imagining things when I hear my name whispered again.

...Eiara Ptheron...

The room spins like a bad case of vertigo, and with a light head, I sway unsteadily on my feet.

Caspian's voice sounds muffled as he shouts my name, and it's like my head is underwater as I succumb to the dark.

~

As I struggle to peel my eyelids open, they feel like they weigh ten pounds each, and my mind feels dizzy and disoriented. The dark around me swirls with ribbons of white fog, and I raise my palms, seeing a thin layer of it glide over my skin.

Where am I?

"Ahhh, so good of you to finally join me."

A deep voice jolts me from my thoughts, and I scramble to my feet, twisting to see a tall man in a dark robe standing mere feet away, his white eyes locked onto me.

Everything about him screams bad news, and red flags with loud alarm bells sound off in the back of my mind as I take a tentative step back.

"Who are you?"

The stranger tilts his head as he tracks my movement and sighs deeply, running a large hand through his long brown locks of hair to pull them from his face.

"My name is Kouros. Pleased to finally meet your acquaintance, Eiara."

His imposing form steps forward, and he holds his hand out expectantly between us. I blink at him before looking at his hand, and a mixture of annoyance and frustration coats my veins.

"What do you want?" Kouros tuts as he snatches my hand from my side, holding it between us. He shakes it with a crushing grip, and I grit my teeth.

Who the fuck does this guy think he is?

He squeezes tighter, "The proper way to greet a fellow god is to show respect, Eiara."

Grinding my teeth against the pain, I suppress a breath of relief when he releases my hand, and it drops to my side.

"Though I suppose having been raised amongst those dreadful humans would have taught you a lack of manners and respect for the gods. Disgusting creatures, really."

I roll my eyes, crossing my arms as phantom pain throbs in my hand, "God or not, what the hell do you want with me?"

Anger flashes across his face, but he quickly masks it, and my gut twists.

"To meet the daughter of Sol and Luna, of course. Your parents and I have such a history; I could almost be considered family," he says coolly. "Say, do you know what the customs are on Meloris for gods to pick their mates?"

My brows pinch together, and excitement paints his features as he leans in, "You see, Eiara, gods are not bound by the laws of humans or Servilians. As superior beings, we do what we want, when we want, and who we want. Females choose the males, males mate to the females, and the world continues to go round."

He tilts his head, "Well, fate would have it that, as of recently, there are arguably fewer gods being born on Meloris, which in turn means fewer mates." His lip curls as a maniacal grin creeps across his face.

"I knew the moment you were born that I would get to claim you for my own if you made it to maturity. Though, I wasn't going to make it easy for you. Not just anyone can mate with another god. Now, who would have thought the chosen daughter would have survived all the trials and challenges set on her path and still managed to be strong enough to find her way back to Meloris."

Challenges? Trials?

I step back again and frown, "What the hell are you on about?"

Ignoring my question, he grows more animated as he continues to ramble. "Eiara Ptheron, the infant transported to Earth, only to later find herself in the clutches of some of the worst foster families on the planet. Regretfully, it took some years to find you, but once I did... It's a wonder you made it through those foster families, never mind my masterpiece with that hunter."

What he says next sends a cold note of dread through my body.

"Watching him tie you to that bed as I whispered in his ear from the shadows of all the things he could be capable of if he just managed to take you for himself."

No. No, this can't be possible.
Is he saying he was the one responsible?
He did all of this?

"What? How? Why?"

The questions come out mumbled and full of confusion. My mind can't comprehend why someone would do this to someone they do not know.

He raises his arms toward me as if I'm an award or statue being revealed, and a broad smile spreads across his face.

"Because it was fun, and watching them break you only so you could put yourself back together brought me so much joy! Look how strong it made you!"

I can only stare at him in disbelief as he continues his tirade.

"Although, some of my best work may have been in all the fun with Samira and those pesky royals on Servilia. Convincing the royals to bind their son's magic to keep him from killing their future king, and I'm the only one who can help them do it? Priceless!"

"Then came Samira. Oh, my dearest Samira. Such a troubled child she was. When she found out her father was giving her up, it was not hard to convince her that she was nothing more than a prized beast to bargain with. Never did I expect her to go to these lengths to drain Servilia of its essence."

She's… draining the world of its essence?

He sighs listlessly, his gaze distant as he reminisces through memories. I'm almost afraid to ask, but he seems more than willing to divulge her plans, so I ask anyway.

"Why is she draining Servilia?"

He looks at me with pure excitement, as if this is the best part he's yet to mention, "To become like us, Eiara. To become a god!"

He gestures between us proudly as if we are somehow the same, and I take another healthy step back, nervous that his egotistical rant may be nearing its end.

"And you approve of this?"

He quickly moves closer to clasp my hands within his as he beams.

"Approve, dear child? I endorsed it. I have cultivated it. I gave her the blueprint to breathe the idea into existence and the tools to ensure its success. Little did I know she would drain nearly all the prominent bloodlines in the process!"

I swallow audibly, trying to withdraw my hands, but his grip tightens, and my question comes out in a whisper, "What does any of this have to do with me?"

His face darkens as his smile grows wider, "You, dear child, have a choice to make. You can join me and see this world burn or die."

"I—" I'm interrupted as he releases my hands only to grip my throat tightly.

"Think carefully about your next words," he growls, squeezing painfully to emphasize his threat.

My head starts to spin as I try and fail to gasp for air before he finally relaxes his grip.

I suck in a ragged breath.

I don't know what to do.

But what I do know is that I refuse to be a part of his plan and would rather die here than give in.

Gripping his wrist lightly, I glare defiantly at him, "Go to hell, asshole."

Spitting in his face, I use my defense training to break his hold on my neck, bringing my elbow down before thrusting it into his nose with brutal force.

Satisfaction rifles through me as he staggers back, holding his face with wide eyes.

"I had a feeling it would go this way," he says before suddenly disappearing.

Next thing I know, his hot breath skates over my ear, "Wrong choice."

My reaction is too late as I whirl to face him, and he lands a punch to my stomach, sending me backward several feet as I cough painfully.

With mere seconds to recover, he charges toward me.

His already large form grows more imposing as he throws his fists in a series of attacks, and I somehow manage to dodge them, saying a silent prayer of thanks for my training with Zayne and the others.

He finally lands a punch that catches my jaw, and I tumble to the ground, landing on my back with a thud before he's on me.

With his weight bearing down on my hips, he quickly uses one hand to tug my wrists over my head before the other wraps a hand around my throat.

I'm effectively pinned to the floor, and no matter how I buck or struggle beneath him, I can't break free.

A sickening crunch sounds out above my head, and a guttural scream crawls out my throat as pain radiates from my hand.

He broke my fingers.

He grins with wild excitement before leaning his body into mine, and I don't miss the hard bulge that presses against my abdomen.

This guy is fucking sick.

His white eyes search my face as he leans down to smell my cheek, "The real question is, do I kill you here and let your companions mourn your empty carcass, or do I break your mind and claim you for my own?"

My pulse rages in my ears, and I desperately try to open myself up to my magic as his lips brush along my skin. My panic heightens even further when it doesn't answer my call.

He laughs as if he knows my thoughts, "Oh, did I not mention? Your magic is useless here, and mine is limited, but I will not need all of it for this."

His body melds against mine as his weight bears down, and he leans in, his lips brushing against my ear, "You're all alone here, and there's no escape. What would be the fun in ending this prematurely?"

As he muses, he brings his hands down to trail his fingers between my breasts and down my stomach slowly.

My heart leaps, thinking he's no longer restrained my hands, but they remain above my head even as I tug on them. No matter how hard I pull, I can't seem to free myself from whatever magic he uses to keep me in place.

His grin widens as he watches me panic as I pull and tug my arms.

When his finger drops below my belly button, I whimper and thrash to try to force him off, but his weight keeps him on top of me.

My actions only grind his erection harder into my pelvic bone, and he groans as he reaches between my legs.

My mind goes distant, and I run through the motion of disassociating, thinking of my companions. My mind wanders from Darian to Val, Kieran, Gray, and Zayne.

Finally, my mind lands on Caspian, and my heart squeezes painfully as I realize all the wrongs done to him.

Kouros glides his tongue along my chest, and I squeeze my eyes shut as he presses himself against me with a husky breath.

All my dreams and hopes of helping Servilia, freeing their people from the darkness in their world... It all stems from Kouros, and Caspian has gotten the shit end of the stick with it all.

He deserved better than this life.

He's called himself a monster—my monster—but I know that, in reality, people like Kouros and Samira are the real ones.

Caspian is not.

Not to me.

Kouros reaches up once more, using his strength and positioning to twist my arm painfully until it snaps with a loud crack that I feel reverberate through my entire body. The white-hot pain shooting down my arm into my shoulder makes me cry out once more, and I buck against him to no end.

But it's no use. He doesn't budge.

Instead, his grin just widens as if this is what he's been waiting for all his life.

He grinds himself against me as if the clothes between us don't exist, "Do you know how often I watched them beat and break your bones? How many times I came from watching them use your body?"

The look in his eyes is feral as he throbs between my legs, and his dry thrusts emphasize his words.

"I watched them fuck you, and every, single, time; it only made me want to claim you more."

His eyes flash as his hand snakes between our bodies, and I squeeze my eyes shut when the sound of fabric tearing fills the air. I try to picture the door in my mind for my magic in a feeble attempt to open myself to it, nearly sobbing when the room is empty.

"No, I have waited far too long not to enjoy this as much as I have needed to. So, while your physical body sleeps, my dear child, I will own your mind and then claim it in ways you didn't know existed."

My brows furrow as he circles my clit.

His white eyes search the confusion on my face as he grins, "Ah, you are still so young for a goddess. For me to claim you and enjoy you how I desire... you must be willing."

Chapter 52

Eiara

Willing.

Holy fuck.

Relief like a warm blanket washes over me but quickly dies out as he laughs, bending my finger in a way it isn't meant to bend as it snaps, and my body arcs involuntarily into him. This pushes his erection against my thigh, and he groans, leaning his head into my chest and licking my skin.

"By the time we're done, you'll forget all about Darian," he says, snapping another finger.

"Valerian," another snap, and my scream comes out silent as my voice breaks with it.

"Kieran." He lists out each of their names as he snaps a frail bone in my hand and my body tremors uncontrollably from the pain. Tears stain my cheeks, and he smiles, placing his hand over mine as all my bones snap painfully into place.

He reaches between my legs once more and circles my clit, "How about this? I'll be benevolent and negotiate. I will stop breaking your bones if you come for me."

As if to emphasize his promise of relief, he snaps three of my fingers in quick succession.

The agonizing pain radiates through my hands, but I shake my head, "No."

His jaw clenches, and he snarls, "Maybe you just need more convincing," he sinks his teeth into the tender skin of my neck and grasps my hips as they break, crunching loudly beneath his strength.

I nearly vomit from the pain as he presses himself harder between my legs, and my screams fill the air.

Kouros' chest heaves as he gets a wild glint in his eyes. "Fine. You will serve me in other ways."

He crawls onto my chest, and a fresh wave of panic fills my mind as he pulls apart his robe, releasing his thick-veined cock that bobs between us each time it pulsates. His fist collides with my jaw, and my head snaps to the side as stars fill my vision.

I don't get any warning before he grips my head with his hands and thrusts into my mouth. My head falls back to escape intrusion, and my skull cracks against the ground as he leans forward, crushing my head beneath the weight of his hips.

Already fighting for air, I gasp against him as he forces himself deeper, stretching my throat in unnatural ways as pain lances down my neck. Between his cock down my throat and his fist in my hair, I'm unable to pull away or turn my head.

He holds himself there for a moment, his dick throbbing as he pants, "I have waited far too long to feel you myself."

My gag reflex triggers, and he groans, pushing his cock in time with the contractions as my throat fights the invasion. Tears spring to my eyes as my lungs beg for air, and I kick, buck, and squirm, ignoring the immense pain in my body from the bones he's left broken.

I think he's about to pull out as he withdraws, and my body craves relief, but he thrusts in harder, slamming my skull against the ground again. His pelvic bone smashes against my face as he reaches a depth that my throat wasn't created to handle.

That's when I realize.

I will die here.

He slams into my throat again and again until my body is limp, twitching from lack of air as he fucks my throat relentlessly. My vision starts to darken as he pulls out, placing his hand on my chest, and my lungs fill with urgency as I cough.

He places his hand on my hips as they snap back into place, but I hardly register it from the shock of nearly dying.

That's when I vomit in earnest.

He takes in my disheveled appearance before straddling my hips, "Now, dear child. This could all have been avoided if you just said yes."

His hand moves between my legs, and he circles my clit once more. The shock has begun to wear off, and I glare at him.

"Go fuck yourself, asshole," I croak.

He tuts and circles my clit faster, "Come for me, Eiara."

"No," I spit in his face, falling short as it hits his chest, and he smiles.

"You will come for me. Whether you want to or not."

He sounds so fucking confident.

I grit my teeth, ignoring the pain in my jaw and throat.

"Either that or your face gets the honor of being my vessel again. Maybe this time you'll learn that this," he gestures between us, and his dick throbs hungrily, "this is inevitable because when I want something, I get it, Eiara. And oh, do I want you."

"For years, I simply watched and guided as your foster parents got all the fun, but once I was inside Cain's mind and felt how perfect you were, I knew that I would claim you."

My body goes numb, and all the blood drains from my face.

"Maybe I've taken the wrong approach," he murmurs, as my own body betrays me and pleasure builds in my core, "Perhaps I will just kill Caspian, Darian, and the others while you watch."

My eyes widen.

He's bluffing.

He has to be bluffing.

Logic tells me he is, but the irrational part of me argues that he could have a trick up his sleeve.

He pulsates between us again, and a wild look takes over his features, "The scent of your arousal is intoxicating," he murmurs, bringing his hand to his mouth and sucking on his fingers.

When he withdraws them, he puts them into my mouth roughly, and I bite down hard, feeling my teeth bury into his fingers until they hit the bone. "You little," He recoils, backhanding me as my head snaps to the side.

Hands grasp the sides of my head, and he forces his cock down my throat again, snapping his hips with no remorse as I fight for breath with each millisecond that he withdraws.

Holding his dick deep down my throat, it pulsates, "I'll kill Kieran first. I will string him up by his veins and watch him bleed out before feeding his heart to you."

The image makes my blood run cold, and my heart pounds as the pressure in my head builds. The lack of oxygen makes my lungs contract as my throat gulps against him in a desperate attempt to get air.

He groans, staring at my mouth, and his lip curls in twisted satisfaction.

Ignoring that I'm suffocating, he continues, "Then I'll kill Gray. I will break every bone in his body before tearing him apart piece by piece. It will be like a puzzle for you, just like the ones you used to love."

Horror washes over me that this sick creep was watching me, even back then.

If he has been able to manipulate everything until this point, there's a chance he's not bluffing about killing them.

The decision between keeping my men alive versus whatever horrors Kouros has is an easy decision to make...

But it's not a decision I want to make at all.

He withdraws from my mouth and quickly leans to inhale against my chest, sighing relievedly, "You are finally seeing reason."

Horror coats my veins as he crawls down my body, circling my clit once more. "Now that you've accepted your fate. Come."

He circles faster, and disgust coats my veins as pressure builds in my core.

I don't want them to get hurt, and I'd do anything to keep them from it.

I know it.

He knows it.

Maybe this was an inevitable choice I'd have to make.

At least I freed them. At least I freed Caspian.

I'm so sorry Caspian.

My chest tightens as I pray the others will forgive me for not being strong enough, and some small part of me wishes I'll get to see them before it all ends.

Or before my mind breaks.

Kouros searches my face with a level of hunger and anticipation I've never seen before, "That's it, Eiara. Accept what must be and let go. Do it for them."

I squeeze my eyes shut, and a tear escapes.

This isn't how it's supposed to be.

I want my men.

I don't want Kouros.

His threats hang in my mind as I'm faced with an impossible decision, and my mind whirls, my orgasm surfacing as he presses harder against my clit.

No, no, no.

No matter how I try to ward off the pleasure, it just continues to build in my core, and I'm dangerously teetering on the edge of an orgasm.

No, please-

He suddenly withdraws his hand and presses the length of his cock between my legs, grinding his bulbous head against my clit relentlessly as the pressure pushes me over the edge. He watches with vicious anticipation as guilt and shame mix with the first wave of unwanted pleasure that washes over me, and my body clamps down against the waves of my climax.

"That's it."

No, I don't want this.

"Yes. Yes," Kouros' breath hitches in excitement as the head of his cock notches my entrance.

Panic rises in my chest.

This can't be happening.

"No. No, stop—"

He's suddenly ripped off me and thrown across the room. My gaze falls upon a furious Caspian, who scans my body with a lethal glint in his eyes as he turns to Kouros.

Every inch of him screams violence in a way I've never seen before, and I've never been more relieved to see it than I am at this moment as tears spring to my eyes, blurring the corners of my vision.

"This can't be possible," Kouros mutters in disbelief, "How?" he demands as he glares at me.

"She does not answer to the likes of you," Caspian says, launching himself at the god with unexpected speed. Kouros's features twist into panic, and he smashes his fist to the ground and disappears into a cloud of fog.

I jolt upright with a desperate gasp for air, tears streaming down my face unbidden as I search the area through blurred vision.

Panicked that I'm locked into another area or room with Kouros, a hand on my arm sends me scrambling forward as my pulse rages, drowning out the voices in the room.

It's not until my gaze locks with a pair of burning emerald eyes brimming with so much rage that my pulse slows and my focus becomes linear.

The look on his face should terrify me, but it doesn't.

Still fighting to catch my breath from the panic clawing at my mind, I crawl off the bed toward Caspian as he quickly steps closer, kneeling until we're at eye level, but he doesn't move to touch me.

I need his touch more than I've needed anything.

Because I still feel Kouros.

His weight. His touch, his threats.

They hang like a knife dangling over my head, and I just want it to stop.

My breath hitches as he holds his hand up to the side with his palm outstretched, and I know it's because the others are in the room with no idea what's happened.

Outside of what I'm feeling, only Caspian knows the truth.

The truth.

Oh gods, he needs to know the truth.

My hand covers his thigh, and the moment I bring my hand down to touch him, a wave of relief crashes over me.

But he does not move to grab me.

No, he simply waits, letting me creep closer of my own accord as tears flow freely.

I pull myself into his lap, ignoring the shame, guilt, and embarrassment that coats every thought, feeling, and emotion as I wrap my arms around him.

I can feel his heart pounding as I bury my face in the crook of his neck.

My entire being feels like it could shatter as if held together by brittle tape that could tear at any moment.

"Please hold me."

My voice is no more than a whisper, but that's all it takes for his arms to wrap tightly around my shoulders as he squeezes me into him.

"You're alright now, little one." I shudder, and he leans his cheek against my hair, "Whoever that was, I will kill him. It may not be today nor tomorrow, but his death is mine." He vows as the room goes silent amidst my sniffles.

I loosen my grip with trembling arms and lean back to look at him, "It's all him, Caspian. The foster homes, your magic, Samira, Servilia's magic disappearing, it's all tied to him."

Someone in the room clears their throat, and Caspian's emerald gaze lingers on mine for a long moment before he looks behind me, "She didn't just faint." His jaw feathers as I shift slightly in his lap, freezing when I see blood on his mouth.

Is that... my blood?

But that can't be what happened. I had to beg him to use my power when Gray and I were injured, and he looked like it was torturous even to ask that of him.

How else could he have found me if he didn't dream-weave?

I feel his gaze shift to me as I stare at the crimson on his lips before raising my eyes to his. He searches my face as if he knows the influx of questions weighing on my mind, and his gaze softens.

"I would do worse things if it meant keeping you from harm, little one. I'm not afraid to be a monster, especially not when you're involved."

My heart squeezes in my chest, and I correct him with my voice no more than a whisper, "My monster."

Emotion flickers across his face, but he quickly masks it, his gaze darting to the others behind me.

"Goddess?" Gray's voice sounds out, and I fight the mental image of his body in pieces.

I shift in Caspian's lap to face the rest of my men as a fresh wave of concern and relief bleeds from them.

Our large bed has been made larger to accommodate our entire party, and the rest of my men, with concern painted across their features, are standing at the foot of it.

I never thought I'd see them again.

Zayne's piercing gaze travels my body, and for a moment, I feel the ghost of Kouros' touch once more. I shudder, and Caspian's grip on me tightens when Zayne's soft voice breaks the silence.

"What was it then?"

My breath catches in my lungs when they look at me for an answer.

I can't voice it.

Not now.

Not when my mind wars between pretending it never happened and allowing myself to acknowledge it.

Tears spring to my eyes when Caspian speaks for me instead, "When I found her, she was trapped with some asshole on top of her seconds from being raped."

Caspian gaze flicks to mine, and I know he's omitting details to save me from embarrassment.

He wipes my cheek with his thumb, "So tell me his name, little one, and I will hunt him down to tear him to pieces with my bare hands." The lethal calmness with which he says it sends a shiver down my spine as Val kneels beside us.

The look in Val's hazel eyes is pure understanding, and my heart squeezes painfully in my chest as I reach out to grasp his arm. Taking that as his queue, he wraps an arm around my waist and hugs me tightly.

"I'll kill him too."

Kieran moves to the wall behind Val, "Count me in too, sweetheart." Darian kneels in front of me, giving his brother a look I can't quite place before he leans in to place a kiss on my temple.

Gray sits on the edge of the bed with a feral look in his eyes, "So, who is this dead man?"

I swallow against the lump in my throat.

"His name is Kouros. I suspect he told me everything under the assumption that I would not leave that place—at least, not in any useful state." A shudder wracks through me, and Caspian's grip on me tightens as my gaze flicks to his.

"He claimed that you actually have magic. He bragged about how he convinced your parents to bind your powers under the guise that you would try to kill Darian."

Caspian blinks and shakes his head, "My magic is absorbing others temporarily, nothing else."

"That's what you have now, but according to him, your magic is bound," he frowns as I turn to Darian, "Samira is trying to become a god. That's why she's draining Servilia. Kouros gave her the idea and then showed her how to do it. According to him, she's been draining the land and all the prominent bloodlines."

Gray leans back and braces on the bed, "Why did she not drain Caspian's then? He's royal blood."

I shake my head, "That, he did not say."

Zayne frowns, "Did he say why he trapped you, Eiara?"

My gaze meets Caspian's, and I feel like I could vomit as I struggle to find my voice.

"He..."

My stomach flips as the memory of Kouros' attempt to claim me flickers through my mind.

"He said gods aren't being born often on Meloris and that he was going to... claim me."

Anger flashes across Darian's face as Zayne steps forward with his hand outstretched between us, "I think the most important question we've not yet asked," I frown, placing my hand in his as he pulls me from the comfort of Caspian's embrace, "Is if you are okay."

Caspian helps me to my feet before Zayne's arms encircle my shoulders tightly. A warm body at my back makes my heart swell as Kieran joins the embrace, followed by Val.

Emotion clogs my throat as I choke out a small laugh.

"I'm okay. I'm just... I'm beyond thankful that Caspian showed up," I say, realization dawning on me. "How did you know to dream-weave to me, anyway?"

Caspian moves to the bed, resting his weight on his palms as he tilts his head. He brings his hand to his chest, where my magic remains within him. "When you fainted, we brought you in here, and you just wouldn't wake up. We were in the middle of discussing how to find Vates when I thought I heard your voice. It was almost as if you were here, but you sounded far away."

Val, Kieran, and Zayne make room for Darian as he wraps his arms around me, "We were sitting here wondering what to do next when Caspian bit into your wrist without saying anything, and then he went unconscious, too."

"What would you have done if you were trapped there with me?"

I stare at him incredulously, and Caspian's lips twitch, "You say that like it's a bad thing."

My heart squeezes in my chest again as I let the thought settle in.

Caspian hates stealing powers, yet he did it to save me without a second thought.

Val crosses his arms, looking between Caspian, Darian, and I, "So what do we do now?"

Darian's baritone voice is low as he rubs his thumb along my skin soothingly, "We still must go to Maximillia to stop Samira from getting the artifact, but once we do that, we find her and Kouros, and we send them both to the depths of the underworld."

Chapter 53

Eiara

After a restless sleep due to the paranoia of falling into Kouros' hands again, I sit in the bedroom watching Caspian sharpen his longsword as Gray plops down beside me.

"Goddess," he passes a slice of melon-like fruit in my direction as Darian steps into the room, "You need to eat."

My stomach turns at the thought of food, so I shake my head, "I'm fine."

"Eat." Caspian and Darian say in unison, and I reluctantly take the fruit from Gray. Looking at it in my hand makes my stomach flip, and I glance up to see Darian watching me.

Does he know the truth?

Would he have said anything yet if he did?

The memory of my body betraying me sends guilt and shame over me once more, and I swallow.

How could I ever tell them?

Lost in my thoughts, I hardly notice when Darian glances at Gray before he sets down the bag he came into the room to get.

"Sunshine."

My eyes snap to him as Val opens the door, "We're all ready to head to the docks, D."

Darian holds my gaze for a long moment, "We'll be right there."

The door shuts behind him, and Darian's jaw ticks before he speaks, "I'm not going to ask you to talk about what happened until you're ready,

Sunshine, but tell me that you understand when I say that none of this is your fault."

The pressure in my chest grows, and I swallow, feeling Caspian's lingering gaze burning into me as I nod, "I understand."

"Goddess," Gray warns, pointing to the untouched slice of fruit in my hand, "Don't make me force that trazcht down your throat."

I feel the blood drain from my face at the thought.

He moves to snatch the fruit from my hand, and irrational panic suddenly takes over my mind. Within seconds, and before I can blink, Darian's grabbed Gray's arm inches from the trazcht.

He knows.

Gray's eyes widen as he stares at Darian's hand, but Caspian's voice sounds out from the other side of the room.

"Gray, do us all a favor and never make that threat again, jokingly or not."

How the hell could they both know?

Ripping his hand from Darian, he pushes off the bed, "Fine! The goddess can starve!"

He storms out of the room, and I hesitantly bring myself to look at Darian as Caspian pushes to his feet, "I'll meet you two outside."

My heart gallops in my chest as he kneels before me, "Sunshine."

"How?"

He frowns at my question, "How what?"

My pulse quickens as he takes my hands into his, waiting for me to clarify. I feel out of breath as I finally manage to find my voice, "How did you know that was going to upset me?"

A sad smile crosses his face as he brings one hand to my chest, resting it just over my heart. "I felt it. Then I put two and two together," his hand cups my cheek, and my mind wars against itself to ignore the memory of Kouros' hands, "Did he do what I think he did?"

His mismatched gaze holds mine, and I feel something inside me crack as tears well up in my eyes.

I don't know how to tell him.

There aren't words to convey that what happened there was more than just an assault on the body.

It was unveiling every wound I'd ever been given, only to learn it had a face, a name, and my only choice was to surrender to him or risk those I love most.

So I don't tell him anything, but instead, as tears pour from my eyes, I let myself feel everything.

The confusion, the terror, the resignation, the defeat, the shame, the guilt, the embarrassment. My vision blurs as my tears run down my skin onto Darian's hand as he searches my face, his anger and regret bleeding into me as he absorbs it all.

Finally, I recall the relief that overwhelmed me when Caspian appeared, and I decide to let him feel that, too. His face flashes in understanding as his own tears trail down his cheeks.

He leans his head against mine, and sorrow washes over me like a tidal wave, followed by a mixture of anger and fear.

There's a long moment of silence between us as we breathe each other in until his thumb wipes the tears from my cheek, "My biggest failure is not knowing what was happening to you or getting you out of there." I shake my head, but he continues, "I made a promise—"

"Without Caspian's ability to steal powers, Darian, I don't think even Vates could have found a way to get me out of there."

Darian searches my face for a moment before leaning in, "I know my brother already claimed Kouros' death for his own, but I'll be damned if I don't get to kill him myself." his lips brush mine before he finally closes the distance.

It's tentative, soft, and cautious, and when he pulls away to look at me, I can't help but feel a little bit lighter than I did when I woke up.

Walking the oddly vacant streets of Trebonia, I glance at each of the men with me to see guarded expressions on their faces as they peer into the windows of houses or shops we pass by.

The city suddenly seems abandoned, like all the citizens decided to pack up and leave overnight as we venture to make the final turn to the docks.

It isn't until the ocean comes into view that we see the first signs of life as people bustle to and from the ships. The closer we get, the more it becomes apparent that the entire city is here as people file onto the boats, lugging crates of weapons and arrows, along with various other items.

Darian curses under his breath as Tiul spots us from the water's edge, and the blood drains from his face as he jogs over.

He bows slightly, his hands trembling as he straightens out, "Your majesty, we are ready to depart momentarily."

Darian's brows pinch together as he surveys the docks before turning his attention to Tiul, "I said we were going to go alone," Tiul nods in agreement, "You mean to tell me that you refuse to remain in Trebonia?" he asks, concern written clearly on his face.

Tiul wrings his hands together, "Respectfully, the people in this city would rather die with their true King than live without him."

Darian blinks, "I will not deny anyone their choice, but I hope to avoid loss of life as much as we can."

Tiul inclines his head with pride on his face before he springs into motion, ushering us towards the loaded boats along the docks.

Darian glances at Zayne, "Does this change our arrival location?"

Zayne's violet gaze scans the boats and townspeople before he shakes his head.

We board one of the larger boats as various workers begin to sprint along the sides of the dock, untying ropes and tossing them aboard as we drift away. Butterflies run rampant in my body as the rumble of whichever magic powers the ships roars to life, and soon, we're flying over the calm ocean surface with four ships on either side of us.

It doesn't take long before the air becomes so frigid that our breaths create clouds of mist, and as land appears on the horizon, we slow our pace. With Caspian on one side and Darian on the other, I peer over the bow toward the city of Maximillia in the distance. But the dark smoke rising high into the clouds makes my heart drop.

We're too late.

Glancing at Darian in a panic, it's clear that he's on the same page as he murmurs something to Zayne and Gray, who take positions beside me, as Val and Kieran place themselves on either side of Darian.

Feeling someone at my back, I don't need more to wonder who it is as warm breath cascades over my ear, "Let's get through this without any bodily injuries this time, little one."

I laugh softly.

*It **is** an ongoing theme for my monster to be there precisely when I need him the most.*

Our ships pull onto the frozen shore, the ice and snow groaning against the weight of the boats as we quickly make our way onto solid ground.

Only a handful of people remain with the ships to guard the supplies while the rest of us trudge uphill through the knee-high snow toward the burning city.

Finally, as we breach the top of the hill, the scene before us is almost out of a movie. Hundreds of Servilians in a sea of blue and black are locked in battle outside the city walls as a large mechanism rams into the front gates.

Soldiers in bright blue along the walls shout as they drop large rocks onto the soldiers manning the battering ram.

Hope is not lost. Not yet.

The tide of battle looks to be in Samira's favor as the number of black-outfitted soldiers outnumbers blue by three to one.

"Now!" Darian shouts, and Tiul releases a long blow from a large horn before slinging over his shoulder and unsheathing his weapon.

The horn has the desired effect, pulling the attention of countless soldiers of Samira's army who have yet to fully engage in battle.

They begin to scramble into position to face us, their arrows and swords held at the ready.

I watch as their archers, no more than one hundred yards away, nock their arrows, raise the tips to the air, and release them.

It's an odd feeling, seeing the arrows released into the air before hearing the whistle on the wind as they hurtle down toward us, and the dread that pools in my stomach quickly turns into relief as Darian uses the snow around us to form a dense sheet of ice, absorbing the impact.

Val's commanding voice booms, and my anxious heart flutters violently, "Ready."

He extends his arm into the air, and I watch as every bow in my vision moves in unison, "Aim."

"Fire!" he thrusts his arm forward, and anticipation builds as the arrows surge into the air.

Hope builds as their aim looks true until the arrows hit some sort of shield before dropping uselessly to the ground.

Val curses as Darian turns to us, "We're going to have to get in close," My heart rattles in my chest as he glances at Kieran, Val, Gray, and Zayne before his gaze falls to Caspian. The concern he feels bleeds out as he holds his gaze. "Keep her safe, brother," he says, glancing at me once before he turns away and sprints through the snow toward the crimson-stained battlefield.

My heart stutters, and before I can follow him, Caspian's arm wraps tightly around my waist, "Easy, little one, my brother knows what he's doing."

His voice is so sure that I can only watch in horror as the opposing forces collide. Swords clash, bodies jerk to a stop, and blood sprays into the air as everything inside of me screams to join the fray.

I squirm against his grip, but he holds me tight against his chest. "Caspian, we have to do something."

I watch as Darian narrowly avoids one strike before he brings down two soldiers, and my heart races.

"Why must you be so insistent on running to your death?" he asks, exasperation clear in his voice.

I twist in his grip to face him, but he doesn't loosen his grip as he squeezes me into his chest. My heart is a war drum on its own, beating to the call of death and battle as I search his face.

"Why must you be so insistent on stopping me from helping?"

I stare at him with wide eyes, and his mouth twitches in anger, "Because we almost lost you in Trebonia–I almost lost you in Trebonia!"

He releases me from his grip, turning away as he curses.

I do not run from him, but I also don't give myself time to fully process what he said as my focus remains on the countless lives winking out behind me.

My hands tremble with anger as he turns to face me with a pained expression.

"What good is being alive if those we love are lost in the process, Caspian?"

Emotion flashes across his face as shouts break out amidst the battle, and we both turn toward it. My pulse hikes as two groups of Samira's soldiers flank the reinforcements from Trebonia on either side, pressuring Darian and the rest as they struggle to maintain their ground.

It's a trap.

I watch in horror as blasts of ice, shadow, water, and flame suddenly burst into the sky as the soldiers block our view, "Caspian..."

He curses as he unsheathes his sword, "You want blood, little one. I hope you still have those claws." He surges forward, and I sprint through the well-worn path in the snow to stay close to him as we charge toward the battlefield.

With our weapons drawn, we dive into the battle, and my vision becomes a blur of blood and battered bodies as we fight through the endless ocean of Samira's army.

I'm not sure how long we've been fighting, but when I finally spot Val and Kieran back-to-back, they're surrounded by enemies as they use their swords and magic simultaneously to block and counterattack.

It's a challenge to keep them in my line of vision as Caspian and I fight through our opponents. From what little I can see, their breathing is labored as they fend off the relentless assault.

"Caspian, I see Val and Kieran," He glances at me as he thrusts his blade into the abdomen of a soldier before following my gaze.

We spring into action, fighting toward them as a whistling sound echoes into the air. I hardly get time to register it when Caspian twists faster than I've ever seen, and he tackles me to the ground.

My head collides with the cold, hard ground, and the wind gets knocked out of my lungs beneath his weight as I groan. I open my eyes as my ears ring, only to see countless bodies littered on the ground around us.

Arrows jut out from gaping wounds in various bodies, indiscriminate between black or blue-garbed soldiers. Horror washes over me anew when I realize that Samira's army released an attack on everyone, including their own forces.

Caspian grunts as he lifts his weight off me, cursing as he holds his thigh where an arrow protrudes from. A black oil-like substance coats the arrow, and my mind flashes to the brute in the mountain as I quickly move to his legs.

"Fuck."

Caspian tuts in feigned disapproval, "Such foul language, little one."

He grunts as I pull the arrow from his flesh, and crimson flows out as I press my hand against his thigh. His blood seeps through my fingers, and I send my magic into his body as he gets a half-surprised, half-panicked look on his face.

I know it's the paralytic wreaking havoc on his body, but thankfully, I can hone in on the microscopic tendrils of dark magic before they spread too far.

Fueled by adrenaline and a sense of urgency, I snuff out the dark magic before it fully takes hold, stitching his wound together with half a thought.

He blinks as I push to my feet, extending a hand between us, "Who knew you were such a quick study."

My lips twitch as he stands, "I always did well in trial-by-fire scenarios."

The earth around us shakes as a blast of water sends a soldier flying, and I'm finally able to see Val and Kieran less than fifty feet away as whistling sounds out in the air again.

Caspian manages to rip a shield off the ground as he pulls me into him and crouches with the shield held over us. An arrow slams into it directly overhead, bending the metal to its shape as the tip of the arrow has torn through.

My gaze slides from the tip of the arrow to Val and Kieran as time seems to slow down.

I watch in horror as Val staggers with his back to me before he looks down, and Kieran's blood-spattered face contorts in pain.

The same look of pain he had when Cade died.

No, Not him too.

Chapter 54

Eiara

My heart feels like it's shattering into a million pieces, grinding to dust before my eyes as I scream Val's name.

I ignore Caspian's warnings and launch myself forward, watching in horror as Kieran collapses onto the ground next to Val with tears in his eyes.

As I run at full speed, every second feels like an eternity.

Every second that passes is a second I lose with him.

Kieran is oblivious to the two soldiers taking advantage of the chaos as they run toward him. Bending to grab a dagger off the ground, I flick it at one of the soldiers, and it buries into the back of his thigh as he collapses to the ground.

The second soldier notices, turning his attention to me.

Each second I spend taking them down is another moment I don't have, and by the time they're both down, my heart is in my throat.

A deep-set arrow protrudes from Val's chest as Kieran uses his magic to keep the soldiers at bay while he attempts to heal him.

His breath hitches, and he fights back a sob as I fall to my knees next to him, "It's not working, I don't understand. Eiara, please, I can't lose him too."

A soldier breaks through the wall of water, and Kieran quickly moves to clash his sword against the attack. I wrap my hand around the arrow as blood begins to stream from the corner of Val's mouth, each of his breaths short and labored.

The way he's looking at me sends a soul-shattering sadness through the very core of my being and threatens to overwhelm me. His tired hazel eyes look resigned as he places a hand on my thigh.

I shake my head, "No. No. I won't lose you."

My heart thrashes wildly as another whistle rips through the air, and I can only hope the rest of my companions are okay as I pull the arrow from Val's torso.

He grunts as blood streams from the wound, seeping out with each breath he takes, and I place my hands over his chest. Pouring my magic into his body, I urge it to mend his flesh as it slowly manages to stitch together and suffocate the remnants of dark magic within his veins.

I search his face as my magic withdraws, nervously counting the seconds between each of his shallow breaths, and relief coats my veins as they become deeper, stronger, and more even.

My heart stops as another ominous whistle echoes amongst the wind, and a layer of water forms a shield above us.

Glancing around at the countless bodies littering the ground, I'm not surprised to see that many of them are from Samira's army, but my gut twists when I see some that I recognize.

It isn't until my eyes land on the lifeless body of the woman from the butcher shop that my heart drops.

We almost lost Val.

We could lose anyone.

We are not winning this without severe casualties.

My heart weighs heavy as I survey the area, spotting Zayne's dark magic not far off and flames spurting into the air in the distance, telling me the others are still fighting with everything they have.

Here I am, fighting with a sword and healing the wounds of those who mean the most to me.

What good is being a goddess if I don't have the power to save those who only wish to live their lives?

My gaze locks with Caspian's, and he searches my face as if he can sense my thoughts, "Lara, what are you about to do?"

"What good is being alive if those we love are lost in the process, Caspian?"

I repeat my earlier question, and he stares at me with furrowed brows before placing his hand over his chest where the small bundle of my magic remains.

The look on his face tells me that he's just now realizing that this is the same sentiment I felt when I saved him. I offer a soft smile before allowing my power to surge through my body.

The rush of energy causes a force of air outward from where I stand, and as my power encircles the area, I hone in on each and every soldier on the field.

I'm hardly aware of Caspian, Kieran, and Val cutting down the soldiers who notice and attempt to make their way to me. The sun peers out from the clouds as I stand straight, tilting my head to the sky.

My power churns as I extend my magic further than ever, allowing it to reach the edges of the battlefield where fewer bodies lay.

It's clear as day to know which soldiers are Samira's.

Their entire bodies are stained with a taint of darkness that my magic rebels against as it dances over their skin. Only when I am satisfied that I have reached them all do I pause to pinpoint my magic, concentrating it on two targeted areas on each soldier.

My eyes snap open as a thud sounds out in front of me, where Caspian has his sword burrowed into the chest of a soldier. Our eyes meet, and the area brightens with beams of light as I open myself to more of my power.

I hold his gaze as I pour my magic relentlessly, funneling it into each targeted destination, and torturous, blood-curdling screams begin to fill the air with the clash of swords. The pinpoints blink out quickly, like hundreds of stars in the night sky that are there one moment and disappear the next until none remain.

Soon, the clash of metal quiets, and only agonizing shrieks linger as I close myself off to my power. Caspian's gaze remains on me, and to his credit, he holds no fear, disgust, or contempt in his expression.

In fact, if anything, I'd say he looks proud.

Tearing my gaze from him, I survey the battlefield as hundreds of soldiers cover their bleeding eyes with their hands. Their pained moans fill the air as they shuffle from side to side and struggle to walk.

"Gods," Kieran mutters as he watches Samira's soldiers stumble around, waving their swords wildly before being cut down.

"Remind me," Val says beside me as he tosses me a grin, "never to piss you off."

My heart squeezes, and I throw myself at him as he catches me in midair. With my face burrowed into his neck, I swallow against emotions clogging my throat, and my voice comes out as no more than a whisper.

"I thought we were going to lose you."

His grip around my waist tightens before he pulls back to cup my head in his hands, "Never."

He glances over my shoulder as relief radiates from him, and I turn to follow his gaze.

Darian, Gray, and Zayne walk toward us with their bodies spattered in blood that doesn't appear to be their own as they cut down blinded soldiers.

I breathe a sigh of relief, knowing that, at the very least, our group remains unharmed. But as the memory of Val dropping to his knees flashes through my mind, I know we came close to the bitter reality of most on this battlefield.

Darian surveys the bodies on the ground and blind soldiers with wide eyes, "What in the gods' names just happened?"

The overwhelming insecurity that he may disapprove of my methods rises to the surface, and my pulse hikes up.

What if they look at me differently now?

"You," Tiul's voice sounds out, and we all turn to him only to find him pointing a finger at me, "Who are you?"

My anxiety skyrockets and I open my mouth to answer, but a warm body at my back snags my attention as Caspian's voice rings out into the still air.

"Her name is Eiara Ptheron. She is the daughter of Sol, the god of the sun, and Luna, the goddess of the moon. She is the reason that we won this battle."

Heat rises to my cheeks as he leans in, his chest pressing into my back as his lips graze my ear, "And she is ours."

My eyes lock with Darian's, and I don't mistake the fierce look in his eyes, snuffing out any insecurities I had about my own actions. When Tiul drops to his knees and presses his nose to the ground, I blink in confusion.

Gray groans, "Tiul, for gods' sake. Stop groveling."

He pulls Tiul up by his shoulders before making his way over to me. His piercing golden eyes linger on my face before dropping to my lips, and my cheeks burn when he stops directly in front of me.

"You're covered in blood, Goddess," He grins, running his thumb across my lower lip before putting it in his mouth and sucking the blood off, "It's a good look."

It's all I can do to keep my jaw from dropping as he laughs and steps aside to run his sword into a wandering soldier.

Darian steps closer, gesturing to the soldiers with a bewildered look, "This was you?"

I nod.

"Well done, little one," Caspian's voice rings out close behind me, and I suppress a shiver.

Zayne takes a few steps closer, glancing around the battlefield, "Not to interrupt, but we should head north to the lake. It looks like Samira took a secondary force and diverted past the city. Tiul and the rest can manage to reinforce the city while we do."

Traveling further north into the deep, snow-covered forest, my fingers and toes go completely numb.

Add that to my exhaustion from the overuse of magic that lags my movements as we navigate the frigid forest, and it's a wonder I'm still managing to remain upright.

I'm nearly certain we all feel drained though, so I keep quiet and stubbornly push through.

We've only been walking for half an hour, but given how stiff my limbs feel, it might as well have been hours. Even rubbing my hands together to create friction does nothing to recover any feeling as I blow warm air into my fists.

Each step of my heavy, numb legs feels foreign as I keep my jaw slack to keep my teeth from chattering.

Thankfully, the trees block most of the wind, but the raw chill in the air feels like it's seeped into the core of my bones, making my movements sluggish as we continue.

How do people live up here?

There was a reason I never moved to Canada, and the lack of feeling in my fingers and toes is a healthy reminder.

Crossing my arms over my chest, I slide my hands under my armpits, wincing as the warmth causes them to burn.

"Our goddess is going to freeze soon if we don't do something." Kieran's warning gets everyone's attention, and I raise a hand to wave him off dismissively, my eyes widening at the deep purple hue of my fingers.

"Oh, I guess that doesn't give me much room to argue," I mutter between my teeth chattering.

Val rubs his hands together before crossing them over his chest, "It is quite cold... There's a reason I preferred living near Lavinium. Even Nomentum never gets this bad."

Kieran places his hands on mine as his magic tingles through my body, bringing feeling and color back to my stiff limbs.

"There. That should fix any damage the cold caused, but we still need to find a way to keep you from freezing—" He's interrupted as Gray pushes past him, hooking his arm under my legs as he lifts me into his chest.

My jaw goes slack, "I—"

Instinctively, my arms wrap around his neck, and the delicious warmth of his body seeps into mine.

"I've got her, let's go."

I can't help but melt further into him.

He's literally the equivalent of a walking furnace with the heat radiating from his skin.

I lean my face into the crook of his neck as he walks, and as my cold nose presses against his collarbone, I can't tell if the resulting shiver is from him or me.

The longer he carries me, the warmer his skin feels, and it takes a few minutes before I realize he's using his magic to keep us both from the cold. Even my toes have finally regained feeling and are no longer blocks of ice attached to my legs.

Clearing my throat, his piercing molten amber gaze flicks to mine, "Thank you for keeping me warm."

His lips twitch before his eyes focus on something ahead, and I follow his gaze. The treeline ahead gets thinner as more trampled snow comes into view with each step.

My stomach twists as I see a giant crater in the center of the frozen lake, with large boulders of white-blue ice scattered atop bodies of crushed soldiers who must have been too close when the explosion happened.

Gray sets me to my feet, and dread settles in my gut, "We're too late."

We slowly reach the large crater, which runs deep and juts down nearly a hundred yards. At the bottom, a large hollow stone lies with marks from where Samira's minions broke into it.

Darian curses as he surveys the area around us, the muscle in his jaw feathering.

"Want me to take to the air?" Gray offers with a broad grin, and my heart drops into my stomach as I consider the last time we took to the air.

Thankfully, Darian shakes his head, "We should regroup. We don't know what this artifact does or how she could wield it. For all we know, she could very well remove you from the sky and this plane of existence. We regroup, recover, and think of another way to cut the head off the snake."

Chapter 55

Eiara

We return to the battlefield outside of Maximillia as they gather around large burning pyres of the dead, mourning the loss of their loved ones as my heart weighs heavy in my chest.

How many of them will we lose in the end?

How many have we already lost due to the machinations of a madman?

A shiver wracks my body, and I cross my arms in an attempt to stay warm. Val's strong arm snakes around my waist, tugging me into a warm, hard chest as his long, dark hair tickles my cheek.

I eagerly melt into him, leaning my head back to his shoulder. I feel his heart beating steadily in his chest as he holds me tightly against him.

It takes a moment before my pulse slows, matching his steady rhythm, and I wrap my arms alongside his.

He angles his head to look at me better, "How are you feeling?"

Taking note of the weariness in my body, I shake my head. "I'm fine. Tired as hell, but otherwise okay."

"You're getting stronger," he says with pride as he glances at the crowds surrounding the pyres. "It wasn't that long ago that you wondered if you could do more than just dream-weave. Many people here wouldn't be alive if it weren't for you."

He presses a kiss to my temple, and I nod slightly.

But it's not until I take in our surroundings that his words truly sink in because that's when I start to notice more than just the carnage.

More than just the brutality of what happened.

A little girl chases, whom I assume is their mother, as she carries drinks to some individuals who are getting their wounds tended to.

Not far from them, two men hug one another, and tears stream down their faces as they embrace.

A few feet from them is a young boy searching the crowd with concern painted across his features. He pauses, and a mixture of relief and joy takes over him as he launches toward an older man sitting on the ground.

I suppose Val's right in that sense.

War is ugly.

It's indiscriminate and unfair, and though I may have taken a route many would deem unconventional... it saved enough that I do not regret my actions.

Val holds me for another long moment as we watch families reunite, and I can't help but remember the phoenix statue as smoke billows into the air.

My heart clenches painfully at the memory, and my mind wanders to Kouros, Cade, and my parents.

"Hey, Val,"

I feel him lean in, "Yeah?"

"Tell me about gods and their mates."

His brows pinch together, "Well, from what we know, they typically only mated with other gods, and their relationships were mostly kept secret to protect one another," he glances at Darian before scanning the crowds around the pyres, "Assuming you're asking this for the reason I'm thinking, we don't know what happens if a god were to mate with someone who isn't from Meloris. I've heard stories, but..."

He trails off, unsure whether the stories are factual enough, and I squeeze one of his arms across my abdomen, "Tell me anyways."

"There's only been rumor of it happening, nothing anyone could ever prove but... Of all the stories and fables of gods who chose Servilians or another god as their mates, they had some kind of connection to their mates in some way, which is why it usually makes the mate a target because if anything happened to one, it would drive the other to madness."

My heart stutters, "Can you tell me one of the stories?"

His arms tighten around my stomach, "There was one story of a woman in the mountains of Nomentum who claimed to have bonded with a god when he saved her after she fell into a ravine. From what the stories say, she died in childbirth, giving the god a son who grew up to curse his father for not saving her. The god had gone insane when his Servilian mate died, and he cursed his son for causing her death."

His thumb glides along my skin soothingly, "The god was cursed to never love again, to never mate with another and the son was cursed to kill those around him. Thus both father and son disappeared into the mountains, never to be seen again."

I laugh softly, "This sounds like an excellent story if you're trying to convince someone not to mate with a god."

Val grins, and my heart flutters dangerously in my chest. "Well, I think that ship has sailed already."

I frown. "What do you mean?"

The look he gives me is uncertain like he's unsure if I'm joking or if he should really clarify.

"Are you trying to say that we're already mates?"

The way his features soften has my head swirling.

"I think there's an explanation behind how we're connected, and mates are one of the most likely possibilities. I'm still not sure how or when it happened, but I'm not mad about it."

What if they didn't want to mate with me?

Is this why Kouros wanted to kill them?

Am I just putting them in danger more by choosing them?

Was Kouros trying to force the mating bond on me?

Panic wells up as the influx of thoughts clouds my mind, and Val turns me to face him.

"Hey, hey!" He cups my cheeks and tilts my head toward him, searching my face, "I know myself and my brothers. Believe me when I say that outside of how much we care about you, the mating bond is an honor, not a burden."

Memories of Kouros' threats echo in my mind, and though I know I should take Val's words as they are, I can't help but feel like I'm putting them all at risk and have been doing so unknowingly.

My eyes squeeze shut, and I suck in a ragged breath as Val's lips press against mine.

The moment our lips touch, my chest swells as adoration, happiness, love, and fierce protectiveness wash over me like a tidal wave.

Tears fill my eyes, and I pull back to look at him as a smile tugs at the corner of his lips.

"I'm sure it's overwhelming, but it feels right to me. It always has, always will."

I lean my forehead against him, breathing him in as I feel someone approach from the side.

Kieran.

"Well, lovebirds, what do ya say we get some food and much-needed rest?"

Chapter 56

Eiara

As the sun slowly sets beyond the horizon, the temperature drops with it, and my teeth chatter as we walk past civilians disassembling the battering ram in front of the large stone gates.

Rocks and boulders of varying sizes lay across the road, splattered with crimson-stained snow that's long since turned to ice.

To my left, Kieran blows warm air into his hands as he steps over a rock, "If I ever complain about Lavinium, remind me of today."

Val snickers behind me as Gray shrugs, "It's not that bad."

The wind blows suddenly, and I squint as the needle-like sensation in my cheeks intensifies, "Speak for yourself."

Gray's grin widens, and the wild look in his eye is only there momentarily before he scoops me into his arms again.

"If you wanted to be carried, Goddess, all you had to do was ask."

"Who said I wanted to be carried?"

He leans in until the tips of our noses touch and wiggles his eyebrows, "Are you saying you want me to put you down?" the heat from his body suddenly intensifies, seeping into my stiff limbs as I narrow my eyes.

"No," I murmur, and he grins widely again.

Caspian and Darian lead the way through the narrow roads filled with people who scream Darian's name or stare at us warily. It's not long before we're pushing through the doors of an inn, and Kieran moves to the counter as the rest of us head toward the largest table in the room.

Gray sets me on my feet, gesturing to a chair before taking the spot next to it, and Val snickers as he takes the seat to my left.

Kieran walks over and takes a seat at the end of the table. "We got the biggest room, but you'll have to work your magic again, Val."

Val grins, "Fine, I'll supersize the bed, but I call center dibs."

Zayne glances around the room as Darian and Caspian sit across from me. I shake my head, "Honestly, with how cold it is... I didn't think I could be happier having so many bodies in one bed, but here we are." Zayne's lips twitch as Caspian takes a sip of his drink.

"Lay next to me, and you won't need the extra body heat, Goddess." I blink, turning to look at Gray as his grin broadens.

Kieran looks between each of us, "So what now?"

There's a long, drawn-out silence as Darian rubs his jaw, and Caspian appears lost in thought as his lips purse.

"We could retake Aveentia from Samira's control, but we would risk much in the process." Caspian offers, glancing at his brother, who shakes his head slightly.

"As much as a war of territory sounds necessary, we don't have the luxury of an army that can contend with hers. Besides, if enough innocents die in this war, we won't have the ability to repopulate. Servilia could become no more than a handful of nomads by the end of that kind of bloodshed."

Gray abruptly stands, his chair falling backward, and the room falls silent as he stalks toward a nearby table. His entire body is tense as he leans down, bringing his face within an inch of an older man sitting with a group of others.

"Say that again," the muscles in his forearms rippling as he tilts his head. He searches the man's face with a vicious look in his eyes, and I glance at Caspian and Darian, though neither of them looks inclined to intervene.

In fact, if I didn't know better, I'd say they condone Gray's aggressive stance towards the individual.

"Say it," His look has gone from rage to taunting, as if he is egging the man on. "Say it for everyone, including my brothers, to hear."

Seemingly accepting whatever challenge he sees in Gray's eyes, the older man sneers, "I said, maybe we should just throw the goddess into Aveentia by herself so she can do her part."

The others at his table nod slightly in agreement and my heart wrenches.

I knew there was general dislike and frustration with the gods, but I didn't think it would be this bad, especially after the battle.

Emboldened by his companions' subtle agreement, the man continues, "In fact, the good-for-nothing goddess can take back Aveentia and then march right back to Meloris, where she belongs with all the other absent gods."

No sooner have the words left his mouth when Gray moves and it all happens so fast that I likely would have missed it had I blinked.

Within seconds, the man is pulled to his feet and thrown onto his back atop the table. Gray reaches into the man's mouth as a gurgling shriek fills the air before he withdraws his hand, holding a large piece of the man's tongue in his hand with half of it blackened and smoking.

Holy shit, he burned his tongue off.

By now, the others at the table are on their feet, and they take a healthy step back from Gray, who holds the man's tongue tauntingly towards them.

"Dragon got your tongue?" His golden eyes burn bright as he clutches the tongue in his palm, and his flames engulf it. He curls his hand into a fist and turns it over, releasing the black dust as it falls to the ground.

The man moans as he holds his mouth, his whimpers catching Gray's attention.

"The goddess saved thousands today, including my brothers. Where were you, I wonder?" he pushes to his feet and glances at the others, "Any other suggestions on what the goddess should do?"

They shake their heads nervously, and he returns to the table with a sweet smile. I can only blink as I look between him and the table of men staring at him with a healthy amount of fear.

Val snickers beside me, bringing my attention to the rest of the table.

None of them look surprised or upset, which has me even more confused since this must be considered typical behavior for Gray.

Kieran must notice my confusion as he laughs slightly, "Has Darian not filled you in on Gray's tendencies?"

"Only the seer and his eye," I murmur, making Gray rear back.

"He stole Kieran's cup!" he gestures to one of the cups on the table in exasperation, and I can't help but laugh as the inn's doors open once more and a handful of people make their way in.

It was just a cup?

"It wasn't even full," Zayne interjects, but Gray waves his hands in front of him.

"He should have foreseen the repercussions. I was simply delivering justice," Gray grins wildly before taking a sip of his drink.

"Hopefully, I avoid a future with such punishments," Vates voice rings out as she approaches the table, lowering her heavy hood to her shoulders.

"As long as you don't steal things that don't belong to you..." Gray warns, wiggling his finger at her before taking another swig.

"Wouldn't dream of it. As much as I'd love to be here with good news, I'm afraid there's a reason I came urgently." She says, moving closer to the table as the tongueless man and his friends leave the inn.

"More urgent than the fact that Samira has the artifact?" Darian asks, leaning forward.

Vates nods, "Though it may be one and the same. Rumors are coming from Sabinia that another dead zone has been discovered near Lavinium. While these rumors are unconfirmed by trusted sources, I fear they are legitimate." She pauses, "I am still unable to see the paths of those affected by Samira's dark magic, but upon looking at yours..." she says, gesturing to everyone at the table, "When I peer upon your paths there, they go dark."

The table goes silent as everyone falls into contemplation.

"What do we know about her operations out of Lavinium?" I ask, looking at Caspian directly.

The muscle in his jaw works as his eyes drop to the table thoughtfully, "Lavinium was mostly her interrogation base. She frequently brought prisoners who had some decent ability to use magic in and brought them to the lower levels near the mountain." his face hardens as he glances around the table, "None of them left."

"The lower levels?" Zayne asks Caspian with a frown, "She never had me interrogate there."

Caspian shakes his head, "You either got them first, or she would have them brought to the cellars. When I was banished, she had Blair bring them to her to be interrogated. She ordered me to deliver two more children after my banishment was broken."

My heart clenches in my chest as Zayne curses, his knuckles turning white around the handle of his mug.

"The children," Zayne chews out between his clenched teeth, "She had me bring her children to the cellars near the library once I had finished with them."

Caspian's jaw feathers and bile rises in my throat.

If Zayne's interrogation of me was any indication, I doubt they would have left him in any state worthy of answering questions.

In fact, the more I consider it, the more it doesn't seem to make sense.

I frown at Zayne, "Why would she interrogate them when you already did that for her? It doesn't make sense."

"I'm not even sure what she was looking for," Zayne says softly, and I know I'm not imagining the shadows in his eyes as he holds my gaze.

As the realization hits me, dread coats my veins like oil, and my heart gallops in my chest, "You said those she interrogated had magical abilities?"

Caspian nods, "Every one, some more capable than others, but all of them able. Why?"

"Kouros mentioned that she was draining all the prominent bloodlines. What if he meant magic-wielding bloodlines?" I ask, staring at Caspian as his eyes widen.

"Why wouldn't she have drained ours?" Kieran asks, leaning his forearms on the table.

"Perhaps it wasn't beneficial, or she assumed her control was unbreakable." I offer before shaking my head, "Regardless, it seems we know that Lavinium is our next destination whether we like it or not."

Though, not knowing what we will find makes me uneasy.

Gray takes a sip of his drink, "Well, seer. How long until we leave?"

My heart plummets as she glances at me apologetically, "Rest tonight, but we must leave for Sabinia at the first light of dawn."

I jolt as Gray stands abruptly, walking over to where I sit and I tilt my head to look at his towering form, "Gr-"

No sooner have I started to speak when he leans down and scoops me into his arms.

"Now, now, Goddess. It's time for you to recharge, and I'm not about to let you freeze to death in your sleep."

His arms flex as he pulls me into his chest, and as if to emphasize his point, warmth radiates from his skin, only melting me further into him.

The scraping wood of chairs shifting fills the air as the others stand, and Gray's eyes slide to mine as he turns toward the back of the inn.

"Thank you for earlier, by the way."

Shock flashes across his face before a grin forms, "Are you thanking me for taking someone's tongue, Goddess?"

I blink at him, and my cheeks burn. "I—"

Caspian's voice sounds out close beside us, making my heart thunder in my chest, "She's got quite a tendency to lean toward violence, isn't that right, little one?"

Gray snaps his head to Caspian as his eyes widen. "Oh?" He casts his eyes down to mine with a grin that creeps across his face. "Is this true, Goddess?"

"I stabbed you one time, Caspian. And you can't tell me you didn't deserve it."

He answers with a reluctant huff, and my pulse jumps erratically as Gray leans in close, "Did you make him bleed?"

Caspian scoffs, "Hardly."

"It took me over an hour to clean the blood off the floor. I don't think 'hardly' covers it."

Gray shifts me in his arms as we near the doors to the room, pressing me closer to his collarbone.

He pushes through the doorway and sets me on my feet near the edge of the bed before taking a step back. "Where did you stab him, Goddess?"

I glance at Caspian, who is only a handful of steps away, tugging his shirt over his head. My eyes track the movement, with each inch of his body revealed before he tosses it to the ground. His sun-kissed skin over the defined muscles in his abdomen flexes and ripples with his movements.

My fingers twitch lightly at my sides, remembering the night at his house when I sat naked on top of him.

The memory of how he felt beneath my touch resurfaces, and my heart stutters in my chest as the image of his head between my legs flashes through my mind.

When my eyes meet his again, his lips twitch as if he knows exactly where my mind went.

"Goddess?" Gray's teasing tone tells me that he, too, knows what kind of thoughts are plaguing me.

My feet carry me forward of their own volition, and my heart thunders in my chest as I lean down to point at the spot on Caspian's thigh where I had once buried my dagger.

"Here."

The moment my hand brushes Caspian's thigh, his breath hitches, and my eyes snap to his.

For a glimmer of a moment, I wonder if the old wound is still tender until his jaw feathers, and I don't mistake the way his gaze darkens as he searches my face.

The look he's giving me makes my stomach flip as my pulse rages.

I know what he wants.

Hell, I know what I want.

But as the ghost of Kouros' hands glides across my skin, mixing desire with guilt and shame, I don't know if it's possible.

Gray walks to the side of the room, kicking off his boots as he tugs his shirt overhead before tossing it to the ground. He takes one look at me before glancing at Caspian, and a dark grin creeps across his face.

There's no way they could both know what I'm feeling yet... Could they?

Gray squats down, dropping to sit on the floor with his legs crossed. He leans back onto his palms and raises his brow at me, "Well, Goddess. Tell us what you need."

My heart stutters in my chest as my gaze flicks to Caspian, and the smile that tugs at his lips makes my insides do somersaults.

"What I need..." my throat tightens, and I try to hide the tremors in my voice, "I need you to erase him."

The mixture of rage and understanding in Caspian's burning emerald eyes sends relief through my veins.

If anyone can help me, it's him.

For all his faults, one thing about Caspian remains a constant, which is that he's not just a monster that can scare away the demons that haunt me.

He's my monster, and I've never needed him more.

Caspian steps in close, and my head tilts slightly to look at him as he tugs the hem of my shirt up, lifting it over my head.

My hair falls against my bare shoulders as he tosses my shirt aside, and I fight the urge to cover myself as he searches my face.

"Get on the bed, little one."

The door opens to the room as Zayne walks through. His gaze flicks to each of us before he steps aside, leaning against the wall.

I ease myself down until my fingers meet the plush mattress and slowly move further onto the bed, positioning myself in the center.

Caspian kneels on the bed, stalking forward until he's stationed at my feet, "Where?"

I swallow against the lump in my throat, my gaze shifting to Zayne against the wall, "He restrained my hands over my head."

The moment the words leave my lips, Zayne's eyes flutter closed, and the muscle in his jaw clenches.

Caspian leans in as his knee slides between my legs, and his towering form slowly covers my body.

My heart races in my chest as his large hand wraps around one of my wrists and brings it to his lips before gently tugging it over my head. I squeeze my eyes shut, fighting the tears pooling beneath my lids as he repeats the action with my other wrist.

Somewhere inside me, there's a conflict of emotions waging war between the memory of Kouros' touch and the mixture of trust and desire that fills my veins.

His dark hair falls forward as he tilts his head, his bright emerald eyes burning into mine with the question.

"He..." My breath hitches as Zayne's magic secures my wrists over my head, freeing Caspian's hands as he leans his arms on either side of me—anxiety, fear, and terror simmer beneath the surface as I focus on my breathing for a moment.

With our faces no more than an inch apart, my voice comes out as no more than a whisper, "Chest, stomach, then lower..."

Chapter 57

Eiara

Anger flashes across his face, and he leans his forehead against mine, "There is nothing I regret more than the time it took for me to get to you."

Being this close, breathing his air, feeling his body on mine, it's overwhelming. My pulse jumps as he presses his lips to my collarbone.

He places a kiss on my chest directly over the stain of Kouros' touch, and my entire body stiffens.

Without missing a beat, he scrapes the sharp point of his canine against my skin, just enough to draw blood before he presses another more fervent kiss, sucking and laving at my skin.

Is he...?

My eyes flick down to where his lips touch the superficial wound on my chest as it stitches together, and a fresh set of tears spring to my eyes.

He's making his mark just to heal them using my power. I feel his lips against my skin once more and brace for my body to react negatively.

But it doesn't.

His emerald eyes meet mine, and it's as if my entire world has narrowed into this room. This man, whom I once held so much anger, disappointment, and frustration toward, has somehow become my salvation.

"If the first time between us was a form of worship, little one, then I will gladly venerate your body as my altar," his breath skates across my skin, and guilt laden desire pools in my core as he holds my gaze, pressing another tender kiss to my chest.

He slides himself lower, his lips trailing down the center of my body to my navel until he reaches the waistline of my pants.

Still, the look in his eyes remains as if searching for any indication of discomfort as he unravels the ties at my waist before tugging the material down my hips.

He leans back to pull my pants down my legs, tossing them next to the bed, and my gut twists nervously, "He—"

My body trembles as I recount the memories, doing my best to ignore the echoes of radiating pain that still seems so fresh.

"He broke my hips, my arm, and each of my fingers repeatedly," my voice is no more than a whisper as Gray curses loudly, sounding much closer to the bed than he was before.

With my throat tightening, I know I need to tell them why.

A shudder runs through me as Caspian glides his hands under each of my thighs, sliding them up to cup my ass.

Tears fall freely from my eyes as my body tremors, "He said he was going to kill each of you if I didn't give in and do what he wanted," I gasp as Caspian's teeth sink into my right hip.

The pain of my skin tearing pales in comparison to the moment his teeth reach the bone, and electric pain shoots down my thigh but quickly diminishes as he uses my power to repair the wound.

The moment his lips kiss the newly healed skin, a sob claws out of my throat, and he freezes as our eyes meet.

I'm probably a hot mess.

My eyes feel swollen from the tears that stain my cheeks and have fallen down my neck to the bed. My throat is tight from the emotion that clogs it, while my chest heaves from the mixture of pain and relief that courses through my veins.

But I don't want him to stop.

With each moment of pain, each second of agony feels like he's claiming that piece of me for his own and using my own power to heal the unseen wound that festers beneath.

Caspian positions himself over my other hip, "What did he want, little one?" his lips brush my skin, and I can't suppress the shiver that sweeps through my body.

"He wanted me to—" his teeth sink into my skin once more until he reaches the bone, and I cry out, gasping deep breaths as I watch him kiss the wound gently.

"Go on, little one."

"He wanted me to accept him in as my mate, and to do so, he used threats... pain... and my own body against me."

Blood trails down his chin as he angles his head to look at me better, "And did you?"

My eyes avert to the side as shame coats my veins like hot oil.

"Look at me," his command jolts me, and my eyes snap to his. "Did you claim him as your own?"

The tone in his voice is oddly comforting, and though my entire being screams guilt and shame, knowing that he managed to coax my orgasm from me, I cling to that comfort with everything I have as I shake my head.

"Words, Sunshine." Darian's voice rings out, and my eyes snap to the side where he stands against the wall with Val and Kieran on either side.

I didn't even notice them come in.

My body trembles once more beneath Caspian as my gaze drags to where he remains between my legs, "No. I did not. But I—"

I snap my mouth shut as Caspian shakes his head.

"Kouros is either mistaken or misinformed. For a goddess to mate, they must claim the other as theirs irrevocably before solidifying the bond... and that is much more than just a manipulation of the flesh. To do such an act would be to bind fibers of your soul together, which you have already experienced."

My heart beats frantically as I soak in his words, glancing at Darian, Val, Kieran, and Zayne. The sixth sense of knowing where they are and the faint echoes of their emotions from where they stand reaffirm that I've tied myself to them in a way I can't describe.

This also reaffirms that I do not share this bond with others outside this room.

My blurry-eyed gaze shifts to Gray, who stands only a few feet away, and my heart thunders in my chest as his molten eyes burn bright.

Heat flashes across his face, "Say it, Goddess."

Pulse raging in my ears with my chest heaving, Caspian places another kiss on my abdomen, and his fingers squeeze my skin.

"If you would both have me-"

Gray tuts, wagging his finger from side to side, "I'll say it again, Goddess. Tell us what you need."

I don't wait before answering, "You," dropping my gaze to where Caspian is as he places another kiss lower, and desire pools in my body, "And you. I need you both."

Caspian eases himself lower, his lips and teeth grazing my skin as he nips along my inner thigh, his breath skating over the trail he leaves with his kisses.

"Valerian," Caspian's hands glide to the small of my back as his attention turns to me, "Why do you need us, little one?"

The bed suddenly shifts as my hips are raised higher, and vines of soft moss tickle around Caspian's hands on my lower back. Caspian's eyes darken as he peers at me from between my thighs, and I nearly forget the question.

"Because you're both mine."

The moment the final word leaves my lips, Caspian's mouth is on me.

Audience forgotten, my back arches as his tongue glides over my pussy before he works my clit, and I tug at my restraints. His movements are slow, like he has all the time in the world.

It's as if I'm a five-course meal, and he intends to savor me bite by bite.

His fingertips dig into my skin as he grips the small of my back in an attempt to pull me further into his face.

With the stubble of his beard grazing against my skin, his nose and mouth press against me like he's determined to eat his way to my soul.

I guess, in a way, he is.

He pauses slightly, "In the centuries I've been alive, never have I tasted something so intoxicating."

My entire body stiffens, and I glance down to find he's already staring at me with a level of rage that borders on terrifying, and I would be scared if it were directed at me.

Instead, it does the opposite, sending a shiver down my spine from the promise clearly written across his features.

He does not simply dislike Kouros for what he's done.

A bolt of dread settles in my stomach.

If he thinks what happened this far was bad...

"What else did he do?" The violence radiating from him is palpable, and I can feel the anger bleeding through from the others in the room.

I swallow against the lump in my throat, "He bit my neck, hit me in the face, and..." my voice trails off as Caspian releases his grip under my thighs.

My hand restraints come undone, and the second my arms go slack, I cover my face with my palms.

I can't say it.

It's too embarrassing.

Saying it makes it real.

Caspian gathers me in his arms as the moss beneath me lowers, and I'm vaguely aware of the others as I feel them shift around the room, their uncertainty and worry creeping through into my mind.

"Eiara," Zayne's voice sounds out, and something inside me fractures.

He knows.

Of course, he does.

Zayne taught me how to truly come to terms with what happened based on his own pain.

Tears stream down my cheeks, falling onto the skin of my bare chest as I pull my hands down from my face to look at Caspian.

If not for me, then I have to face it for them.

"He sat on my chest and forced himself on me," my voice cracks as his grip on me tightens, almost painfully, "I nearly died from it, but he healed me before doing it again," my voice is barely audible, trembling from getting the words out by sheer force of will.

Val and Kieran curse from either side of me, and fury engulfs the room. It nearly overwhelms my senses, and it takes everything I have to push it from my mind.

"I will peel every inch of his skin from his body," the edge to Gray's voice is lethal, yet still, somehow, it brings a sense of calm to me as my gaze locks with his.

"This is enough," Caspian's voice sounds out, "We're not going to push things further than we need to right now. You've been through enough."

I shake my head, "No."

"Goddess," Gray warns, but my stubborn mind has been made up. I'm not letting Kouros take this from me.

He's already manipulated my life in some of the most heinous and awful ways.

Allowing him to keep me from bonding with Gray and Caspian is akin to him winning, and I refuse.

My heart thunders in my chest, and my stomach twists anxiously as determination settles into my veins.

Pushing out of Caspian's arms, I crawl further onto the bed before turning to look at Gray.

The look on his face sends butterflies through my body but bolsters the confidence I need.

His molten amber gaze burns into mine from where he stands a few feet from the bed as I upturn my palm between us.

"Come here," heat flashes across his face as he steps forward, stopping abruptly as I hold my palm out, "Ah, ah, ah. Crawl."

The surprise mixed with excitement that dances across his features sends a thrill down my spine, and I watch with rapt attention as he sinks to his knees.

He stalks past Caspian on the bed, stopping mere inches before me as he searches my face. I glance at the soft mattress before me, and he follows my gaze.

"Lie on your back," his pupils blow wide as he positions himself, and my gaze slides to Caspian.

I can tell from the look on his face that he's still apprehensive about doing this now, for my sake.

But I know what is best for me and what I want.

I won't sleep tonight until these men are mine in every sense of the word.

"This is my decision to make if you do not wish to—"

I hardly get the words out before he swallows audibly, "I am not forcing myself on you, little one."

"It's a good thing I'm not asking you to, then. I'm going to sit on Gray's face while you fuck my throat because it's what I want. Unless that's not—"

My words get caught in my throat as a flicker of emotion flashes across his face.

It stopped when Caspian returned.

My gaze flicks to Zayne before landing on Caspian once more. "Do you want this?"

The guarded surprise on his face as he searches mine tells me everything I need to know, and my pulse hikes.

What if he doesn't want this?

What if he was only doing this for my benefit?

What if-

"Answer her, asshole, or else I'm burning you to a crisp."

Caspian pauses, and his gaze flicks from Gray to the others before landing on me. "I haven't stopped thinking of what it would be like to fuck you since I tasted you that night and you came around my fingers. It's kept me awake at night and driven me to the edge of madness nearly every day. You were the sole reason I didn't give in while Samira had me under her control. If you think the answer to your question is anything but yes, you severely underestimate the unrelenting grip you've unknowingly held over me from the moment I first laid eyes on you."

My heart thunders as he holds my gaze, and as if to emphasize his point, he cocks his head slightly, "There's not a language alive or dead on either Earth or Servilia that could describe the way I have needed you."

The corded muscles in his body flex as he moves to the edge of the bed, towering over a smirking Gray, whose molten gold eyes slide to me with a level of desire that flips my stomach.

My nerves are frayed, but this insatiable desire to bind myself to them, to meld my soul to theirs, surpasses and drowns everything else out.

It's like each of these men, their presence, their very core selves, speaks to my soul in a way I can't comprehend.

Every person I met prior had a normal relationship with me, a normal friendship in which you can go days, weeks, or months without hearing from one another and be perfectly fine.

My relationship with my men is different.

It's raw, innate, and it feels just right.

Gray's eyes track my movements as I crawl up the length of his body; my hands graze the bare skin of his abdomen, and my fingertips glide over his chest until I'm bracing myself over him with my hands on either side of his head.

With my heart galloping in my chest and our faces merely inches from each other, his hands grip the back of my thighs firmly, holding me in place.

I'm about to speak when he interrupts, "Whatever you're going to ask, Goddess, just know I'm thirty seconds away from hauling you over my face."

My gaze drops to his mouth as he talks, and as my mind wonders how his lips would feel on mine, he suddenly closes the distance between us.

His hands squeeze the back of my thighs, and I'm vaguely aware of the bed shifting slightly, but the way he's kissing me sends my mind into a tailspin.

Everything about the way Gray kisses is chaotic and so entirely him—intense, wild, and consuming. Our kiss breaks only for his canine to sink into my lower lip, and I gasp through the sharp pain as he draws blood before his lips move against mine once more.

His fingers dig into my skin as if restraining himself, and just the thought sends a heady mix of desire deep into my core.

As if the raw, unfiltered desire raging through my veins wasn't enough, my attention turns to Caspian standing in front of us, and the moment I break apart from Gray, he pulls me by my thighs onto his chest.

Seeing his mess of dark hair below me, the feral glint in his bright eyes sends heat through my body.

Subtle movement in front of me catches my attention as my gaze flicks to Caspian's.

Chapter 58

Caspian

My dick throbs painfully against the fabric of my pants as she glances up at me, still seated high on Gray's chest.

The smear of crimson where Gray bit her is a stark contrast against her full lips and fair skin as her blue eyes pierce into mine.

Her body is bared to us from where she sits like she's a carved statue of eternal beauty itself.

She claimed a space inside of me I didn't know existed.

It was like being awoken from a long dream into a life that had for so long felt as though it wasn't my own, and each step I've taken since then has been toward her.

I imagine each person in this room feels the same.

Though, perhaps they deserve the honor more than I do.

My gaze rakes down her body, taking in the curves of her breasts, her nipples, and the way her hips dimple and widen from where they rest on Gray's chest.

She's a physical embodiment of the gods in every sense.

I catch the shiver that runs through her, and my gaze snaps to hers again. "Take those off," she gestures to my pants, and my dick pulsates beneath the material as if echoing her sentiment.

It's an odd sensation being commanded but doing it of my own volition.

It's liberating, if nothing else, and as I untie the string keeping them at my hips before tugging the material down where it falls to the floor, and I still feel more in control than I ever have.

My gaze drops to her mouth, and my dick throbs once more.

Well, in control in some ways.

A smile tugs at my lips as her gaze drops to my cock between us, and as it bobs once more, she swallows before looking at me.

"Last chance to change your mind, little one."

She opens her mouth to answer as Gray pulls her over his face, hooking his arms around her thighs as a surprised sound escapes her, and her hands brace against my thigh and hip to keep herself upright from the sudden movement.

Her eyes nearly roll to the back of her head as Gray groans in satisfaction, and I pull the lock of hair that had fallen in front of her face if only to watch how she reacts to him.

My dick throbs again as if it needs to remind me that the woman who has invaded every orifice of my being sits before me, wanting that which I've craved more than air itself.

Gray grips her thighs tightly as the muscles of her legs tense, and she sways her hips to grind against his face, releasing a soft moan before her eyes flutter open.

The half-lidded gaze she levels me with sends more blood straight to my dick, and her hand slides from my thigh to wrap around the base of my cock.

My knees nearly buckle as she glides her hand from base to tip while fighting to keep her eyes from rolling.

She's fucking perfect.

I take a small step to close the distance as she leans forward, licking the length of my cock as her nails dig into my hip almost painfully.

But I don't give a shit about that.

Hell, she could stab me again, and I wouldn't give a flying fuck if she kept touching me the way she is now.

Who knew the path I was on would lead someone as lost as me to a soul so pure and immensely strong as hers.

None of us in this room is worthy of her, yet we all claim her in our own ways.

And here I am still trying to figure out where my place is in all of this.

Her silver hair falls into her eyes as she wraps her mouth over the tip of my cock, and I forget how to breathe, watching my dick disappear inch by inch as she takes it deeper into her mouth.

Val curses under his breath beside us, and my hands mindlessly move to hold her long strands of hair, forming a fist at the back of her head.

She gets halfway down the length of my cock before withdrawing with a pop, and her blue eyes collide with mine, "I—" she manages to get out before a husky moan escapes her.

It takes every last ounce of willpower not to ease myself back into her mouth as I wait impatiently for her, and my hand squeezes the hair.

"Caspian, I need you to fuck my throat, ah-"

My balls tighten, and I'm nearly about to come as her hand grips the base of my cock tightly, squeezing it as Gray continues to devour her beneath us.

If I weren't enjoying her expressions so much, I'd have already ripped her off of him and sunk my face between her thighs.

"I don't think I can be gentle, little one." My voice is strained, and I'm fighting for my life as she gasps, and her eyes lock onto mine beneath strands of silver hair.

"If I wanted gentle, I'd ask for it. I said I want you to fuck my throat." she cries out. Her eyes roll fully back, and she gyrates as an orgasm takes over her body.

Just like that night in the house, her body trembles with each wave of pleasure, but this time she doesn't fight it.

There's no uncertainty in her movements, and a sense of pride washes over me, knowing I was among the first to give her that experience.

Even considering the circumstances of that night.

That's when her words when she dream-walked sink in.

She is no longer the same woman she was when all that happened.

No, she's much, much more than that.

The waves of pleasure appear to subside as her eyes flutter open, locking with mine, "The moment it becomes too much, little one, tap my hip."

Heat dances across her half-lidded gaze, and she moves at the same time as I do, wrapping her mouth around my cock as I squeeze her head further down the length of my dick.

I hit the back of her throat and squeeze her head further into my dick as her nails bite into the skin of my thighs. Her throat constricts against me, and as tears spring to her eyes, I withdraw for her to suck in a breath.

The moment she does, my fingers tighten in her hair, and I'm thrusting into her throat again. Her tongue glides against my length with each stroke as I keep my pace, allowing her a short breath before I bury myself into her mouth.

Tears stain her cheeks, and I feel myself getting close as her throat works to accommodate my size with each thrust. My pace quickens as my dick throbs against her, and a quick tap at my hip sends my heart into my throat as I withdraw quickly.

Did I hurt her?

Had she been tapping, and I didn't realize?

Fuck.

She gasps and sputters, her chest heaving as she swallows. Gray even releases her thighs, letting her slide to the side slightly as she catches her breath.

Fuck, if I hurt her...

"Gray, stand up," she whispers, "Caspian, come lie down with your feet on the floor."

Surprise rifles through me, but Gray climbs off the bed with his face glistening with her arousal, and I turn to seat myself on the edge. Hardly a second passes before she's easing herself into my lap, with the length of my dick pressed against her as she wraps an arm around my shoulder and neck.

"I want you both at the same time."

My dick throbs against her, and her lips twitch as if knowing that's me answering.

Gray positions himself behind her as she reaches between us to angle the tip of my dick at her entrance, and I've entirely forgotten how to breathe and think.

She searches my face with those bright blue eyes, and my chest tightens, "In case it wasn't clear, Caspian Cathorn, I claim you and Gray both as my own. Nothing in this world or the next could keep me from you, and I would gladly lay my life down if it meant keeping either of you from harm."

My heart nearly stops beating in my chest as she leans in to press her lips to mine, and I groan against her as she sinks onto my cock.

Her soft lips move against mine, and as the taste of honey and lavender overwhelms my senses, something inside me cracks.

My hand finds the smooth skin of her hip before snaking around her waist as she eases down inch by inch. My tongue finds the seam of her lip before she opens for me, and I have to fight the urge to thrust up into her the rest of the way as she gyrates with each movement.

If watching her orgasm was a storm passing, then I am amidst the swell of the ocean in a tsunami of everything that is her as she settles herself fully seated on me.

Each movement of her mouth against mine has me squeezing her tighter into me, and when she suddenly tenses, I almost forget that there are others in the room until she pulls back.

Her fair skin is flushed as she glances over her shoulder where Gray stands fully nude, and when she tightens around my dick and gasps, I groan.

Chapter 59

Eiara

I lean further into Caspian until we're skin-to-skin, our lips a mere hairs-breadth apart as Gray continues to ease his fingers into my ass.

Caspian remains still, allowing me to breathe through the pain of being stretched.

The bed shifts on either side of us again, and I glance over to see Kieran move closer. He places his hand on my lower back as magic dances along my skin.

With the pain gone, I groan with the next stretch, "Thank you."

I pepper kisses along Caspian's collar and his neck as I feel the head of Gray's dick against my ass.

My gaze meets Caspian's once more, and my chest tightens as he presses his forehead to mine, "Are you going to come around both our cocks, little one?"

Gray pushes in, and though Kieran's magic keeps the pain at bay, I still gasp at the pressure.

"Yes," I breathe, "And you're both going to come with me."

I cry out as Gray snaps his hips, bringing them flush with my ass, and in that same moment, Caspian withdraws slightly before pushing back in.

The three of us groan in unison as their movements begin in earnest, thrusting in time with one another while I cling to Caspian for dear life.

Pressure builds in my core each time they piston into me, and my limbs tremble as they hit every spot that sends pleasure through my body.

I lean into each of their movements, trying to chase the building orgasm as their thrusts become more forceful.

"I-"

My orgasm crests as they drive into me, and my nails bite into Caspian's chest as he uses his hand twisted into my hair to tilt my head, baring my neck to him as he sinks his teeth into the sensitive skin of my neck.

The pain mixes with pleasure in a heady mix that throws me over the edge, sending my orgasm crashing over me as both men tense, burying themselves deep as they pulsate, filling me with their release.

My limbs tremble as Gray places long, drawn-out kisses along my spine, and that's when I feel it.

The sixth sense of their presence, the unseen knowledge of their existence in the back of my mind, like a piece of them woven into the very fabric of my soul.

Relief washes over me, mixed with adoration, lust, and...

My eyes flick to Caspian only to find him already searching my face.

Reverence.

Love is a term I may have once used to describe the emotions radiating from him, but this is so much more than that.

It's so overwhelming that my chest tightens, and I let myself feel it all.

The feeling fills my heart to the point where I don't know where my emotions end and his begin, but it's not until I start to feel it from every corner of the room that I look around to see Val, Kieran, Darian, and Zayne all staring at me with the same look in their eyes, mirroring what I feel from Caspian and Gray.

My throat constricts as both men withdraw, and Gray settles onto the bed next to Caspian.

"Looks like you'll never be able to get rid of us now, Goddess."

Gray's voice is oddly quieter than usual, though the contentment radiating from him says more than words perhaps ever could.

A smile tugs at my lips, "Uno reverse, Gray. Now you're stuck with me."

He grins as I toss him a wink, and Kieran hooks his arms under me to lift me from the bed, "Let's get you cleaned up, sweetheart. We've got a long trip back to Sabinia in the morning."

And just like that, reality comes crashing down over the slice of heaven we carved out in this room together.

I suppose so long as we're together, perhaps that slice of heaven will remain with us wherever we go.

- 390 -

Chapter 60

Eiara

We spend the next few days at sea on a boat large enough for our group as we make our way to Sabinia. The town is nearly deserted as we venture off the docks and into the almost empty streets. The few people wandering the roads eye us warily as we step further into the city.

The devastation caused by Samira when we last visited is still prominent, with strong, wooden buildings toppled and broken down all around us. A few have been restored to functionality, though remnants of the battle are evident all over the wood beams that hold them up.

"It'll be years before we can rebuild," Kieran's gaze tracks the movement as a man nearby clears rubble from the ruins.

Val glances at me with a wink before turning his attention to Kieran, "Maybe by hand, yes. But there's always magic."

My gaze flicks to Caspian, and though his eyes remain on our surroundings, the muscle in his jaw works, and the hint of concern bleeding from him sobers me.

Magic is as much at risk as everything else.

We turn a corner to see the remnants of the toryian stables, with the main beams standing around a handful of the giant creatures and a thin wooden roof overtop.

It's just enough to protect them from the elements, though with their wiry fur, I doubt they'd mind a bit of cold.

Following Kieran's lead toward the toryians, a breeze picks up, blowing dust through the empty street.

Shielding my eyes from the wind, I glance at the small, bare-bones buildings erected from the ruins. "Where is everyone?"

Zayne follows my gaze as he grasps the reins of a toryian, "Most of the repairs here will need lumber and other supplies, so I'd imagine most have gone to either Gremn or Wrennock to find some."

My brows pinch together, "Gremn or Wrennock? Are those neighboring cities?"

Val walks his toryian over with a grin, and my heart skips a beat as he leans in, "Sometimes I forget you aren't from here until you get that look on your face."

Kieran holds his hand out to help me onto the toryian, laughing as I gaze at him.

"What is so funny? What face?"

Darian's laughter fills the air as his baritone voice sounds out, "The face you make when you learn something new."

My cheeks burn as I glance between them, "I do not make a face!"

Their laughs collectively fill the air, and I purse my lips to keep from joining in as I hoist myself onto the creature's back.

"Sweetheart, the faces you make are beautiful..." Kieran pulls himself into the seat behind me, wrapping his arms around my body in a tight hug, "No matter the reason you're making them."

"I can think of a few particular faces that are my favorite," Val sounds out, his grin evident in his voice.

My cheeks burn as Kieran's arms tighten around my shoulders, "I can think of a few, too," his voice is no more than a whisper as his breath brushes against my ear, and a shiver runs through my body.

His arms glide lower, his hands grazing my arms before settling on my thighs.

I lean back into his chest, "And what faces might those be?"

Kieran steers his mount from the building onto the street as his free hand glides up my inner thigh, stopping as his thumb reaches my clit, and my heart feels like it's beating in my throat.

"This one. The face you make when you know you want more of something."

His hand leaves my thigh only to tilt my face toward him, bringing our lips no more than a hairsbreadth apart, "But more often than not, it's the face you make when you're coming that I might just love the most."

My heart thunders as raw desire courses through me, and I close the distance between us.

I'm not sure where my desire ends, and his begins as I return everything he offers. My tongue grazes the seam of his lip in a silent request, and as our lips move, it's as though my entire body is aware of him.

His touch, his breath, his taste, his very being.

I'm not sure when his hand left my chin, but just as I feel it between my legs, his magic pours from his hand into my clit, and I cry out as my body tenses with the waves of my orgasm crashing over me.

Kieran breaks our kiss, his gaze searching my face as his magic continues to send euphoria throughout my body. My eyes threaten to roll back in my head as he cuts his magic off.

The look on his face is pure satisfaction as I catch my breath, "That sweetheart is by far my favorite one."

I lean in to place one lingering kiss on his lips when Val's voice rings out into the air behind us. "Assuming we find Samira in Lavinium, how are we supposed to stop her from draining our powers like she's been draining the others?"

The question sobers me from riding the high of my orgasm, and it's clear Kieran feels the same as he wraps his arms around my shoulders once more, resting his chin atop my head.

We slowly gain distance from the ruined city as Zayne's soft voice carries in the air, "Well, I have a theory."

Every head turns to look at him as the road continues, lined with thick forest on either side.

It's a conscious effort to remain focused as my anxiety heightens.

"Over the course of time, since Eiara has been able to use magic, she has exponentially grown in power. I suspect that this is due to a multitude of reasons, but given that she managed to cleanse the altar that held Caspian for hundreds of years so soon after learning to use her power..."

My brows pinch together, and my gaze shifts to Caspian, who is already looking at me as if he is gauging my reaction more than listening to Zayne's theory.

"We already know that her power is not as limited as ours. Where most Servilians can use their reserves and pull small amounts under duress, Eiara showed she can pull directly from the source of gods' power, putting her life at risk of losing control more than burning out of power. Though she's managed her well of power better with time, there's something else I suspect may be contributing to both her well of power and ours."

Val and Darian nod as Gray raises a brow at Zayne, "Well? Spit it out already."

Kieran's arm wraps tighter around my waist, "What do you mean ours?"

Zayne's violet gaze turns to me, "I suspect that the bond between us does more than simply allow us to feel each other's presence and emotions. I suspect that it has expanded the well of power we all can pull from, and each bond has strengthened your magic."

I blink, "But that would mean all our magic wouldn't run out as quickly as it has in the past."

Zayne inclines his head, "Many of the times we were drained, you had not opened yourself to magic, so we may have pulled from the limited reserves you had. I admit, I hadn't caught on until you freed Caspian. When you were at the altar and losing control, it felt like my power was almost limitless. I wondered if it were due to the urgency of the moment, but it wasn't until the fight afterward, when you were fully drained, that I started to connect the dots."

Val rubs his chin thoughtfully, "I still don't understand how this will help keep us from being drained by Samira once we're there."

"What Zayne is trying to say," Caspian's voice rings out, "is that Eiara just bonded to Gray and me, which will have increased her well and strength. She already had enough power to free me from a blood magic that would have otherwise consumed any of us."

"How do we know that bonding to you increased her strength or well when your magic is supposedly bound?" My attention snaps to Val, and he puts his hands up, "Allegedly!"

I roll my eyes as Zayne responds, "I doubt the bond relies on that distinction rather than simply being a chain reaction to the connection between them."

"What happens if we get there but she's not strong enough? Or if she burns herself out?"

Silence falls over us, and Kieran's thumb glides soothingly along my thigh. I'm not sure whether it's meant to soothe him or me, but I lean into him as my anxiety rises.

When none of us respond, Gray laughs, "It's one of those 'We'll cross that bridge when we get to it' type of things." He grins and gives me a wink before looking ahead again.

Val glances at us with worry etched across his features. I know he has more to say, but surprisingly, he says nothing. He passes one lingering stare in my direction, his concern bleeding into me from where he sits atop his toryian before surveying the forest around us.

We ride for some time before the road crosses a river with a weathered bridge. Instead of going over it, we turn and continue along the river's edge in relative silence. The sounds of wind and water fill the air as Darian and Caspian take the head, guiding us further into the wilderness.

Half the day goes by, and with the sun at its peak, the trees around us, which were once varying colors of green, red, and yellow, begin to look haggard and decrepit.

It's as if all the nutrients in the soil have disappeared with the withered, leafless branches, and despite the river running alongside them, the cracked and dusty soil that swirls in the wind makes it seem like rain hasn't fallen for years.

Dread coils in my stomach as I glance around nervously, and when my eyes lock with Zayne's, I'm sure we both have the same thought.

The last thing we want to see is another one of those creatures, even if we're better equipped now to handle it.

Luckily, whether one wanders the lands or not, we manage through the remainder of the day unscathed, and as the sun sets, the river gives way to a lake with a connecting river across from us. Zayne and Val scan the trees cautiously, with the quietly rushing water on one side of us and the decrepit forest on the other.

Darian and Caspian murmur to one another in front, and as Gray glances to the sky, I can't help but wonder what each of them is thinking.

It's hard to reconcile that this time last year, I was just a regular scientist researching various topics, and now I'm...

Heaving a sigh, I lean further into Kieran's chest. His arms encircle my body, holding me closer to him. "Everything alright, sweetheart?"

The first moon rises slowly on the horizon of the trees, shining in the reflection of the water and casting an eerie glow amidst the starved forest.

I nod, unsure how to answer his question.

On one hand, things have never been alright in any sense of the word.

On the other, with each of these men coming into my life, things have been better than I've ever known.

It's an odd paradox.

His arms tighten around my body even more, and I nestle into his warmth, shutting my eyes as the world fades away.

By the time dawn breaks, the impressively pristine white marble of Lavinium is on full display over the tops of the trees. As we draw near, a cloud of fog thickens in the forest with each passing moment, and unease settles in my stomach like a bag of rocks.

I have no idea if I'm ready for what's to come or what to expect.

It's as if I'm on the edge of a cliff in the middle of the night, staring into an endless dark abyss with each of these men tethered to me.

If I fall, so too shall they.

But that cannot happen. I will not allow it.

Darian and Caspian veer our path from the river into the heavy mist, which has become a thick miasma, filling our lungs with each breath. We slow to a stop in front of a large aperture in a low rock face, where water slowly seeps from the bottom.

Darian nods to Zayne before he dismounts, and the rest of us follow suit.

"We'll use this to gain access to the servants' quarters, then we'll hope that we can slip by unnoticed before we find wherever this lower level is."

We encircle the opening as Darian moves towards the entrance, abruptly coming to a stop as Caspian's hand juts out in front of his chest.

"Perhaps it's best if the leader of our people doesn't go head first into the unknown," Caspian says, his voice dripping with sarcasm.

Darian's jaw works, but he concedes with a nod as Caspian takes a few steps into the crevice. My anxiety builds as he disappears into the shadows, and my magic brims beneath the surface on instinct.

Darian moves to go inside, but Gray grips his arm.

"Goddess first. Between Caspian and her, the two of them will be able to defend against whatever bullshit is waiting for us."

My eyes meet Darian's mismatched gaze, and my heart stutters at the worry on clear display in them.

"One Goddess guard, coming right up," I whisper with a forced smile before turning and walking into the dark after Caspian, keeping my eyes glued to his back.

The narrow rock tunnel is just wide enough for the men to squeeze through. Twisting to the side, the clothes on their chests and backs scrape against the jagged rock as we file through one by one.

It's so dark that I can hardly make out any shape beyond Caspian in front of me, and it takes all my mental effort to tamp down the trepidation building in my chest.

Our footsteps slosh loudly in the eerie silence, and slowly, the path widens enough that the scraping of cloth and leather against rock ceases.

It doesn't take long before the tunnel takes on a firm, rounded shape. Even though my eyes have grown accustomed to the dark, the low light allows me to track the movement of Caspian's form just barely.

I don't notice when he suddenly stops moving and collide with his back, bracing against him with my hands, "Uh, sorry."

He turns slightly, and though I can't make out his face, I hear a slight chuckle under his breath, making my face flush with embarrassment.

The outline of his arm in the dark points upward, "Here."

I squint into the abyss as his outline moves, and a loud scraping sound fills the air as he pulls down what I assume is a ladder.

"This brings us to the cellars. We will have to take the servants' corridors," he grasps the side of the ladder and pauses. "Stay close to me, little one," he whispers before climbing up.

My heart thunders in my chest with each step he takes, bringing him further away from me. He lifts a large panel above him a sliver, casting light into our entrance, and I squint against the intrusion to my senses.

The coast must be clear as he pushes the thick panel open further to crawl out and positions himself over the hole, reaching down toward me.

"Let's go, it's clear for now." I swallow audibly, gripping both sides of the ladder as I haul myself towards him. The others rustle behind me as they follow in close. My pulse slows as I reach Caspian's outstretched hand, and he eases me over the ledge onto solid ground.

My gaze travels the dimly lit tunnel with sconces that flicker an eerie light against oppressive shadows, and my stomach flips with unease as the others cover the hole in the floor with the panel once again.

Caspian and Zayne lead us slowly down the well-worn servant's corridor, and as we venture further, the air thickens. The tainted magic hangs heavy around us as if the very air we breathe wants to choke out any form of life as we come to an abrupt halt.

Peering around Caspian's large form as he turns to face the wall, confusion pulls my brows together. The hallway continues past him, but I follow his gaze to the wall, and it takes a moment before I notice it.

A thin line on either side and top marks the opening of a hidden doorway, but it's the drag marks against the dust and dirt on the floor that disappear into the stone, with chips and scratches along the side of the wall that send a cold chill down my spine.

Images of innocent people being brought here against their will flash through my mind, and my imagination runs wild as a heavy dose of anger courses through my veins.

Years of bloodshed.

Years of torn apart families.

Years of torture.

Years of lies and deceit.

All this tragedy is for the machinations of a madman toying with those he feels are below him.

Kieran's hand slides into mine, squeezing it as sadness bleeds from him. His gaze stays fixated on the marks on the wall as my heart clenches in my chest.

Caspian moves to the doorway and feels around for a way to open it before stepping back with a frown, "I've never gone inside before. She was always here waiting for them."

Val's hand on my waist catches my attention as he steps past me, "Let me take a look,"

He places his hand on the wall and shuts his eyes. A few moments pass before the ground shudders, dirt and dust kick up from the ceiling, but slowly, the stone door opens, revealing another dimly lit hallway.

Once the door stops moving, Caspian steps inside with Zayne close behind him. As I move to follow suit, Val motions to us with urgency.

"Hurry, someone is coming," his voice is hushed. His eyes are trained behind us, and I hurry past him, Gray, Darian, and Kieran trailing me.

Val shuts the door behind us, and the air is even more opposing once we're sealed inside. The sour taint of Samira's dark magic penetrates the space like a cloud of rot.

"We should hurry. We don't know how long we have until we're discovered," Caspian says, his voice betraying his own nerves as he glances down the corridor that curves to the side.

We quickly follow Caspian and Zayne down the hall into the unknown, with only our soft footfalls against stone filling the air to announce our presence. With each step, the already oppressive dark magic grows heavier until my lungs and very being feel like I'm being squeezed from within.

We're definitely in the right place.

After what feels like an eternity, Caspian and Zayne come to an abrupt halt, and my pulse rages in my ears as I peer past them to the open doorway at the end of the corridor.

Grey cloth-covered stones and weathered, brittle branches scatter the floor, coated in shades of deep brown and red. We take a few steps closer, allowing more of the room to come into view, and a loud gasp claws out of my throat as a hand quickly covers my mouth.

Horror coats my veins.

They're not cloth-covered stones and branches. They're fucking bodies.

Hundreds of them in different phases of decay lay stacked on one another across the room. Their blood-stained clothes are in tatters, entangled with one another as if they were trying to escape through the sea of bones.

It wasn't until the most recently deceased bodies at the top came into view that it became apparent what this room was filled with. Their skin is leathery and wrinkled, blood dried on their clothes, and their faces etched with terror has my chest heaving with the adrenaline coursing through my veins.

"If we're noticed too early, this becomes much more difficult, Goddess," Gray whispers against my ear, "We don't know what awaits us in that room. Compose yourself."

He releases my mouth gently, and I grind my teeth against the bile rising in my throat.

My eyes are glued to the countless withered bodies as we slowly make our way closer, and it's not until ribbons of crimson catch my attention that I manage to tear my gaze off the bodies to scan the room.

It's enormous, with five symbol-marked, towering pillars that encircle the ominous bloodstained altar emanating Samira's twisted magic.

Atop the altar is a glass bowl filled to the brim with blood and swirls of blood ribbon through the air from the bodies, as if somehow continuously feeding into the bowl.

My stomach flips as we step into the room, and Gray rumbles from behind me in a low growl, "What the hell is this place?"

"Somewhere that shouldn't exist," Zayne answers quietly, his eyes scanning the bodies.

"Were all of these people...?" I trail off, unable to finish the question.

Caspian's voice is cold and detached as he answers, "These were the magic wielders, yes."

Turning, I follow his gaze to the center of the room. "The sooner we get this over with, the better."

The second I move to take a step toward the altar, Darian's hand on my arm halts me in my tracks.

"Shield yourself first. We don't know what could happen." His gaze flicks from me to the altar, and though he doesn't outwardly show it, the concern radiating from him speaks volumes.

I nod, berating myself internally for being ill-prepared. Calling forth my power, I ease it into a cocoon over my body as I take another step closer. But nothing happens.

With each step forward, I brace for a blow, for some type of attack to come from the altar, but nothing happens. The strands of blood curling through the air don't even appear to acknowledge my existence as I side-step one when it curves to the side.

When I finally reach the center of the room, death has settled in my gut, and I twist to look back at the others. They've moved close to the center and remain mere feet from where I stand. With swords drawn as if preparing to join me at a moment's notice, my heart clenches in my chest.

Only when there's movement behind them do I realize we're not alone.

Two gargantuan soldiers stand in front of the doorway, stepping aside as Samira walks past them and steps closer.

"My, oh my. What a pleasant surprise. If I'd have known you'd deliver yourself to me, I'd have waited here instead of sending my pets." A sly smile creeps across her face as she winks at Gray tauntingly. "How is your neck, by the way? I heard you took quite the spill."

I don't miss Gray's knuckles turning white as he glares at her.

Movement to my side catches my attention, and Zayne's smoke forms his scythe.

The next few seconds happen in slow motion as the pressure from the magic in the room becomes crushing.

Within the blink of an eye, Zayne is thrown across the room into the far wall, and dust and debris from shattered bones fly into the air, obscuring our vision of him.

Darian takes a step toward the cloud of dust, his eyes wide as a heady mix of rage and worry radiate from all sides of the room.

Chapter 61

Eiara

"Zayne," Darian calls out as his gaze darts from Samira to the wall, and the room goes silent outside of Samira's raucous laughter.

Soft footfalls sound out as Zayne steps over the mounds of bodies towards us. The bones crunch beneath his weight, kicking dust up with each movement.

As his figure comes into view unscathed, the magic in the room pushes against the faint shimmer of my shield, and Samira's laughter falls flat. Zayne's violet gaze finds mine and inclines his head before continuing to my side.

"You-" Samira growls, her blood-red eyes trained on me, "You've ruined everything," she chews out, her voice shrill, "You're supposed to be dead!"

She steps closer, and the men before me snap into defensive positions, with Darian and Caspian unsheathing their swords. The weight of the magic in the room crushes deeper against their shields, and I allow my magic to flow freely through me into the space around us, equalizing the pressure in the room.

"Eiara," Zayne says softly next to me, and my heart beats like a war drum, "Whatever happens, you must focus on only one thing. We will handle Samira and her minions. Do not allow them to distract you."

Time slows, and I glance between them nervously, my gaze lingering on Kieran, his sword held ready as he gives me a wink.

"Don't worry about us, sweetheart. We'll be just fine."

They're right.

My men can handle this.

They've seen more than their fair share of bloodshed.

If I don't do my part, we're all dead anyway.

The quiet voice in the back of my mind tells me that there are worse fates than dying and that it's a serious possibility with the situation we're in.

Meeting Zayne's bright lavender gaze, I nod.

Going against all instinct, I turn my back to Samira, and she screeches as my gaze lands on the bowl sitting mere feet away at the top of the altar.

"Stop!" Samira shrieks behind me, "Kill them! Kill them all!" Heavy footsteps crunch behind me before metal sings in the air, and chaos ensues.

A sense of urgency takes over me, and I quickly close the distance to the bowl, taking large steps up the blood-stained stairs. Ribbons of crimson weave around it as if suspended by the air itself as it flows in from the bodies around us.

From the center of the bowl, my gaze lands upon a gold handle sticking out from the viscous liquid, and I frown. My magic surrounds me protectively while maintaining the shields I placed around the others early on.

I'd been so caught up in shielding them that I had nearly forgotten my own.

I reach forward in an attempt to grasp the bloodied handle just as a surge of power thrusts against the shield, sending my hand into the air as if smacked away by some unseen force.

Light catches my eye as the symbols carved into the pillars glow before returning to normal. I solidify my shield around my hand once more and attempt to grasp the handle, quickly looking at the five pillars as they glow in response.

They're protecting the bowl. It's a shield.

Chaos fills the air between shouts and the sound of steel singing, but Zayne's words repeat in my mind like a mantra.

Don't let them distract me.

Streams of my power surround the first pillar as it activates once more. The darkness thrashes against it as I squeeze the pillar, my hands mimicking the actions as I reach toward it and squeeze my fingers into a fist.

A loud crack echoes into the room, and the ground shudders as the pillar fractures down the center. Pieces crumble from the top as a surge of power erupts from it.

My chest heaves in exertion as the dark power collides with my shields scattered across the room, and I pour my magic into them to defend against the assault, repairing the gaps in them.

Four more and the altar.

Samira's shouts echo into the air as more heavy footsteps fill the room, but all I can do is turn my attention to the next pillar. My magic swells around me, looking for an outlet as streams of light form, and I send them around the pillar as it begins to glow.

The dark is a startling contrast to my power as tendrils of it lash out from all directions. My shields block the first series of strikes that hit myself, Gray, Darian, and Val.

I'm in the middle of pouring my power into regenerating their shields when a second strike of dark power hurtles toward my arm, where my shield has yet to regenerate.

Panic fills my mind, and all I can do is brace as the dark collides with my arm, sending a searing pain throughout my limb and into my shoulder as I cry out, trembling as I repair the hole in my shield.

"Eiara!"

Tears stream down my face as I shake my head, "I'm fine."

I need to be faster.

Pain lances through my arm, but I don't have time to inspect it as another wave of darkness lashes out against my shield. Sweat beads down my forehead, and my brows pinch together as I reinforce shielding layers around each of us.

Anger builds in my chest as Samira's laughter fills the air, "You'll never win if you can't even protect yourself. You might as well give up now. These pets are mine, anyway."

Fuck this shit.

Energy surges from me as I fully open myself to my power, sending decrepit bodies flying outward from where I stand at the altar as rage continues to brim within me.

Layers and years of rage, anger, wrath, and fury coat my veins as the pillars and altar become the focus of my ire.

That's the thing about emotions.

You can bottle them, box them away, or stomp them into an abyss, but the moment you're faced with an appropriate outlet...

I'd be a fool not to accept this gift that fate has given me.

I turn, and my gaze meets Samira's as she grins with some sense of false triumph.

It's not until I turn my palm upward and lift my hand that the humor falls from her face, and she glances between each pillar with panic.

Satisfaction rifles through me as my power crackles in the air, and the room brightens. Her eyes widen, and even from here, in the reflection of her gaze, I can see my power encircling the four pillars before I squeeze my hand into a fist.

A ghost of a smile creeps across my face as my magic crushes against the remaining pillars at once. Each one sends its own defensive assault out in response, but in the few seconds it took to crush all three at once, I prepared for this.

The attacks lash out from the pillars repeatedly, striking the layers of shield I've formed around myself and each of my men. Each assault shatters a layer, but there's another just beyond it.

Samira shrieks in frustration as my lip curls, and I hold her gaze with a lethal calmness as the ground tremors, sending the bones of the deceased around us rattling, and in quick succession, each pillar cracks with a boom that sounds akin to thunder.

My gaze flicks to each of my men, still fighting against her tainted minions, before settling on her empty, blood-red eyes, "These men are mine. You would do well to treat them respectfully... though I doubt you'll manage to live long enough."

My limbs tremble as my power surges, but I turn toward the altar as a heady mixture of pride and rage radiates from each of them.

Samira's frantic shouts fill the air inaudibly, and the sounds of fighting ring out with renewed vigor as I turn my focus to the altar.

I shield my hand once more before reaching into the bowl of viscous liquid and wrap my fingers around the wet metal hilt. Tugging upward to lift the artifact does nothing.

It's as if the item is glued to the bowl, weighed down by some unseen force of gravity, or as if the liquid is suctioning it.

Panic from Darian bleeds into me, and I shut myself off from their emotions as a renewed sense of urgency clouds my mind. Fighting the urge to turn to see the source of his panic, I brace my foot against the altar, pushing off from it as I lift the artifact with both hands, but it does not come free.

Stupid piece of sh-

Panting from exertion, I feel the exorbitant use of my magic deep within my bones.

I know I'm going to hit my limit soon.

Using my emotions was effective in the moment, but now, as I face the final task, I can't help but regret using such a large amount in such a short time.

But I refuse to fail now.

Not when I've already gotten us this far, with so much at risk.

I won't fail them.

My chest tightens, and I funnel my power into the bowl, flooding it until my magic surrounds the artifact from all sides, but I'm somehow unable to penetrate the surface.

It's as if there's a barrier around it.

I frown, allowing my power to encircle the artifact carefully, starting with the blade's tip. Looking for any weakness, my magic probes along the surface to no end. My teeth grit as my power glides along the edge, finding no traction or gaps.

Movement in my peripheral catches my attention as Gray intercepts a dagger hurled in my direction. His blade collides with the hilt as It jerks to the side and falls into a pile of corpses.

My gaze flicks to Gray, already locked into battle with another soldier, then to Kieran and Val standing back-to-back, their faces focused as they fend off the continuous assault.

Each looks just as drained as the last and nearly as exhausted as I feel.

I need to hurry up.

Adrenaline courses through my veins, and I return my focus, sending my magic along the handle, determined to find an opening as my magic glides against the surface and reaches the end.

Reflecting on the attacks on my shield, I drive tendrils of my power into the barrier before using another tendril to test the points of contact.

The shield is intact, and with the distraction of my disappointment, I nearly miss it.

The tiniest pin needle of an opening disappears as my magic covers it, and the triumph washes over me with renewed vigor.

I can do this. We can win.

Repeating the test, I drive multiple tendrils of magic-like screws into the shield before testing the areas of contact once more. A pin needle opening where the blade meets the hilt appears, and I seize the opportunity.

My magic eases in bit by bit to clear the dark magic. The trickle of my power making its way into the dagger ever so slowly begins to take hold, and my pulse rages in my ears as I weigh the rate at which I'm dispelling the dark magic.

My eyes scan the carnage as soldiers pour in from the doorway.

Zayne and Caspian fight on either side of Darian, sweat dripping down their skin as they fight in unison to protect him.

The tiny ribbon of my power flows in bit by painful bit.

Kieran is only feet away, facing off against a soldier who looks over a foot taller than him, wielding a giant mace adorned with spikes.

Val and Gray fend off attacks on either side of me. Each of them looks drained, dripping with sweat and blood that's not their own.

I continue feeding my magic into the knife at a painfully slow rate.

It's as if I'm easing a single thread into the darkness within, and it's resisting, battling for dominance as my power collides with it.

A shout breaks through my focus, and just as my gaze lifts in that direction, Val throws himself between me and the arrow aimed at my head as it burrows deep into his shoulder.

Horror coats my veins as he drops to his knees, clutching his injury as his blood begins to ribbon, slowly lifting towards the bowl.

No.

Where was my shield?

No, this can't be happening.

Panic wells within me as each moment passes, bringing more of his blood from the wound toward the bowl.

"Val!" Darian's voice rings out as his ice freezes around Val's blood, but it doesn't stop the stream.

"Shit," Gray mutters, blocking another attack before burning his assailant to a crisp.

Val's blood has crept a quarter of the distance to the bowl, and I've only managed to trickle no more than a handful of threads of my magic into the artifact.

It's not enough.

I need more.

I glance around frantically before my gaze lands on Caspian, and as if on queue, our eyes lock.

For a moment, it's as if time stands still.

As if everything around me has come to a halt.

I don't miss the concern etched on Caspian's face as my gaze flicks to Val again, and my soul feels as if it's being torn into two.

I refuse to lose anyone to this.

Desperation coats my veins as my magic swirls in the room, chaotic and dense as I urge my power to answer my call, pulling on it with all my might.

Having only allowed magic to flow through my body as a gateway, I'm not prepared when my call is answered, and the entire room shudders as my power fills the air, turning it heavy and thick.

It's as if time doesn't exist as adrenaline pumps hard through me, and I look at Val from where he kneels, an arrow protruding from his shoulder with his wide eyes locked onto the ribbon of his very life essence.

His blood is nearly halfway to the bowl, but with each passing second that feels like an eternity, it's hardly making any progress toward it. I focus on the knife, not wasting another moment as I force my power inside the minuscule opening.

At first, the hole doesn't give, and sweat beads down my temple as I pour all my strength into stretching the pinpoint gap in its defenses. The strain is immense, and it feels as though my power could tear me in two from the force of it driving into the pin-prick-sized hole.

It's seconds before I grasp the knife with both hands, and columns of white light erupt between my fingers around the hilt.

My hair lashes against my face from the chaotic energy surrounding me, and when the opening finally gives, widening a small amount, relief courses through my body.

Riding the high of triumph, I urge my magic to push harder against the gap in its defenses. Pouring more magic into the blade, my anxiety sky-rockets as Val's blood appears in my peripherals, only a few feet away.

I've nearly cleansed half the blade, but I'm still forcing the opening in the barrier wider to allow more of my magic to enter.

Val's blood creeps closer, and more adrenaline pumps through my veins.

Too close. I'm not going to make it.

I know it's now or never as the ribbon of his blood slides closer through the air, and in desperation, I urge my power through me, begging it to hurry as I squeeze everything I have into the weapon.

The sudden surge of energy in the room sends everyone and everything flying against the outer walls, turning the room blindingly white. I hardly recognize the cry escaping my throat as I funnel as much power into the artifact. The darkness within it rages against my attempts to dispel it as if battling an ocean.

Val's blood is inches away from the bowl now, and my power swells one final time from a place deep within me that I've never felt before. It clashes against the last remnants of dark magic within the weapon. The moment the two forces collide, one last wave of energy hurtles out to the edges of the room, and I drop to my knees at the altar.

Clutching the knife in my hands and panting in exertion, I raise my head to scan for Val's blood.

Relief washes over me when the ribbon has disappeared, and Val's chest rises and falls from where he lies on the ground.

It's done.

My attention catches on Samira from where she staggers to her feet. She glances around the room with a mixture of desperation and panic.

I can't say seeing her terrified is not a pleasant sight.

Her soldiers are no more, her artifact is no more, and she controls none of my men.

She cuts into her palm roughly, "This isn't over!" She shouts, drawing a series of symbols on the ground beside her. She slams her hand into the center of the symbols, and a small circular form takes shape.

It takes a moment to realize she's teleporting away, but none of my men are in a position to stop her, and neither am I.

Hell, I don't even think I can stand up on my own yet.

Inside the circular portal is a large castle in the distance, with hylia ilvrost scattered amongst the background. She drags herself to her feet and throws herself head-first into the portal before it disappears.

Val stirs on the ground with a low groan, and I drag myself to his prone form. His dark hair has fallen in front of his face from where he lies, and the moment my hand covers his wound, his eyes flutter open.

I send the meager remnants of my magic into his body just as I wrap my fingers around the arrow's base and pull it from the meaty flesh of his shoulder.

I lean onto his chest, still unable to bear my weight, and take his face into my hands, "Val, are you alright?" I whisper, my lips twisting downward as tears threaten to escape.

Val's mouth opens, "Can't breathe," he chokes out, and I quickly push off of his chest as he sucks in a deep breath.

I sigh deeply, and tears of pure relief stream down my cheeks.

He's okay. He's going to be okay.

"Eiara," Zayne's soft voice fills the air beside me, "Is it done?"

I raise my eyes to meet his, but his gaze is fixed on the blade next to us. Reaching over to grasp it in my hand, my magic flows freely into the artifact, no longer hindered by the constraints of the barrier, and I nod.

"The dark magic is gone," my eyes find Val's as another wave of relief crashes over me. "We were almost too late."

Val's gaze softens and he shakes his head, "You were right on time, Eiara."

Swallowing thickly against the emotion clogging my throat, the slash of a sword catches my attention, and I twist to see Gray lobbing off the head of a nearby soldier.

Our eyes meet as he lifts his head; his sun-kissed skin is stained crimson as he grins triumphantly, driving the sword into the body on the ground next to him.

"So," Caspian begins as he sheaths his blade, "I don't suppose any of us know where she went?"

He's answered with shaking heads and frowns from the others, and the room spins as exhaustion weighs heavy in my bones.

My voice is no more than a whisper as I fight to maintain consciousness, "She went to Meloris."

"Meloris? You're sure?" Kieran says, crossing his arms.

I nod my head, "Positive. I could see the hylia ilvrost when she took the portal out."

Darian rubs his chin thoughtfully, "Then we go after her."

"We have no idea how to get there," Val inserts, "Not to mention the small problem that we have an entire realm to protect and run."

Darian opens his mouth to respond as Zayne chimes in, "He has a point. If we all leave, Servilia will be in chaos."

Gray crosses his arms, "It's already in chaos."

"Even more reason why we must begin securing Darian's return to the throne," Zayne finishes as the room falls quiet. Everyone's gaze turns to Darian, who sighs in resignation.

"It pains me to think of separating, though I understand it is the right thing to do." he says, the muscle in his jaw feathering as his gaze settles on me, "We rest first. If we run head-first after her now, we risk it all. We rest up and then find her."

Gray's features are rife with excitement, and he grins, "Assuming we find a way to follow her to Meloris."

"I know how to follow her. She's used the spell a few times before," Caspian's voice rings out, and everyone's attention turns to him as he stares at me, "You've been to Meloris?"

I nod as Zayne says softly, "Gray, Caspian, Eiara, and I will go after her."

Darian steps closer and nods, "Val, Kieran, and I will remain here to rebuild and smother out what is left of her following."

"If there is any," Kieran's voice rings out as he grins, and I can't say I don't share the sentiment.

Chapter 62

Eiara

My eyelids droop as I follow closely behind Caspian and Darian through the tunnels, with Gray, Val, Zayne, and Kieran at my back.

Every step is labored, as my feet hardly manage to leave the ground, and my limbs feel as if they're weighed down with lead.

I stubbornly declined to be carried when Kieran offered earlier, and I'm thoroughly regretting my decision.

My toe catches on an uneven stone, and I tumble forward as a hand wraps gently around my bicep.

"Come on, silly goose," Val tugs me into his chest and lifts me until I'm straddling his waist with his hands under my thighs, supporting my weight, "Was this so hard?"

The grin that dances across his features makes my heart clench as I search his face.

I nearly lost him.

My arms snake around his neck, and I lean to rest my cheek against his shoulder.

The very shoulder that nearly took him from me.

My blink is slow, and it takes a conscious effort to open my eyes again as I fight the sleep my body craves. "Think we'll run into any trouble?" Darian's baritone voice rings out as the path turns into a winding staircase.

"Unless Tamara is here, I doubt it."

My eyes snap open, and I rear back, "Tamara, as in...?"

There's a brief pause, and concern radiates from Darian while Caspian responds, "Yes, your friend Tammy."

I squirm in Val's arms until he sets me on my feet, "What the hell do you mean she could be here?"

Exhaustion forgotten, my pulse skyrockets until it rages in my ears.

They said she was safe.

Darian said she was safe on each, and he called a rescue team.

I would have gone after her first if I had known she was under Samira's control.

We come to a stop as I grasp Darian's forearm, and his sad, mismatched gaze meets mine. "You lied to me!"

He shakes his head, but Caspian responds, "He didn't know, little one."

Caspian's jaw works as I search his face, "But you did? I don't know if that's worse."

He steps closer, "There was no easy way to tell you who she really is or what we were wrapped up in."

No easy way?

He made me think she was kidnapped and then neglected to tell me that she was one of Samira's pawns.

Oh, gods.

My heart squeezes as I hold his gaze.

Judging from his pained look, he can feel it all, and though it kills me to voice it, I have to know the answer.

"Was any of my friendship with her even real?"

His lips twitch, "I cannot speak for her, but I'll tell you that the night Blair broke the binding on magic and I finally found where she had lured you, Tamara was already awake."

Surprise bleeds from Darian as Caspian continues, "She knew what happened, and if Samira hadn't bound us both to return to Servilia, I'm positive she would have killed me right then and there."

I frown, "Why?"

Caspian's tongue clicks, "Because while I was exacting my revenge on Dolly, Blair found the last key without me knowing. Tamara saw my priorities for what they were and rightfully blamed me for what she thought was surely your death. She is fiercely protective of you, which speaks volumes to the depth of your friendship."

Tears well in my eyes, "How can we know if she's okay? Does Samira know that she and I were friends? What if she's hurting her?"

Caspian splays his palms up between us, and my mouth snaps shut, "There was a reason Tamara kept her distance, little one," He steps even closer, cupping my jawline with his hands, "The less she saw you, the less information she'd have for Samira to use against you should she ever uncover the truth. Up until the point I was released from her control, Samira had not discovered how close the two of you were, and from what I know of Tamara, she would have done everything possible to maintain that."

His expression hardens as his thumb glides along my cheek, "If she's still in the castle, there's a chance she's been ordered to kill you, and on the chance she is—"

I shake my head, "We're not killing her!"

"I wouldn't dream of it," his lips twitch slightly, "but right now, I doubt we're prepared to face her in our current state. So, as much as I suspect she's not in the castle, we must consider the dangers we might be walking into."

I nod lightly but frown as the realization dawns on me.

"Did you even kidnap her when I was collecting the amulets?"

His brow raises as if my question is ridiculous, "I had to keep her from responding to you, but no. She was comfortably living in a safe house on the coast."

Darian's head tilts, "What about the warehouse?"

A ghost of a smile creeps over Caspian's features, "That is where I made it seem like she was being held," he tilts his head to look at his brother, "It seems like the distraction was effective."

My head swirls with all the overwhelming information, and I soothingly rub my temples.

"Alright, alright," Val tugs me out of Caspian's grasp, pulling me into his chest as my legs instinctively wrap around his waist. "Time to find a bed or a room at least suitable for a goddess."

"We can use mine," Caspian whispers, and I don't miss the guarded look in his eyes as he turns to walk down the corridor.

"Don't worry, Eiara," Val murmurs against the shell of my ear, "I won't let anyone hurt you."

I blink slowly as another wave of exhaustion looms, "You, my dear Valerian, are banned from my protection until further notice."

He rears back with wide eyes, and his dark hair sways with the movement, "Uhh, are you serious? Why?"

"Because this is the second time you've gotten injured during battle and nearly scared me to death."

"But—"

I shake my head, "No 'but,' Valerian. I'm not risking you anymore."

Kieran laughs under his breath next to me as I yawn deeply, "She has a point, Val. You are quick to use your body as a shield."

Gray slaps his hand on Val's shoulder, grinning, "It's alright. You can support us from the sidelines in the next fight."

"It's official, we're benching Val," Darian chokes out as Caspian huffs a laugh beside him.

Regardless of the humor from the rest of them, a hint of concern and annoyance radiating off Val makes my chest tighten.

"We will protect her, Val." Zayne's soft voice catches my attention, and my gaze flicks to his from behind Val. "Besides, assuming Tamara is not in the castle, there may very well not be any danger to protect her from."

"Unless you plan to protect her from us," Gray asks, and I feel Val's breath catch in his chest.

Caspian chuckles as we breach the top of the staircase, and we all fall silent as we venture further down the hallway.

My eyelids weigh heavy enough that each blink forces my eyes closed, and my arms around Val's neck struggle to remain locked as I fight the urge to fall asleep.

We come to a stop in a large room, and I'm jolted awake as unease washes over me from where Caspian stands next to us. His emotions instantly dissipate as quickly as they came, and I know he's masked them for my sake.

His jaw works, and I turn to follow his gaze to the bed.

Bile rises in my throat, and when I look at him once more, his guarded emerald gaze is already locked onto me. "We don't have to—"

"It's fine. You need rest, and I doubt the other rooms have much to offer in terms of comfort."

One could argue that this room offers little comfort, too, but I'm too exhausted to debate semantics.

Not when we can make this room into something other than what it has been.

I reach down to slide my hand along Val's forearm, and he brings his hand up to meet mine as I intertwine our fingers.

"Val, I think this room needs some remodeling."

"Ah, lucky for you, that happens to be my specialty."

Caspian holds my gaze, and my cheek rests on Val's shoulder. Vines begin to cover the walls all around us. A splatter of red roses and white lilies sprouts from the vines in my peripherals as emotion clogs my throat.

"Not disagreeing that this is your specialty, but one could argue that self-sacrifice is up there with it," Kieran murmurs, followed by a shrill sound I've never heard him make before, "Hey! What was that for?"

Val's chest rumbles with laughter, "Whoops, vines didn't see you there."

A smile tugs at my lips as Caspian's gaze tears from me to glance around the room, "This is..."

The look on his face is a mixture of awe and something I can't quite place. I lean back, squirming as Val moves to set me on my feet.

As I turn toward the bed, my heart clenches in my chest.

Beautiful vines of varying colors rise from the four corners of the bed, which has grown in width to accommodate all of us. A thick bed of moss has replaced the bedding with a soft blanket of woven vines and other soft, leafy pieces to make it comfortable. The four posts meet at the top in a bell-like shape, with the luminous moss woven throughout.

"You really weren't kidding about this being your specialty," Darian whispers, his mismatched gaze scanning the room.

I squeeze Val's hand before stepping toward the bed, but Kieran's voice halts my steps, "I believe it's a fair request that we clean off before getting into the new bed, don't you all?"

I blink, scanning each of us before wincing.

He has a point.

Each of us is caked in bone dust, blood, and various other things, but my exhaustion isn't going away on its own, so I'm debating the choice of a bath when Kieran laughs.

"Sweetheart, there are other ways to clean off, you know." He lifts his palm, and water streams from the bathroom, cracks and crevices in the marble and through the window frame.

The ribbons of water rush toward us, gliding over our skin and clothes before turning shades of red, grey, and brown. I watch in fascination as the water clears the scuffs and caked-on dirt from our skin and clothes before disappearing into the bathroom.

"That was amazing," I breathe, glancing at Kieran, who winks before crossing his arms over his chest.

"Well, this bed isn't going to break itself in," I say, grasping Val's hand as he snickers. I pull him and Caspian to the edge before turning to face them.

"Will you all do the honor of joining me?"

Val grins, "You'd have to bury me alive under a mountain to keep me from it, and even then, I'd manage to join you."

A smile tugs at my lips as he moves past me to get on the bed, and I turn to Caspian, who stares at the center of the bed with an expression I can't quite place.

"Come," I say, squeezing his hand. I kneel on the bed and move toward the center, where Val lies comfortably with his hands braced behind his head. I can feel his apprehension as he pulls his shirt over his head and follows me into the center.

My gut twists.

The last thing I want is to force him to be somewhere he doesn't want to be.

"Would you rather—" My jaw snaps shut as he shakes his head.

"No, little one. This is fine." He settles on his back next to me, his muscles tense as his teeth grind together, and I sigh.

"Turn over."

His emerald gaze slides to mine, and he frowns, "What?"

My cheeks burn, "Turn onto your stomach, Caspian."

He raises a brow at me, "Why?"

What is this, 20 questions?

"For someone who claims to be a monster, you sure are concerned by turning your back on a little thing like me. Now, turn."

His eyes flash as surprise bleeds out of him, but he concedes, turning onto his stomach. "Little, yes, but you have stabbed me before, you know."

The muscles along his back ripple with his movements as he settles himself down, and the others file into the bed on either side of us.

Pushing to my knees, I lean over his back, trailing my fingers along his skin from his neck to the line of his pants. Goosebumps break out over his skin, and he shivers as I fight the smile tugging at my lips.

Giant ol' brutal monster getting goosebumps from lil ol' me.

My fingers trail up his back until I reach his shoulders and press my thumbs into the thickly corded muscles.

I watch his side profile as his eyes flutter shut, and he relaxes into my touch as I massage my way from his shoulders to his lower back.

Fuck Samira for making him do things he didn't want to do.

I yawn deeply, and his eyes snap open, "Thank you, little one, but you need rest more than anyone here," he turns over, wrapping his large hand around my wrist before tugging me into the soft moss bed.

Laying on my side with our hands between us, I search his face while lifting a piece of his dark hair from his eyes before sliding my hand into his and intertwining our fingers.

"Sleep, Eiara," Val shifts closer, the length of his body melding with mine as his arm wraps around my waist.

Each blink comes in slower than the last as Caspian's gaze lingers on me until I finally fall asleep.

Chapter 63

Eiara

The peaceful sound of deep, even breaths from each of my men slowly wakes me from sleep as my eyes open. With the light pouring into the room, it's hard to say how much time has passed, but I remain still.

I watch Caspian's relaxed expression, seeing the rise and fall of his bare chest.

It's all so serene.

A stark difference from the hell we just went through.

Sometime during our sleep, the blanket became crumpled and pushed to the end of the bed. Val rolled onto his back, leaving me with an opening to sit up... which is good news considering that my bladder feels as though it's about to explode.

I crawl out of bed without waking anyone and slip into the bathroom unnoticed before sneaking to the edge of the bed again. From where I stand, looking at the half-nude men splayed on the bed, each of them looks like a piece of art.

They're beauty and strength, forged into vessels that contain the very souls of those I've come to cherish more than anything else.

They're more than just regular Servilians.

They're everything.

They're the very fabric of my soul, torn from the cloth of my tapestry long before my birth when the threads were still being wound.

Each of them has taught me a valuable lesson in the short time I've known them, yet I feel I still need a million lifetimes more.

Each of these men has given me so much that I can't help but feel like I've returned so little.

Perhaps it's time to change that, one day at a time.

The moment my knee leans into the bed, Val's eyes scrunch, and he cracks them open before his gaze lands on me. He opens his mouth to speak, but it snaps shut as I shake my head slightly, glancing at the others who are still fast asleep.

Kneeling at the foot of the bed, I lean down onto all fours and slowly ease inch by inch toward Val, keeping myself positioned between his legs. His hazel eyes hold my gaze, and by the time I reach his knees, his eyes are dilated, with the fabric of his pants lifting every few seconds.

Fighting the smile tugging at my lips, I sit up and reach forward to untie the waist of his pants. He lifts his hips, letting me tug them down his thighs.

As I pull the last pant leg down off his foot, Gray turns onto his side with a sleep-laden sigh, and we both freeze, staring at one another as if what we're about to do must be kept secret.

Gray's breathing is even as he snores slightly, and I pull the material down Val's foot, dropping it to the edge of the bed with a soft thud.

He's already hard, his dick bobbing every few seconds in anticipation.

I bring my finger to my lips, indicating for him to keep quiet before leaning down to place a kiss against the inside of his knee. With each kiss I place higher on his thigh, his hands squeeze the moss, and by the time I reach his balls, his chest is heaving.

The veins protruding from his dick look like they could explode as he throbs, and as the skin at the base of his cock brushes my nose, I'm nearly certain it's taking every ounce of restraint he has to remain quiet and still.

His hazel eyes watch with rapt attention, holding my gaze as I flatten my tongue, licking him from base to tip. Taking his bulbous head into my mouth, I swirl my tongue over it, tasting the pre-cum as it mixes with my saliva.

Satisfaction rifles through me as his mouth drops open and his head tilts back, but his eyes remain locked onto me as if refusing to miss anything in this moment.

Chapter 64

Valerian

When her lips wrapped around my dick, I nearly came then and there.

Since that moment when time stood still in that blood-stained hellhole of a room when light erupted from her hands, and she made the impossible happen, I've needed her close.

It's why I stayed near her the entire way to the room.

The reason I covered this space in her favorite flowers to respect those she loves.

It's entirely why I waited until her soft snores filled the air before falling asleep.

I should have died today.

My body should have been drained of its essence and turned to dust just like the rest of Samira's victims, but because of this woman...

No.

Because of this goddess, I remain whole.

My mate.

Our mate.

Her tongue swirls, and I nearly come undone as my breath catches and my heart pounds as if it's trying to escape. I tilt my head back but can't tear my eyes off her.

Silver hair falls in front of her as she glides her hand up the length of my cock, and she brings her head down as far as it will go.

Watching my dick disappear in any capacity into her mouth is like having an out-of-body experience, and my legs twitch with the urge to thrust into her mouth.

But I won't take that control from her.

My balls tighten as if warning me that there's no way I'll be able to last long. She buries my cock down her throat once more, hollowing her cheeks as pressure builds in my body, my legs go numb, and I'm gripping the moss on the bed as if it's my fucking lifeline keeping me from unloading down her throat.

As if by the grace of the gods themselves, she pulls back, and it's only then that I realize she's been squeezing her thighs together the entire time.

Fucking hell.

The sight of her trying to ease the desire in her own body while pleasuring me nearly sends me over the edge, and I blow out a breath. My magic seeps out, and when the vines glide over her skin, causing her to jolt, her eyes wide with alarm until she realizes what it is.

I fight a grin as goosebumps break out over her skin, and when the vines creep up her thighs, her ocean-blue eyes collide with mine.

The heat that flashes across her face as the vines curl around the curve of her breast before reaching her nipples sends a fresh wave of blood to my dick.

It takes half a thought to send another vine between her legs, pressuring against her clit as a soft gasp escapes her, and her eyes dart to the others.

The snoring on either side of me continues as Caspian's breathing pauses almost imperceptibly, and my grin widens.

He's waking up to one of the rare wonders of this world.

Eiara covered in vines and soaking wet.

The best part is that she's all ours.

She wraps her mouth around the head of my cock again, and this time I can't stop my eyes from squeezing shut.

Chapter 65

Caspian

Waking up to the soft gasp initially had me worried until I sucked in one breath and smelled her arousal mixed with Val's.

I didn't even have to open my eyes to know.

But fuck am I glad I did.

Her focus is locked onto Val as she glides her hand along the length of his dick and takes him deeper into her mouth. I track each of her movements as my own dick throbs against the fabric of my pants.

She buries his cock down her throat as far as it will go, and the muscles in his thighs flex beneath her hands with restraint. His vines squeeze her nipples, and a muffled whimper sounds out, sending a fresh wave of blood to my dick.

Gods damn it all.

The breathing around us has changed, and I can already tell that Darian and Kieran know precisely what's happening between them as Val's eyes squeeze shut.

His vines tighten around her legs, and she dips her head toward his pelvic bone as his hips thrust.

My dick throbs painfully again as his mouth drops open, and he stares at her with a mixture of awe and pure desire. Between the look on his face, the way he's thrusting into her throat, and the difficulty she is having with each move he makes, I can tell he's seconds away from coming.

Somehow even that knowledge doesn't lessen the urge to pull her onto my lap and fuck her myself.

As the thought crosses my mind, my mental barriers slip and her eyes snap open.

The moment our eyes meet, Val's hand weaves through the hair at the top of her head as he pushes deep into her mouth and comes. My eyes track the movement as her throat works, and she swallows against him as he pants.

In my peripherals, Kieran sits up and leans on his elbows, "Well, isn't this a sight to wake up to?"

Her gaze averts to Val as she withdraws him from her mouth, making a 'pop' sound before crawling up his body and looking into his eyes.

This moment between them feels too intimate to be shared, and I nearly avert my gaze when her mental shields drop, and a wave of emotions crashes over me.

Relief.

Love.

Desire.

Happiness.

Gratitude.

These emotions and everything in between nearly overwhelm my senses as Gray and Zayne shift on the bed, waking up to the seismic activity mere feet from them.

The realization hits me as she leans in to press her lips to his, with a hunger indescribable from any words in any language I know.

She wants to break down the barriers between us, if only for today. I can manage that request.

For her, I can.

Their kiss breaks apart, and after a lingering moment, her gaze flicks to mine as I drop the walls erected around my mind. Her eyes widen, mirrored by the surprise that bleeds through the bond before the other emotions over-take it.

Val's vines recede into the bed as she crawls onto me until we're chest-to-chest.

My lips brush hers as I lean forward, "Is this what you wanted, little one?"

I can feel her heart racing through her breasts as she leans in, rubbing her nose against mine from side to side playfully before a smile tugs at her lips, "Yes, and more."

My hands hook under her thighs, positioning her to straddle my waist before pressing my lips to hers. The mix of her with Val fills my senses, and the urge to replace his scent with mine takes over my mind without warning.

No. Not replace.

She pulls back to search my eyes as if giving me time to process that revelation, and my eyes flick to Val.

All the time I'd been with them, I'd somehow convinced myself it was to be close to her only and that they'd never accept me.

What if I was wrong?

As if reading my thoughts, her voice is no more than a whisper as my gaze slides to hers, "You belong here as much as each of them, Caspian."

My chest tightens, and I'm about to argue, but to my surprise, Darian interrupts me, "Brother, if you don't believe her, then listen to me very closely."

Everyone's head in the room turns to look at him, but his green and white eyes fixate on me, "You may be capable and willing to do questionable things, but I trust Eiara's heart, and I've seen what you will do to those who oppose us. If I had any reservations about you, they died in that cave when you had my back as much as any of my brothers would."

The others nod in my peripherals, but Eiara's gaze turns to me, "Now that that's settled," she sighs wistfully, leaning in once more with her eyes focused on my lips, "I believe I was about to properly thank you for saving my life and Gray's."

Chapter 66

Eiara

The emotions barreling down the bonds from each of my men only heighten those already within me, and my chest feels like it could explode at any moment.

In the corner of my eye, Val leans back onto the bed as I shift back and ease myself lower.

The desire coursing through Caspian feeds into me as I hold his gaze and lean down to press my lips to his bare chest.

Heat flashes across his face, and his emerald eyes darken as I move lower before placing another kiss.

Each time I repeat the action, the line between our emotions blurs further, and by the time I'm between his legs, tugging his pants down to his ankles as his dick bobs between us, I've lost track of where he ends, and I begin.

Yet somehow, I couldn't care less.

No, I'm going to enjoy every single second of this.

I place a kiss on his inner thigh, and his dick throbs once upward before I move to his other thigh, pressing my lips to his skin before frustration radiates from him, mixed with the overwhelming desire he's feeling.

"Little one."

His voice is a warning, but a smile tugs at my lips as amusement courses through my veins, and I place a few kisses up his thigh to the V line before tracing down it with my tongue.

Satisfaction rifles through me as his breath hitches, and he weaves his hand through my hair, fisting it at the top of my head with one hand.

"Yes, my monster?"

My lips press against the skin at the base of his dick, and the length of him grazes my cheek as he throbs.

Butterflies soar chaotically through my body as I bring my lips lower until I'm peering at him from behind his cock.

The bulging veins that feed it make desire pool in my core as I remember how good they felt, and it takes a conscious effort to focus as my breath skates over his balls.

"Do you enjoy torturing me?"

The liquid heat in his eyes as he tracks my movements makes my thighs clench together to stave off the desire raging within my own body, and movement sounds out behind me as I press my lips to his skin once more.

His breath catches in his chest as it heaves with anticipation, and I savor the way his eyelids flutter.

"I think you know the answer to that."

There's not a damn thing in this world that I wouldn't give if it meant seeing that look on his face again.

Hell, I'd easily spend the rest of my life doing this to get these reactions from them.

A fingertip traces up my leg as I flatten my tongue, dragging up the length of his dick. By the time I'm at the tip, the taste of him has overwhelmed my senses, and I nearly moan when his desire crashes over me like a tidal wave.

Large hands glide up to my hips, and Darian nips at my skin before easing my thighs apart. His breath skates over my exposed pussy, and his mouth is on me as I take Caspian as deep as he will go.

His size stretches my throat as I work the base of his dick with my hand, pausing now and then for a desperate breath as Darian pushes me closer to an orgasm.

It takes everything in me not to chase my pleasure as Caspian's breaths come in shorter. His hands pull my hair back from my face, and I use my free hand to cup his balls as he moans.

The sound reverberates throughout his body, and I keep my pace even though I'm dangerously teetering an orgasm of my own.

A flicker of guilt passes over me as I consider the thought that I want to be the one to give them pleasure, but my guilt is overtaken as Caspian's cock thickens in my mouth.

His balls tighten in my palm, and I quickly take him as deep as possible as he comes.

The emotions radiating from him as he pulsates against my tongue are maddening. Many of them echo everything I feel, but there's one emotion I can't quite place that makes my heart squeeze painfully in my chest.

It's as though my body recognizes the emotion, but it's so overwhelming in every sense of the word that my mind can't grasp it.

While Caspian comes, his fist squeezes my hair as if refraining from squeezing my head further down his cock, and I swallow roughly against him as tears roll down my cheeks unbidden.

My chest swells with emotion as he gently withdraws from my mouth and pulls me into his chest.

That's when I realize that, with this two-way street of emotion, he's feeling everything I am, too, and tears spring to my eyes anew.

This man, the one who had been trapped his whole life, made into a criminal, a villain, and murdered his parents against his will... the sheer amount of serenity and fulfillment pouring from him is almost too much to handle.

As he wraps his arms around me, my orgasm is entirely forgotten.

He takes my chin between his thumb and index finger, tilting my face toward him as his deep emerald eyes search mine. "I once thought salvation was finding my end after getting revenge on those who stole my life and my future from me," wonder takes over his other emotions as he continues. "But my true salvation lies at your feet, where I plan to spend the rest of my days worshipping the ground you walk."

My arms wrap around his torso, and he shudders, his half-lidded eyes locked on my lips as I whisper, "Then we will be spending the rest of our days on the ground together, Caspian."

He tightens his grip on me and closes the distance between us as his lips collide with mine.

The way he kisses me is a heady mix of greed and savoring as if my touch alone is the answer to all the questions he's ever asked.

He shifts his grip, breaking our kiss just as Darian kisses his way up my leg. Anticipation builds in my body as a smile tugs at his lips, and I turn to look down the length of my body only to see Kieran, Gray, and Zayne already watching us with a level of desire in their eyes that sends a shiver down my spine.

"Sweetheart, I think we all know and love that you want to spoil us more than you already do, but if we have to wait one more minute..."

"It's a good thing we're not waiting then." Zayne's voice is soft, but the heat in it is unmistakable as his dark magic hooks around my waist, and Caspian lets out a dark chuckle as he leans back, resting his arms behind his head comfortably as he watches.

"Z, help her into a more comfortable position," Gray's husky voice sounds out as Zayne's shadows wrap around my wrists and ankles, lifting me off the bed as I squeal in surprise.

I'm floating.

I'm fucking floating in the air, suspended by magic.

Oh, gods.

"Zayne, don't you dare drop me."

He laughs softly, "You wound me, Eiara. I'd never."

Darian chuckles as he stands at the foot of the bed, "I'd be more concerned about other things right now, Sunshine."

I blink at him as Zayne's magic encircles my thighs, lifting them to chest height before my arms are gently pulled over my head. My muscles strain as his magic bends me more than I'm used to, and the burn slowly ceases as I feel Kieran move to stand behind me.

"Are you comfortable, sweetheart?" His fingertips glide across my bare ass, and I hum in approval as his magic tingles under my skin before he eases a fingertip into me.

His magic eases the pain of the stretch, but as he pushes his finger deeper into my ass, I can't help the husky moan that escapes me.

My head dips forward as his lips press against my shoulder tenderly, and Darian moves in close, cupping my cheeks with his palms as his mismatched gaze searches my face.

"You might think we've given you everything and received nothing in return, but you don't see the hole in our very souls that you have filled with yourself. That is a gift we can never repay, but we will happily spend our lives trying, Sunshine."

My chest tightens, and as I inhale, he presses his lips to mine. His body pulls flush against me in a desperate attempt to be close as his tongue glides against my lower lip, and I open for him.

His kiss is all-consuming, and beyond the pressure of Kieran stretching my ass, I'm hardly aware of any discomfort. It's not long before the pressure recedes completely, and I feel the tip of his cock against my ass just as Darian grinds his length against my clit.

I gasp at the bolts of pleasure just as Kieran pushes his tip in first. The sting quickly diminishes as his magic encircles the area, and he rubs his thumb soothingly along the skin of my hip.

"That's it, Sunshine," Darian's baritone voice is thick with heat as he notches himself at my entrance, "We're not waiting for another second to feel you."

Darian pushes the thick head of his cock in as Kieran eases in deeper, and my eyes nearly roll to the back of my head. My mouth drops open, and my eyelids flutter before focusing on Darian, whose expression mirrors mine.

With my mental barriers down, the need and euphoria radiating off me bleed into him as his chest heaves. A glance at Caspian and Val tells me they're just as affected, with their dicks both bobbing as they watch.

"Do you feel how perfect you are for us, sweetheart?" Kieran's voice sounds out as he nips at my shoulder. His hips line flush with my ass, and Darian continues to work his way in.

I feel like I could explode.

It's nearly too much.

"Z, squeeze her throat," Gray's voice is thick, and my heart pounds in anticipation.

Zayne's magic glides over my breasts and up my collar until it's around my neck, pressuring the sides as Darian gets to the base of his cock.

My orgasm is nearly at the surface, coaxed by the echoes of their pleasure mixed with mine as they stretch my body to its limits. Darian and Kieran withdraw slightly, and I can't help the moan that crawls out of my throat as they push in again.

Val's hand glides along his length as he strokes himself on the bed, "Fuck, that's hot."

"The sounds you make," Darian says huskily, "drive me to the brink of madness."

"Us," Gray corrects him from behind us, "Drives us to the brink of madness."

Darian and Kieran find their rhythm as they pump into my body, and even though it feels as if they could tear me apart, my orgasm still crests.

Something cold against my thighs catches my attention, and I glance over to see Darian's magic as it swirls over my skin before curling around my breasts, teasing my nipples as the mixture of cold against the heat of their bodies sends my mind into a jumbling mess.

"Darian," I gasp between desperate breaths, "I-"

Zayne's magic suddenly releases my neck as blood rushes to my head, and Darian's baritone voice sounds out, "Come for us, Sunshine."

The command echoes into the depths of my core, and as the building pressure of my orgasm crashes over me. Each wave of pleasure comes, and my body tenses around them as they both bury themselves deep before finding their release.

My pulse rages in my ears as they both pause, placing tender kisses on me before withdrawing as Zayne's magic eases me into my unsteady legs. My gaze slides to Zayne and Gray, and though my legs twitch in the aftermath of my orgasm, I manage to maintain my balance.

"Zayne, restrain Gray for me, please."

Gray's eyes flash in surprise from where he lies on the bed as Zayne's dark magic wraps around Gray's ankles, securing them to the bed before pulling his arms taut over his head.

"Goddess," Gray warns as his dick bobs between us, "Are you sure you know what you're doing?"

I crawl on shaky legs between his knees, easing myself higher on the bed, peppering kisses along his thigh as his golden eyes burn bright. The need to taste him sends desire through my veins like hot oil, and as if on queue, his gaze collides with mine.

The thing is, I don't know if that desire is his or mine.

I couldn't care less, either.

My tongue flattens, and I drag it up his length, ignoring the come dripping down my thighs as the salty taste of him invades my senses, making me even more wet.

Val groans, "This is torture."

"Zayne," I whisper, my eyes meeting his for a moment. Without further instruction, he moves forward on the bed until he's positioned himself behind us.

I swirl my tongue around Gray's tip before taking him into my mouth, and his hips buck upward into me, hitting the back of my throat as tears spring to my eyes, and I suppress a gag.

Zayne's magic encircles Gray's abdomen, securing his hips to the bed as he notches the tip of his cock against my soaked pussy.

"Goddess, release me right now so I can fuck—" his words die on his lips as I take him into my mouth fully, pushing him as far down my throat as possible, and he groans.

Breathing through my nose proves difficult as Zayne slides deeper, and I struggle to remain focused as his and Gray's emotions radiate into me through our bond.

It's like navigating a maze in the ocean blindfolded.

I can't figure out up from down and left from right.

All I can do is tread water.

Working Gray's shaft as he tugs against his restraints, Zayne's thrusts push me deeper onto Gray, and it doesn't take long for my orgasm to crest again.

"I'm going to fucking—" Gray gasps as my throat works to accommodate his size.

Zayne's magic glides across my skin, ribbons of his smoke squeezing my thighs, pressing on my abdomen as he thrusts. It is too much to handle, and I'm close to coming as he suddenly thrusts deep, throbbing and pulsating as he comes.

Zayne's magic dissipates, and within the blink of an eye, Gray has withdrawn from my mouth. The 'pop' sound echoes in the room as he hoists me into his chest and launches us off the bed.

"Gray." Darian's voice warns, but in the corner of my eye, Caspian holds his hand to calm him.

Gray slams us against the stone wall with a thud, hooking his arms under my knees as his dick presses against my pussy already leaking Zayne's release mixed with Darian's.

"Did you have your fun, Goddess?" Gray's voice is chilling, and any normal person would be afraid of the wild look in his eyes as his molten lava gaze searches mine.

But I am not a normal person.

"Absolutely."

Heat dances across his features, and his gaze darkens as he grins, "Great. Now it's my turn."

In one brutal thrust, he slams into me, and I cry out at the sudden intrusion. He doesn't give me a moment reprieve before withdrawing, only to slam himself into me once more.

Darian murmurs from the other side of the room, and I want to tell him it's okay, but Gray's lips crush against mine.

His teeth tug at my skin as he keeps his brutal pace, slow and hard. Each thrust squeezes his pelvic bone against my clit, and my head swirls in the mixture of pain and pleasure.

He must feel it as his pace picks up ever so slightly, and my toes begin to twitch with the orgasm that's starting to crest once again. He leans down and bites the skin above my breast, drawing blood as I cry out, but it comes out as nothing more than a husky, throaty moan.

"My brothers and I might all own your pleasure, Goddess, but I alone own your pain," He digs his fingers into my ass as he drives into me hard as if to prove his point.

My nails dig into the skin at his back without restraint, and he groans as I whisper between gasped breaths, "I own yours too, dragon."

A low growl escapes him suddenly, and he thrusts hard in quick succession, each one squeezing against my clit until my orgasm crashes over me, and he squeezes me tight to him.

His cock thickens as he comes, and I can feel him as if he's in my stomach with how deep he is.

We're both panting, breathing each other's air as we come down from the waves of euphoria, and he presses his forehead against mine.

"You weren't even afraid for a moment," his voice is barely a whisper, though I know everyone in the room can hear him.

A smile creeps across my face, "Not a chance."

He leans in, pressing his lips to mine as I taste the metallic tang of my blood, "That's our good little Goddess. We'd only hurt you if you want it."

Chapter 67

Eiara

My heart weighs heavy as we say our goodbyes.

Caspian stands in the center of the room waiting with Gray and Zayne, graciously giving me a moment as Val and Kieran sandwich me in a tight hug.

"Make sure you give her what she deserves, sweetheart," Kieran says with a wink before placing a tender kiss against my lips, still slightly swollen and sore from Gray's bites this morning.

"Just make sure you watch out for those buffoons," Val laughs, tilting his head in the other direction, "Without Darian to keep an eye on them, they're unpredictable," he says with a laugh, resting his forehead against mine. "And make sure you all come back in one piece."

I give him a half-hearted smile, "We will be fine. I think the hardest part is over," My eyes close for a moment as he kisses my forehead, his lips lingering as he takes a deep breath against my skin.

When my eyes open again and Val takes a small step back, my gaze tracks Darian's movement as he approaches. His stride stops just before us as he gives a nod to Val and Kieran.

"Eiara." The sound of my real name on Darian's lips sends my heart fluttering in my chest.

"It goes without saying that they'll protect you," he says, running his hand through my hair and fisting it behind my head, "But regardless of that, I need you to be careful."

His arms envelop my shoulders in a tight hug, and the familiar scent of forest rain washes over me as I nod against his chest, "I will. Promise."

My throat tightens, and I know it's because I'm making promises before heading into the unknown.

It's hard to be careful when you're not entirely sure where you're going or how to get there.

But for him, for them, I will do my best.

His lips brush the top of my head, and my heart rattles in my chest, "When this is over," he says, pulling back to cup my face in his large hands, "I'll understand if you wish to remain in Meloris with your family, but I'll admit, I selfishly want you to live with us."

His gaze is soft as he searches my eyes, waiting for me to choose.

As if I'd ever want anything different than them.

"Home is where the heart is, Darian. I wouldn't want to be anywhere else."

My voice is no more than a whisper, and the moment the last word leaves me, his lips crash against mine. The passion in his kiss ignites with mine as our lips move against one another.

My body acts on its own as my arms reach around his neck, my hands entwining through his hair as he squeezes me against him.

If it were up to me, I would never leave their arms and spend the rest of my days repeating this morning.

But unfortunately, we don't have that luxury.

Not when Samira and Kouros are still here.

The sound of someone clearing their throat halts us in place, and I feel Darian smile against my lips, "We'll have to pick this up later," he murmurs, glancing behind me to the others before placing one last tender kiss against my lips.

My nerves are frayed as I go to the center of the room where Caspian, Gray, and Zayne stand. Caspian reaches out toward me, and I notice the silver dagger held firmly in his hand before spotting the gold dagger at his hip.

"You're the only one of us who has been to Meloris. I will cast the spell, but you must remain focused on where we are teleporting."

My heart feels as if it could beat out of my chest as my nerves get the better of me, "Right."

"Lara," He squeezes my hand slightly, pulling my full attention to him, "This will work."

He looks so sure that I can't help but believe him, and I blow out a breath with a nod, "Let's go, then."

Gray and Zayne move in closer as the cold edge of the dagger presses against my palm.

Cradling my hand in his, Caspian squeezes the blade in gently just as a sharp pain jolts up to my wrist and he creates the inch-long incision. He withdraws the blade to his belt as my blood pools in our hands, and Caspian quickly gets to work drawing symbols.

I shut my eyes and picture the room where I met Sol and Luna—the bright, pristine marble room with curtains waving in the breeze from the open window where countless hylia ilvrost stood.

When I open my eyes, a shimmering portal appears before us with the room I pictured on the other side.

It's now or never.

Zayne and Caspian step through first before Gray and I follow closely behind. My head begins to spin, and I'm starting to wonder if the spinning sensation is from blood loss or magic when Gray's voice murmurs into the space around us, and a hand wraps around my arm.

"It worked."

Chapter 68

Eiara

My eyes open to the familiar view where I met my parents.

Everything seems... brighter.

It's like with my real vision; the details of the room are more crisp and clear. I didn't notice it then, but I'm more awestruck than I was the first time I saw it.

Zayne surveys the room, "This place is..."

"Fitting for the gods," Caspian's eyes find mine from where he stands before me with a hint of reverence in them and my cheeks warm.

A clattering sound reverberates through the room, and I twist to see Gray inspecting a vase before placing it back down.

"Let's just go find—" I stop abruptly as glass shatters a few feet in front of Zayne and Caspian, where I can make out the top of Luna's head, which the men in front of me mostly obstruct.

"Who are—?" She starts to say as I angle myself to get a better view of her. She glares at Caspian before taking a healthy step back and out of my direct line of vision, "You."

Zayne shifts defensively, and Gray's hand wraps around my bicep as if bracing to tug me away from danger at a moment's notice.

"Luna?" Sol's concerned voice echoes from the hall, followed by quick footsteps before he appears in the doorway next to her, "Impossible."

Though his body is mostly obscured behind Zayne and Caspian, the warning in his voice is clear, "You shouldn't be here."

The sing of metal fills the room as I yank free of Gray's grasp, pushing past Caspian and Zayne with a grunt.

Both gods look at me with wide eyes, but Luna's shrill voice fills the air.

"You brought him here?" She gestures at Caspian, and a mixture of anger and disbelief flashes across her face.

The nervous boulder in the pit of my stomach feels like it drops even lower, and a note of dread creeps up my spine.

They wouldn't hurt him, right?

"I can explain," I manage to say calmly, but I hardly get the last word out as Sol lunges with his sword aimed directly at Caspian's chest. On instinct, he moves with unexpected speed to unsheathe the silver dagger from his hip, pausing as Sol's sword collides with my shield.

Caspian blinks at the shimmering barrier before glancing at me, and the look on his face makes my heart flutter wildly as he returns the dagger to his hip.

Sol's face turns red, and the vein in his forehead bulges as he shouts, "You would protect him after all he has done?" He steps back, keeping his sword ready between us and Luna.

I narrow my eyes at Sol's sword, surprised that he hasn't tried to use magic against us yet, but I shove my concern away.

I sigh, gesturing to Caspian, "I told you I could explain. Clearly, he's not here to hurt anyone."

"Well, actually," Caspian interjects, "I am, just not either of you,"

I look at him, horrified, before the realization dawns on me.

"Oh, for gods' sake," Zayne mutters beneath his breath as Gray cackles.

"Correction," I state loudly, "We are here for one individual."

"Two, possibly," Gray corrects with a wide grin.

I frown at him, "Two?"

"Kouros," Zayne clarifies, and I rub my temples.

"What does Kouros have to do with anything?" Luna asks, stepping closer to stand beside Sol, her eyebrows pinched together.

"Oh, you mean besides trapping your daughter inside her mind and assaulting her?" Caspian's voice is lethally calm as he continues, "He's at the top of my shit list, right next to Samira."

Luna pales, "He did what?"

Sol eyes Caspian warily before turning his gaze to me, "Is this true, Eiara?"

I can't help but notice the muscle in his jaw pulsate with tension as I nod, "Samira is guilty of many crimes, which she will answer for, but Kouros has just as much, if not more, blood on his hands."

Luna wrings her hands together nervously, "Sol, this is so much worse than we thought."

Sol sheaths his sword as he scrutinizes us before his gaze flicks to Caspian's hip, "Where did you get that dagger?" The alarm on his face sends a jolt of panic down my spine.

Though, if any of my men notice, it doesn't show.

Zayne is the first to answer as he crosses his arms, "We got it when we broke some spell Samira was using to drain prominent magic wielders in Servilia. That dagger was in the center of a ceremonial altar, and Eiara cleansed it."

Surprise flashes across Luna's face, "Alone?"

Gray steps up to stand next to us, "That's right. We were with her, but she hardly needed our protection. If anything, it was the other way around."

Sol's jaw ticks, "You have much to learn about our ancient relics, Eiara. They should remain buried where they belong."

Anger coats my veins like hot oil, "You act like we were the ones who unearthed it to begin with."

"It's alright, little one. They were just about to get to the part where they tell us why this dagger worries them so much."

Sol looks between us before conceding with a sigh, "The dagger was one of a few weapons created by Cronus in one of his many moments of madness. It has the ability to sever the soul from the body, and the wielder then absorbs the essence of the soul."

"Thus eternally purging the soul from rebirth," Zayne says softly under his breath before shaking his head. "No wonder it was sealed away beneath that lake."

I frown, "Does this mean that any souls of those prominent bloodlines after she got the dagger were were..." I don't bother finishing my sentence as Sol and Luna's faces fall.

"Caspian," Luna's voice trembles slightly, but she quickly masks it, "You said Kouros went after Eiara. Did he say why?"

She wrings her hands together nervously before glancing at Sol, and in my peripherals, I see Caspian's jaw feather before he answers, "To force the bond on her."

Sol's features are painted with a mixture of surprise and rage as he rears back, "Impossible! It is not possible to force the bond. You must be lying!"

As I rush to interject, Caspian's frustration bleeds out, "He is not lying."

Sol deadpans, "Eiara, Kouros has been around for millennia. He knows how bonds work between gods. The only benefit would have been increasing both your pools of power."

There's a tense silence before Zayne's voice fills the air, "Unless he was trying to reign in the only power that could destroy everything he has built. If he managed to convince her to accept the bond, to accept him, she would not be able to stop him."

Sol blinks as the realization hits him, "He tried to bribe you?"

The dry laugh from my throat is more of a scoff, "Blackmail, actually."

"The situation is more dire than we thought. If what you say is true, we must find them quickly."

He takes long strides to the shelf along the side of the room with glass artifacts on top as he searches for something with urgency. He fumbles with items as they clatter against the shelving, and my gaze slides to Zayne's as we both share a look at Sol's odd behavior.

"I believe it is your turn to explain, Father," the moment the word leaves my lips, Sol abruptly stops, turning to look at Luna before sighing in resignation.

Luna steps into place next to Sol, her white hair and gown flowing with the movement.

Her quiet voice rings into the still air around us. "When we bound magic on Earth, the cost was great, Eiara."

Concern etches across their features as Sol whispers, "I'm afraid we will be of little use in confronting them. We lost most of our powers soon after the spell was cast to bind magic on Earth. We've yet to see them return. They flicker at times but are volatile and unreliable."

His expression is unreadable as he returns to the shelf, finally grasping a small crystal.

They... they don't have magic anymore?

How can that be possible?

"What does that mean for you?"

Luna nods her head, "Meloris has been suffering for two and a half decades."

"How many gods took part in the ritual?"

My head snaps to Zayne, "Do you mean how many gods lost their magic?"

Luna's hair shifts side to side as she shakes her head sadly, "Twelve of us were needed for the binding, but only eleven participated. In the chaos that followed, we could only determine that the spell was tampered with once our magic was gone. To change the results, the requirements were also changed," Luna places her hand on Sol's tenderly, "I'm uncertain whether we will be useful without our power, but we can try. We must."

Zayne's gaze slides to mine before flicking to both gods, "Your knowledge alone has been useful."

Sol grips the crystal tightly, and his knuckles turn white, "Listen to me, Eiara. Killing Kouros will be impossible. He can be wounded and trapped but not killed."

"Everything can be killed." Gray grins as if Sol's statement is more of a challenge than anything.

"You don't understand," Luna whispers, "You cannot kill him because we, and the other gods who participated in the binding, risk everything if we do."

My throat tightens, but I manage to give them both a nod. "Is there a way to strip him of his power?" Zayne asks, and Luna inhales sharply.

Luna inhales sharply, "To strip another god of their powers is strictly forbidden."

"Or we could kill him," Gray suggests again with a grin, and in the corner of my eye, Caspian's lips twitch.

Sol searches another shelf of rolls of parchment, "Banishment is one of the most common ways to strip a god of their power if one is looking to avoid the most permanent form of power stripping, which is a forbidden art we've avoided for millennia on the sole fact that it causes a ripple effect in the magic of the realm. If even one god's powers are permanently severed from them, it can tilt the balance of nature in irrevocable ways."

Gray sighs wistfully, but I ignore him, "How would we banish him?"

"It typically requires more than one to perform unless the one is of immense power. There are various banishing methods, but to banish another god from his realm would essentially be tearing his power from him and using your own to thrust him out of his domain."

When he sees the confusion on my face, he chuckles, "Imagine you are squeezing and pulling his magic from him until nothing remains, cutting off the supply and forcing his physical being beyond that of this world."

I blink at the description, which oddly makes sense, and give a single nod.

"We need to find him and Samira," Zayne says quietly, "We could leave now to look, but any help being pointed in the right direction would be appreciated."

There's a long pause as Sol eyes us before sharing a look with Luna, "Scrying may be our best option if they're here on Meloris, but you will need to do it."

He places a scroll on the table and rolls it out before setting weights on each end. The scroll is huge, with two large continents on it. Various symbols mark cities amidst the mountain ranges, the sea, and everything in between.

It's a map.

Sol holds the crystal outstretched in his palm between us, "Allow the crystal to dangle as you focus on the individual you wish to locate."

Blowing out a breath, I take the cool, dainty metal chain into my hands. The crystal drops, dangling over the left continent first as it swings freely.

"Repeat after me," Sol's voice resonates, "Iltrin mrot ven lurivys vraght mghen."

I repeat the phrase slowly, letting the unfamiliar words chew their way out before Sol nods, "Again."

The second time is easier as my mouth memorizes some of the movements, and by the third repetition, they come out with ease. My magic begins to stir as lines of light web across my skin toward my hand holding the chain.

The crystal circles the area of the map, jerking here or there but not seeming to land on a place.

Sol gestures to the other continent, "Try there now."

"Iltrin mrot," the crystal jerks violently as it spins. "Ven lurivys vraght mghen," I repeat it once more. By the time I finish the next sentence, the crystal has frozen over a castle with the chain pulled taut from my hand. There are various symbols on top of the castle, which I assume are the names.

Luna gasps across from me, and I look at Sol, "Where is—?"

"Here," Sol's eyes flick to the door, "They're in the castle grounds."

Zayne shifts closer, and I quickly drop the crystal, sending it clattering to the surface of the map.

"There must be countless places she could be hiding here," Gray's neck muscles tense as he looks at Sol, whose face has paled. "Yet I have this strange feeling you already know where she is."

"I hope I am incorrect," he whispers, "You must go to the tree."

Sol and Luna lead the way down the brightly lit halls of the castle. Hues of gold and silver twist and swirl throughout the white marble, sparkling against the rays of sunlight streaming in through the ornately carved windows, with sheer curtains that billow amidst the breeze.

Nervous sweat slicks down my spine as we turn a corner, the echo of our quick steps mirroring the roaring sound of my pulse raging in my head.

Kouros was trying to remove his only opposition.

The dagger rends the soul of the one it's used on.

My head swirls with more questions than I can muster as they guide us down a flight of stairs and across an empty courtyard before the oddity hits me, "Are there no others living in the castle?"

Luna glances back with a small smile. "It is nearly solstice. Much of the realm is preparing for the celebrations and will be for days." Her smile turns sad as she turns forward once more.

"Isn't solstice supposed to bring happiness?" I ask pointedly, and she shakes her head.

"Solstice is historically a time of celebration to honor one another and our families while those we've blessed honor us. What once was a time-honored tradition filled with love has become one filled with pain, suffering, and discontent. When we lost you, it was like we finally understood the loss the Servilians have felt for centuries, and the ceremony hasn't been the same since." Sol's arm snakes around her shoulders to comfort her, and a lingering question burns at the back of my mind. I don't know when I'll get another chance to ask.

"Where is Cade?"

I feel heads snap in my direction from each of my men as Luna's face brightens, "He was sent to help with solstice preparations, but he is here on Meloris."

My heart stutters, "How did you save him?"

The tentative hope that filled my body dies out as Sol answers, "Let me be clear, Eiara. We did not save him. His body decays on Servilia. We simply allowed his soul to come to Meloris, where it belongs, and when you claimed him as your own, we heard your prayer."

I frown, but Luna chimes in, "We were visited by Vesta when we heard you. She has always enjoyed being owed favors, so she gladly stepped in to bring him 'home' for you."

"What does that mean for my brother?" Zayne's voice wavers as Luna's smile widens.

"It means he will remain here until he's ready to be reborn. If he's ever ready to be reborn. He seems to like it here."

Gray takes two steps closer and looks at her incredulously, "Does he even have a body?"

She rolls her eyes, "Of course he does. What did you think was going to happen?"

He shrugs in response, "I don't know! Maybe he was just this transparent image of him walking around. I've never seen it happen before."

"No one has," Sol interjects, "This is the first time a demigod has been allowed passage to Meloris after being claimed by one of us."

I feel the blood drain from my face as surprise echoes from Zayne, Gray, and Caspian. "Demigod?"

Luna's gaze flicks to each of my men before settling on me with a raised brow, "Eiara, are you telling me that you didn't know the ones you took as mates were demigods?"

I shake my head, and Sol chuckles, "You are the goddess of elements, Eiara. Did you not find it strange that you were drawn to the most powerful beings in the realm who wield fire, earth, frost, shadows, and water?"

Holy shit.

Luna's quiet voice fills the tense air, "As much as I want to continue this conversation, we must hurry. I promise we will answer all your questions after this is all done."

That's enough for us to fall silent as we continue forward. Finally, we come to an enormous set of doors wide enough to fit double our party at once.

Sol grasps the handle firmly and pushes, revealing the impressive trunk of a hylia ilvrost.

Ribbons of gold and silver adorn the ground, leading up the roots to the tree itself. The base of the hollowed base of the tree has a cave-like entrance wide enough to fit two to three people at a time, and the mouth of it only seems to get bigger as we come closer.

By the time we reach the opening, the nervous butterflies in my stomach have begun to flutter throughout my limbs, and it takes a conscious effort to keep my breathing even.

This has to be it.

"What is this place?" Zayne asks softly as they lead us down a winding pathway in the tree's center.

"This is our main connection to the other realms," Sol whispers. "When we had our magic, this tree would allow us to portal to various locations in other worlds."

Shock rifles through me, "Like Haven and the lake I was researching on Earth."

A look akin to pride flashes across his features, "Yes, it would make sense that you managed to find a way to be close to us."

Sol and Luna pause, "If they are there when we get to the room, we will wait outside until it is done, and we are ready to seal the banishment."

My stomach flips nervously as I nod, and they continue to lead us down the passageway.

Right. Easy-peasy.

Chapter 69

Eiara

Sol and Luna's footsteps slow as the faint sound of voices echoes in the distance. We follow the sound down into the depths, keeping our footfalls near silent as the voices get louder.

It's impossible to make out what they're saying, but the male voice accompanying Samira's is unmistakable as dread settles into my bones.

Kouros.

We reach the bottom of the winding pathway, and my heart lurches into my throat as I struggle to maintain a hold on my nerves. Flashes of memories make their way to the forefront of my mind, and I struggle to shove them away as my lungs feel starved for oxygen.

It isn't until my eyes flick to Caspian's that my lungs manage to fill from what I see there.

His body is tense, but an air of violence radiates from him, sending a nervous wave of relief through my veins. Everything about the way he's poised screams the promise of death as Zayne moves to stand beside me.

I shouldn't feel this attracted to the murderous look in his emerald eyes as he stares down the corridor into the room where the voices are coming from.

But I am.

My heart stutters in my chest as his gaze slides to mine, and his anger intensifies as Kouros speaks.

That's when I realize it's not Samira's presence affecting him this way. The sole cause of his years of servitude and torture stands not far from us, but the promise of revenge for him pales in comparison to drawing blood with the god he saved me from.

The realization is almost too much to take, and I tear my eyes from him to remain focused.

Slowly, Caspian and Gray lead us into the room, with Zayne and I close behind them. It isn't until my mind registers the third person standing next to Samira that shock and relief rifle through me.

My eyes scan over the bombshell of a brunette with bright green eyes that widen as they stare back at me, and my heart lurches in my chest.

"Tammy?" I whisper, as if speaking her name too loud would make it more real than it is.

"Well," Kouros exhales loudly, "You certainly are a tenacious group, aren't you?" His power thrusts outwards toward us in a rush as Caspian, Zayne, and Gray move to brace themselves, pausing when my shield over them shimmers before becoming transparent once more.

The only outward sign of displeasure from Kouros is the tick in his jaw, "I think it's past time for you to be done away with," he glances at Samira and nods, "If you won't join us, then you will all die."

"Tamara, kill Eiara." Samira juts her finger in my direction, "Now." Tammy's small form takes a step closer before she suddenly disappears.

That's when all hell breaks loose.

Movement at my right catches my attention as Tammy reappears, her form coiled as she lunges for my throat with a dagger gripped tightly in hand. Panic rifles through me when I realize she can reappear within my shield's barriers.

Her movements are fast, but there's something odd about them as she surges toward me. It's like she's somehow stuttering her movements.

Gray reacts instantly to her assault, twisting her arm to block her attempt as I take a nervous step back.

Her eyes flash with relief for a moment as she disappears again.

She's trying to slow herself down.

My heart thunders in my chest as I watch Gray swipe his hands at the air where she stood seconds ago. Darkness swirls around me from Zayne as he moves closer to my back, and as she reappears, his shadows stretch out and grip her limbs, freezing her in place mere feet away from where I stand.

My gaze snags on Kouros and Samira as they move toward the portal, but before I can call out to the others, Gray has already lunged at Kouros, with Caspian quickly engaging Samira.

I don't have time to think before Kouros's power surges, and he hurls a blast in our direction. My shields deflect it, leaving him and Samira with no choice but to use physical weapons.

Tammy disappears once more, and Zayne's shadows disperse, only to return as she reappears in front of me. But the moment his shadows surge towards her, she disappears once more.

"Eiara," Zayne's violet eyes flick to either side of me. You must banish Kouros now. This is our only chance," he rushes out as Tammy reappears again at my side. Within a moment, his shadows have her restrained.

He's right.

If they escape now, it could be impossible to find them again without knowing which realms they've gone to.

I need to trust that the others can hold Tammy and Samira at bay while I try.

I open myself up to more of my power, and it swells as if my body alone were holding the entire force of the ocean within. A cold sweat slicks down my back as I encircle Kouros with magic and wait, uncertain of my next steps, as I ease my power closer to him.

My shield around Gray bends and shimmers as Kouros' magic pulsates outward before absorbing into my shield and dissipating. I slowly inch my magic toward Kouros, and sweat beads down my temple as I look for a way to pull his magic from him.

Chaos continues around us as Tammy maintains her relentless assault, and Caspian strikes repeatedly at Samira, only to hit her own shield.

My magic glides along Kouros' skin just as a wave of power surges from him. The magic rushes toward Gray, leaving a small trail disappearing within the blink of an eye.

I poke and prod along his skin, looking for an opening, a thread, or a ribbon of his magic to grasp.

But I find nothing. There's no stream of power, only curves and edges. There's nothing for my magic to hold on to. Another wave of power pulses from him, absorbing into my unseen vortex, and the realization hits me.

I can use his attacks at Gray as my leverage.

My heart thunders in my throat, my blood roaring in my ears as I prepare my magic. It coils between Gray and Kouros, like a predator waiting for an opening to pounce on its prey.

One...

Tammy appears in the corner of my eye, her abrupt movements coming to a halt as Zayne again holds her stationary.

Two...

If I can get this right, this could all be over.

Three...

My pulse rages in anticipation as Kouros sends another wave of power at Gray, and I thrust my hands forward as if they were grasping his magic within them. His attack rushes outward as I surround it, following the small tendril of power as the rest breaks off from its source and hurtles at Gray.

My window begins to close as the tendril pulls back, and I curl around the small thread, raveling it around my own. Like a string wrapping around an invisible hand, I pull it taut, and satisfaction rifles through me at the resistance. I can do this.

Tammy appears in my peripherals again, and it takes all my concentration to ignore her, trusting in Zayne's ability to keep her at bay.

With a firm grasp on Kouros' power, I slowly pull it towards me. My hands mimic the motion as if pulling on an invisible rope. His magic eases closer, and I wrap the length around my invisible hand, gathering more of his power before I repeat the action.

Kouros' white eyes snap to mine as he deflects a strike from Gray, and the panic in them reassures me that he knows exactly what I'm doing. Using the momentum of my success, I repeat the action as he tries to withdraw it. The resistance pulls my magic taut from my body, and beads of sweat run down my cheek.

This could be dangerous.

I've also opened the door for him to do the same thing to me.

No wonder they say it usually takes more than one.

Kouros tugs on my power again as Gray lunges at him with a cry, and I use the distraction to yank on his power, pulling a long portion from him before raveling it around mine.

Kouros screams as he blocks another strike from Gray, and the sound is music to my ears.

But we're not done yet.

The exertion begins to settle in my bones as I squeeze more and more of his magic out. Ribbons of light surround my limbs, and my skin feels like it's on fire as I continue to pull until, finally, it comes free from him.

The last of it snaps apart from him and dances in the air between us like a cloud magnetized to return to him as I keep it contained.

Now, to cut him off from it.

I surround it, weaving my power around it as I did within Caspian, and Kouros shrieks, thrashing his weapon at Gray wildly to get to me.

Gray doesn't miss a single step in his deflections, and as I finish encircling Kouros' power, I use a surge of my own to thrust him against the awaiting portal.

It ripples against his weight as he struggles, "You can't do this!" his shrill, panicked voice echoes against the stone walls, "We could have been great together, Eiara." He chokes and sputters as my power cuts off his air supply.

"I have no desire to become your puppet," though my voice is unwavering, I feel close to losing control as my power swirls within me, looking for an outlet.

My power completes the last weave over Kouros' magic, and I sense the moment when something tears from him. It's as if a rubber band that linked him to his power has snapped, and the ball of his power floats freely between us.

"Tamara! Kill her now!" Samira's shrill voice echoes as I start forcing Kouros through the portal. He gasps, clawing to remain in the room as the portal shimmers at his back ever so slightly.

It's going to take a lot more power than that to force him through.

My power swirls once more, threatening to make my knees give way as I hurtle it toward the portal. Time feels as if it slows when the cold edge of a blade suddenly presses against my throat and my heart thunders.

Gray's amber eyes meet mine, and I see them flash with panic for the first time as the metal bites into my skin.

This can't be it.

This can't be how it ends.

A loud bang sounds out, jolting me as the blade digs further into my neck before clattering to the ground. My attention flicks to the other side of the room where Samira and Caspian are.

His back is to us as my pulse races.

Was it a gunshot?

No, it wasn't the same kind of sound.

It was a loud crack, like someone had taken a wooden stick and slammed it on a surface over a megaphone.

It sounded like thunder.

Kouros gasps frantically and strains against my power at it presses him against the portal, but the distraction of Samira and Caspian keeps me focused as my power begins to overwhelm me.

Samira's steps shuffle backward before she falls to the ground, holding her abdomen, looking at the gaping black hole in her body as steam rises from it.

The smell of burning flesh reaches my nose, and I suppress the urge to vomit.

"Caspian, what—" I'm cut off as my gaze flicks to the tiny bolts of electricity dancing along his arms and upturned palm as he stares down at them with awe.

"Your power..." I whisper, "Sealing Kouros' magic freed your power," my nervous excitement takes over as my power swells again.

Luna's voice sounds out, and within seconds, a chest slides in front of me, "Eiara, push him through and place it here. Hurry!"

I nod, throwing my hands out as my power hurtles once more toward Kouros. At that exact moment, Caspian launches toward the portal, and my heart skips a beat.

What the hell is he doing?

I watch with wide eyes as he unsheathes the golden dagger and in one fluid motion, drives it into Kouros' abdomen. My power is still surging in their direction as blood spurts from his wound.

No.

NO!

Caspian withdraws the dagger and quickly dodges to the side as my power crashes against Kouros, forcing his wounded visage through the portal.

Relief crashes over me that Caspian wasn't sent through the portal as Luna steps forward, gesturing with shaking hands toward the shimmering barrier, "What did you do? If he dies, his power needs a vessel!"

"I did what was necessary! She was never going to be safe until he's dead!" Caspian shouts at a fearful Luna before his burning gaze turns to me, and I know what needs to be done.

My power swirls once more, forcing me to my knees, and I quickly squeeze the ball of chaotic magic smaller.

It riots and presses against my grip, but I finally bring it to Caspian. "Do it, little one."

The little voice in my head screams that this is dangerous and that we don't know what could happen, but I ignore it. The certainty coming through the bond is enough to silence any doubt.

I squeeze the dense ball of power into a small opening in the weaved vault within Caspian as he shouts various curse words. Using the ball of my magic as a second layer of protection, I seal it thoroughly before testing the boundaries.

My power swells chaotically inside me, and I'm forced to close myself off with a gasp.

It will have to do. It should hold.

Fuck, I hope it holds.

My limbs shake as I brace myself, panting to catch my breath, and my gaze lands on a very dead Samira as a strangled laugh bubbles up within me.

We did it.

We fucking did it.

Caspian takes strong strides to stand before me as I fight to contain my laughter, and my gaze locks with his relieved emerald eyes as his lips crash against mine.

He kisses me like the world is about to change, like there's a promise for tomorrow, and I'm his salvation.

Although, in a sense, it is, and I am.

"Lara?" A nervous, feminine voice sounds out behind me, and my heart stutters as Caspian breaks apart, searching my eyes before placing one final lingering kiss against my lips.

Zayne supports me with a hand on my arm, and I twist to see Tammy's bright green eyes filled with tears. Wisps of Zayne's smoke dissipates from the grasp he had on her as she glances at my neck.

"Oh my god, Lara," she gasps, covering her mouth as the tears spill over, "I could have killed you!"

I shift closer, gathering her in my arms and pulling her into a tight hug, "But you didn't," I whisper, placing a hand against her head as I squeeze my best friend into my chest, "It's all over."

Another laugh bubbles out of me, and Tammy pulls back, looking at me as we laugh with tears streaming down our faces.

I glance at Luna and Sol, seeing the concern and relief etched on their faces, before looking at my men.

There's no way to know if I'll have to replace or repair the seal around Kouros' magic or what the future holds, but for now, we're all alive, free, and ready to build our future free from tyrants like Kouros and Samira.

Gray steps closer, extending a hand between us as I smile at Tammy as she slides her palm into mine, "Let's go home."

The portal behind Caspian shimmers, and the faint outline of an unfamiliar mountain range comes into view through it, with a handful of large castle-like buildings nestled between.

Whatever that place is beyond the portal, hopefully they rest easy tonight knowing Kouros and Samira are not within their borders.

At least, hopefully not alive anyways.

I glance at Luna as she whispers pensively to Sol, "Kouros is gone right? Like, there's no way he could have survived that large of a wound with that dagger..."

Luna's hands wring together nervously, but she nods, "I don't know of any magic that could save him from the blade, especially with his own power unavailable to him."

"Well, Eiara," Sol's voice echoes in the room as he steps closer, "Goddess of elements, savior of realms... We hope you'll consider Meloris as the second home to you and your mates. Welcome home, daughter."

The end... for now.

<u>Acknowledgements</u>

I have to first, again, say a huge thank you to Amanda Dumky for the insanely gorgeous cover. I will forever be thankful for your input, honesty and talent for bringing my vision to life.

A huge thank you to my husband, who unwaveringly supports all my chaotic hobbies, endeavors and passions without a second thought. I love you to the moon and back.

Thank you to my street team for being so supportive, hyping me up even when I was lost in the sauce, and always bringing excitement to my life. Alysse, Megs, Laura and Carysnn... you are all beautiful humans and I cannot tell you how thankful I am to have you all in my life. I mean this with all the sincerity in the world when I say, that if nothing else has come from this journey with writing the unbroken series, I am eternally grateful for this path leading me to the four of you.

Lastly, much like with Shadows of Dusk, thank you to all the readers who decided to give this series a chance. I can't promise it's the most well written, or well written at all... but I, as with many authors, put a piece of myself into my work, and taking the time to read it... well that may be the best gift of all.

It's just my hope that you enjoyed it, even if only for a moment before you move on to your next adventure.

Stay tuned for my next upcoming dark paranormal romance standalone books in the Prince of Hell series, and my dark paranormal academia series.

The first books from both are estimated for release in fall of 2025.

www.ingramcontent.com/pod-product-compliance
Lightning Source LLC
Chambersburg PA
CBHW032105310726
48972CB00001B/100